David Huebner

Heart of a Beast, Soul of a Woman

"There is something about the outside of horse that is good for the inside of a man."
Winston Churchill

PREFACE

The breed is ancient. Images of Sorraia horses dating back to 25,000 BC, decorate the walls of caves near La Pileta, Spain. The animals appear to be virtually unchanged from their descendants of today. They are the principal ancestor of the Lusitano, Andalusian and Warmblood. Their DNA permeates almost every modern breed, to produce dun, buckskin and grulla colored horses in them.

The horses were not tall by today's standard; rarely exceeding 14.2 hands, but they were tough, able to survive harsh environments. They were also smart, quick and agile, with the ability to flex at the poll and work off their hindquarters. Local farmers used them to herd fighting bulls and domestic cattle. They were almost always dun or grulla colored. They had black ear tips, black manes and tails fringed with lighter colored hair and faint black stripes on their legs and shoulders.

They came to the Americas with the Spanish Conquistadors. Many escaped and quickly reverted to the feral state, prospering and reproducing on the plains of the wild American West. Some were captured and re-domesticated. Some mingled with other imported breeds and came to be known as American Mustangs. Some of their blood filtered into the American Quarter Horse and gave that breed the agility and ability to work cattle.

Now they are mostly extinct. About 150 head still survive, held on private lands in Spain, Germany, France and Switzerland. Unknown others still remain however, basically unchanged since the days of the Conquistadors, in small herds scattered throughout Nevada, Utah, Oregon, and Wyoming in what is left of the American Wild West.

The cow wants to be in the herd. It feels safe in the herd. The man wants the cow out of the herd. He needs to handle it. Maybe to be branded or inoculated or shipped; whatever the reason, the man has to separate it from the rest of the herd. But the cow does not want to leave the herd. Enter a rider on the back of a horse, a horse with special agility and intelligence; a horse that can explode in one direction for two strides, stop, pivot on a dime and explode in the opposite direction; a horse with no fear of the cow; a horse that senses what the cow will do almost before the cow itself knows; a horse with an attitude, a cutting horse. It is their job, the rider and this cutting horse, to separate the cow from the herd. The cow does not want to leave the safety of the herd; the horse wants to cut it out of the herd. This is the game.

The confrontation between cow and horse has inspired competition among cowboys since cattle have been worked on horseback. The first US official cutting competition for money was held in 1898. The prize money totaled one hundred and fifty dollars. Now, every year the national futurity for three-year-old cutting horses is held in Fort Worth, Texas. The total prize money currently exceeds two million dollars.

Once in a long while a horse is born who becomes a benchmark whereby to measure all others. Over the years there has been Hub, Steeldust, Flo, Poco Lena, Doc O'Lena, Doc Per, Smart Little Lena and Smokin' Joe. These have remained the epitome, leading a remuda of great cutting horses, distinguishing themselves by having something extra—great heart and great soul.

Chapter 1, Jolena

Jolena came into the world in the usual way, front feet first, closely followed by her nose. Pete watched quietly from the darkened aisle in front of Smart Smokin' Kitty's stall. He had been a party to this process several hundred times, he'd even helped a time or two, but it never failed to thrill him. Birth of a horse, or anything else for that matter, was an outright miracle as far as he was concerned. How could you witness this and not realize there is God?

The silver-blue amniotic sac shimmered in the pale March moonlight coming in through the big slider door down the aisle. Then, as Kitt's belly trembled with another contraction, the foal oozed a little farther out of the mare. Tiny pointed hooves tore a hole in the sac and for the first time, the foal's nose was exposed to the air outside the mare.

Pete looked at his watch. Ten minutes had slipped by since Kitt had gone into labor. "Right on schedule, Old Girl," he whispered.

Pete knew only too well that the foal had to have air within twenty minutes of the start of the birth process. Longer, and there was risk of brain damage. He had seen several foals that either died or were put down because they had been too long coming into the world.

Even though he'd given up training professionally, Pete had been anxiously waiting for this baby more than any other he could remember. He had been praying for one more good horse before he died. In anticipation, he'd started sleeping in the barn a week before Kitt was due. She was a maiden mare, and sometimes maiden mares foaled early. Pete didn't want to miss the delivery. Kitt however, had shown no indication of urgent motherhood until four hours ago.

Pete had kept her separated from his other horses for the past two weeks. He'd put her in a half-acre paddock he could watch from his kitchen window. For the first few days Kitt had resented the separation, constantly calling to the rest of the herd, who after a few hours mostly ignored her. However, each day she whinnied less and by the third day she came to accept her confinement. Pete lavished attention on her. He fed her the finest alfalfa and gave her extra rations of grain. He concocted his own special supplement blend of amino acids, vitamins, calcium, phosphorous, and molasses that she ate greedily from his hand. If she were inclined to think about much of anything, she was thinking life was good.

Every evening, just before sunset, Pete brought her into the barn. He had a special foaling stall twelve feet wide and sixteen feet long. He didn't want his foaling mares to be cast by a wall in one of the smaller stalls when they were in the middle of labor. A bigger stall gave them room to roam and find the right spot to lie down and enough room to get back up.

Every morning when he turned her out and every evening when he brought her in, he checked both her teats, feeling for wax. This evening, he found some. A small drop of congealed colostrum was clinging to each nipple.

"It's time," he announced to the mare and put an extra helping of fresh pine shavings in the stall. He ate dinner quickly and hurried back to the barn to wait. Later, his daughter, and the twins, and Woody came out to sit with him, but when Kitt showed no big hurry to deliver, they all became bored. This was normal behavior for both humans and horses. The foaling mare really didn't want an audience and Pete's family, although interested, were not dedicated. By eight o'clock Pete was on his own. At nine o'clock he turned off the lights and settled down on the cot he'd set up in the aisle. He covered himself with an old goose-down comforter and snuggled into its warmth. One of the barn cats jumped on his chest and started purring. He was asleep in minutes.

Sometime before midnight Pete awoke with a start. He'd heard the soggy splash of the mare's water breaking. He flipped the comforter over, rolled off the cot, and peered into the stall. He did not turn on the lights. Kitt was fidgeting, lifting her hind legs slowly, one at a time, as if marching in place. There was a dark wet spot behind her in the blanket of shavings on the floor of the stall.

"Come on, Baby," whispered Pete, "You got twenty minutes before I call the vet. And I am the vet."

The mare circled round a couple of times and then went down. She stretched her back legs out, lifting the leg that was away from the floor. She strained hard. Nothing happened. She rested for a moment and pushed again. The foal started to slowly emerge. The mare then attempted to stand, gathering her legs beneath her. Just as quickly, she gave it up as another contraction took her. Now Pete could see the foal's front feet and the tip of its nose. It was forty-five degrees in the barn, but the mare was sweating, her coat darkening along her withers and flanks. Pete was sweating too. The mare's breathing was deep and fast, as if she had just run a twenty-eight second, quarter mile. She convulsed again and the foal squirted forward, beyond its front shoulders, its hooves splitting the amniotic sac at the seams.

This gave Pete his first real look at the baby. "I'll be," he whispered, "we got us a paint horse, Kitt! How'd you do that?"

The foal had a white snip, stripe, and a star, and Pete could see more white on her front legs and shoulder. He did some recollecting and vaguely remembered something about Doc O'Lena, Kitt's grandsire, producing an occasional crop-out on solid quarter horse mares.

"Well it sure doesn't matter to me, baby, as long as you can cut a cow. I'll register you as a paint horse and if nothin' else you'll be worth some money to those paint people. They're always tryin' to put color on cow horses."

Once again Kitt attempted to stand, this time succeeding. The foal was hanging half out of her and Pete didn't like to see that. He hoped she would lie down again and soon.

The mare turned once, rethought her position and settled back down. She discovered it was much better to take the contractions lying down. Two minutes and several contractions later the foal was out. Kitt stayed down and relaxed briefly. The umbilical was not yet broken and she still retained the placenta. Then the mare heaved a sigh of relief and stood. The cord was snapped and the baby started life on its own. Almost immediately, the foal began kicking with its fore legs. The back legs however were still imprisoned in the amniotic sac. It was hung up around her hocks. Pete took a towel and slowly entered the stall. He began his brief ritual. Thirteen minutes had elapsed since the mare's water broke.

The first thing he did was to stroke Kitt's neck. "Easy, Kitty girl, I'm here to help." He spoke quietly in soothing tones and moved slowly, deliberately, careful not to give the mare any reason to spook. Kitt nickered and nuzzled her baby's neck, inhaling the smell of her.

Certain she was okay with him next to the baby, he turned his attention to the foal, quickly stripping the sac away from the foal's back legs. He whistled softly. "Aren't you a pretty little beast," he said. "You a filly or a colt?" He reached carefully between the baby's back legs.

Finding nothing he told the foal, "You're a little filly then."

He put one hand on her shoulder to hold her down and started toweling her off, rubbing vigorously with the rough towel. The foal fought his touch only briefly and then relaxed. She seemed to enjoy the rubdown. Pete eased up on the pressure he was using to hold her down and put more effort into the towel.

"I'll be, you seem to like this." He thought back on past deliveries. "You're about the friendliest new baby I can remember."

He finished toweling the foal on one side and then flipped her over to dry the other side. She was beautifully marked with generous splashes of white radiating up from her belly. She had a dark dorsal stripe and none of the white crossed her back.

"You're an overo," Pete told her. "A frame overo, in fact, but I'm not sure what color you are yet."

The filly's coat was still damp. The toweling was more to get her used to his touch than to get her completely dry. She looked brown, but Pete knew she would be lighter in the morning when she was dry. She had dark points, meaning her ears, mane, and tail were black. It also appeared as if her eyes had been heavily made up with mascara.

Pete had seen a lot of horses in every color variation possible. He knew there were actually only two colors of horses, black and red; everything else was either a dilution or modification of those two, even white. The variation Pete was now looking at had him a bit puzzled. The filly's dam, Kitt, was a blood bay. In bright sunlight she looked like polished mahogany. She had dark points and no white except for a small star on her forehead. She did not have a dorsal stripe, but her sire, Whiskey Joe, was a dun. He had a dorsal stripe and the genetic factor that produced dun was supposed to be dominant, but the bay factor was strong also. Pete had seen a lot of dun and bay crosses in which the dun factor was not expressed. In this foal however, the dun factor had won out.

"My guess is you'll be buckskin or dun or maybe even grulla once you lose that baby hair," he told the filly. If she were listening, she didn't acknowledge him. She just lay quietly while Pete worked.

The towel was thoroughly soaked when Pete put it aside and started to rub the foal with his old, but still strong hands. He touched her everywhere. He put a finger in her mouth and rubbed her gums, feeling the first blunt points of her teeth barely protruding. He rubbed her ears inside and out, he rubbed her nose, under her jaw, her neck, withers, and gradually worked his way all the way back to her butt. He even pulled gently on her tail a few times. Then he picked up each foot, in turn and rapped on the hoof with his knuckles several times. He repeated the hoof treatment three times.

All this fondling and massaging served to accustom the foal to the human touch at the earliest possible age. Later when it came time for hoof trimming, shoeing, grooming, and general handling and training, the foal would remember. Anyone who had to deal with the horse should have an easier time.

Less than ten minutes later, Pete backed away from the foal. She had accepted all the handling with patience, and if he could use the word, dignity. Pete didn't want to overdo it. Some breeders didn't bother with this initial handling at all; others spent much more time on the newborn. There were those who spent over an hour, doing all sorts of things Pete considered foolish. You could get the opposite effect of what was intended if you weren't careful. Many experienced breeders did little or nothing. Pete had used this same basic technique for almost sixty years and it had served him well. He referred to it as a first lesson rather than imprinting. "Okay, Baby," he told the foal, "time to get up and start bein' a horse."

Kitt was waiting patiently. She had passed the placenta a few minutes earlier and standing close by, had watched Pete intently. She was concerned about what he was doing, but she trusted him and had allowed him to handle her baby. As soon as Pete stepped back, she moved in and nuzzled the foal, pushing on her hindquarters with her nose. The baby responded by propping her front end up with her forelegs. With that done, she attempted to get her back legs under her, struggling to lift her butt. About half way up she lost her front legs and dropped back to the floor. On her next few attempts she got her butt a little higher each time before her front legs slid apart and she went down on her chin. She turned her head to regard her back legs.

Pete watched closely, noticing the way she moved and how hard she tried. From his experience, the faster a foal stood, the more coordinated it would be as a mature horse. That wasn't infallible however, only a general observation. He'd been personally associated with several late bloomers who took forever to stand and nurse that went on to be first rate performance horses.

This little filly seemed different though. It appeared to Pete almost as if she were concentrating intently, trying very hard to determine how her legs were supposed to work rather than just trying to stand.

"That's impossible," he told himself, "she can't reason, not at this age."

But on the next attempt, she gathered all four legs together and stood. She flicked her tail and looked at Pete.

"Well you little sprite, you figured it out. Now pay attention to your mama and drink some milk."

The filly tossed her head, turned and wobbled toward the mare. Within two minutes she was nursing lustily, sucking in the colostrum that would give her the antibodies she needed to survive. Pete used a shovel to retrieve the placenta from the stall. He examined it briefly, laying it out flat and poking it with his forefinger. It was of uniform texture and color and the organ was intact. Pete decided mother and daughter foal were healthy and fit. Then he cleaned all the wood shavings out of the stall and replaced them with clean straw. Sometimes a foal would eat shavings and colic. If this one ate the straw it wouldn't hurt her.

He watched the little filly nurse a while longer. "Smokin' Jolena," he announced for the mare and foal to hear. "Your name is Smokin' Jolena. Lena in honor of your great grandsire, Jo in honor of your sire, and Smokin' in honor of your dam."

Having made this proclamation, he left the barn and went in to bed. It had been a long evening for him, but even so he was still puzzling as to how this new little filly had come by her color. The overo gene that produced white markings in horses was not dominant. In order for little Jolena to have it, at least either her sire or dam should be a paint. Neither of them was. Pete would have to consult the pedigrees of Kitt and Joe to see if there had been any paint horses in their history. It wasn't a problem for he liked paints. He didn't think they were any better or worse than quarter horses, just more colorful.

"Old Zip had a little color on him," he told himself. "I can't remember exactly how much, but he was about the best horse I ever had." He fell asleep fast that night, trying to recall all he could about Old Zip.

Chapter 2, Pete

Pete Browning owned a ranch in Montana. It lay tight against the knobby-toed, rock-calloused feet of the Cabinet Mountains to the west of Kalispell, and was cut down the middle by Rogers Creek. The ranch wasn't big, only the width of the creek valley and a bit shy of two miles long. It was a total of six hundred deeded acres with first water rights on Rogers Creek. The ranch had never made any serious money, but it was what Pete did. He raised cows and horses, cutting horses. He trained them too, although now he was completely retired from any serious participation. He was eighty-one years old and per his own evaluation, "I've never done anything else of consequence except graduate from Vet school and successfully help defend the freedom of the United States." For his part in the Korean War he'd been "shot in the ass" to hear him tell it.

Actually, the bullet entered his torso in the soft flesh slightly above and to the left of his right pelvis, missed everything of consequence and exited through the top of his right buttocks. He subsequently managed to kill the "Commie" who'd shot him. The wound got him off the front lines, but not out of the war. He was back in the field with his unit six weeks later.

When the war was over, he came back to where he'd grown up, his parent's ranch in the Bitterroot Valley south of Missoula. As a young man he loved ranching, except for the money, or lack thereof. There was a living to be made raising cows as long as you didn't mind living poor. So in 1958, shortly after returning to his parent's ranch, he decided to go to college. Vet medicine seemed like a reasonable choice.

Vets made more money than most small ranchers and they had a measure of respect in the community. It was a lucky choice for Pete as it was in college he met the love of his life.

The young lady's name was Renee and she came from out east, which to Pete was anywhere east of the continental divide. She was from Trenton, New Jersey, but by the time she was eighteen, she hated the crowded, dirty city, longing for some fresh air and wide-open spaces. Going to college in Montana, the Big Sky State, was the most exciting thing she could imagine. It was, too, until she met Pete, and he introduced her to horses.

They dated for several months before Pete decided he should bring Renee around to his folks, to see what they thought of her. It wouldn't matter to Pete if they didn't approve, only make things easier if they did. They did approve, but that wasn't the most important thing in the long run. The big deal was that Renee fell in love not only with Pete, but also with horses. She'd never been on the back of a horse prior to the day she came to meet her boyfriend's parents.

It was after lunch when Pete's mother suggested, "Pete, why don't you saddle up four horses so we can all go for a ride. Let Renee see the ranch." Pete's mother was no dope. If this pretty little, city girl couldn't learn to handle a horse, she was no good for Pete. There was no need for concern for to the delight of Pete and his parents; they could hardly get Renee off the horse's back. Astride the powerful animal, she quickly succumbed to the spell of equus.

Renee had started college as a history major. She wasn't all that interested in the past, although at the time, it was an acceptable endeavor for a woman. She could be a librarian. But, after her exposure to horses and cows, she turned her attention to vet medicine as soon as she could. Even though Pete had a year's head start, she was a better student and they eventually graduated in the same class. She also turned out to be a better vet than Pete. Possessing keen powers of observation for any abnormalities in animal behavior, she became a diagnostic genius. It seemed only normal after they bought their first and only ranch that Pete did the ranching while Renee made the ends meet by practicing vet medicine. It was a partnership that lasted until the end of Renee's life.

For years, Renee told everyone who asked about when she would retire, "I intend to take care of sick horses and cows until I tip over." She was as tough as a rawhide-covered, wooden saddletree inside and out, and a perfect lady.

She came home late one afternoon and told Pete she was tired.
"I'm going to lie down and rest a while."

Later, when Pete had supper on the table, he checked in to call
her to dinner. She was already cold. She was sixty-six. Pete had loved
her dearly. He scattered her ashes on the ranch near a lovely little riffle
in the creek where the two of them had often picnicked. The headstone
Pete erected over her final resting place had both their names chiseled
into it. Pete didn't intend to leave the ranch either.

Now, twelve years after his beloved Renee had died, Pete still
ran two hundred head of cattle and twenty horses, but had a hired man to
help him. The hired man, Woody, was sixty-eight years old. He'd been
a sheepherder, and he and Pete had been friends for nearly forty years.
The two of them, plus Pete's divorced daughter and her nine-year old,
twin girls, lived together and worked the ranch. They had five hundred
acres of hay to bale at least twice every summer, but with modern
equipment they could handle it. In fact, for the past several years, they
made more money selling hay than they did selling cattle. If Pete didn't
need cows to work his horses, he'd have sold them all.

The attraction for Pete, beyond the land itself, was horses. His
earliest memories were not those of sight and sound, but of motion, the
motion of riding horseback. On his parents' ranch, he'd come within
five minutes of being born in the saddle. His mother had taken
childbirth as a natural event not an illness. For the entire nine months of
her pregnancy, she carried on her day-to-day activities while she carried
Pete inside her. This was not always easily done, but it was always
done. Her help on the ranch was needed. When her water broke, she
was trailing a few head of cattle down from the hills to the winter
pasture in the valley. Her husband delivered the baby on the spot.
Within the hour, she and little Pete were back in the saddle headed home.

Little Pete spent most of his first year either on his mother's
back, Indian style, while she rode, or in the crook of his father's arm
while he rode. Pete truly could ride before he could walk. By the time
he was two, he was riding solo on the back of a steady, old gelding that
Pete's father had acquired twenty some years previous as a three-year
old mustang, fresh off the range.

The mustang was what was called "green broke." It was an
interesting term for describing a horse's level of training and could
mean a lot of different things. At worst, someone had been on the
horse's back at least once. The duration of that ride could have been a
few minutes or only a few seconds. At best, the horse had been ridden
some, was reasonably steady, and would respond to basic cues.

This mustang fell into the worst case category. In the process of capture, the horse had been seriously mistreated. It was spooky and mean, but after months of work, he gradually came to trust Pete's father, eventually becoming a partner. Zipper was a tough, smart, line-backed dun, and he'd been one fine, cutting horse. He'd also seen some accidental stud service before Pete's father discovered Zipper could jump a five-foot fence. Now, his big days were over. He was twenty-four when Little Pete came to ride him. Old Zip was gray-faced, sway-backed, and had a slight limp on his right front from a broken knee he'd suffered five years earlier, but he was alert and still loved life.

Someone once asked Pete's father if he wasn't doing the horse a disservice by not putting him down since it was obvious that he sometimes appeared to be in pain.

"Hell no!" he thundered. "I'm full of aches and pains and nobody's going to put me down! I've got too much livin' yet to do."

At the time, Old Zip was about 14.1 hands high and Little Pete was about 9.2 hands high. Pete's father built a platform with a couple steps for Little Pete to walk up and from there, climb on Zip's back. After the first couple attempts, they both got the hang of it. It wasn't long before Zip started standing by the platform in the morning after he'd had his oats, waiting for Little Pete to show. The two of them, little boy and old horse, became inseparable. Unless his father was around to tack up Zip, Pete rode him bareback, with no bridle or bit. He just got way forward on the horse's neck and tugged on the halter in the direction he wanted Zip to go. They didn't go far or fast, but they were always going somewhere.

Old Zip had been in the ground over seventy years and Little Pete was now Old Pete, but the love he had for horses was just as intense as it had been then. He'd mourned the death of Old Zip until his father had threatened to spank him so he could bury Zip. Little Pete clung to the dead animal for hours before his mother finally pried him away. Even now, after all the horses he had known, Old Pete missed the old gelding.

He still remembered in great detail, how Zip, even while dying, had taken care of him. They were chasing a calf, not fast, but not merely poking along either, when Zip quickly slowed. Little Pete gave him some leg pressure to get him going again, but Zip didn't respond. He just stopped. Pete knew immediately something was wrong. He could feel Zip's posture change and sense his attitude diminishing. He slipped off the horse's back and went forward to his head.

"What's the matter, Zip?" he asked the horse.

Zip wasn't talking, but he nuzzled Pete's shoulder, nickering softly. Then he lifted his head, turned to look to the west and his legs piled up under him. He settled to the ground in slow motion.

"A heart attack," said Pete's father. "It's a good way to go, Petey. Old Zip didn't suffer a lick. Now he's free, runnin' with the big herd in the sky."

"I wanna go with him!" Little Pete wailed between sobs. "I wanna ride Zip in the sky!"

"You will someday, Pete, but not for a long time yet," his father consoled. "You're only five. You've got a lot more horses to ride here on this ground before you can ride with the herd in the sky. Old Zip will be waitin' for you."

"And now," mused Old Pete, "I've ridden a lot more horses and Old Zip is still waiting."

He smiled to himself as he closed the door on the pickup. *I guess he won't mind waiting a little longer. There's still a few rides left in me.*

"What you grinnin' about?" asked Woody from the other side of the pickup.

"Just thinking about my first horse."

"Is horses the only thing you can think about?" Listening to Woody, it was hard to believe he was college educated.

"No, horses aren't the only things I think about. Sometimes I even think about women!"

Woody smiled. "Yeah, I still think about women too, 'specially the ones I knew."

Woody butchered his English on purpose, or at least that's how it'd started. Now it was a habit, and only by conscious effort, or when he'd been drinking, did he speak properly. He actually had a doctorate in physics from MIT, but after he fled the city, to come out west, he wanted to fit in so he learned to speak like the natives. In Woody's circle, those natives were mostly uneducated, rarely finishing the eighth grade; ranchers, cowboys, sheepherders, and the women with whom they associated.

Pete and Woody were leaving the ranch for a few days. They were headed out, going to a horse sale in Oklahoma. It could be a long drive if Woody got to talking about women. Sooner or later the discussion would get around to Ellen, Woody's late wife. She had been murdered when she and Woody lived in New York City. Her death put a huge hole in Woody's life. He'd never refilled it, but he had managed to learn how to navigate around it.

"You got everything we need?" asked Pete.

"If it ain't in all the stuff we got, we're certain to not need it."

Pete put the pickup in gear. They started away. He glanced in the rearview mirror to check the horse trailer hauling Jolena. He wasn't going to this sale just to look. The trailer was getting smaller.

"Oh for the…! Who was supposed to hook up the trailer?" Pete demanded of Woody.

"You, a'course. You backed up on it."

Pete slowly shook his head. "Sweet Jesus, forgive me, but it's going to be a long trip." He stopped, put the pickup in reverse and went back to collect the trailer.

Chapter 3, Connie

Conrad Allen Bradley III, Connie, to anyone who knew him, was in trouble. It had been almost two years since the great evil had taken his wife. She had fought valiantly for ten long months, but in the end the cancer prevailed. During the long process of suffering her beautiful body had been laid to waste. Her spirit however, had refused to yield. For that Connie was grateful, but watching the suffering she'd had to endure nearly killed him as well as her. The day she died she tried to tell him so much.

"I don't want to leave you." Her voice was tiny and frail in Connie's ear. He had to put his head close to her lips to hear her speak. She was trembling. Her breath came in short, shallow rasps.

Connie cradled her head in his hands; tears filled his eyes to overflowing. He put his lips to her ears and whispered, "I don't want you to leave me."

Then she told him what she'd finally come to accept. She had strongly resisted admitting it. "I can't go on. I want to, but I can't. I can't fight the pull any longer."

Connie was sobbing, "I know, Sarah. I know. I love you." He desperately wanted her to live and be healthy, and they had both fought so long, but he knew she was right. "I release you, Sarah. You have to go." He didn't know exactly what made him say that, but after all the heartache they'd gone through together, it seemed right to tell her.

Sarah tried to smile, "Don't worry, I'll always be close." Her voice was nearly inaudible. Connie strained to hear. "I've come to terms with...." but before she could explain her last thought, her voice trailed off. She was gone. The smile on her lips remained.

"Goodbye, my friend," Connie told her and he sat, holding her hand until it was cold.

Now, two years later, Connie had not reconciled her death. Once again he was contemplating eternity and infinity. To ease the pain he drank. His drinking had evolved quickly since Sarah had left him. He'd always enjoyed a little alcohol; a glass of wine with a special dinner, a beer and a cigar on a lazy Saturday afternoon, and occasionally, a taste of single malt. In the entire twenty plus years since he'd been discharged from the Army, he could count on the fingers of one hand the times he'd had more than two drinks. But that was before Sarah died. In the past six months, he could count on the fingers of one hand, the number of nights he'd not gone to bed in an alcoholic stupor. He likened his drinking to a two-stage rocket blasting away for a trip to the moon. The first stage was a bottle of wine or a six-pack of beer. Consumed quickly, it got him moving upward, away from the gravity of despair that held him down. Then as he was beginning to rise above his grief, he switched to scotch or bourbon to start drinking seriously. As this second stage kicked in, he left his pain just as a rocket would escape the earth's gravitational pull. Connie was free. The earth and its harsh reality receded while the moon and stars lured him on, burning bright with the promise of new hope.

He continued on his rocket ride to nowhere, drinking until he could no longer think. Only then would he sleep. But, in the morning, his head ached more than the night before and now, twenty-two months after Sarah had died, he realized he couldn't continue. Most days he started drinking in the morning to relieve the shakes from the night before. After catching a buzz, he stayed with it all day long. By evening he was becoming incoherent. He'd alienated all but his sister and closest friend. If he couldn't learn to cope with Sarah's absence and his private emptiness, he'd either become a hopeless drunk or take his life.

"I have to do something," he said out loud. "This grief will kill me if I allow it. I've got to do something to help myself and I have to do it soon!" He affirmed this to the ceiling, which he regarded from his bed. The bed he and Sarah had shared for almost twenty years.

They'd met at a party. It was an FTA party for him, hosted by his twin sister, Suzy, and her husband. In polite society, FTA stands for "Forget The Army". In a conversation between two or more soldiers, "Forget" is usually replaced with a different word. Connie hated to blow off four years at West Point, but his military experience was not what he'd hoped it would be. Suzy had started planning the party as soon as he told her of his decision to make his exit. Initially his father, a thirty year man and a retired general, had been disappointed with his son's decision, but he was also aware a military career was not for everyone.

Most of Connie's friends and all of his family were there. Most of Suzy's friends were there too, including a woman the likes of whom Connie had never seen. She was so beautiful he could not help staring at her. He wasn't alone.

An old classmate tapped him on the shoulder. "It's not polite to stare."

Connie turned, "Yeah, I know. Who is she?"

"You're asking me? I don't know any women who look that good. Ask your sister."

Connie noticed the woman was holding an empty glass. "Maybe I should see if I can get her another drink." He was speaking more to himself than his friend.

"Good idea, none of those other guys around her are getting anywhere, and since I'm spoken for, you just might have a shot."

Connie turned, not speaking, giving his friend a look that could curdle fresh milk

His friend lifted his hands in surrender, "Hey, just joking. She's all yours." He slapped Connie on the back.

He quickly walked away without comment. He needed to find his sister, which in this house full of people wouldn't be easy. Suzy and her husband were in the advertising business and had built the house for entertaining. The "great room" gave new meaning to the term. It took several minutes to finally find Suzy chatting animatedly with a young couple he didn't recognize.

Suzy was always chatting with someone. Since she was old enough to talk, she chatted. Connie used to call her JJ, short for Jabber Jaws, until at the age of fourteen, she told him the nickname hurt her feelings. Connie smiled, he'd never called her JJ since, but watching her now, he thought he might remind her of her old nickname. He also thought she'd be chatting all night. If he waited for her to mingle back to him, he could be waiting for a long time. He decided to approach the beautiful woman without Suzy's help.

Since puberty, pretty girls, by mere proximity, tended to intimidate Connie. Even now, at the age of twenty-six, after all he'd lived through, pretty women still made him nervous. He hoped he wouldn't make a fool of himself. The woman was talking to three men arranged in a semi-circle facing her, supplicants petitioning the master.

Strange, I don't recognize any of those guys. For a party in my honor, there are a lot of people here I don't know. He decided a frontal attack would be best. *If I'm going to get shot down, let's make it quick.*

"Excuse me, sir," he told the man directly in front of the woman. "I need to talk to the lady."

The man eyed him warily, but since Connie was physically imposing he quickly shifted to the left to allow Connie room to slide between him and another mesmerized admirer.

Connie reached for the woman's wine glass. "Miss, could I possibly get you a refill?"

She looked him directly in the eyes. "Yes," she told him, "I'd like that. Thank you."

And then, rather than hand him the glass, she moved forward, took his arm, and excused herself from the present company. "Do you mind if I go with you?"

Connie's respiration and heart rate jumped at her touch. "I'd like that," he managed to croak, "Yes, of course."

"You must be the guest of honor." It was half statement, half question.

"Yes, I guess that would be me," he replied as they moved towards the bar Suzy had set up at the back of the great room. "And you are?"

"I'm Sarah. I'm one of your sister's clients."

"Sarah, I'm Conrad, Suzy's brother." He spoke confidently now. Talking had relaxed him.

"I know, I wondered how long I'd have to wait before I met you."

"Really, what has Suzy been telling you?" Sarah had green eyes.

Sarah smiled. "She told me you were a nice guy."

"So, you probably know a lot of nice guys." Her hair was dark reddish, brown, the color of polished mahogany.

"No, you're wrong, nice guys are extremely rare. So rare, I thought I'd come to your party to see for myself."

Connie made a mental note to thank Suzy. "Well, Sarah, I hope I don't disappoint you and I'm pleased to meet you." She was almost as tall as he was, but she was wearing high heels.

They smiled at one another and shook hands. The rest was history. They were married six months later. The honeymoon had lasted over eighteen years.

The phone was ringing. Connie snapped his eyes open to regard his bedroom ceiling again. He groaned a middle-aged groan. "God help me," he moaned softly, more like a prayer than a complaint. Rather than answer his cell phone on the nightstand, he got up and slowly walked to get the phone in the kitchen. With a little luck whoever was calling would give up by the time he reached it. They didn't.

"Hello."

"Hey, Connie," said the voice on the phone, "What's happening on this beautiful morning?" It was his best friend, John, trying to be cheerful.

"You tell me. I'm dying to know." Connie didn't need cheery right now.

"Okay, I will. What are you doing for the next few days? And don't lie."

Connie thought fast, but last night's alcohol had dulled his wits. Nothing came to him for a believable excuse. John and his wife Paula were always trying to involve him in one thing or another. Usually it had something to do with horses. They kept a few quarter horses for diversion and tried to include him in their life. Paula and Sarah had been friends. Connie knew Sarah's death had been hard for Paula, too.

"Time's up, Buddy."

"Uh, nothing, I guess. What's up?"

"I want you to go to a horse sale with me. Paula can't go. She nominated you."

"So why do we need a few days? Where is it, Montana?"

"No, Oklahoma."

"They have horses in Oklahoma?"

"There'll be at least seven hundred, performance bred horses at the sale. That's all I care about."

Connie again tried to think of an excuse for not going. *Montana or Colorado maybe, but Oklahoma? That's desolate country.* He wavered, "Ah, I really should stay here. I've got some stuff to get done."

John wasn't hearing it. In spite of what Connie thought, his drinking was no secret. "Stuff! Yeah right. I'll pick you up at five tomorrow morning. We'll be gone five or six days. Bring your checkbook."

"I don't know, John, I'm really not interested."

John had anticipated Connie's reluctance. He was well prepared to argue his case. He had a speech ready. "Listen up, Connie, all you've been doing for the last six months is moping around, feeling sorry for yourself, and getting hammered. You're sorry Sarah is dead; I'm sorry Sarah's dead, everyone who ever knew her is sorry she's dead, but she is dead. The issue is you're still alive. She wouldn't want you to carry on like you are."

"What do you know about it?" Connie demanded. He was surprised at John's remarks, shocked actually. "You have no idea what she went through and what I'm feeling! I'm trying to get through this. It's just not that easy." *Pretty lame.* His head hurt more than normal.

John didn't want Connie mad at him, but if that's what it took for him to respond, so be it. "Connie, that's the wimpiest thing I've ever heard you say. You were a leader of men, not a pathetic whiner. Look, I realize how much Sarah meant to you and how hard she fought to live. She had the most beautiful spirit of anyone I've ever met, but what about you? Where's your spirit? You just going to roll over and drink yourself to death? Is that the way you want to honor her memory? If it is, say so. I won't bother you anymore."

There was a long period of silence. John thought he might have lost the connection. Finally, Connie broke his silence. "Okay, okay. I'll go. I'll see you at five." Something John said had penetrated the alcohol induced fog. "Why should I bring my checkbook?"

"Who knows," John answered, much relieved Connie had agreed to go, "you might want to buy a horse." With that he hung up. He wasn't going to give him time to change his mind.

Connie held onto the dead phone for some time. Staring straight ahead, his eyes focused on nothing, he was wondering a lot of things. First, what had just happened? *Did I agree to go to Oklahoma with John? Why does John need to go to Oklahoma to find a horse? There must be half a million horses in Indiana.* He thought about calling John back for more details, or better yet, begging off altogether. However, as he considered the situation, he knew John was right. He had become pitiful, and he was the only one who had some control over the situation. Sarah wouldn't approve of his behavior. Actually, he didn't approve of his own behavior. He'd always been upbeat. He'd never allowed himself to feel depressed, at least for long.

It's different this time though. She meant so much to me. I have a right to grieve. He finally hung up the phone. *Who the hell am I kidding?*

There was half a bottle of single malt whiskey sitting on the kitchen table, left over from last night. It tempted him mightily. The low alcohol warning system his body had developed over the past six months was blinking rapidly, screaming at him, "I need a drink!" He stared at the bottle until he broke into a cold sweat. He made fists of both hands and clenched them until his wrists ached. Several minutes passed before he was able to recall what John had said about Sarah's spirit, "She had the most beautiful spirit of anyone I've ever met."

True. She had a beautiful spirit. Physically and spiritually she was the most beautiful woman in the world. Tears blurred the whiskey bottle.

Connie remembered the night he met her. All the men at his party had been staring at her. "Does it bother you?" he'd asked her.

"Not any more. I'm used to it. Actually, it's given me confidence." She said it as a matter of fact, without pride or arrogance. It was merely a statement. "When I was a teenager, I thought I was pretty hot stuff and I acted like it. My mother straightened me out. She told me I was pretty, but she also made me understand being pretty wasn't an accomplishment. I wasn't responsible for the way I looked. That was heredity, not achievement. She said, 'If you want to do something, make yourself beautiful on the inside. That's where it's important. Then when you're old or your health fails and your physical beauty is gone, your beautiful soul will still be there.' I've tried to take her advice."

She'd been successful. Everyone who knew her had to agree, she was truly beautiful inside and out. *So what am I?* He wasn't certain, but he suspected he was becoming very ugly on the inside. He didn't want that.

Okay, I'll go. A little road trip will be good. He left the bottle of scotch undisturbed and started moving. He had a few things to do before the tomorrow morning.

Financially, Connie had done well. He'd been a partner in a plastic plumbing supply business that, while not very glamorous, certainly had treated him right. He and his partner had bought the business from his partner's father. At the time, it was financially sound, but small and faced a lot of competition. His partner had the idea to carry a huge inventory so customers wouldn't have to wait. He believed it would make them the plastic pipe supplier of preference. The partners borrowed every dime they could, rented a large warehouse, stocking it with every imaginable plastic fitting any contractor could ever need. He'd been right. Their success was phenomenal, but after twenty years,

Connie was more than bored. Also, Connie's partner had a son and Connie didn't. It seemed reasonable to sell out. He sold his half of the business for slightly less than eight million dollars.

He was at the apogee of middle age, forty-six, but still fit and tough. He and Sarah planned to travel and enjoy the money. The first trip they made was to Africa where they climbed Mount Kilima'Njaro and visited game parks in Tanzania and Kenya. Sarah wasn't feeling well when they returned home. For as long as she could, she dismissed the nausea, thinking her discomfort was related to the trip and would pass. A month later her condition had not improved, and at Connie's insistence, she visited her doctor. That started a two-month ordeal of tests and retests at the end of which she received the bad news. It took another seven months and several different "cures" for her to die. Connie would gladly trade every cent he had to have Sarah back, but that wasn't going to happen.

John's admonition to bring money would be no problem. His only concerns would be Fritz the cat and clean clothes. Connie hadn't been doing much laundry lately.

Actually, Fritz won't be a problem. I'll take him to Suzy's and clean clothes won't be a problem either. I'll just go buy some new blue jeans. What else would I wear to a horse sale in Oklahoma? He smiled at the thought.

Boots too, I'll need some boots. Maybe some snakeskin or alligator or whatever cowboys wear now days. He was getting into the idea and it surprised him.

It'd been a long time since he'd ridden a horse, although it wasn't necessary to be an actual cowboy to wear the outfit. In fact, the last time he was on a horse, he was only eighteen. *Twenty-eight years! I wonder if it's like riding a bicycle, or can you forget how?* Not that he intended to find out. He was going to a horse sale, not a dude ranch.

At one time he'd been a decent rider. Every summer, between the ages of thirteen and eighteen, he'd worked on a dude ranch in Montana. The owner of the ranch was a World War II buddy of Connie's father. They'd been in combat together. Connie's father had been captivated with the stories his friend told of the Wild West, but not quite enough to relocate after the war. He stayed in close touch with his friend and they visited each other often. When Connie was old enough, he was invited to spend summers on the dude ranch. The work had been hard, but he liked it. He planned to be a rodeo cowboy first and a rancher later. However, his father had other plans for him and when

Connie received a nomination to West Point; he gave up his cowboy dreams.

Thinking about boots had awakened long sleeping memories. In particular, he wondered what had happened to Patsy, the pretty little brunette he'd met on the ranch the summer he was seventeen. At the time, he'd loved her desperately. She was five-foot-two, with short, dark, curly hair that framed her face in the most beguiling fashion. She had a physique that made Connie weak with young lust. It was the first time he'd thought about her or any other woman since Sarah had come into his life. Suddenly Connie discovered he was looking forward to this trip to Oklahoma.

Oklahoma! Good grief, I'm excited about going to Oklahoma! I'm in worse shape than I thought.

Soon he was cruising down the highway to the closest Western wear and tack shop.

Chapter 4, Pete and Woody

"So you reckon you'll be gettin' big money for Jolena?"
Woody asked Pete through a yawn.

"Yes, I do. Don't you think I should?"

Woody had stayed awake but silent for the first hour or so.
Then, right after they passed through Polson at the south end of Flathead
Lake, he dozed off for about a hundred miles. Shortly after Pete turned
off US 93 and onto Interstate 90, headed east, Woody woke up and
wanted to talk. It didn't matter what he talked about, he just wanted to
hear himself and Pete make conversation.

"Well, I dunno. You obviously think she's pretty capable. My
question is do you think other people will think she's as good as you
do?"

Pete thought for a minute. As usual with Woody, it was a
loaded question. "So what you're really asking me is why do I think
I'm such a great judge of horse flesh?" Pete looked over at Woody who
was looking out his window.

Woody turned to catch Pete's eye. "Yup, that's what I said."

"When you were herding sheep, how many did you have in a
flock?"

"It varied some. Could be one summer I'd have only three
hundred, then next season it'd be double that. Just depended on how
many the company wanted to keep and how many herders we had."

"Could you tell them apart?"

"Yeah, mostly. Usually by the end of the summer, I'd maybe learn 'em all, unless it was a real big flock, but still I'd know a lot of 'em. What's your point?"

"My point is simple. In spite of the fact all sheep are born just lookin' for a place to die, they're all individuals. Some of them are actually dumber than others. And I suppose, they don't all look alike either."

Woody laughed. "I'll grant you they ain't Rhodes scholars, but neither are horses. I'll bet if you was to scale a sheep up to the size of a horse, it'd be just as good—smoother ridin' too. You wouldn't need no saddle, just sit up there on that soft fleece and grab a hand full of wool. Hell, you wouldn't need no reins or a bridle neither."

"Yeah I could see you checkin' into the local hotel. 'Hi, Pardner, my name is Tex. I need a room for the night and my faithful steed, Fluffy, needs a stall in your stable.'"

"You just gonna make fun of me or you gonna answer my question?"

"Geez I'm sorry, Woody. What was the question again?"

"It's a simple question. What makes you think Jolena is so great?"

Woody might really be thinking it was a simple question. Pete wasn't sure. With Woody it was hard to tell. Woody was scary smart and had a sneaky sense of humor. Things were seldom as they seemed when talking with him. This time Pete decided Woody really did think it was a simple question—maybe. Pete decided to give him his best answer. "A horse like Jolena doesn't happen very often. She's one in a million or maybe even one in ten million. I'm not sure, I've never had one like her before. I've never even seen another like her. First off, she's smart. For a horse, she's a genius. How often does a true human genius come along?"

"You askin' me?" Woody looked at him critically.

"You're the only one in the truck besides me ain't you? Who do you think I'm asking?"

Woody pointed up at the small TV monitor hanging from the roof of the cab. It showed a wide-angle view of the interior of the horse trailer they were towing. Jolena was watching them watch her. "For a minute there I thought you might be talking to her."

Pete slowly shook his head. "I'd probably get straighter talk from her. Maybe I should hook up a two-way radio so we could communicate."

"Might's well. You're always talkin' to her anyway. I think sometimes you believe she understands what you're tellin' her."

Pete ignored him. Sometimes he did think the little mare understood him, but he wasn't about to admit that to Woody. "To finish what I was saying, I think Jolena is a very rare horse. She's smart. I can tell that because she learns what I'm trying to teach her very quickly. Horses learn by repetition and most of them need lots of repetition, especially to learn something complicated. Jolena catches on fast, much quicker than any horse I've ever worked with. She's well coordinated. She moves with the grace of a ballerina and the speed of a cat. She's also the most mature three-year old I've ever known. I'm telling you straight, Woody, I've worked a lot of horses in the past sixty some years and she's the best yet. I wish I were a younger man."

"Is that why you're sellin' her?"

"Yeah, mostly that's why. She can be the next world champion, but it won't happen with me on her back. She needs a younger rider. That and I need the money to put the twins through college."

"The twins ain't even outta grade school yet. How much you figure Jolena's gonna bring you?"

"If I don't get at least fifty thousand, she's comin' back home with us." That thought didn't particularly bother Pete. He had grown as attached to this horse as he had to none other, except maybe his childhood buddy, Old Zip.

Woody shook his head slowly. "I seen her work. Can't say as I think she's all that great. Good, yeah, but not great."

Pete laughed. "Woody, no offense, but you wouldn't know a great cutting horse from a painted pony on a merry-go-round. Not only that, nobody has seen this horse work yet. You think the fifteen or twenty minutes a day I've been spending on her back the last six months is any indication of what she'll be able to do by the end of this year?"

"Well I dunno. You're telling me how good she can work. What are you basin' your opinion on?"

Pete rubbed his jaw. He realized Woody couldn't understand how he knew what a great horse little Jolena was and how good she would be.

"I came within five minutes of being born in the saddle and in the past eighty years, I've spent near as much time riding as I have sleeping, maybe more. I can't explain it to you, I can just feel it. I can feel it in my thighs and hips when she moves. It's deliberate and purposeful and there's intelligence behind it. You'll just have to take

my word for it. That little mare has the heart and soul to be the best
cutting horse that ever walked God's green earth."

"Well, if you say so, but just because she can chase a chicken
into a bag don't prove nothin' to me. Except of course, she can bag a
chicken. What's a chicken got to do with a cow?"

Woody was referring to a trick Pete had taught Jolena. Years
earlier, there had been a Texas cutting horse by the name of Rooster
whose owner allegedly made a fair amount of money betting his horse
could cut a chicken into a burlap sack. Legend had it he never lost a bet.
Before Jolena was a year old, she took a big interest in the flock of
chickens Pete kept on the ranch. Anytime they came within range she
pinned her ears back and went after them. She never hurt any of them,
but she never let any of them walk past her either. The first time Pete
noticed, he remembered the story of Rooster. Enlisting Woody's help,
he decided to give Jolena a chance. He positioned Jolena in the middle
of his round pen and had Woody set a chicken in front of her. Holding
open the door to a medium sized, portable dog kennel, he positioned
himself about twenty feet away. The first attempt fizzled when the
chicken flew out of the round pen. The second chicken was a little more
cooperative, making a complete orbit of the round pen before she too,
flapped up over the fence. The third chicken was a real trooper and
within thirty seconds, Jolena had chased her into the dog cage. Chicken
cutting became a frequent game for Jolena and after a few successful
tries; the dog kennel was replaced with an old pillow case, burlap bags
being all but extinct. Pete intended to demonstrate Jolena's chicken
cutting ability at the auction. Jolena shared the horse trailer with two
chickens in a big dog kennel.

"The fact she can maneuver a flighty, neurotic bird into a bag
means she's intelligent, quick and agile. Those same characteristics
make her a great cow horse. She's already better than almost any
finished three-year-old and she's got eight months to go." Pete had
started working Jolena on cattle almost a year ago, but wasn't pushing
her very hard. Pete didn't like to work his young horses too hard until
their knee joints matured. He never had accepted the conventional
thinking that allowed three-year olds to seriously compete and run the
risk of being lame at an early age. On paper Jo was a three-year old, but
in reality she had a month to go before her third birthday. All horses
born in a given year are automatically a year old on the first day of that
year. A horse born on December thirty-first officially became two years
old the next day.

"Well maybe you're right. Fifty grand, you say? Seems like a lot of money for a little cow pony."

"Woody, fifty thousand is nothin' in the cutting horse business, and even less when you start talkin' race horses. Some stud fees are double that and more."

Woody shook his head slowly. "A hundred grand, just for swimmers?"

"Well you're not paying just for the semen. There is a live foal guarantee."

"There's a comfort."

"Money is no object for some people."

"Yeah, it never was for me either. That's why I ain't got any." Actually, Woody was lying. He had well over six hundred thousand dollars in various bank accounts back East. It was money he had inherited from his parents and an uncle. He'd never spent any of it, preferring to let it grow. When he died, Pete's grandchildren would get it. Pete had no knowledge of Woody's plan.

"How far we goin' today?" Woody changed the subject.

"Why, you bored already?"

"No, I want to know is all."

Well, if we want to get to Oklahoma City before the sale starts, I'd like to get to Sheridan by tonight. That's about seven hundred miles." Pete glanced over at Woody. "Sure you're not tired of riding already are you?"

"No, course not. I like watchin' the country go by."

"Looks to me you like inspecting your eyelids for holes more than you like watching the scenery."

"You got me up too early. I need my beauty rest you know."

Pete regarded Woody with a critical eye. "Yes, you do! In fact, if you go to sleep now and don't wake up until we get to Oklahoma City, you might just break even."

"What's that supposed to mean?"

"It means you're ugly, and I don't see much that tells me you're going to improve."

"I used to know a woman or two in Sheridan who thought different. One of 'em was real fine lookin' too."

"Used to know? What happen, they move away?"

"I'd guess they're still there. I'm just not sure either one of them would be happy to see me after all these years."

"Why not? You love 'em and leave 'em?"

"Sorta. Though I almost married the one."

"Why didn't you?"

"Well, not only was I sure I could live without a woman's charms, she was awful demandin'."

"How about the other one. You come close to marrying her too?"

"Naw, she said she had no desire to get married. She said she'd been married once and that was all she needed."

"That doesn't sound all bad. Why'd you dump her?"

"I didn't, she dumped me. Some old cowboy started hangin' around and she found him more her style than an old sheepherder. I seen him a couple times. Looked more like a drugstore cowboy than the genuine article. For his age, he didn't look near busted up enough to be a real cowboy."

Pete shook his head in mock sympathy. "Bet you hated losing out to a scissorbill like that."

"Initially it didn't set right, but after I come to my senses, I realized that cowboy done me a big favor. See I was gettin' kinda comfortable with that old gal. I come close to losin' my head."

"How so? You just said she didn't want to get married. What was the danger?"

"She claimed she didn't want to get married. After I come to my senses, I realized she was lyin'. A woman that don't want to get married ain't natural."

Pete laughed. "That's about the silliest thing I've ever heard come out of your mouth. There are lots of women who, for various reasons, prefer not to get married."

"Yeah? Name one we both know."

"Well my daughter for one. She was married once. The guy was a dope and I doubt if she'll ever remarry."

"I'll grant you her husband was a dope, not to mention a fool, walkin' away from a fine lookin' woman like Cally, but I'll bet you even money she's remarried within five years." Woody thought for a second. "Naw, make that two years. I got a hundred bucks says she's married again within two years."

Pete took his eyes off the road for an instant to look at Woody. He appeared serious. "What makes you so sure of that?"

"Easy. You know horses, I know women."

"You're on. Write it down or we'll both forget." Woody rummaged through the glove box until he found a pencil and a piece of paper. Licking the lead of the pencil, he wrote down the terms of the wager. He passed the paper and pencil to Pete. "Make your mark."

"How about I just initial it, or would you prefer I made an X?"

"Yer initials would be just fine."

"Hold the paper on the dash and give me the pencil."

When the agreement was duly authorized, Woody folded it in half and committed it to his wallet. "When we get home, you can lock it up in your gun safe."

"Deal," Pete agreed.

Pete's pickup truck and the horse trailer seemed to sit still on the interstate while the country flowed past. The two old men continued to discuss horses, women, and the things they had done together when they were younger; boasting and laughing until the Montana college town of Bozeman slid into view.

"You hungry?" Pete asked Woody.

"Yeah, my stomach thinks my throat musta been slit."

"Why didn't you say something earlier?"

"I figured you was on a tight schedule."

"We're on a schedule all right, but it ain't that critical." He looked at his watch. "It's not quite one, we're doin' good. You can take enough time to eat as much as you want."

"Glad to hear it. You 'spose this town still got a decent steak house or have all the intellectuals filled it up with café latte bars and vegan restaurants?"

"I don't rightly know." Pete started braking for the exit. "Let's find out."

They found a bar and grill with a big parking lot not too far off the freeway. Pete wheeled the pickup through the lot, parking well away from the other cars. "You go ahead in and find us a seat," he told Woody. "I'm gonna let Jo out for a minute."

"You want coffee?" Woody called over his shoulder as he made for the door.

"Yeah, that'd be good."

Unlatching the back door of the trailer, Pete called out, "Hey, Jolena, how you doin'?"

The horse nickered in response. Pete walked into the empty side of the trailer and unsnapped the mare's trailer tie. He clipped a lead rope on her halter. "Back, Jo." The horse backed out of the trailer. "How about we go for a little walk?" Pete led the horse towards the back of the parking lot. He attracted a fair amount of attention with patrons going into and coming out of the restaurant.

"My God, Jo," he told the horse when he put her back in the trailer, "you'd think they'd never seen a horse before. What kind of a Montana town has this become?"

Later, after a passable steak, Pete expressed his concern to Woody. "I'm worried about this country, Woody."

"How's that?"

"When I had Jo out in the parking lot, we created quite a stir.'

"What'd ya 'spect. Folks ain't used to seein' horses in the parking lot of restaurants."

"This is Bozeman, Montana, Woody, not New York City!"

"How'd ya know the people doin' the gawkin' weren't tourists from New York?"

"Yeah, I never thought of that. But still even if they were, they'd have to realize they were in Montana. The sight of a horse gettin' a little exercise shouldn't be a big deal."

"Maybe Jolena's just a lot flashier than you know. Maybe them folks just never saw a paint horse that color before."

Pete thought about that for a while. "Maybe you're right." Then he started thinking maybe fifty grand was too cheap a price for a horse like Jolena. After all, he was the one who had said it, "A horse like her is one in a million."

Later that evening, after Jolena was settled in a stall at the "mare motel" and he and Woody were settled in their room close by, he was still thinking about it. "I really don't want to sell this horse," he quietly told himself. He thought about turning around tomorrow morning and heading home. He'd keep her and finish her training. Maybe get Cally to ride her and enter her in the futurity himself. No, that'd be stupid. Although he was sure Cally could ride her, how would she find the time? Those twin girls of hers were firecrackers. Some days they kept everybody hopping. There was no way she could do all she had to do and still seriously train for a major event. And it was "The Event." Last year the winner in the open division picked up a check for over two hundred thousand. No, Cally wasn't an option. He'd have to find another way. He fell asleep searching for a plan.

Two thousand miles east of where Pete, Woody, and Jolena slept, Conrad Bradley was tossing and turning at the rate of one complete flip every six minutes. He hadn't had a drink all day and he was missing it badly. He knew it was more than a psychological thing. It was also a powerful physiological addiction. He'd never imagined he could ever be so weak as to become dependant on alcohol. He was sorely tempted to get up and start to work on the bottle of scotch that was still sitting on his kitchen table.

He looked at the bedside clock for the fiftieth time and moaned, "Oh for the love of God, why can't I just fall asleep?" He itched all over. No position was comfortable and he was getting hot. He wanted to scream. Throwing back the blankets he got out of bed. He walked into the kitchen to regard the whisky he craved.

As he sat at the table, he pulled the bottle close to him and wrapped both hands around it. It would be real easy to yank the cork and have a nice long pull. He put his fingers on the cork. "Be strong!" He heard a voice. He snapped his gaze around the room as the hair on the back of his neck rose up. A chill skittered across his shoulders and slipped down his spine.

"Good, Lord! Now I'm hearing voices." He released his strangle hold on the whisky bottle and retrieved a bottle of milk from the refrigerator. It was about the only thing left in there. After pouring a cup, he heated it in the microwave. When he was a kid and couldn't sleep, his mother would stir a big spoonful of honey into a glass of warm milk and by the time he'd finished it, he was rubbing his eyes to stay awake.

"Let's see if it still works!" More than forty years had passed since the last time he'd tasted the potion. It was more cloying than he remembered, but he managed to finish it. Ten minutes later he was back in bed, sleeping soundly, dreaming about horses.

Chapter 5, Connie and John

"Nice boots," John told Connie when he stepped up into John's pickup. It was first light and the already warm air was heavy with the sweet scent of lilac. It was going to be a hot, humid, spring day in Indianapolis.

"Thanks, Buddy. Genuine Luccheses."

"Nothin' but the finest. Keep this up, you'll be on horseback before the week is over."

"I doubt it, but I want to get a hat. I figure there's got to be a Western store somewhere on our way. I couldn't find one I liked around here. Everything I tried on looked stupid."

John put the truck in gear and pulled out into the street. "Maybe it's not the hat," and he quickly added, "but I know there's at least one Western store in Oklahoma City. If they ain't got one that makes you look smart, we'll go to Fort Worth. I guarantee we'll find one there."

"That'd be good." Connie ignored the cheap shot and pointed his thumb over his shoulder. There was a horse trailer behind the truck. "You must be serious about buying a horse."

"Yeah, two even, if I can find two I like at a price I like. Paula and I rode cutting horses for the first time about six weeks ago. Now it's all we talk about."

"That great, is it?"

"It's kind of hard to describe, but Paula thinks it's the most fun we've had since our honeymoon."

Connie considered John's statement. He tried to remember back to the long summers of his youth working on the Montana dude ranch. He didn't recall anything he did on horseback to be as exciting as what John was talking about. He thought back on the little brunette again and decided it would have had to been one wild horseback ride to thrill him the way she had. And they had never taken off so much as their shoes. "Sounds interesting. Maybe I'll have to try it."

"If I can get a couple of horses, plan on it."

"What about cows? You planning to get some of them too?"

"Don't need to. We go to this place where you rent them by the minute."

"Rent cows by the minute?"

"Yeah. There's this farm about forty miles west of town. Actually it's a feedlot, but it's not your typical, muddy, cramped operation. The guy has a hundred acres and always has about a thousand head of cattle. You get space in an arena and twenty-five cows for twenty minutes for half a C note. We go with two other couples and do three twenty minute sessions. Costs fifty dollars a couple. That's cheap, a good bottle of wine can be twenty bucks, and there's no hangover associated with chasin' cows."

"The no hangover part is good. Isn't that kind of hard on the guy's beef cattle, getting chased all day long?"

"I asked him about that. He's got it figured out. Each cow gets chased less than five minutes every week."

"Okay, makes sense. Five minutes a week shouldn't affect them. Is he busy all the time?"

"You wouldn't believe it. You have to make reservations at least two weeks in advance. We figure he's making more money renting the cows for cutting than he does selling them for meat."

"I never would have guessed there are so many closet cowboys out there."

"Wait 'til you try it." John continued to enlighten Connie on the more subtle aspects of cutting cattle on horseback as the first hundred miles slipped by them.

Over the course of those hundred miles, as they talked, Connie finally started to relax, to give up a little of his pain, and begin to forgive himself. The death of his beloved, even though he knew it was coming, was like a kick in the groin. It took his spiritual breath away and left him doubled over with an intense ache in his psyche. It would be much longer for his complete recovery, but it was then, in the truck, going down the road with a good friend when his deliverance from the prison

of pain he'd locked himself into finally started. Maybe it was the
realization he could think and talk about something other than Sarah's
death. Maybe it was rediscovering the world had not stopped for
everybody else, and maybe it could start again for him. Or maybe it was
simply the stimulus of moving smoothly down the highway with an easy
destination in mind. Later, when Connie realized he was getting past
Sarah's death, he was grateful to his friend, John, for convincing him to
come along.

"I've never been to an auction," Connie told John.

"You're serious? Never?

"Nope. Never. If I want something, I just go out and buy it."

"What if you wanted a genuine antique? Where would you
go?"

"Antique store or my sister's. She's got a house full of them."

"Where'd she get them?"

"I have no idea. Antique stores probably."

"I doubt it. I'll bet most them came from estate sales. If you
want the good stuff, you've got to go to the source. I don't do estate
sales, but every horse I've ever bought, I bought at auction."

"How do you know what you're getting?"

"It's like buying anything. You have to know what you're
looking at. You were in business, how'd you pick your suppliers?"

"We bought direct from the manufacturers. It was plastic pipe
and fittings, they're all the same."

"Regardless, the manufacturers were all different. Some had to
be better than others and you had to learn which ones were the best."

"Yeah, okay, but it wasn't that difficult. How much time is
there to judge a horse at the auction? Five minutes? How can you tell
anything about a horse in five minutes?"

"No offense, but you probably can't tell much of anything
about a horse in five minutes other than what color it is. I'm fifty-one
years old and have been playing with horses for more than forty years.
It isn't something I can communicate, but I can tell enough about a
horse in less than two minutes to know whether I want to own him or
not. My wife has an even better eye than I do. Her only problem is
she's afraid to bid."

"If you can do this, what about all the other people at the
auction? Do they all have an innate ability to judge horse flesh?"

"Most of them do, in varying degrees. It wouldn't be much of
an auction if they didn't."

Connie thought. "Good point. Glad I'm not bidding."

"You want to bid, let me know what you're looking at before you start. I'll keep you straight."

Connie reached down to the control on the seat. Tilting the seat back, he stretched out and closed his eyes. "That's not going to happen. I need a horse like I need a bad case of amoebic dysentery."

"Be careful. Where we're going, we could get that too"

Connie sat back up in his seat. "What God forsaken wilderness are you taking me to? I thought you said Oklahoma."

"Relax, I'm kidding. I've never gotten anything worse then a mild case of heartburn where we're going."

Connie leaned back into the seat. "Comforting. Wake me if you need me to drive." Closing his eyes, he thought about the little brunette of long ago on a Montana ranch outside of Livingston.

The truck and trailer were hitting the expansion joints in the concrete freeway with a certain, disjointed rhythm. Due to the difference in the length of the wheelbase of the truck and the distance between the truck's rear wheels and the trailer's wheels, every fourth expansion joint produced a gentle tugging motion that quickly hypnotized Connie. Thump, thump, thump, tug. Thump, thump, thump, tug. He was asleep in minutes.

He woke when John pulled off the freeway to get gas. Sensing a change in the rhythm of thumps and tugs, his eyes snapped open. He jumped against the seatbelt.

Connie's reaction was so intense, John was startled. "You okay?"

Connie's eyes were wide, darting wildly. He was trying to determine whether to run or fight. As realization dawned, he exhaled slowly. "Geez, I hate that. You'd think after twenty years, I'd be over it."

John knew he was referring to the time he spent in combat. "You scared me. I'm glad the seatbelt held."

"Scared you. I scared myself." And then he smiled. "You should have seen Sarah the first time it happened. I don't think she slept the rest of the night."

John thought Connie might lapse into some kind of depression if he talked about Sarah, but to his surprise and relief, it didn't happen.

"Yeah, I'm sure she was wondering what she had gotten herself into. But after that first time, she seemed to be able to handle it. I don't think she ever got used to me flying out bed, positive I was under attack, but she got pretty good at calming me down."

"She was definitely a class act." And then he changed the subject. "You hungry? How about we get some breakfast?"

"Yeah, what good is a road trip, if you can't stop long enough to sample the local cuisine?"

"So you're saying you don't want to go to a franchised eatery?"

"Yeah. Get away from the highway, at least a little ways. Let's find some little joint with a lot of cars in the parking lot."

John cruised up to the stop sign at the end of the exit ramp. "That's a contradiction in terms. How can a little joint handle a lot of business?"

"You know what I mean. Go right."

The freeway had bypassed the town years ago, leaving it to survive by its own devices without the benefit of the traffic the old highway had provided. Once John and Connie had passed by several combinations of gas station, convenience store and restaurant at the freeway exit, it took them five minutes to get to town. They cruised the three-block-long main drag, up and down. There were two restaurants in the little town, one on either end of the strip.

"Okay, Smart Guy, which one of these two, fine, local establishments is it going to be? Neither one of them has a parking lot."

Connie didn't hesitate. "Go back to the one on the other end of town. It's on the corner and you can park on the side street."

They had to park a block away and walk back, but the food was worth it. They sat at the counter, on stools that swiveled. The red plastic upholstery was buffed pink and smooth from years of use. The original pattern in the vinyl and its color could only be distinguished on the sides of the stool.

"Just think of how many different butts have graced these stools," John said as he dropped his onto the long-suffering resting place.

"Probably just the same couple dozen thousands of times over the last fifty years." Connie looked up at the high tin ceiling with its stamped pattern of bumps and ridges. He tapped his toes on the worn pine floor beneath his stool. "Check your watch, see if the hands are still moving. This looks like the place time forgot."

"Hey, Buddy, you picked it."

"I know; I just hope the food's better than the place looks."

The waitress, a pretty, young woman, looking like she should still be in school, brought them water, empty cups and a pot of coffee without asking if they wanted it.

She poured coffee in the cups. "Good morning, Fellas. What'll it be?"

"Shouldn't you be in school?" John asked her.

She glanced at her watch. "I got another forty-five minutes before I have to leave. It's only quarter past seven. I get credit at school for work."

"Good for you, I'm impressed. Can we have a menu?"

"Not for breakfast." She gestured behind her. "Everything's on the board."

And so it was, the daily fare, printed in colored chalk on a blackboard. There were pancakes, eggs, toast, waffles, French toast, sausage, steak, pork chops, bacon, hash browns, American fries, cold cereal, hot cereal, pastries, and several combinations of these things with names like The Lumberjack; three eggs, hash browns, two, six-ounce, pork chops, toast and coffee. Connie settled for The Rancher, two eggs, eight-ounce tenderloin, American fries, toast, coffee, and orange juice. John had boring bacon and eggs, although he did finish it off with a hot apple dumpling, a small dollop of ice cream on the side. Thirty minutes later, they waddled back to the truck, toothpicks hanging from the corners of their mouths.

"Now that's what I'm talking about breakfast," Connie told John.

"Yeah, you did good, but how about driving for awhile. I might need a little nap. I shouldn't have had that apple thing."

"You mean that sweet, juicy, apple dumpling with the ice cream melting all over it?"

"Yeah, that thing." He tossed Connie the keys.

Back on the freeway, behind the wheel of the pickup, with John zoned out, Connie had time to think. He felt blessed. Something he hadn't felt in a long time. He had just consumed at least three times the daily recommend amount of protein for a male of his size, and it had cost less than three gallons of gasoline. He was glad to be an American, living in America. The people who thought he should be eating nothing but bean curd and taking the bus everywhere he went, were nuts. But, he speculated, those people probably didn't like him, the American life style, Americans in general, and maybe not even themselves. As far as Connie was concerned, social engineering was something those who considered themselves to be the social elite should keep to themselves. But, on the other hand, freedom had to hear all the voices. He just didn't have to listen.

Connie had another realization. The last time he had breakfast on the road was with Sarah. It was shortly after she'd been diagnosed with cancer. They had traveled to a prestigious Chicago hospital to get a second opinion. In spite of the purpose of the trip, it brought back fond memories. They had searched out obscure restaurants, snuggled in strange beds in good hotels, played stupid car games as they went down the road, and they talked, not of cancer, but of their future. "We didn't have a clue about what was coming," Connie whispered. A few months later, Sarah weighed less than ninety pounds and could barely sit up. In another two months she was dead. Truly, cancer was the disease straight from hell. Yet even this thought did not depress him as it would have just a day ago. I've turned the corner, he thought and realized he was doubly blessed.

When the gas gauge demanded attention, he found a station. When John woke up, they talked. When he grew sleepy, they traded seats. They moved across the countryside in a blur of hazy colors and the incessant thumping of tires. Noon came and went followed by afternoon and early evening. Finally, when the sun began casting long shadows they could not outrun, they debated driving straight through or finding a motel.

"Whatever you want," Connie told John. "I can drive or I can stop."

"We've got time if we want to stop. The auction doesn't start until tomorrow morning at eleven, but I do want to get there a little early to look at what's for sale."

"Whatever you decide, although it would be nice to find the place in the daylight. Unless you already know where you're going."

"Nope, never been there before. I've got directions though."

"Well then, what's the big rush? Let's find a place to flop, get up early, and be there before ten. We can even stop for another gut-busting breakfast."

"Okay, start looking for a motel."

An hour later they found one in the little town of Miami, Oklahoma, seventy-five miles east of Tulsa. They slept the sleep of the righteous, neither of them suffering the slightest hint of insomnia. In the morning, Connie again felt blessed. It was the best night's sleep, unaided by alcohol, he'd had in a year.

The site of the auction was about thirty-five miles east of Oklahoma City and the directions John had been given, proved to be nearly worthless. Actually, the directions weren't bad, it was the fact the local roads were so poorly marked. It took them almost an hour to find the place after they turned off I-40 at the Shawnee exit. Even the truck's GPS was confused. They had to stop for directions, something neither of them considered manly, but still finally arrived by nine.

As Connie got out of the truck and stretched, he watched two old men unloading a pretty, gray colored, paint horse from a trailer with Montana plates. The filly backed out of the trailer, turned to look Connie in the eye, and gave a quick, high-pitched, whinny before the two men led her away toward the sale barn.

Chapter 6, The Auction

There were certain horses John wanted to see before the sale started. He'd been studying his catalog since he'd received it in the mail two weeks earlier, annotating the horses in which he was interested, according to a specific code. Horses with pedigrees he felt to be worthy of his attention were marked with a check. Horses marked with two checks were horses with good pedigrees and had some amount of cutting training. Horses with three checks had worthy pedigrees and had earned money in cutting contests. Thirty-eight horses had one check. Twenty-one of those horses had two checks and nine horses had three check marks. It took two hours for John to see them all. Most of them looked the same to Connie, although he did see one well-built, flashy, buckskin, paint gelding that interested him. He asked John what he thought.

"Nice looking. Well balanced, but too big for a cutting horse." Then he looked at the horse's pedigree stapled to the front of the stall door. "You probably wouldn't want him."

"Oh, yeah. Why not?"

"He's related to Impressive."

"Who's Impressive and what's his problem?"

"He was a big time show horse with a genetic aberration called HYPP. He sired over twenty-five hundred horses and his extended get list is over a hundred thousand horses. I don't know all the details, but somehow HYPP affects the horse's ability to metabolize potassium. The worst cases are fatal."

"Is there a cure?"

"No, but there's a test. Not all of his descendants carry it. Usually, anybody trying to sell an Impressive bred horse will have had him tested. If the seller isn't advertising negative test results, don't buy the horse."

Connie read through the flyer stapled to the stall front. "Doesn't say anything about it."

"Forget him," John told him and continued moving down the aisle between the rows of stalls. "He's a show horse. Show horse people are different."

"What about cutting show horse people, are they different too?" John stopped. "Huh?"

"What's the difference between people who show horses and people who show cutting horses?"

"I'm talking about the difference between halter horses and performance horses."

"What's a halter horse?"

"It's a horse whose specific purpose is to be led around an arena on the end of a lead rope. It's usually big and muscular with little feet and can't do much of anything but look pretty."

"What do you mean by can't do much of anything? It's still a horse."

"Barely. They usually end up with hoof and leg problems. They've been bred for big bodies and little feet. All that weight pounding on those minimal hooves eventually leads to problems."

"Why breed them that way."

John shrugged. "Who knows? It happens to be the present style. Maybe in another twenty years the judges will realize horses were meant to run."

Connie continued to look at the gelding after John walked away. According to the pedigree taped to the stall door, the horse's name was Texas Zipper. "Sorry Zip," Connie said to the horse, "The man says no." He moved on to catch up with John. Texas Zipper continued chewing hay, totally unconcerned about his questionable pedigree or a potentially painful future filled with lameness.

Finally finished with looking, John at horses and Connie at the people looking at horses, they were ready to get a seat in the part of the barn where the auction would be held. The facility was two buildings connected by a short, wide, covered walkway. The sale horses were stabled in stalls in a large barn with an adjoining arena. The auction was conducted in a smaller barn with a twenty by fifty foot show ring

surrounded on three sides by bleachers. By the time John had finished
looking at all the horses he was interested in, the best seats were filled
and they had to take seats high up, towards the top of the bleachers, in a
corner. Not the greatest seats in the house, but John had already decided
on which horses he wanted to bid. He could bid on them just fine from
where they'd be sitting.

Connie had a big cup of bad coffee and had sipped about half of
it as they were inspecting horses. What was left was now cold and
totally undrinkable. "I need to get rid of this swill," he told John. "I'm
going back to the concession stand to get something better. You want
anything?"

John thought for a minute. "I don't know, maybe a soda."

"What kind? What size?"

"I don't know. Surprise me, but make it small."

"You got it. One small surprise comin' up." He began picking
his way carefully down the bleachers through the crowd.

The concession stand was in a corner of the big barn by the
arena, and as Connie moved through the walkway between the buildings,
the first sellers were lining up with their horses in the predetermined
order of sale. Connie glanced at his watch. It was ten minutes past
eleven. The sale was supposed to start at eleven.

As he came to the end of the walkway, he noticed the two older
men with the pretty little paint horse he had seen earlier in the morning.
He swore one of the men had tears in his eyes, but what really threw
him was the look he got from the horse. The little filly was staring at
him and as he walked by, she turned her head and held eye contact until
he was well past her. It was like a girl watching a guy who was
watching her, nothing subtle about it. When Connie got to the end of
the aisle, he stopped. There was a line in front of the concession stand
twenty people deep. He looked back towards the two old guys with the
little filly. The horse's head was still turned in his direction. If he stood
in line long enough to get served he might miss the sale of the filly.
Why that should matter to him was not readily apparent, but for some
reason he suddenly decided he wanted to be there when she went
through the sale.

He turned and headed back down the aisle to the bleachers. As
he passed by the horse, she nickered at him. He shook his head and kept
walking. He counted eight horses in line in front of her. He had left his
sale catalog on his bleacher seat next to John. He'd have to check out
lot number nine.

"That was quick," John said when Connie got back in the bleachers. Noticing his empty hands, he commented, "You didn't get anything."

"You said you wanted a small surprise. Well, that's it. Surprise, I didn't get anything. The line was too long and there was a horse, number nine, standing in line that I want to see go through."

John looked at him and laughed. "You getting into this or what?"

Connie was thumbing through his sale catalog. "Here it is, number nine." He held the catalog and waved it at John. Her name is Smokin' Jolena and she's not quite three years old and..." His voice trailed off as he read her birth date. She was born on the same day his wife had died. He stared hard at the paper, the words blurring through the tears that welled up without regard for his attempt to stifle them.

John had found the same page in his catalog and was studying it, not looking at Connie. "She's got a dynamite pedigree, too bad she's a paint." He looked over to Connie. "Hey, you're not thinking about buying a horse, are you?"

Connie swiped the back of his right shirtsleeve across his eyes. "I doubt it. What would I do with a three year old horse?"

John couldn't help but notice Connie's wet eyes and looked back to his sale catalog. Jolena's foaling date jumped out at him. Then he understood the reason for the tears. The crackle of the sound system saved them from embarrassment. The auction had begun.

"Ladies and gentlemen, cowboys and cowgirls, and horse lovers of all persuasions," the announcer paused and looked around. "Did I leave anybody out?" A more than polite chuckle rippled across the audience.

"Okay now, I assume you all came here for the sale and we're gonna start that right quick. We do have a few formalities to cover before we can actually sell some horses, however. The very first thing is I want you all to look in your sale catalog on the second page where it says, 'Terms and Conditions.' Read that carefully, because you, me, and the consigner will all be held to those terms and conditions. Next is money. If you can't pay for a horse, don't bid on it. You will have to make full payment before you can take your horse home. Don't give us a bad check. I don't care if you don't have the money in your account today, but Monday morning when I put your check in my account, it has to be there. Enough said about money. There is no smoking in this barn or the other barn. Don't make me come and put out your smoke because I won't come alone. Even I have to go outside if I want a cigarette."

It was apparent to Connie that he owned the facility. He continued on for another two or three minutes before he finally introduced the auctioneer.

The auctioneer was a chubby, short man, who looked to be in his late fifties, maybe even early sixties. He wore a tan colored hat with a high crown and the hair at his temples was white. After acknowledging the introduction, he rapped his gavel on the top of the elevated podium behind which he sat. "You all know the drill. Let's trade some horses. Now remember, you people are the judge and jury. We're gonna start these horses out at what we consider to be a fair price. If you think it's good, then I want you to bid. If you don't think it's good, then I reckon I can figure that out and I'll adjust. Okay, let's go here. Show me lot number one."

A man standing off to the left of the auctioneer's podium, at one side of the sale ring, pushed open a sliding door and a woman on the back of a sorrel quarter horse rode in. She walked the horse to the center of the ring and stopped.

Another man, seated to the auctioneer's right, read the horse's pedigree and some of the same information that was printed in the sale catalog. When he finished, the auctioneer started.

"Isn't she pretty and look here, she's only five years old and she's already won a bunch of money barrel racin'." A 'bunch' in this case was about twenty-three hundred dollars, but for a five year old barrel racer that was a reasonable start. "Who'll give me five thousand?" There were no takers at that number and the auctioneer backed down to twenty-five hundred. Still no one made a bid. "Okay, let's get down where everyone can play. Who'll give me a thousand?"

If Connie hadn't been paying close attention he would have missed it. The man whom Connie assumed to be the owner of the facility made a subtle motion, just a slight nod of his head. He was standing in the sale ring next to the podium where the auctioneer was seated. He looked up and tipped his head almost imperceptivity to the auctioneer. "I got one thousand, now who'll make it eleven hundred?" His voice rose in volume and intensity and the speed at which he spoke tripled. Somebody in the stands gestured. "Come on, I got 'leven, 'leven, 'leven, gimme twelve, twelve, twelve,"

One of the spotters in the ring saw a motion and yelled out, "Here!"

Without taking a breath, the auctioneer continued rapid fire, "Twelve, I got twelve, I'm looking for thirteen, thirteen, come on gimme thirteen. Okay thirteen, now fourteen," a hand went up, "now fifteen," another hand, "now sixteen, now seventeen, seventeen, now eighteen, gimme eighteen, eighteen, now nineteen, now twenty."

The bidding continued fast and furious, Connie trying to understand the words and keep track of the price. From what he could determine, there were at least four interested parties bidding for the horse. During the bidding, the woman was riding the horse back and forth in the sale ring, doing sliding stops, spinning and turning on a dime. Connie thought the horse and rider looked good. He had never seen anyone ride a horse like that in such a small space.

"Fifty-seven, I got fifty-seven, gimme fifty-eight, fifty-eight, fifty-eight, come on now, wontcha give me fifty-eight?" He stopped then and pointed to a young woman in the lower section of the bleachers. "Come on now, you know you want this horse and I know you're gonna look good on her. Split it with me. Give me fifty-seven-fifty." He spoke quietly and sincerely as if she were the only one at the sale. When she nodded, he quickly said, "Okay, now fifty-eight." A hand shot up. He turned back to the woman, "Okay, Miss, now give me fifty-eight-fifty."

She smiled and nodded again. He stopped and spread his arms. "See, it's not that hard. One person bids and then another person bids and so on and so forth." The audience laughed.

"Okay, now fifty-nine. Who's gonna give me fifty-nine, fifty-nine, fifty-nine, thank you, now six thousand." Meantime, the horse and rider were still spinning and sliding in the ring.

Connie leaned over towards John, "This guy is good. I never thought he'd get over two grand the way it started."

John laughed. "Wait. It's early. You'll get a chance to see some real bidding when the crowd gets warmed up."

"Okay, I got sixty-three-twenty-five. One last time, sixty-three-fifty. Anybody, sixty-three-fifty?" He took his time looking around. The horse and rider had stopped. "Sixty-three-fifty?" He banged the gavel down hard. "Sold the horse for sixty-three-twenty-five. What's your number, young lady?"

The woman who had made the winning bid held up a card with a number on it. "One eighty-four," the auctioneer said. "Lot number one goes to buyer one eighty-four. Thank you, Ma'am. I'm sure you'll get along just fine with your new horse."

The woman on the horse rode over to a door on the opposite side of the ring from which she had entered and rode out. The entire process had taken about six minutes. As soon as she was out of the ring, the auctioneer called for the next horse. "Okay, boys and girls, now that you know how this operation works, let's see lot number two."

The process was quickly repeated and by the time lot number seven came into the ring, Connie was getting nervous. His palms were sweaty and his respiration rate was up. He was beginning to fidget, curling up his sale catalog tightly and then unfurling it again, over and over. What's wrong with me? I feel like I'm ready to explode. I'm not going to buy a horse. Relax, just relax, he told himself.

Number eight came and went. The selling prices had not been particularly high. The fifth horse through had gone for eighty-eighty hundred, but John figured it should have gone a lot higher. It was a horse he was interested in, but thought it would go for much more money. He had bid on it twice, but stopped at seventy-five hundred because he felt like it was more horse than he needed. Now, he was thinking he had made a big mistake, although if he had continued bidding, it might have gone for a lot more.

The flat crack of the gavel popped over the loudspeaker. "Have we got a treat for you all. This next horse is definitely one of the finest young horses I have ever seen. And you better believe me, I've seen horses." He pointed to the man working the entrance door. "Slide that door open, young man, and let lot number nine in here."

Chapter 7, The Auction Continues

When the door slid open, Pete, riding Jolena, entered the sale ring. John leaned over to Connie, "She looks good all tacked up."

Connie had to agree. The horse looked real good. In fact, she was about the prettiest horse Connie had ever seen. He suddenly flashed back to the first time he'd laid eyes on his bride to be. *She was the prettiest woman I had ever seen, and I knew immediately I had to have her, dependant of course, on if she'd have me. But this is a little different, what do I want a horse for? Just because she's pretty is no reason. If I really want this horse, it shouldn't be a problem, I've got eight million dollars in the bank, but what am I going to do with her?* Then a flash of what he thought was inspiration came to him. *I'll buy her and give her to John.*

He turned back to John. "Yeah, she's gorgeous, if I can use that term for a horse. You think she'd be a good cutting horse?"

"She's got one of the highest powered, cutting horse pedigrees I've ever seen. If she can't do it, I'd be real surprised."

"Oh now, just y'all lookee here," the auctioneer intoned. "What we have is my old friend Pete Browning, one of the country's finest cuttin' horse trainers and my, oh my, he has brought us about the prettiest filly I ever did see." He tipped his hat to Pete and Pete waved back as he walked Jolena across the sale ring.

The auctioneer's voice dropped about twenty decibels and he spoke slowly and sincerely to the crowd. "I want to tell you people something, before we start. I've known Pete here for about forty years. We were younger when we first met, but just as smart and as good lookin' too. Pete had just won his first futurity and I was a young, second string auctioneer selling horses for a big outfit in Texas. Me and Pete have crossed paths many times since then and if I know one thing, it's Pete knows cuttin' horses. Oh yeah, one other thing, unlike most other horse traders, Pete always tells the truth."

He paused briefly for effect. "So when Pete tells me he's offering for sale probably the best cuttin' horse prospect he's ever seen, I got to believe this filly we're all lookin' at here, is gonna be something spectacular. Could even be the next futurity winner."

Pete continued riding Jolena back and forth across the sale ring as the auctioneer had his little "heart to heart" with the audience. Connie watched, practically hypnotized, as Jolena gracefully carried Pete on her back.

"Remember people, it's far better to own one good one than it is to own twenty bad ones—cheaper too. Don't be afraid to bid on this one. If you don't own her, you're gonna have to beat her, and I've got a hunch she might just be unbeatable." He nodded to the man seated next to him. "Go ahead now and tell the people all about this little filly."

As soon as the pedigree reader stopped, the auctioneer started. "Okay, I'm gonna open up the bidding where you can all play. I'm lookin' for five thousand, who's gonna give me five thousand?" The words were barely out of his mouth when the bid was made. "Five, now ten." Someone else bid. "Ten, now fifteen, fifteen, now twenty, twenty, twenty, twenty."

"Here," yelled a spotter, pointing to a woman in the third row back from the ring.

"Okay, who'll make it twenty-five, twenty-five, twenty-five, come on gimme twenty-five?"

"Here," from a spotter on the other side of the ring, looking at someone directly in front of him.

"I got twenty-five, I'm looking for thirty, thirty, thirty, come on gimme thirty, thirty, thirty."

Connie was dizzy. The price of the horse he was looking at had gone from five thousand to twenty-five thousand in less then thirty seconds. He looked at John. John was grinning from ear to ear, watching the spectacle. Pete was riding Jolena casually across the ring. The auctioneer was flapping his gums a mile a minute and the spotters were feverishly scanning the crowd for signs of bidding. Connie was caught up in the excitement. He stuck up his arm and hand as if he were back in Miss Anderson's third grade classroom volunteering to answer a question she had just posed.

"Hey, I got thirty, thirty, thirty," The auctioneer paused briefly, "You can put your arm down now, young man, I have you at thirty thousand."

His ears burning red hot from embarrassment, Connie dropped his arm like a stone. John looked at him. "What, are you doing?"

"Bidding on a horse."

"Let's go here, I got thirty, I'm lookin' for thirty-five, thirty-five, thirty-five, come on why doncha gimme thirty five." He hammered at thirty-five for a few more seconds and then stopped. "Look here folks, this could be the next national cuttin' horse futurity champion and I've only got thirty thousand dollars and don't tell me she can't possibly win because she's a paint. She's out of two quarter horses and I don't care if you're a hundred years old and ridin' a white Arab stallion, if the horse can cut a cow and you can stay in the saddle, the judges are gonna pay attention. Don't let this one get away."

The auctioneer took a healthy pull off a bottle of water, smacked the top of the podium with his gavel and started in again. "I got thirty thousand, who'll give thirty-two-five."

"Here," from the spotter on the auctioneers right.

"Okay, now thirty-five, thirty-five, thirty-five, yup, now thirty-seven-five."

"Here."

"Now forty, forty, forty, come on gimme forty, forty."

Connie raised his hand, but not so high this time. Not counting him, there were five parties in the audience who were seriously interested in Jolena. Two of the parties were breeders who specialized in breeding performance paint horses and both had come to this sale especially to see Jolena. The other three parties were cutting horse trainers who knew Pete's reputation and if he thought the horse had championship potential, well then by God, she could be a champion. Three of the interested parties had deep enough pockets to match any bid from Connie.

The auctioneer pointed at him, "Forty here. Thank you. Okay, I got forty, forty, forty, gimme forty-two and a half now."

"Here," from the spotter on the right again.

"I got forty-two and a half, I need forty-five now, come on, forty-five, forty five, forty-five." He was looking at Connie.

Connie slid his hand up even with his head.

"All right, now, I got forty-five, gimme forty-seven- five now." He tried for a while at that price and then stopped. He again addressed the audience in his 'sincere' voice. "I didn't think we were gonna have to do this, but I guess none of y'all did your homework. I gotta tell you a little story. Some years back, even before my time, there was a Texas cuttin' horse by the name of Rooster. Rooster was the best around and his owner, just an ordinary poor cowboy, taught Rooster a trick whereby this aforementioned poor cowboy could make a buck. He taught

Rooster to chase a chicken into a burlap sack and then he bet any and all takers five dollars that Rooster could cut a chicken into a sack. Now this is the truth or at least it's what's been passed down, Rooster never lost a bet. Each and every time, he'd chase that chicken into that sack."

He paused to regard his audience. He had them. "So what, you say? So Rooster could chase a chicken into a bag? Well. I gotta ask you. Have you ever tried to herd a chicken? You just can't. They are all over the place. But Rooster could, and you know what else? This pretty filly right here in front of you can do the same. And Pete's gonna show you. Pete, take it away."

Pete and the auctioneer had talked prior to the sale. Pete's reserve was fifty thousand. If he couldn't get that, he'd "no sale" Jolena and take her home. While that was okay by Pete, the auctioneer was working for the house. He wanted to sell the horse, the more money, the better. Pete had told him about Jolena's special ability and they had agreed to do the chicken trick if the bidding bogged down before Pete got his price.

Pete dismounted. "You want me to leave her tack on or take it off?"

The auctioneer chuckled. "You go ahead and leave it on her. I don't want you to have to carry it out after the sale."

On cue, Woody, who had been standing near the door, brought out the portable dog kennel containing one of the chickens they had brought with them. Pete knotted Jolena's reins together and dropped the loop over the saddle horn. Woody removed the chicken and carefully handed it over to Pete. He then picked up the kennel and walked to the opposite side of the sale ring.

Pete waved at the auctioneer. "We're ready."

The auctioneer smacked his gavel on the podium. "Let the game begin."

Pete told Jolena to stand and walked about ten feet in front her. He set the bird down on the floor and moved away quickly. "Cut the cow, Jo," he commanded.

Jolena whinnied and the chicken stood still, inspecting the ground between its feet. Jolena stamped the floor hard with her left front and the chicken made a mad dash to her right. Jo cut left, the chicken dashed left and Jo cut right. The chicken turned and ran, Jo right behind her. Ten seconds later the bird was back in the box and the crowd was cheering.

"See now how pretty that horse moves," the auctioneer chastised. "And I've only got forty-five thousand." Again he whacked the gavel down. "I got forty-five, who'll gimme fifty. I'm lookin' for fifty, fifty, fifty."

"Here."

"Here."

Both spotters had bids from opposite sides of the ring. The auctioneer pointed to the spotter on his right. "I've got your bidder at fifty." He turned to the spotter on his left. "Will your bidder go fifty-five?"

The spotter looked at his bidder. The bidder nodded. "Here." The spotter yelled, raising his arm.

"Now sixty." The auctioneer was looking at Connie.

Connie nodded.

"You're getting real good at this, young man," the auctioneer told him. "Now sixty-five."

Of the five bidders Connie was challenging, one had dropped out at forty thousand and a second made his last bid at fifty. The remaining three bidders were looking around in the direction pointed out by the auctioneer's eyes every time Connie made a bid. They all knew each other, but were wondering who it was immediately countering their bids. Didn't this guy know you were supposed to play it coy, drag things out a bit? Maybe he didn't care what the price was. All three of them wanted Jolena, but not at any price.

"I have got sixty thousand and I'm telling you, she's a steal at that. Look, you can wear the wheels off your pickup drivin' around the country and you'll not see a finer prospect than what's standing right in front of you. And I have only got sixty thousand dollars. Who'll give me sixty-five? Okay, make it sixty-two and a half."

"Here." The spotter on the right.

"Now, sixty-five."

Conrad nodded.

"Well, it's' not your turn, but I'll take it. Now sixty-seven-five. Come on, gimme sixty-seven-five, sixty-seven-five, sixty-seven-five. Okay, I'll make it easy, gimme sixty-six, make it sixty-six."

"Here," from the spotter on the left.

"I got sixty-six, now sixty-seven, now sixty-seven, sixty-seven."

"Here," from the spotter on right.

"Sixty-seven, now sixty-eight." Pointing with the handle end of the gravel, he looked up to Connie, "Now it's your turn. Gimme sixty-eight." Connie nodded. "Sixty-eight, now sixty-nine. Sixty-nine, sixty-nine, sixty-nine, don't let this one get away. When you think about how much twenty bad ones can cost you, this one's a bargain. Come on gimme sixty-nine."

The bidding continued at a slowed pace, a thousand dollars at a time. The auctioneer maintained his coaxing as the price rose to seventy-eight thousand dollars.

The auctioneer was watching the man down in front, three rows back. He saw him nod his head and before the spotter could call it out, he announced, "Okay! I got seventy-nine. I'm askin' eighty, eighty, eighty." He focused on the bidder who the spotter on his left was watching. "Eighty, come on, give me eighty. It's only a thousand more than seventy-nine."

He saw the bidder shake his head no and he immediately turned up to look at Connie. "Don't let this one get away now, gimme eighty. I got seventy-nine, now eighty."

Connie nodded. Turning back to the man down front, the auctioneer pleaded. I got eighty, now eighty-one." A nod. "Eighty-one, now eighty-two." Connie nodded. Turning his eyes back to the front. "Now eighty-three."

Staring at the bidder in the third row, he stopped talking fast. "I don't want you going home to tell them you almost bought the best horse at the sale, gimme eighty-three now."

The man wanted the horse and he didn't think eighty-three was too much, but the way his competition was bidding, he doubted he'd get the horse at any price. Oh well, one more shot. He nodded.

"Thank you, eighty-three," and turning his attention to Connie, "Now eighty-four." Connie wasn't thinking, he was operating on adrenaline and instinct. He nodded. "Thank you, young man, now you just keep doin' what you been doin'."

"I have, eighty-four thousand, now eighty-five." The man down front decided to give it up. Whoever he was bidding against appeared to be unstoppable. He shook his head no. "How about I make it easy, eighty-four and a half." The bidder shook his head no again. "You're sure? eighty-four-five is only five hundred more than eighty-four."

When he was certain the bidder was finished, he looked around. "Anybody else. Now's a good time to bid because I'm gonna sell this filly." He waited. Nothing. He smacked his gavel down. "Going once." He smacked the gavel again. "Anybody else? Last chance." The gravel came down again. "Sold the filly to number... Sir, what's your number?"

Connie suddenly realized he'd bought a horse. He'd felt detached during the bidding, as if it really wasn't him making the bids but some other guy who just happened to be occupying his body for a while. It also dawned on him that he didn't have a number. He'd never registered to bid.

"Loan me your number, John."

John handed him the stiff paper card with the number two hundred, eighty-eight emblazoned on it. Connie held it up for the auctioneer to read.

The auctioneer saw John hand Connie the number and chuckled, "Good trick, you gonna get him to pay for it too?" The people sitting near John and Connie had been watching Connie as he bid. They laughed at the auctioneer's comment.

Connie was a bit confused. "No, I'll pay. I've got the money."

The auctioneer laughed again, "I'm sure you have and I'd like you to come down here and introduce yourself. And we'd like to get your picture with Pete and this nice filly you just bought. Oh, yeah, bring the other guy down here too, the guy with the number."

Connie looked to John. "They want us to come down there. Why? None of the other buyers had to get their picture taken."

John started to stand and grabbed Connie by the arm, pulling him up too. "You just spent eighty-four K on a horse that's why. I'd guess that's probably their top selling horse in a long time. Let's go."

The crowd on the bleachers parted in front of them as they made their way down and into the sale ring where they were met by Pete, Jolena, the owner of the facility, and the auctioneer. Connie and John gave their names, had their hands shook, had several pictures taken with Jolena, were given a round of applause, and then followed Pete, Woody, and Jolena through the exit door of the sale ring.

As soon as they were outside the ring, John made his getaway. "Nice meeting you fellows, but I have to get back inside. There's a horse coming through that I'm interested in and I don't want to miss her. Connie, you know where to find me."

Pete nodded and Woody said, "Nice meetin' you too."

Pete turned towards Connie. "What do you intend to do with this horse? You don't strike me as bein' a cowboy."

Connie was taken by surprise. "Well, I think this is a public auction. I don't believe I have to be a cowboy to buy a horse."

"No, you don't, and don't take offense, but I'm curious as to what you intend to do with Jolena. You see, she's no ordinary horse. I was hopin' whoever bought her would campaign her."

"What do you mean, exactly, by 'campaign her'?"

"What I mean is show her in the cutting arena. This horse has the potential to be the next national futurity champion. I sure hate to see her miss a chance at the title."

Connie's mind was racing trying to determine what Pete was saying. He just won the auction for Jolena and therefore he now owned her. It appeared as if Pete was telling him what he had to do with a horse he no longer owned. "I'm a bit confused here, Pete. Did you or did you not just sell me this horse?"

"Yes, I did sell you this horse."

"Okay, if that's the case, why do I have to show her in the cutting arena?"

Pete slowly shook his head. "Let's start over. I fear we have a failure to communicate. He held out his hand. "Howdy, I'm Pete Browning."

Connie felt silly, but he shook Pete's hand anyway. "Howdy Pete, I'm Conrad Bradley and I just bought your horse." *I'll play your game.*

Suddenly Pete's countenance developed a foggy, far away expression, as if he were in deep thought. "Conrad Bradley? Not a junior are you?"

"No, actually I'm a third. Both my father and grandfather were named Conrad too."

"Was your father a Major Conrad Bradley?"

"Yeah, at one time he was. He was a general when he retired."

Pete grinned a huge grin. Placing an arm around Connie's shoulder, he said, "Come with me, young man, we have to talk."

Chapter 8, The Decision

As Pete, Connie and Woody walked Jolena back to her stall in the big barn, a plan was forming in Pete's mind. It was more than a little desperate, but if it didn't work, he was seriously thinking about refusing the sale, and that would be difficult if not impossible now. When he had consigned her to the auction, he hadn't considered the possibility that someone who had no intention of developing her talent would buy her. It would be like buying a sports car and locking it in the garage, never driving it, only worse because Jolena was a living, breathing creature, born to work cattle.

Had she come from lesser breeding, with fewer innate abilities, okay, make her a pasture pet, but that wasn't the case. Jolena was the brightest, most tractable horse with the biggest heart Pete had ever experienced. Horses like her, as he'd told Woody, were exceedingly rare. She had to be developed and shown. If he could communicate that much to her new owner, he had a chance. When he learned Connie's father had been Major Conrad Bradley, he prayed Connie might be reasonable.

At the door to Jolena's temporary home at the sale, Pete handed the reins to Connie. "Hang on to her for me while I pull off this saddle."

Connie took the reins. Jolena nickered and nuzzled Connie's shoulder. He reached up and scratched her head. "She's friendly," he commented more to himself than Pete.

Pete wanted to launch into a tirade about her not only being friendly, but smart and able and everything else that was good about her, but he held back. "Would you believe it if I told you that your old man was my battalion commander in Korea?"

Connie scrutinized Pete. "You're not old enough. And he was a Colonel in Korea."

"He was still a major when the hostilities started, and how old do you think I am?"

Connie studied Pete's face. "Maybe early seventies. Seventy-five at the most."

"Thank you, son. I do appreciate that. If I were still in my early seventies, I wouldn't be selling this horse. I'd be headed to Fort Worth in December." He shook his head. "But I'm not goin' to be ridin' this horse in the futurity and I won't be seein' eighty again either. I'm eighty-one. I got out of high school in nineteen fifty-one and immediately joined the army. I served with your father when he was still a major; he was promoted towards the end of the war. Just in case you don't know it, he was a great soldier and a fine officer. He didn't lead from the rear. He was right out front where you could see him and I'd have followed him to the gates of hell. In fact, I believe we did follow him through the gates of hell, and he led us back out the other side."

Pete threw the left stirrup of the saddle over the horn and loosened the cinch strap. "I'll never forget the little speech he gave one afternoon. There were literally two hundred thousand crazed Chinese in front of us. We were hungry, tired, wet, and thoroughly miserable. Guys were sick, wounded, some of them dying. It was a real snafu if you know what I mean. We were low on everything; rations, ammo, luck, and morale. The Chinese had been assaulting in what were called short attacks, small fire teams of five guys, over and over, until we had them stacked in front of us two feet high and twenty feet deep. That was bad. Bad, but awesome." He looked Connie in the eyes. "You a military man like your father? You ever been in a serious fire fight? Not that anytime somebody's shootin' at you it isn't serious."

Connie nodded. "Nothing like you saw in Korea, but I've been in one or two."

"Well then, you know what I mean. Scares you witless, but if you don't get killed, it's awesome. It might be awesome if you get killed too, I wouldn't know. But, back to my point. Your dad went around to each and every position and gave us all a pep talk. Must have taken him half the day and I don't believe he did it for career enhancement. He asked us if we were cold, wet, hungry, scared and when we said we were, he told us he was too, but he also felt blessed.

One of the guys wanted to know what the hell he could feel blessed for. You know what he said?"

Connie smiled. "He told you he was blessed because God had chosen him to support and defend the constitution of the greatest country that had ever been or was likely to ever be, and everybody back home was counting on him."

Pete was in the process of pulling the saddle off Jolena's back and nearly dropped it. "It's exactly what he said."

"Yeah, I heard it a time or two from him. Used it myself more than once, except for the 'everybody back home was counting on me' part."

Pete set the saddle on the floor with the cantle facing up. "Son, that's amazing. But I guess it's to be expected, it's in your pedigree, just like chasing cows is in this here horse's pedigree." Pete suddenly felt as if the odds on his gamble had greatly improved. "You married?"

"I was. My wife died two years ago."

Pete nodded. "Yeah, mine passed on about twelve years ago. That was tough."

Tough? If he only knew. Then again, maybe he does know. I'm not the first guy who's lost a loved one.

"So there we were, holed up on top of that miserable ridge in the middle of winter waiting for the Chinks to attack again. We all figured we were dead. Then this fool major ambles over to our position and tells us how blessed we are for being there. His words didn't make a lot of immediate sense. He mentioned how Washington and his troops suffered during the winter at Valley Forge. He said adversity is what defines you. 'How hard will you try to overcome? How much 'try' have you got inside you?' he asked us. Then he walked off to talk to the guys on the next position. I've thought about it ever since. It has helped me to survive." There was more he could have said. Hard memories, he'd put behind him. Memories of lighting cigarettes off the machine gun barrel red hot from gunning down Chinese troops who ran at them with no weapons, piles of corpses in front of their lines almost too high to see over, and the fear of running out of ammunition before the crazy troops gave it up. His best army buddy was never able to resolve what he'd done, committing suicide five years after the end of the war. Pete had said enough. Conrad would or wouldn't cooperate.

He took the reins from Connie and slipped off Jolena's bridle. Opening the door to the stall, he commanded, "Get in the box, Jo." Jolena dutifully obeyed. "You mind grabbing that saddle and following me out to my pickup? Then you can buy Woody and me a cup of that wretched coffee. We got a lot more to talk about.

"Here's the deal, Connie," said Pete as they sat on folding chairs next to the concession stand. Someone must have brewed a fresh pot of coffee because this stuff was much better than what Connie had bought earlier. "I really wanted Jolena to go to someone who would use her in the cutting arena. The only reason I sold her was to give someone that chance because I'm feeling too old to compete. That's irritating enough, and I realize you bought her fair and square, paid a good price too, but if you don't intend to use her for cutting, I'd like to buy her back. If I didn't care so much about her competing, I would have kept her."

"I bought her to give her to my friend, John, the guy who you met. He's into cutting."

Pete scratched his head. "Into cutting you say? How far into cutting is he? Does he ride every day, seven days a week, thirty days a month or does he play around on the weekend for an hour or two at some rent-a-cow place?"

"Ah, I'm not sure. I don't think he rides every day. Maybe two, three times a week."

Does he have cows or easy access to cows? Does he compete?"

"I don't think he competes, at least, not seriously. I know he doesn't own any cattle."

"How about you? Do you ever ride?"

"At one time I did. I worked on a dude ranch outside of Livingston every summer when I was growing up."

"Did you just saddle horses and fetch iced tea for the lady dudes, or did you actually ride?"

Had Pete not served under Connie's father and spoken so highly of him, Connie would have taken Jolena and shoved off at this point. However, knowing some of Pete's history, he figured he owed the old man something.

"The first year I mostly just did chores, but I did manage to ride a little. The next four summers, I rode a lot. I was planning to be a cowboy until my father told me I had an appointment at The Point. He said he was counting on me to take it."

Pete chuckled. "I imagine he was. So you gave up the dream of bein' a cowboy to go to West Point. How about now? You have any dreams of bein' a cowboy or are you still in the army?"

Connie laughed, "Jeez, no. I got out of the army more than twenty years ago. As for being a cowboy, I ain't exactly a spring chicken either."

"Got a steady job?"

"Nope, I gave that up too, sold out my share of the company to my partner four years ago. My wife and I were going to see the world." Connie paused.

"And she didn't make it. I'm sorry," Pete told him. "All three of us have lost our sweethearts. Woody lost the love of his life after only a year."

Connie looked at Woody. Woody said, "Some godless bastard killed her during a stick up at a jewelry store. Shot her in the face. She had a beautiful face. I never filled the hole she left and it's been fifty years."

"So here we are," Pete said, "Three survivors. What are we gonna do about it?"

"About what?" Connie asked, suspecting he knew the answer.

"About you bein' a cowboy, and Jolena goin' to the futurity?"

"How about we find a capable rider, you keep training the horse and I'll pick up the tab. Jolena goes to the futurity and after that I take her home."

"Well, that's not bad, except any rider I'd want to see on her back has his own training setup and is probably already committed to riding at least one and maybe two horses. It's gettin' late. This is a big deal. The top riders are tied up years in advance."

"You make this thing sound like the World Series. I never heard of it until just a while ago."

"It's bigger than the World Series as far as I'm concerned, but that's not the issue. The issue is, we have a horse, we have a trainer, and we need a rider. Now my daughter is a good rider, but with her two little girls, she can't spend the amount of time necessary. So I've decided you're gonna be the rider."

Connie was in the middle of swallowing a mouth full of coffee. "What?" he said, almost choking.

"Well, it's obvious to me. You're not strapped for cash. You're footloose and fancy free. You have one of the best trainers in the country to teach you, and you've got the horse that can do it. Though it would be nice if you were twenty years younger and had been riding for at least twenty years. However, we'll all just have to make do."

"You can't be serious. I'm too old."

"No you ain't. There's lots of men and women your age and a lot older riding cutting horses. The night Jo was born I slept in the barn, waiting for her birth. Just before I dozed off I asked the Lord for one more good horse. I got that horse and I was gonna ride her too, but sometimes not everything works out the way you planned it. What I'm trying to say is, if you're healthy, you're not too old. The horse is doin' most all the work. It's not about age. It's about 'try'. How much 'try' you got inside you, Son?"

Old Pete was sharp. He knew the one thing he could say that would hook Connie. He could have talked all day about Jolena's attributes and how exciting cutting cattle was and how it was addictive; once you started, you couldn't get enough. But he knew all that would be mere hyperbole; he had to hit him in the vitals. Maybe it was a cheap shot, but it worked.

Connie was silent for a good minute. To Pete and Woody it seemed like half an hour. "What's the deal?"

"I take Jolena back to my place. You go home, get your stuff together, and come on out. You stay with me and Woody and Cally and the girls while I teach you how to ride Jolena. We'll feed you and put you up in the bunkhouse. In your spare time, when you're not riding, you'll help out around the ranch. It'll be a full day, six days a week. We won't train on Sundays."

Connie remembered ranch work. It was hard, but you ate well and slept well. Did he really want to get involved with Pete and from the sounds of it, his entire family? Why had he ever started bidding on that horse? He was searching for the words he could use to refuse Pete's offer. As far as Jolena was concerned, he'd let Pete keep her. He hadn't written any check yet. And then, from somewhere deep in his consciousness, came a single, strong, thought, "Go." That was it, "Go." It wasn't like hearing a voice, just a powerful thought. He wasn't certain where it came from, certainly not from the reasoning, rational part of his brain, but he knew from experience it was not to be ignored.

It was odd that he should have this experience now. The last time it had happened was about twenty years ago. At that time the thought had been, "Get down!" and when Connie yelled out, "Take cover!" his platoon hit the dirt. The Republican Guards, their ambush blown, opened fire anyway, but instead of annihilating Connie's platoon, they received far worse than they gave. The firefight lasted less than five minutes, just enough time for Connie to rescue a wounded point man and take two bullets through his left arm and wrist. He had been wounded twice before, but this one sent him home.

His earliest memory of the "thought" was as a child of eight. At the time, his father was stationed at the Pentagon. His mother had taken him and his sister shopping at a large department store in downtown Washington, D.C. On the way back to the parking lot, he and Suzy were running down the sidewalk when Connie noticed a car careening down the street much too fast. The thought, "Get back!" shouted at him. Grabbing Susie's hand, he stopped and pulled her back, just before the car jumped the curb, flew down the sidewalk and smashed into the corner of the department store.

The experience was rare, but he knew better than to ignore it. *Funny*, he thought, *that I should have it now, in this situation. It doesn't seem to be life threatening.* Then, before he could think about it any more, he said to Pete. "Deal, you've got yourself a rider. I just hope I can do it."

Pete stuck out his hand and they shook on it. "You'll do it. I don't know if we'll win, but you will learn how to ride."

"So now what?" Connie asked.

Pete looked at his watch. The auction had gotten off to a late start. It was now almost one. "I think Woody and I and Jolena will hit the road. We can make at least three hundred miles yet today before we have to stop. How soon can you get your affairs in order, turn around, and get out to my place?"

"I'm not sure. Two weeks maybe. How long will I be there?"

"Don't plan on gettin' back to your home until Christmas. The futurity won't be over before the middle of December and we've got a lot of work to do.

"What do I need to bring with me?"

"Your clothes and your wallet is all. Oh yeah, you might also want to consider gettin' a pick up truck and a horse trailer. Riding cutting horses is a thrill, but it ain't a cheap thrill."

Connie laughed. "In for a penny, in for a pound. I will need your address."

"And you're gonna get it. Let's go to the office so you can pay for your horse and I can get my money. Then we'll go back to the stall, exchange addresses and you can say goodbye to Jolena, temporarily that is."

"What about a saddle? Don't I need a fancy saddle?"

It was Pete's turn to laugh. "Not just yet. I got plenty of saddles for you to learn in. When it's time, we'll find the right saddle. I know a good saddle maker in Coeur d'Alene; maybe we'll get one built special."

They pitched their empty cups into the closest trash barrel and went to the sale office to take care of business. Back at Jolena's stall, Connie brushed and fretted over his horse while Woody and Pete gathered up their stuff. It didn't take long and Connie felt a sting of sorrow when Pete and Woody pulled out of the parking lot with Jolena in tow.

"I can't believe it," he said quietly to himself. "Two weeks ago, I was well on my way to becoming a dead drunk. Now I own a cutting horse and I can't wait to learn how to ride her."

Sarah's image as a healthy, beautiful woman came to him, unbidden, but strong. "Thanks, Babe." He waved at the back of Pete's horse trailer as it turned to the right, making its exit from the parking lot. He headed back to the sale arena to find John.

Chapter 9, The Move

Connie sat back down next to John in the bleachers of the sale arena. "Spend any money yet?"

"Yeah, actually, I did. A four year-old gelding that I think will be real good for Paula. I didn't spend quite as much on him as you did on that little filly, though."

"How much is not quite as much?"

"Fifty-seven hundred."

"Yeah, that is a bit less, but you don't know the half of it. I should have my head examined."

"Don't tell me, let me guess. He sold you his pick-up and trailer too."

"No, I'll have to buy my own pick-up and trailer. I'm moving to Montana."

There it was. Right out in plain view. If Connie had not realized what he and Pete had agreed to before, he absolutely did now.

John had been paying attention to the bidding, but now he turned toward Connie. "You serious?"

"Yup, I'm serious." He was unprepared for John's reply.

"Good for you. I'm jealous. When are you leaving?"

"Soon as we get back, I'll pack up my stuff, get my sister to take care of selling my house and head out. I hope to be in Montana in two weeks."

"You going to have that old man teach you how to ride your horse and go to the futurity?"

"That's the plan. You think I'm crazy?"

"Yeah, but not for doing that. God, what an adventure. I am really jealous."

"You don't think I'm too old."

"Of course you're too old, but what is life for, if not living? And I can't think of a better way to live it than what you have in mind. Even if you never get to first base, what an adventure you'll have. Did I tell you I was jealous?"

"Yeah, I believe you did. Come on out with me."

"If I only could." He thought for a minute as his eyes developed a faraway look. "Maybe what I could do though, is come and visit later in the year. Me and Paula could pull a couple horses out in August or September and we ...." He stopped. "Or not, we'll have to wait and see. But if you do go to the futurity, we will come and watch."

Then the auctioneer called for lot number forty-six. It was a horse John was considering. "Time out, I gotta see this one."

While John watched the sale, Connie was considering his last comment, "come and watch". It dawned on him. He'd have to ride in front of an audience. He hated to do anything in front of an audience. He had given speeches and presentations and done just fine, but he didn't enjoy it. Performing on horseback in front of an auditorium full of spectators was something he didn't even want to think about. The last time he had performed anything for an audience was at a violin recital.

There had been a time he thought he would never use his left hand again. Two 7.62 mm bullets from an AK-47 had shattered the ulna and radius of his left arm. It had taken several army surgeons and three operations to put all the pieces back in place, or at least most of the pieces. One of the doctors later told Connie they threw away all the smaller chips and then to make up the difference, they used titanium and stainless steel and all their collective skill to reconstruct and reconnect everything back together.

After all the surgery, Connie spent months in therapy, trying to regain full use of his hand and fingers. When he complained about the slow progress he was making, one of the therapists jokingly suggested he take up the violin. Connie thought he was serious and decided to do just that.

He found a terrific old gentleman who gave private lessons. After another year and a half, Connie's wrist was working much better and his teacher suggested he play in a recital that was given for the parents and other interested parties of all his students. Connie balked. He was the oldest student, although there was a young lady of twenty, but the rest were all kids. However, the old man was persistent, and Connie finally acquiesced. He practiced a simple Irish jig for weeks and worried mightily about blowing it in front of a bunch of eight year olds and their moms. He need not have agonized. His instructor introduced Connie by telling the story of his injury and explaining it was a miracle he could hold a violin in his left hand, let alone actually play it. Connie could have missed every third note and the audience would have approved, but he actually gave the fiddle tune a respectable rendition and received a standing ovation.

Forget it, he thought. *I might never get to the futurity and if I do, I can worry about it then. I have enough to consider.* He wanted to start home right away. There was so much to do. He'd decided to sell his house. He might never go back to Indianapolis and if he did, he'd want to downsize. There was also Sarah's memory. It permeated every cubic inch of the place. She had designed the house, decorated it, furnished it, and loved it. Connie loved it too, but primarily because Sarah did. It could never be the same. It needed to pass to another family. They'd refill it with their memories.

All his furniture would have to go into storage; he'd need to find a reputable real estate agent, and then decide what to do with all his and Sarah's personal stuff. All the photos, mementos, books, trinkets and everything else two people collect over twenty years would have to be dealt with. He'd avoided disturbing Sarah's things; her clothing still hung in her closet untouched. He'd not even opened her armoire and chest of drawers. *Silly, I knew she wasn't coming back. What have I been waiting for?* A wave of melancholy washed over him, leaving tears in his eyes. He put his head down and squeezed his eyes hard with the thumb and forefinger of his right hand, attempting to push back the tears. When he lifted his head, his eyes were dry. *I'll just deal with it when I get home.* And he realized he could.

He sat quietly for the next half hour, watching horses go through the sale and thinking private thoughts. He didn't see any that looked as good as Jolena. He wished he could have gone straight to Pete's ranch with him and Woody. He needed to get moving. John hadn't bid on a horse lately, and Connie wondered how long they'd be here. It was a two-day sale with seven hundred horses. In three hours, they were only on number fifty-nine. If they continued at this pace, they'd be at this continuously all the way through tomorrow until nine at night.

"Hey, Buddy," said John getting up. "Let's go get us some lunch. There's no horses coming up I need to see for at least an hour, probably more like two hours. Then there are three of them in a row. If I can get any one of them, I think we're out of here."

Connie stood and they threaded their way down the bleachers and out of the sale arena to John's truck. "Sounds good to me. How long is this going to go on?"

"It'll be late. Maybe ten, eleven, but if you haven't noticed, the auctioneer has picked up the pace. He's spending a lot less time on the lesser quality horses and working the crowd a lot harder for the better ones. I'll bet by ten tonight, they'll have sold at least half of them."

"What happens if nobody bids on a horse?"

"Somebody always bids. The guy that introduced the auctioneer, I believe he either owns the sale barn or is running the sale, or maybe both. If you noticed, he usually makes the first bid."

"So if no one else bids, he's stuck with the horse?"

"Yeah, but he's not really stuck because he never bids very high. If no one else bids, and the consigner lets it go, he's got himself a horse at a serious bargain price. He'll wait until the next auction and probably make a healthy profit when he runs it back through the sale."

"So he never gets burned?"

"I wouldn't say never, but I imagine it doesn't happen often. I'm sure he knows horses and the horse market better than he knows his wife. If he didn't, he wouldn't be around long."

"So, are these prices high, low, average or what?"

"I'd say, other than the one you bought, most of what I've seen has been about what I expected. There have been some bargains and there were a few I thought went too high, but on average, prices are about where I figured they'd be."

"You think I paid too much for Jolena?"

"I don't know. If you weren't bidding, I don't think she'd have gone as high, but she's so far out of my league, I can't say. I didn't expect a horse of her caliber to even be here. If I'd have been Pete, I would have taken her down to Fort Worth last December and consigned her to one of the sales at the futurity. That's where all the big players go to shop."

"He said he'd wanted to ride her himself. His decision to sell her was a last resort, something he didn't want to do or even think he'd have to do. I got the distinct impression he'd waited as long as he could before the big realization hit him that he was no longer able."

"What a horrible predicament. You have huge success as a young man, you're a great trainer and when you finally get your last big chance, you're too old."

"Stop, you're scaring me."

"Why would you be scared? You don't owe Pete anything. You can change your mind. I wouldn't like to see you do that, but you could."

Connie walked a few steps in silence, regarding his boot toes. "I told you earlier you didn't know the half of it."

"Yeah?"

"Well, if you can believe this, Pete served in Korea under none other than Colonel Conrad Bradley."

"No. Not you're old man?"

"Yes."

"Aw, man, that's too incredible to be true."

"Believe it. He told me a story about my dad giving him a pep talk during the Inchon campaign and I told him exactly what my dad had said. Then, if that wasn't enough, he used one of my dad's favorite motivational tricks on me. I mean, my God, I've heard it since I was five years old. You'd think I'd be immune, but no, not old Conrad, I sucked it up like a puppy would a bowl of cream. He says, 'How much try have you got in you?' and I lapped it up. Can't believe how dumb I am."

"Hey, it doesn't matter what he said or what you said. The thing that counts is you get to try something new and different, and whatever else happens, I guarantee you won't be bored. I'm as jealous as possible, and I think you're going to have a blast."

"Yeah, you're probably right, but I really hate to get manipulated like that. Even though I'm looking forward to it, I feel like such a sap."

"Try seeing it from Pete's perspective. He's got a great horse, but no rider, so he decides to sell the horse so she can get to the big time. Then some dude with a lot of money, but no clue, buys her. He really wants the horse to compete, so he offers to not only finish the horse, but also to train her new owner, and all in less than nine months. You tell me, who's the sap?"

Connie waved his hands over his head. "I surrender. You're right. No one's holding a gun to my head for any of this. I did it all on my own. If I can pull it off, I'm a hero, if I can't, the only thing I've lost is money and that doesn't bother me in the least. All I can say is that Pete better have as much 'try' in him as I've got in me."

John punched the remote to unlock the doors of his pickup. "Amen, Brother. Let's get us a hamburger."

After lunch they came back to the sale barn. In their absence, the place had become more crowded and the noise level was noticeably higher. Their seats were long gone so they had to stand off to one side of the sale arena, at ground level. Connie soon noticed not everyone was intent on the auction. Just off to his left was a middle-aged rodeo queen putting the make on a cowboy who thirty years earlier might have modeled blue jeans for Calvin Kline. Looking up into the bleachers, he saw people talking intently to one another, completely ignoring the sale, and others who stared blankly ahead, hypnotized by the auctioneer's prattle, and incapable of response. It was a scene of seeming total disorder, yet through it all, business was somehow being conducted. It was fascinating.

"Connie."

"Yeah." He quit staring at the crowd and turned towards John. "What?"

"I bought another horse. We can go now. Unless you want to stay?"

"Oh, no. That's good. Let's go."

After paying up, John and Connie loaded the two horses John had bought and made a plan. The horses seemed relatively unconcerned about their change in fortune and loaded easily. John watered them, gave them each a handful of oats for loading, and a thin flake of good grass hay. He didn't want either of them to colic in the trailer.

"I think they'll be just fine," John told Connie. "It's almost five. How far down the road you think we can get?"

"Up to you, Buddy. We can go all night if you want, although I'd rather not. Where can we be in two or three hours?"

They decided to drive to the northeast side of Tulsa where there was a mare motel in which they could not only put up the horses for the night, but themselves as well. From there, if they left at early in the morning, they could make it home by dark. By nine, Connie and John had the horses tucked in for the night and were lingering over a six-pack of Lone Star and the remnants of a huge pizza. They were settled into a rustic cabin adjoining two horse stalls.

"It's been a weird day," Connie said.

John agreed, "Weirdest day I can remember since, ah, since, well, since I can't remember when."

"Yeah, if I hadn't been here, I wouldn't have believed it."

"If you hadn't been here, it wouldn't have happened."

"Good point. I don't think I'll regret it. I had to do something. You know. I was in trouble."

"Yeah, I knew. It was pretty obvious. You weren't all that subtle."

"Really? I thought I was doing a good job of hiding my despair."

"Not hardly. That's the thing about desperation, the only people you can hide it from are other desperate people."

Connie laughed. "And I thought I was so smart. Why is it every time I think I'm smart, I find out what a dope I really am?"

"Because you're blessed. Most people who think they're so smart, don't usually learn the truth until it's too late."

"You really are profound." He tossed his empty bottle into the trash. "Last one is yours."

They crashed before ten and were back on the road at sunrise. They were home before sunset. John had two new horses and Connie had a brand new start at life. He started scrambling to get ready to live it.

Chapter 10, The Move

"Have you started drinking already?" Suzy wanted to know.

"Come on, Suzy, it's eight o-clock in the morning."

"So what, I've seen you drunk before noon plenty of times in the last six months. It's a legitimate question."

"Yeah, it used to be, but I gave it up."

"Drinking? You totally stopped drinking? When? For how long?"

"No, not totally. I've had two beers in the last week. What I've given up, totally, is feeling sorry for myself and binge drinking."

"And you bought a horse?"

"Yes."

"And you want me to sell your house so you can go move to Montana?"

"I don't want you to actually sell my house, I want you to recommend a good real estate agent and then deal with that agent when there's a buyer."

"I'm coming over there. Right now. Don't go anywhere." His phone went dead.

Not quite the same reaction he received from John, but not anything he didn't expect. He and Suzy might be twins and look alike, but they certainly didn't think alike, nor share many personality traits. Connie wasn't exactly agoraphobic, but he preferred small gatherings, trips to the country, and quiet restaurants. He was a member of no social organization or club. Suzy was hugely gregarious, the more people around, the better. She thrived on constant social interaction and was involved with dozens of organizations. It was only normal for Suzy to think her brother had lost it when he announced he was moving to Montana. It was the wilderness.

It didn't take her long to arrive at his house. She looked at him critically. "Well, you look okay."

"What did you expect? A five day beard, dirty fingernails, and BO?"

"You know what I mean. What's going on?"

"Let's go in the kitchen and sit down. I've got fresh coffee, although I'm not sure you should have caffeine. You seem about ninety-five per cent wired already."

"Don't try to give me decaf. It's not coffee without caffeine."

In the kitchen, Connie poured them each a cup and then he poured out his heart. He told her about his struggles of the last two years and how close he came to completely losing it, not that she didn't suspect as much. He told her all about Pete and Jolena, as least as much as he knew, and he talked about having the ability to start a second life, a life without Sarah. He realized this would all seem sudden and crazy, but it had been coming for two years and would prevent him from going insane or worse.

When he finished, he looked her in the eyes. "Still think I'm drunk?"

"No. No, I really didn't think you were when I was on the phone either. I just had to make sure you knew what you were telling me. You can't fault me for that."

"I don't fault you for anything. Everything I've done since Sarah died, I've done to myself. I just finally realized only I could change me. Next I realized how lucky I was. I could do almost anything I wanted to do and believe it or not, at one time, I really wanted to be a cowboy."

"Yeah. I heard Dad tell Mom after he twisted your arm to accept the appointment to West Point that he hoped he didn't regret not allowing you to stay out west."

"I never knew that, but he was right. I had to go to West Point and I believe it was the best thing I could have done. I learned an awful lot. I learned I wasn't as strong as I thought, but I was tougher than I ever imagined."

"Yeah, you got all shot up, too. Do you have any idea how worried I was for you while you were over there?"

"Yes, I do, and I appreciated your concern more than you knew. But, hey look." He held out his left hand and rotated it around in circles at the wrist. "Not so bad for bein' all shot up. I'm even thinking about digging out my old fiddle and taking it with me."

Suzy shook her head. "Men. None of you ever grow up."

"So that means you'll help?"

"Yes, and I know an excellent real estate agent. I'll get her over here tomorrow. What are you going to do with all the furniture?"

"I've got a moving company coming to give me a price to pack it up and put it in storage."

"Who is it?"

He told her.

"No, you don't want them, I have a company in mind that'll do a better job and may even be less expensive. What about Sarah's clothes and personal items?"

"I'm not sure. Could you use some of her clothes?"

"I wish, but unless you're blind, you don't really think I could wear her clothes. She was a perfect eight and at best, I'm a bad twelve, but I know someone who could." Suzy was spooling up to speed. "Her oldest niece, the tall, pretty one who made so many bad decisions, has finally started to straighten out. She could use some help, and Sarah's two sisters should be allowed first choice if you ask me. I can handle all that for you if you want."

Connie laughed, "Now you know why I called you. Not only would I like you to handle it, I'd be eternally grateful, and if there's anything you or your kids would like to remember Sarah by, please, be my guest."

So it went, or almost all of it, Sarah's personal accumulation of a lifetime. Connie kept only the high tech parka she'd worn for their assault on Mount Kilima N'jaro, a souvenir of their one and only trip to see the world. The rest of Sarah's things went to sisters and nieces, that when Connie thought about it, was right.

Just over a week had passed since he'd returned from the auction. He was alone, for the last time, in his almost empty house. The pile of stuff going with him; four sturdy, canvas suitcases, a slightly battered violin case, an M-1A1 rifle inside a hard plastic case and a medium sized, plastic tote box, sat on his kitchen floor next to the door to the attached garage. The only other remaining item was a metal toolbox in the garage containing a collection of tools Connie thought could come in handy. Everything else including Sarah's car, was given to family member, or donated to a charity.

Connie had just returned from the automobile dealership where he'd picked up his new truck. It was a beauty, a one-ton, crew cab, with dual rear wheels, a diesel engine and every conceivable option; a regular cowboy Cadillac. He stashed the rifle behind the back seat and everything else either on the back seat or the floor of the backseat. The thing was cavernous. He walked through his empty house one last time. The agent Suzy had found for him had already shown it several times, twice to one party who had seen it both with and without the furniture. The agent told Connie she was expecting an offer from them. "If it doesn't come in the next five minutes," Connie said out loud, "Suzy will have to handle it." Not wanting to fly back and deal with the sale, he'd given her power of attorney. Now that the place had been cleared out, Connie was in a hurry to leave. He wasn't depressed about leaving, but there were powerful memories here. If he hesitated for a few days instead of immediately making his departure, he might not leave, and the last thing he wanted was to slip back into his depression. He was ahead of it now. *Time to go.*

As he walked through the empty rooms, rather than remembering details of their life together, he kept focused, looking for anything he'd missed. He had the place thoroughly cleaned three days ago so he doubted he'd find anything, but when he looked in the study, he saw something lying on the floor in the middle of the room. He recognized it immediately. It was something Sarah had acquired on their trip to Africa, an ostrich shell necklace about eighteen inches long. It had been hand made by a tribal woman living on the shores of Lake Turkana in the Great Rift Valley. Sarah had found it in an upscale souvenir shop in Nairobi that offered "museum grade" artifacts.

This type of necklace was traditionally made by a mother for her baby and was a symbol of wealth, the longer the necklace, the wealthier the woman's husband. One this long would have signified upper middle class, but some years ago, the women who made these discovered they could sell their handiwork to the tourists and get some of their own wealth. Sarah bought it and wore it home. After she became ill, she had misplaced it and, although she and Connie had searched for it frequently, it remained illusive. Now it was there, lying in the middle of an empty room, in the middle of an empty house.

Connie picked it up. "I'll be." He didn't finish. Instead, he put it around his neck. *It'll be my talisman.* There had been some overstuffed leather furniture, massive and comfortable, in that room. It must have been stuck in the couch or chair and fallen out when the movers took them away. Why it had not been found by the cleaners,

was puzzling, but his finding it was a stroke of luck. He quickly
finished his inspection and with a smile on his face, locked the doors
and departed, never to return. Four hours later he was over two hundred
miles west of Indianapolis, coming up on St. Louis.

His plan was to drive west to Denver, then turn to the north
through Wyoming and into south central Montana to Billings. From
Billings he'd drive west-northwest until he reached Missoula. In
Missoula, he'd finally lose the interstate and go north on US 93. That
would take him to Kalispell and US 2. Pete's ranch was somewhere just
west of Kalispell, not far off US 2. There were probably shorter routes,
but he had to stop in Denver to pick up a horse trailer.

He and John had shopped for trailers five days ago. John
showed him the one he'd buy if he had to do long distance hauling and
Connie liked it. It was a three-horse slant with living quarters. It had a
queen bed, shower and dinette, plus a refrigerator, stove and microwave;
all the comforts of home only a lot more compact. It was thirty feet
long and priced at forty thousand dollars. So far, Connie's start at a new
life style had set him back over a hundred and seventy thousand dollars.
He had a feeling it was just the beginning, although Pete was training
him and Jolena for free.

The trailer that the dealer in Indianapolis showed Connie had
been sold the day before and it would take a week to get another one in.
"Where is it coming from?" Connie asked.

"The factory is just north of Denver, town of Longmont. If they
have this model in stock, it'll take about a week to get it delivered."

The solution was instantly apparent to Connie. "Call the
factory. Tell them I'll be there in a week to pick it up. If they don't
have one in stock, I'm sure they can build one in a week. I mean how
many of these things do they sell every day?"

The salesman hedged, "Well, they just introduced this model
last spring and it's been very successful."

Connie looked him in the eyes, "I'm sure it has, but you call
them and tell them I'm ready to buy this model today, with cash and I
want to pick it up, in Denver, a week from tomorrow. I'll bet they can
do that."

The salesman called, the company agreed, and Connie wrote a
check. The salesman was happy, the dealership was happy, and the
company would happily build another trailer. If everything went
smoothly with the delivery in Denver, Connie would be happy, too. The
arrangement also meant he would be on a less busy highway when he
started practicing driving with a big trailer, a new experience for him.

He calculated that his truck and trailer would be over fifty feet long, not much shorter than a typical over the road, tractor-trailer rig. He'd rather get used to it out west than in the busy corridor between Indianapolis and St. Louis.

His plan for the first day was to drive as far as Kansas City, Kansas and stop there for the night. He hadn't left home until slightly before noon and it was after eight when he finally stopped. He was surprisingly tired and asleep by nine. The next morning he was on his way well before seven. Denver was six hundred miles away. He wanted to get there early enough to find the place where he was to pick up his new trailer while it was still light. He wasn't planning to be there in time to take delivery, but if he did, that would be okay too.

The space between Kansas City and Denver was not well known for spectacular scenery, but it was new to Connie. It was a part of the Great Plains he had never seen and at this time of year, the landscape was saturated with twenty different shades of green. Shortly after noon he drove through a series of powerful thundershowers with lightning bristling all around, leaving the air tinged with ozone. Then a huge rainbow appeared and gave the illusion he could drive right through its arches. It remained in front of him for thirty miles, staying just out of reach until it finally faded and the skies cleared, completely blue. He wondered briefly what determined the steepness of a rainbow's arch. After the rain, visibility was endless, traffic was light and he drove hard, pushing past the speed limit as much as he thought he could. Even after two pit stops, at four-o-clock he was approaching the Denver city limits. He got on his cell phone and called his contact at the factory where his trailer hopefully awaited his arrival.

It was a pleasant sounding woman who directed him to the northwest, bypassing Denver. "Honey," she said, "you sure don't need that traffic at this time of day. You go like I tell you and I'll wait for you. You can spend the night right here in your new rig."

He went the way she directed him and he was there before five-thirty. She was waiting. She was a petite blonde woman, no more than five foot two and if she weighed much more than a hundred pounds Connie would have been surprised. She was wearing blue jeans, boots, and a short sweater that ended just above her belt. Connie guessed her to be in her late thirties and found himself staring. He thought she was cute, if that word could be used to describe a woman of almost forty.

She shook his hand, "Howdy, Conrad. I'm Cindy. I see you can follow directions."

'Howdy?' Did she say, 'Howdy?' "Ah, yes I can and you can call me Connie, Cindy."

"Connie then. Come on, Connie, let's go look at your new trailer."

An hour later, Connie's trailer was hooked up to his pickup and his rig, as Cindy referred to it, was parked in what she called the holding area. She had demonstrated all the trailer's features and amenities. The last thing they did was to drop it down onto the fifth wheel hitch in the box of Connie's pickup.

"You want to go for a little drive, see how it handles?"

Connie looked at his watch. It was a quarter 'til seven. "Yeah, if you wouldn't mind, but it's getting late. I don't want to keep you."

"Honey, don't you worry about that. I own this place and if you're not happy, I'm not happy. Come on, get in your rig and take me for a ride."

They got on the freeway and drove north for a few miles. Initially, Connie was alarmed by the way the trailer affected the truck. He had been used to flying along smooth and slick at eighty miles per hour. Now everything had changed. Acceleration seemed stuck in molasses, changing lanes was nerve racking and he felt the tug from every expansion joint in the highway. John's trailer hadn't felt like this when he had driven on their trip to Oklahoma.

"It's gonna seem a little rough for the first couple hundred miles, but you'll get used to it." Cindy told him, seemingly reading his mind. "After a while, it'll be no big deal. The only thing you'll notice is how bad other people drive."

When they got back, Cindy showed him where to park and then plugged the trailer into a hundred and ten volt outlet. "Might as well run your lights off my nickel while you're here."

He thanked her and she gave him all the documents transferring ownership. "You eat anything lately?" she asked.

"Ah no, as a matter fact I haven't. I was thinking about walking over to that place across the street over there and getting a hamburger." He waved his arm at a roadhouse with a blinking neon sign that proclaimed, "Great Steaks".

She took him by the arm. "Forget it. You look like a class act. Let me take you to a place where the food doesn't bite back."

He went without protest and they drove a few miles to a restaurant with a log cabin motif, a wide front porch running across the front. The weather was mild and all the tables on the porch were occupied. There was a discrete neon sign above the door that spelled out "CINDY'S" in blue. Cindy pulled open the door for him. "After you."

Connie said to his escort, "Nice place you have here."

She smiled and winked. "Thanks. Let's see if I can get us a table."

It didn't prove to be a problem and they were quickly seated in a quiet corner next to a fireplace garnished with an enormous elk head above the mantel. "Now there's something you don't see in Indianapolis," Connie commented.

"What, the elk or the fireplace?"

"The elk."

Cindy looked up at the trophy. "I shot that one seven years ago over towards Creede."

"You're kidding?" But as soon as Connie said it, he realized it was true. Cindy was not the average homemaker type.

"No. I shot a bigger one three years ago, but I kept that one for my house."

Dinner turned out to be more interesting than Connie could have imagined. Cindy had married young to an older and wealthy man; she was just eighteen and he was thirty-two. "It was only fourteen years," she said. "No big deal now, but at the time, all my friends thought I was nuts. I didn't care. He was quite a prize, tall, handsome, rich, and he had the most wonderful manners. We went everywhere and did everything together. He died five years ago and I still miss him. He left me with more money than I could ever spend, and four businesses. I have good managers for three of them, but I can't seem to find anyone worth keeping for the trailer factory. I spend a lot of time there. I built this restaurant three years ago so I wouldn't have to go home and cook for myself."

"Yeah, I know what you mean," and he told her about his previous life, and buying Jolena, and Pete's plan for him to win the futurity. "I'm not sure I know what I'm doing, but I'm sure about trying."

It was after eleven when she dropped him off at his trailer. Before he could get out of her car, she took his arm and pulled him over. She kissed his cheek. "I expect you to win the futurity, Cowboy, and if you're ever lonely, you come back and see me."

Cowboy. He smiled as she drove away. He fell asleep as soon as his head hit the pillow and didn't wake up until the sun was shining in the narrow window of his new bedroom.

Chapter 11, Cally

Cally was surprised when her father and Woody arrived home a day early. She had just chased the twins off to bed when the headlights from Pete's pickup flashed through the kitchen window as he cruised past the house. Pulling on an old sweater, she hurried out the door down to the barn where Pete had parked the pickup.

"Hi, Dad. Hi, Woody. You two are home early. What's up?"

"Hi, Cally. Your father couldn't handle the excitement so we cut 'er short."

"Not true, Sweetie," said Pete as he swung open the trailer door and dropped the butt bar so Jolena could back out.

"You didn't sell her," Cally said, and there was no disappointment in her voice.

"Did so," said Woody.

She looked at Pete. "If you sold her, why'd you bring her home?"

Reaching in the pocket of his shirt, Pete pulled out the folded check he received from the auction barn. He handed it to his daughter.

"Can you bank this tomorrow?"

Cally unfolded the check and under the dim light from the light fixture mounted at the peak of the barn, she looked at the numbers to the left of the decimal point.

Wow, Dad, I've never seen a check this big before."

"Ain't no bigger than no ordinary check," Woody told her. "It ain't like one of them checks the golf pros get that takes two people to carry."

"Oh, Woody, you know what I mean. But, Dad, if you sold her for over eighty thousand dollars, why did you bring her back home?" Jolena backed out of the trailer and nuzzled Cally. "I don't get it." She petted Jolena's neck.

"Well, it seems I sold her to a fella who wants me to teach him how to ride her."

"And he's coming here? Where's he going to stay?"

"I figure he can stay in the bunkhouse. It's not going to be forever."

"Oh, jeez, Dad, the place is a mess. I don't even want the girls playing in there anymore. Nobody's stayed in there since Scrufty left."

"I know, I know. Don't you worry. I'll clean it up."

"Yeah, sure. I guess I'll be cooking for him too."

"Well of course. He's going to be working when he isn't training."

Cally shook her head. "It's a real good thing I love you, because otherwise you'd be on your own."

"Come on, Cally, we've had hired men before. This ain't different. None of us are getting any younger and an extra set of hands will help."

"Only if I can get him to help with the housework."

Pete put his arm around Cally, "Give me a break, Cally. Who knows, you might even like him."

She considered her father. He was old. She'd never seriously thought about it because he'd always been hale and hearty, and his decline had been gradual. But recently, she'd thought he looked different, more tired and worn than she had ever before noticed. Not surprising, he was over eighty. Not many men his age were still working horses.

"How old is he?"

"I'm not certain. Mid forties, I'd guess. He went to West Point."

"A little old for me I'd say."

"I don't expect you'll be marrying him. Although, he's a decent looking widower and I believe he's got a pile of money."

Cally laughed. "Oh money, that's different. Why didn't you tell me that right off? You know how I love money."

Pete ignored her mockery. "I like him. I believe he'll try hard. I think I can teach him to ride Jolena. And there's something else too, something that I still don't quite believe."

"Oh yeah, what's that?"

"He is the son of the man I admire the most."

Woody picked this particular moment to chime in. "I thought that was me, but I ain't got no son."

"A good thing for the gene pool," Pete shot back. "I'm talking major coincidence here, Cally. He's the son of my commanding officer from Korea."

Pete had never discussed, to great extent, his war experiences with his daughter. She knew he'd had to use his rifle and she knew he had a Purple Heart and some other medals, but he'd never told her the details. He'd never told anyone. It was something he did not discuss. She did know, however, he held a man by the name of Major Conrad Bradley, in high esteem, although she wasn't certain why.

"Well, yeah, I guess that would be a coincidence, but what surprises me more is you said you were going to teach him to ride. Can't he ride now? Because if he can't, there's no way you or anybody is going to teach him what he needs to know to ride in the futurity."

Pete put his right arm under Jolena's neck and rested his hand against the right side of her face. "Walk with me, Jo," he commanded softly. "Course he can ride," Pete told Cally as he walked away with Jolena. "I'm just not certain how well he rides."

Cally shook her head. "Come on, Woody, I made a couple of pies this afternoon. You look like you could use a snack before bed."

In the barn, Pete gave Jolena half of a three-pound coffee can full of oats and stood by while she ate. His arm draped across her back, he talked quietly to her. "You know, Jo, I'm probably crazy for doing what I'm doing, but I believe it could work. I know you can do it, and if Connie has any ability at all we might just pull this off. Course, you're gonna have to take care of him and I'm gonna have to convince him to listen to you, not get all goofy and insist on jerkin' you around, but that shouldn't be impossible. He seems like a reasonable sort. I just hope he ain't got a big ego. I've seen a lotta cowboys lose because they were too smart to pay attention to their horse."

He pondered what he had just said. "Yep, that'll be the big trick; teach him to read you and let you have you're way. Course he's also gonna have to stay in the saddle, but I suspect that'll be the easy part."

Jo finished her oats and nuzzled Pete's hand, looking for more. "You had enough for now." He pushed open the door to the paddock next to the barn. "You go on out now and run around some. You been stuck in that noisy old trailer way too long."

She did, and after retrieving his bag from the truck, Pete slowly walked to the house, pondering how he'd handle Conrad. Woody was already on his second slice of pie when he got to the kitchen. He looked at the choices, apple or cherry. He was partial to both.

"Think I'll have cherry," he announced to Woody.

"Why not have one of each? You ain't on no diet. That's what I'm doin'."

"Yeah, that's an option." He pulled a dinner plate from the cupboard and helped himself.

"Where'd Cally go?"

"She heard one of the girls wandering around upstairs and went to check."

Pete was quiet until he finished the slice of apple pie. He stopped with his fork poised just above the slice of cherry. "You think I'm crazy for trying this, Woody?"

"What, tryin' to eat two pieces of pie?"

Thoroughly in tune to Woody's humor, Pete didn't miss a beat. "I mean, how hard can it be to teach somebody to sit on the back of a horse? That's all he'll have to do, stay on her back."

"Easy for you to say, you been ridin' since you were in diapers and if you get much older, you'll be ridin' in diapers again." He got up to get another sliver of pie. "Might be a lot easier trainin' horses than humans,"

"Seriously, Woody, I even taught you to ride."

"Yeah, you did, but I ain't gonna be in no fancy competition on no high-powered cuttin' horse in front of fifty thousand spectators neither."

"There's never going to be fifty thousand spectators."

"Fifty or fifty thousand, what's the difference? When they get to hootin' and hollerin' maybe your boy will come apart."

"You don't know that. Hell, he was in combat and he didn't come apart. Getting shot at is the ultimate test of your cool."

"Well you oughtta know about that, but all he told you is he was in combat, not how he held up in combat."

"True, but I'm thinking if he's anything like his old man I got no problems in that regard."

Cally had come down from upstairs, and when she heard the two of them talking, she stopped in the living room and listened to their conversation. It made her sad. She wished her father were in good enough shape to ride Jolena himself. But she understood that he didn't think he was up to it. Why he thought he wasn't was a different matter. He never complained. He merely said he couldn't do it and Cally accepted his decision. She knew she couldn't do it. She could ride just fine and had won a few saddles and some prize money when she was younger, but now it wasn't possible for her to spend the time that would be necessary. Her kids, her dad, and Woody, and the ranch took up more time than she had. There was no way she could squeeze another four hours out of the day for training unless she took it out of her sleep time, and she wouldn't be able to do that for long. No, at this point all she could do was hope this guy, Conrad, wouldn't be too big a let down for her father.

Pete was almost forty-eight years old when Cally was born. Her mother was forty-one. Pete and Renee wanted children, but Renee couldn't seem to conceive. They were both checked out medically and were told there was no apparent reason they couldn't have children. After several years of agonizing over their inability to conceive, they finally stopped worrying and accepted their childless fate. Then, after they'd been married almost twenty-five years, Cally was born. She grew up having the oldest parents of any of her peers. She was aware of it, but never paid much attention to the fact. She loved her parents and since her mother's death, felt very protective of her father. She did not want to see him disappointed or hurt by anyone. She would do whatever she could to prevent that, and God help the unfortunate soul who tried to take advantage of Pete.

"Well, Petey," Woody continued, "If that's the case, maybe you got a shot at it. Course I still think you're crazy, but you're also about the most blest man I ever seen, so maybe there's a prayer."

Cally walked in and put a hand on her father's shoulder. "I don't think you're crazy, Dad. I just hope you won't be disappointed."

"Thanks, Cally. I'll only be disappointed if Jolena doesn't get to go."

"Oh, Dad, Jo's just a horse. She won't know the difference. As long as there's oats and grass and somebody to scratch behind her ears, she'll be happy."

"Yeah, I know she just a horse, but she's a horse like I've never seen before."

Woody jumped in to finish for him, "Yeah, we know, 'And I've seen a lot of horses.'"

Pete shrugged and decided to forego explaining again what was so special about Jolena.

"We believe you, Dad, but she's still a horse."

"Okay," Pete acquiesced, "She's got a horse's heart, but she's also got a soul and it ain't the soul of horse. It's bigger than that. I've never told anyone and I hesitate to say it now, for fear of bein' ridiculed by you two, but sometimes she reminds me of your mother, Cally. That horse has the soul of a woman."

"Well," said Woody, "I certainly hope this Connie fellow is as good as you think he might be, because it don't do no good to disappoint a woman."

"You speaking from experience or is that just another one of your famous opinions?"

"It's the truth. It's no good to disappoint anybody and if you're a man, it's worse to disappoint a woman. A woman might forgive you, but they'll never forget. Right, Cally?"

"I don't know, Woody. I've forgiven you two so many times, I've forgotten at least half of them."

Pete laughed. "I'm going to bed. I've come seven hundred miles today and I can't handle any more of this scintillating conversation. See you all in the morning." He put his plate and fork in the sink. "Thanks for the pie, Cally."

"You're welcome, Dad. Good night."

When he was gone, Cally turned to Woody. "You notice any difference in him lately?"

"I don't know for sure. He's still just as sassy as ever. Maybe he's movin' a little slower than usual, but he's been busy fussin' over that horse. She might as well have the soul of a woman. He's in love with her."

"Yeah, you could be right. I wasn't all that surprised to see you come back with her."

"After he told me he wouldn't part with her for less than fifty big ones, I assumed we'd be haulin' her back. I never figured he'd get it. The amazin' thing is that he got all that money and still gets to keep her."

"What do you think about the guy that bought her? He's not a dead beat is he? I'd hate to see Dad be disappointed by some jerk that doesn't have a clue."

"I don't know about him bein' able to ride. I'm mostly certain Connie ain't a dead beat, or at least not your ordinary dead beat. He might be a lot a things, but any man who can cough up eighty-four grand for a horse he's fixin' to give to his buddy ain't no piker. I liked him."

"What do you mean? He bought Jolena for a friend?"

"Yep, when Pete asked him what he planned to do with Jo, he said he was figurin' on givin' her to his friend. Seems his buddy was lookin' for a couple cuttin' horses and Connie came along for the ride."

"Where is he from?"

"Indiana. Said he had sold his business a few years ago and then his wife died. I got the impression he was sorta at loose ends. Seemed a little disjointed."

"Disjointed? You don't think he's unstable or anything, do you?"

"No, course not, nothin' like that. He just seemed like he was lookin' for a purpose. I know that feeling, or I did once, after my wife was first gone."

Cally laughed. "That's funny. I didn't feel like I had a purpose until I finally told my husband to get lost."

It was Woody's turn to laugh. "Purpose is all in your head."

"Maybe, but it's a good thing to have."

"Mighty hard to carry on for long without. If Connie's lookin', I hope he can find it."

"What's he look like?"

Woody learned back in the sturdy kitchen chair until he had the two front legs off the floor. "Bout six feet tall, solid, no fat, good head of hair, strong jaw, looks to be some over forty. More like early forties, I thought. He was real polite. Your dad gave him the third degree and he took it like a gentleman, didn't get surly or nothin'. Seemed like a class act to me."

"Well, I guess we'll find out soon enough. When's he coming out?"

"Two weeks he said. I'm lookin' forward to him gettin' here. The rest of you have heard all my stories."

Cally smiled. "I'm going to watch him real close, Woody. Listening to all your stories will be a good test of his character."

Woody feigned insult. "Aw, Cally, that really hurts. All this time I thought you genuinely enjoyed listenin' to my tales."

"I do, Woody, I really do, but it's going to be an experience for the new guy. The way he handles it will be enlightening."

Woody pushed back his chair and stood up. "Always glad to be of assistance, but I'm beginnin' to feel all those miles. I gotta get to bed. Night, Cally."

"Good night, Woody. See you in the morning."

She made herself a cup of tea and picked at a sliver of pie. *Things were always changing,* she thought. *Now I have to adjust to another man around the house.* The last man they employed was a character her girls nicknamed Scrufty. He was a weasely looking man with a pinched face and dirty blonde hair that had a perpetually bad day. He did everything he was asked, but never very well, and he was always looking back over his shoulder.

Cally caught him leering at her more than once. As long as it was her, she wasn't worried, but when it appeared he was leering at the girls, she went after him. It was a hot summer afternoon and the girls were running through the lawn sprinkler. They were only seven and they'd pulled off most of their clothes. Cally was washing dishes and watching them when she noticed Scrufty peeking at them from around the corner of the barn. She watched him long enough to realize his interest wasn't healthy.

She went after him. Grabbing Pete's Winchester Model 94, she marched him down to the bunkhouse at gunpoint where she supervised his packing. She paid him off in cash and sent him out the driveway in his old truck.

That had been almost two years ago and she was quite happy with their present living arrangements. A new man would mean adjustments and more work. The first thing she'd have to do would be to clean up the old bunkhouse. It was one big room with a sink, a wood cook stove, table, and three sets of bunk beds. There was no bathroom, only an outhouse thirty feet from the back door. The girls used to play in the bunkhouse on rainy days, but lately the place was so dirty Cally had told them to stay out.

She held her cup in both hands and sighed. Maybe she just ought to burn it down and Pete could go out a buy a nice, second hand trailer. They could probably find one for a few thousand dollars that would be a lot nicer for this Connie character, not to mention a lot easier for her. Cally looked up at the clock. "Ten-thirty already," she remarked out loud. "I gotta get to bed."

When she said her prayers, she included Conrad. "Lord, make him someone I can handle."

Just a few minutes earlier when Pete said his prayers, he'd included Conrad also. "Lord, make him someone I can work with."

Chapter 12, The Arrival

By eleven o'clock, four hours after leaving the parking lot of the trailer manufacturer, Connie had passed Casper, Wyoming. Sheridan was a hundred and fifty miles ahead and he wanted to make it to Bozeman, Montana, three hundred miles beyond that, before he packed it in for the night. If all went well, he'd be there before seven. That would give him time for a relaxing dinner and find a place to park while it was still light.

The freedom of pulling his accommodations more than made up for the extra driving tension. Besides, he was beginning to feel almost comfortable towing the big trailer. He had discovered the diesel engine under the hood of his pickup had plenty of power to accelerate with the trailer; he just had to step on the gas pedal with a little more authority. Maneuvering the rig wasn't all that difficult either as long as he paid close attention to the surrounding traffic. Cindy's prophesy of discovering how bad other people drive, had already been proven in a number of instances. Lane jumpers were the worst. Connie quickly came to believe that some drivers must have serious death wishes, whether they knew it or not, and young women in small imported cars seemed to be the most suicidal. Then he came to the realization that all conscientious drivers of big rigs eventually come to, "Drive as safely as possible and if some one wants to be stupid, that's their problem." He might have added, "It's also what insurance is for."

Once he grew accustomed to pulling the trailer, he began speculating on his arrival at Pete's. He hoped there would be no issues with Pete's daughter. He felt if there were to be a problem in any of this, other than his riding abilities, it would be with Cally. It was his opinion, and he didn't believe he was being chauvinistic, that women tended to be less tolerant to changes in their lifestyles. Of course that was a generalization based on his experience with women who did not work outside the home. Cally fit that category. She probably worked harder than he'd ever worked, but she worked at home. Home was different than an office. A woman working at home was the boss and, therefore, naturally less inclined to accept externally imposed changes.

Then again, Connie thought, I might be all wet and Cally will be the least of my problems. He wondered how Sarah might have reacted in the same situation. After ten miles he decided, he wasn't certain of how she'd handle the situation, but he felt she would at least be externally gracious. After another twenty miles, he decided the best he could hope for was that no matter how Cally really felt about his intrusion into her home, she would be externally gracious.

"Well," he told himself, "I'm a nice guy. She'll recognize that and in no time I'll be just a member of the family."

There weren't many towns between Casper and Sheridan, and it was one in the afternoon when Connie was able to stop for gas and lunch. The town was Buffalo, some four thousand souls, and at least one good café that served breakfast all day long. Having eaten only a banana and two, Little Debbie, oatmeal cream pies washed down with vending machine coffee, Connie went with pork chops, fried eggs, toast, orange juice, and real coffee. It was a taste sensation. After topping off both fuel tanks, he was ready to take on the highway all the way to Bozeman without stopping.

The scenery was fascinating, mostly high country prairie with rolling hills and huge vistas that are never seen back east. After a wet winter, the hills vibrated to the horizon with a vivid green that was calming and invigorating, exciting and peaceful, a weird combination.

Connie remembered the prairies from his trips to the dude ranch as a teenager, but he had never seen them this green before. In late summer and fall they were a dull brown, beautiful only to cows and antelope. Connie couldn't even imagine how bleak they would be in mid-winter, snow white and slashed with howling winds. But for now, the prairies were absolutely gorgeous, fresh, virgin, and green galore. The miles oozed past and soon he was running along the southern edge of Billings. Nothing inspiring was to be seen from the road, but on the west end of town, the highway started up a long grade. There was an indication the countryside would be changing.

While Connie was contemplating the diversity of country he had seen so far, Cally was finishing up with the bunkhouse renovation. It had been a major challenge, but she, Woody, and Pete had prevailed. They had swept, scrubbed, vacuumed, washed, dusted, painted, and repaired until the bunkhouse was once again fit for human habitation, although none of them would have traded their place in the house to stay there. The thirty-foot trip to the outhouse in the dark of night was still not desirable or convenient. But the lights worked and it didn't take long for the wood stove to make it toasty warm on a cool spring evening. Cally had even sewn new curtains for the windows. She hoped Conrad would understand the situation and accept it. After all, he'd been in the army and fought in a foreign country. Living in the bunkhouse should be cake. Besides, she knew she was a good cook and he would eat better than he had probably ever eaten. She didn't know that for twenty years, he'd lived in a house that was now on the market for almost a million dollars or that his wife had been a gourmet cook.

She gave the place one last scrutiny. "Looks better than it did twenty years ago," she told herself. That was true enough, but even when it was first built, it wasn't much. Pete bought the ranch over fifty years ago; right after the original house had burned down. And if it hadn't burned down, Pete and Renee would have torn it down. It had been carelessly built sometime around 1900, and was junk. Pete built the bunkhouse and he and Renee lived in it for six months while their new house was completed. He built the bunkhouse to be durable, not beautiful, and so it remained today, sturdy and square, a wooden box with no concession to style. Cally locked the door on her way out. She wasn't certain when Conrad would arrive and didn't want the girls making a mess of all her hard work.

Walking back to the house, her thoughts were on the stranger who was coming to stay with them. If her father trusted him and Woody thought he was okay, how bad could he be? She had to admit Pete was a better judge of character than she was. Eleven years ago, immediately after meeting her ex-husband, he'd correctly predicted he was no good. It had taken Cally a year of courtship and a year of marriage to discover what Pete had seen instantly. She still remembered the words Pete had used to describe him, "He'll break your heart, Cally. He wouldn't look me in the eyes. I don't trust him."

"Oh, Dad," she had replied, "He's just shy. You'll see."

Eventually, after she caught him with another woman, she realized her father's assessment had been correct. So there she was, twenty-four years old with twin baby girls, no husband and no means of support. Pete had invited her back home, to be a partner in the ranch, and she'd been here ever since. Initially it had been extremely difficult, not just physically, but emotionally, too. Moving back into her childhood home with two kids and no money was demoralizing. Fortunately, Pete was not judgmental and Cally eventually forgave herself. After that, everything got better. Now they were real partners. Cally had difficulty imaging a life without the ranch.

She told herself this was just another temporary arrangement and come the end of November, or maybe even sooner, the stranger would be gone. Everything would be back to normal. Actually, it might even be good to have him around for a while. There were a few things that could use some work and there was always fence to mend, a job she hated. *Okay,* she thought, *we'll all make this a positive experience.*

Later that afternoon, as she was preparing supper, Lindsey, one of the twins, asked her, "So when does the new guy get here?" It was at least her tenth request since Pete had given them the news.

"I'm not sure. Did you ask your Grandpa?"

"You always tell me to ask him and he never knows."

"How about Woody, did you ask him?"

Lindsey rolled her eyes. "Puh-leeze, Mother. Woody never knows anything."

Cally smiled. "You'd be surprised the things Woody knows. Did you ask him?"

"No, but I'll bet he doesn't know either."

"What do you want to bet?"

"Dishes?"

"Whose turn is it?"

"It's my turn to wash, Danni's turn to dry. Why don't we just get a dishwasher?"

"Why spend all that money when I've got two healthy girls?"

"Aw, Mom, everybody's got one."

"Well, we're not everybody, but I'll bet dishes Woody knows."

"Be right back," and she ran off to find Woody.

An hour later she was back. "I guess I'll have to wash dishes."

"Oh yeah?" Cally was surprised. "What did Woody say?"

"He said he'll be here tomorrow, but he wasn't sure about the time."

"See, I told you Woody knows a lot."

"Yeah, maybe, but I bet him dishes the guy wouldn't be here tomorrow."

"You've become quite a gambler. How about you deal out some plates and silverware on the table?"

As Pete's extended family was sitting down to supper, Connie was squinting into the sun and slowing for the first exit into Bozeman. It was six o-clock when he stopped at the top of the exit ramp. Looking to his left, he saw a huge Wal-Mart staring down a giant strip mall on the other side of six lanes of street. Not much like the Montana he remembered from the late seventies. "Cowboys are probably wearing shorts and drinking latte now days," he mumbled. Hooking a big left turn, he eased into the back of the Wal-Mart parking lot. He parked near a guy selling organic beef from a large trailer. I'll bet he knows where there's a good steak house, he thought.

"Hi," Conrad said, "I'm just passing through and I wonder if you can tell me where I can find an RV park and a good restaurant."

"Howdy," replied the beef salesman. "Your best bet would be to stay parked right where you're at and grill yourself a good steak you bought from me. If you don't have a grill, they sell 'em right down there. Potatoes too." He waved at the Wal-Mart.

The suggestion was tempting, but Connie was tired, he wanted to be waited on. "You know that sounds real good, but I've been driving since Denver and I really don't want to cook."

"I hear ya. There's an RV Park right off the freeway on the other end of town, and the Big Sky Brewery in the middle of town is a fair restaurant. By the way, where you headed?"

"Kalispell, or actually about fifteen miles west of Kalispell. I bought a cutting horse from a rancher out there."

"Pete Browning?"

Connie's jaw dropped to his belt buckle. "Yeah, you know him?"

"Oh sure, him and his daughter buy meat from me when I'm out there. I'm in the Kalispell Wal-Mart lot every other Wednesday. Good looking woman, his daughter."

Connie was confused. Why would a rancher buy beef from somebody else? "I thought Pete raised cattle."

The man in the trailer smiled, "Oh, they don't buy beef, they buy pork." He turned and waved to the sign behind him that listed all his wares. Besides beef, there was pork, lamb, and free range chicken. "I only raise the organic beef, but I sell the rest for some of my neighbors."

Connie had a sudden inspiration on how to endear himself with Pete's daughter. He would bring her some meat. After all, what good-looking woman could resist forty pounds of pork and a dozen free-range chickens? Twenty minutes later and two hundred dollars lighter, he was back on the freeway looking for the RV Park.

It was right where it was supposed to be, just to the north of the freeway. It wasn't high tourist season, so Connie had his choice of parking places. He selected a spot in the back, well away from anyone else. For starters, he didn't want an audience when he parked and dropped the trailer. This was the first time he'd be doing it and he could only hope it would go smoothly. Also, he wanted to be as far away from the freeway noise as he could be. Parking and releasing the trailer proved to be ridiculously easy, especially with the optional electric winch on the trailer's fifth wheel hitch assembly.

After getting directions from the park operator, Connie cruised into downtown Bozeman. It was a warm Friday evening and the city sidewalks were littered with college kids. The man at the RV Park told Connie that Bozeman had a state college that was popular with both local and out of state students. It was beautiful here and many college grads decided to stay. "Competition for local jobs is intense," he'd said. "There's construction workers with PhDs and ranch hands with MBAs, not a lot of them, but it happens."

Conrad was impressed with the downtown area. It was clean and well preserved. He'd be willing to bet the tourist trade during the summer was impressive. He drove past the restaurant at least twice in the process of inspecting the town.

Finally, overcome by hunger, he stuffed the big pickup truck into a spot between a Mini-Cooper and a BMW. "Jeez," he mumbled to himself as he carefully extricated himself from his big Detroit iron, "the least they could do is buy American cars."

Inside the Big Sky Brewery, he was escorted to his table by a young, leggy blonde woman. When she said, "Follow me please," he was prepared to do just that, to the ends of the earth if she asked.

Oh, to be twenty-five again. He rubbed his eyes and consulted his menu. Everything looked good. If his sister, Suzy, thought Montana was a wilderness, she should see this menu. If only half of the food creations lived up to their names and descriptions, this place was surely in competition with the best places Suzy frequented. The only notable difference was a lack of pretension. The place had a back room with six pool tables and a microbrewery.

A couple hours later Connie was back at the RV Park. His belly was comfortably full and his trailer had been reunited with his truck. He tried to stay awake and watch TV while he sipped a bottle of

Moose Drool ale from a twelve-pack purchased on his way back to the trailer. Fighting sleep after finishing the first beer, he flicked off the TV, the lights and crashed. He didn't wake until well after seven.

He took his time showering and dressing and on his way out of the park, dumped the trailer's holding tank. It was almost nine before he hit the road. *Two hundred miles to Missoula and a hundred and forty more to Kalispell, I'll be there by four thirty.* Coming down the entrance ramp he pushed his foot smoothly to the floor. He merged onto the freeway at seventy-five miles an hour.

"Do you really think he'll be here today?" Lindsey asked Woody.

"I bet you, didn't I? Why'd I bet you if I didn't think I was gonna win?"

"I don't know, maybe you just wanted to give me a break from doing dishes."

"Ha, that's foolish. I like you a lot, but I hate doin' dishes. I believe I'll be winning this bet."

"What makes you so sure?" Danni chimed in.

"I am confident in my abilities as a judge of human character."

The girls looked at each other. "What's that supposed to mean?" Lindsey asked.

"It means the man said he'd be here in two weeks. Yesterday was two weeks to the day since we talked and I'm bettin' he'll be here today."

"Well," said Danielle, "if he's so good, he should have been here yesterday. That was two weeks, not today."

"I'm afraid you're wrong about that."

"What do you mean? You just said."

"Forget what I just said, how old were you on your first birthday?"

"That's a dumb question. I was one."

"No, think about it. How old were you on your first birthday."

Danni scowled, screwing up her brow, "One!"

"I'm not talkin' about when you had a cake with a candle and everybody sang, I'm talking about your first birthday, birth-day. Get it?"

"You mean the day I was born?"

"Precisely. How old were you on that day?"

"Ah, well, I don't know. I was just born."

"Would I be safe in sayin' you were zero years old on your first birthday?"

The twins pondered this question. "I suppose," was the tentative answer.

"Okay, now that's settled, pay attention. The day Conrad told me he was coming out in two weeks don't count. It's like your birthday, so two weeks is really up today, not yesterday." Woody smiled, secure in his logic.

"I don't get it," said Danni.

"I do", said Lindsey. "It's like a countdown on a rocket ship launch. They always count to zero before they push the button because that way, they get all ten seconds."

"I still don't get it."

"It's like one from ten equals nine and zero from ten equals ten."

Danni was still a bit confused by the concept. "Whatever, he'll be here today, right, Woody?"

"I'm bettin' on it, Sweetie."

Connie was betting on it too. While Woody and the twins wrestled with higher mathematics, Connie was just west of Kalispell, only ten miles away. He was watching the odometer and counting down from fifteen. When he got to zero, he turned into the next left he saw. The house was hidden from the road by a thick stand of pines, but when he cleared them, he knew he was there. The house was a boxy, bulky, two-story affair with a hip roof and a big porch across the back, just like Pete had told him. He wheeled in next to Pete's pickup and killed the engine. Getting out from behind the wheel, his palms were sweaty.

Woody watched him from the kitchen window. He was helping Cally with their dinner by peeling potatoes. "He's here," he announced.

Cally hurried over to the window, quickly joined by the twins.

"Nuts," said Lindsey. "You win, Woody."

"Nuts," said Cally.

Woody turned away from the window to regard her. "I can understand Lindsey's 'Nuts', but I don't get yours."

"All that work we put into fixing up the bunkhouse. Look at his horse trailer. It's the kind you can live in."

"Maybe you can, but for how long? I 'spect sooner or later, he'll be bunkin' in the bunkhouse"

Cally watched as Connie put his hands together behind his back and stretched the miles out of his neck and shoulders. "I suppose I ought to go out there and welcome him."

Woody handed her the potato peeler, "I'll go fetch him. Where's your father?"

"He said he was going to ride down to the south gate and make sure that piece of fence you two replaced last fall was okay. I told him to be back by five."

Woody glanced up at the kitchen clock. "Ten to four now, I'm certain we can entertain Connie 'til Pete shows up."

Still wearing his apron, Woody left Cally and the girls to fetch their visitor.

Conrad was still standing along side his truck deciding his next move when he heard the slap of the screen door. He turned to see a short man with curly gray hair, wearing a long-sleeved flannel shirt, blue jeans and an apron, headed his way. From the little he knew about Woody, the apron wasn't a surprise. Woody had said he'd herded sheep, alone in the mountains of Wyoming, every summer for forty years. All summer long, he was self-reliant, cooking his meals, washing his clothes, and keeping his flock on good pasture, entirely on his own. If he wanted to wear an apron, it was his business. Maybe, Connie speculated, he was making apple pies. He'd mentioned when they were leaving the auction that he'd bake one of his world famous apple pies for Connie's arrival.

Connie walked toward Woody and stuck out his hand, "Hello, Woody, good to see you again."

"Hello, young man, likewise to you. Your timely arrival has saved me from doin' the dishes tonight."

Connie wondered if he had committed some sort of faux pas. "Should I have called?"

Woody waved his right hand. "Oh no, course not. One of the twins wanted to know when you'd be here. She didn't believe me when I told her today so I bet her dishes. Well, you're here and she'll be doin' dishes. That's all. Come on in and meet the crew. Pete's off somewhere lookin' at fence, but he'll be back before long."

As they walked to the house, Connie was impressed with the view. In every direction except south, where the meadow snuggled on both sides of the creek, the ranch was surrounded by high, pine covered hills. The trees stood out in sharp relief from the blue sky as if they were vividly colored, cardboard cutouts. There was a breeze and the scent of pine was prominent. To a city dweller, it was surrealistic. The clear air belied distance and foreshortened perspective, giving the illusion he could almost reach out and stroke the trees. That was hardly the case.

The closest hills were on the west side of the creek, across a wide hay meadow, a half a mile away.

Woody led him into the kitchen, a big square room with a yellow and green patterned linoleum floor. The ceiling was high and the cupboards went right to the top. There was a sturdy oak table off to one side with six chairs around it. The refrigerator, oven and cook top were all stainless steel and appeared to be new. That was a bit surprising to Connie; he could have easily imagined avocado green appliances. Then when his eyes traveled to the wide arched opening to the kitchen from the living room, he got a real surprise.

He blinked hard. Entering the kitchen was the little brunette heartthrob from the dude ranch of his youth. Impossible, he thought. That woman would be forty-six, the same as him. The woman he was looking at was barely thirty. He heard Woody making introductory noises, but he wasn't sure exactly what was said. However, he managed to extend his hand to shake hers. It was wonderful.

Chapter 13, Introductions

Patsy was the name of the girl Connie had loved during his seasonal tenure at the dude ranch. Cally, the woman with whom he was now holding hands, could have passed for her twin. "Pleased to meet you," he told her, finally relinquishing his hold on her hand. Cally was smiling at him with her whole face, exactly like he remembered Patsy smiling. Her eyes laughed and sparkled, and her voice was clear, like notes from a bell.

Cally thought he was a handsome man and hoped his personality would be as pleasant as his looks. "We've been expecting you," she said. "And these two," she put a hand on each of the twins' shoulders, "are dying to meet you."

"Are you going to give me a few weeks to get your names right?" Connie asked after Lindsey and Danni were introduced.

"Oh, sure," said Lindsey. "Even our teachers have trouble telling us apart."

"Actually we're a lot different," Danni told him. "We just look alike."

"I know how that is," Connie confided. "I have a twin sister and we're very different."

"Wow, that's pretty weird. Does she look like you?"

"No, we aren't identical like you two. She's much nicer looking than I am."

Danni smiled, "You're not so bad."

"Yeah," Lindsey added, "you don't really even look like a hired hand."

"Really? What's a hired hand supposed to look like?"

"Lindsey, that's not very polite." Cally was blushing. "Mister Bradley isn't exactly a hired hand."

"That's what you said he was. Grandpa is going to teach him to ride Jo and he's going to help out with chores."

Cally was about as embarrassed as she'd ever been. "Yes, but that doesn't make him a hired hand." She saw no way out of this.

Connie laughed. "I don't mind being a hired hand. I just want to know how I should look."

"Well, you should look more beat up, rougher."

"Yeah," Danni decided to help her out. "You should look like forty miles of bad road, and your name should be Old Jack or Old Sam."

"Well, I guess you could call me Old Connie."

"No," Danni said, "that's not good. Besides, Connie is a girl's name. "

"Isn't Danni a boy's name?"

She thought a minute. "Danni's just my nickname. My real name is Danielle and besides Danni is spelled with an i not a y."

"Okay, my real name is Conrad, but all my friends call me Connie. Spelled with an i e not a y."

"Girls, girls, girls. How about you wash your hands and help me with dinner?" Cally's color was returning to normal and she thought she would try to call off the girls before they could embarrass her again.

"Oh, Mom, it's just after four and we never eat before six," protested Lindsey.

"Yeah, and Woody's already helping," Danni offered.

"Well, Woody is going to show Connie around and get him settled in, so you two are taking over for him."

Connie couldn't help but wonder what happened to this woman's husband. According to Pete she was divorced and had been for more than eight years. If her ex had left her for another woman, that woman must have been a real beauty. Cally was about as cute as a grown woman could be. His wife, Sarah, had been a regal beauty, elegant, and stately. Her features were well defined, smooth and precise and her complexion was flawless.

Cally was freckled, her features were muted and soft. He couldn't tell exactly what color her eyes were, sort of greenish hazel gray, but they sparkled and danced with an internal intensity. She was shorter than Sarah had been. Connie guessed she wasn't more than five-four, not that her height was critical because her physique was just as impressive as Sarah's and Patsy's had been. Connie never thought he'd meet a woman as physically desirable as his deceased wife. Now he was talking to one.

Woody handed his apron to Cally, "Come on, Connie, I'll show you around."

"Okay, that would be good." He hated to leave.

Outside, Woody said, "Those two girls are real firecrackers. Actually, all three of them are firecrackers." He chuckled. "But, I guess you'll find that out for yourself soon enough."

"Ah, is there something I should know?"

Woody waved his right hand in the air a couple of times. "No, I suspect not. You look like you can take care of yourself all right."

"You'd tell me if there's something I should know, right? I don't want to step on anybody's toes."

"Well, toes were made for steppin' on. Cally can be a little possessive of the twins is all. They have to toe the line, but she's gonna be the one makin' sure they do."

When they reached Connie's trailer, he pulled open the door for Woody. "I've got a couple of cold beers if you're interested."

"Always interested in cold beer." Following Connie into the living quarters of the horse trailer, he took a long look around. "Better than the bunkhouse."

Connie put two of the cold Moose Drool bottles on the dinette table and the men slid in across from each other. "What happened to Cally's husband?"

"Nothin' special happened to him, he was just a dumb cluck. Lotsa men are dumb clucks. It's in their genes or their hormones, or maybe both; I ain't figured it out yet. Still got some of my own hormones. Cally met him at a rodeo. She was barrel racin' and he was ridin' bulls. You know, I never thought about it before. Maybe he wasn't always so stupid, maybe he just got throwed off on his head one too many times. That coulda been it. Brahma bulls made him stupid."

Connie was intrigued. "So how long did it last?"

"Well," said Woody, "Pete figured it out right away. Took Cally about two years."

"Figured out what right away?"

"That he was a dumb cluck. Lyin' bastard, too. Right after she had the twins, she chased him off. Seems as if he'd been payin' a lot of attention to about four different women besides Cally."

"He must have been one busy, lying, dumb bastard."

"Kinda what I thought. Pete and I ran into him about a year ago. Never told Cally. He had a woman on each arm and all three of 'em was tighter than ticks. Pete was gonna talk to him, but I steered him away."

"What did you think he was going to say?"

"Probably somethin' like, 'Where's the six hundred a month for child support you were supposed to be payin' for the last eight years?' But it wouldn't a done no good. The guy ain't merely a dumb cluck, he's a dead beat, too."

"So she's never even seen him since she divorced him?"

"Nope and I suspect that's a good thing. I'd like to see all kids have a father, but in a case like Cally's, it's better they don't have the one that made 'em. Some fathers are worse than no father."

"It appears as if she's doing all right with them."

"Oh yeah, Cally's capable. Smart too. She keeps the ranch in the black. Without her, Pete woulda had a hard time survivin' this long."

"Is the ranch in trouble?"

"Oh no, it ain't gonna make Cally rich, but her and the kids'll never starve. If it'd been up to Pete, we'd be raisin' lotsa horses and losin' money on every one. Cally's got us puttin' up hay 'til hell won't have it. Last year we baled up the most part of two thousand tons and sold it all for about a hundred and twenty bucks a ton. We sold a hundred head of cattle too and got a few more bucks, but it's the hay keepin' us solvent." And he added, "Course if we had all horses like Jolena and could find buyers like yourself for all of 'em, we wouldn't have to cut no more hay."

There was a rap at the door. Connie looked over to see Pete peering in. He got up to open the door. "Come on in. I drove twenty-five hundred miles to see you." They shook hands. "I have more of these, if you're interested." He pointed at the beer bottle.

"Sure," Pete replied. "I just happen to have a thirst that needs relieving." He sat at the table next to Woody and looked around. "Nice place. Beats the bunkhouse."

"Same thing Woody said. What's wrong with the bunkhouse?"

"Actually the bunkhouse is just fine. It's the bunkhouse latrine that's not so good. It's slightly detached from the bunkhouse which makes it a bit inconvenient."

"Slightly detached?" Woody questioned. Since when is thirty feet away slightly detached?"

Pete grinned. "Okay, it's a little more than slightly detached, but I suspect with this rig, you won't be staying in the bunkhouse anyway."

"Well I don't know, but I think living in this thing full time could get oppressive. I should probably check out the bunkhouse. I can always stay in there and use the bathroom in here."

"You can shower at the house," Pete said. "I've got my own private bathroom. People thought I was crazy when I built that house, putting in three full baths. Now I wish I had five."

"I got a shower in here, too. It's a bit cramped, but it works. I shouldn't have to bother you at all."

Pete was relieved. He had been concerned about how Connie would react to his rather limited accommodations. "Well, that's settled then. We'd best inspect the bunk house."

Connie genuinely liked the bunk house. The ceiling and walls were all blue pine paneled and everything was neat and clean. It was cozy and reminded him of a Canadian fishing cabin. "I like it," he announced. "I'm moving in."

Pete knew Cally would be pleased. She'd put a lot of effort into cleaning the place. "Woody and I can give you a hand."

"Okay, if you do, we can probably make it all in one trip."

Thirty minutes later, Connie was firmly established. His socks, underwear and jeans were in one of the old pine dressers, close to his bed. His shirts, slacks, two sport coats and one suit hung in the big closet at the back of the room. The few groceries he had carried with him were in the little refrigerator in the kitchen area. There was a broad bookshelf upon which he placed his violin and the picture of Sarah he had brought along.

"There, that does it. Where can I drop the trailer?"

"I figure you can back it in right along the side here." Pete told him, pointing to east end of the bunkhouse. "Then you won't have far to go when you have to go."

When he had the trailer in place and separated from the truck, he invited Pete and Woody back in the bunkhouse. "I've got at least three beers left and there's three of us."

"Sounds like a mathematical equation," said Woody and they sat at the bunkhouse table while they drank another.

"Oh, by the way, I ran into a friend of yours in Bozeman," Connie told Pete.

"Is he from Bozeman or you ran into him in Bozeman, because I don't know anyone who lives there. In fact, when Woody and I drove through there about three weeks ago, I hardly recognized the place."

"I'm not sure if he's from Bozeman or not, but he said he knew you and Cally. Said you bought meat from him."

"Oh, sure, you mean Rocky Roberts. Cally has a thing about organic meat. Says it's better for you."

"All meat is organic," Woody announced. "Vegetables too."

"I know that, but Cally is concerned with the twins getting too many hormones. Seems like little girls are growing up way too fast and nobody knows why. There's a theory it's because of all the growth hormones that are fed to meat animals and dairy cows."

"I don't know," Conrad admitted. "Sounds reasonable."

Woody snorted. "I disagree. I think it's all this adult television and video game crap kids are exposed too. Messes with their minds and causes their own hormones to kick in earlier."

"That sounds reasonable too. Glad I don't have to worry about it. Regardless, I brought you some pork and chickens."

Woody chuckled. "Ah, organic pig meat, the fastest way to a woman's heart."

Just then there was a rap on the door. It was the twins. Connie waved them in. The girls looked around. They hadn't been allowed in since it had been reconditioned.

"Wow," said Danni.

"Yeah, wow. This is the best it's ever looked," agreed Lindsey.

"Are you gonna live in here, not in your trailer?" Danni wanted to know. "Cause if you don't, we can play in here."

"I hate to disappoint you two young ladies, but I'll be staying in here."

"Why'd you get such a fancy trailer if you're not gonna use it?"

"Because your grandfather told me we'd be doing a lot of traveling with horses so I thought if I had a horse trailer I could stay in, it would be handy. It's my understanding it's what all rodeo cowboys do."

"Oh. Okay," she said and then she spied Connie's violin case on the bookshelf. "What's in the blue case?"

"A violin," Connie told her.

"Can you play it?"

"I used to. I think I'm going to be a little rusty for a while."

"Is it like a fiddle?" asked Lindsey.

"Yes, it is a fiddle."

"You told us it was a violin," Danni said.

"They're the same. A lot of things have more than one name."

"Like what?"

Connie ran his hand through his hair. "Like, ah, like..."

"Like cows and cattle," Pete came to his rescue. "Did you two come down here for a reason or just to harass us?"

"Mom said to come and get you because dinner's ready."

Pete pushed back from the table. "Let's go fellas. Won't do any good to keep Cally's dinner waitin'."

The girls blasted into the kitchen. "Connie plays the fiddle," Danni told Cally, "and it's the same as a violin."

"That's nice. Go wash your hands."

"He's gonna stay in the bunk house," Lindsey said. She sounded disappointed.

"That's nice. Go wash your hands."

The three men followed close behind the girls.

"You all go wash your hands."

The twins chattered like birds while they ate. Connie didn't pay a lot of attention to their conversation as he hadn't eaten since he'd stopped for a late breakfast somewhere around Butte. That had been eight hours ago and it hadn't been all that tasty. This meal, however, was wonderful; nothing fancy, roast beef, mashed potatoes, gravy, green beans with cheese sauce, homemade biscuits and salad

"Everything is terrific, Cally. I haven't had food like this in years."

She was slightly embarrassed. "Well, thank you. It's pretty basic."

"Yeah," Lindsey agreed. "We eat like this all the time."

"Wait 'til we have fried chicken," Danni told him. "It's my favorite, much better than KFC."

Cally rolled her eyes. "You two are hopeless." She looked at Pete. "Who's feeding them fast food?"

Pete held up his hands. "Not me, I know the rules."

She looked at Woody. "Don't look at me. I don't drive. How would I get to town without you or Pete?"

She looked back at Danni. "When did you have KFC?"

"Never, I just heard it was good, but I'm sure it's not as good as what you make us."

"You're right, it's not and I don't want you eating fast food. Not until you're eighteen anyway."

"While we're on the subject," Pete said, "Connie brought us some meat from Rocky Roberts."

"Where did you run into him?"

"Bozeman. I stopped in the Wal-Mart parking lot and asked him for directions and in the course of conversation he said you and Pete were customers."

"Yeah," Pete said, "we won't have to visit him for a while. Connie brought about forty pounds of pork and a dozen chickens."

"Oh, yum," said Danni. "Can we have chicken soon?"

"You haven't even finished this meal. It's way too soon to be worried about the next one."

And so dinner continued an unceasing stream of mostly meaningless prattle. It was the idle chatter of a happy, even if somewhat unconventional family. Later that night, as he lay in his bed in the bunkhouse, a little fire crackling in the woodstove to stave off the chill of a late spring evening in the Rockies, Connie tried to recall all that was said. He couldn't. The girls chattered like squirrels. Connie's sister had kids, but they were older now and Connie didn't remember eating many meals with them when they were young. He assumed it must have been similar to what he had just experienced. He enjoyed it. Danni and Lindsey seemed to be good kids. Also, based on the first meal, he didn't think he'd go hungry. Maybe this would all work out fine.

Later that night, or maybe it was early morning, Connie had to relieve himself. Remembering he had to either go to his trailer or to the outhouse, he pulled on his jeans. Then he fumbled his way to the bunkhouse door. "Wow," he whispered when the night air hit his bare chest. Inside the trailer, he took care of business and as he walked back the few steps to the bunkhouse, he was stopped dead in his tracks by the most god-awful, blood-curdling scream he had ever heard. It seemed to be coming from close across the creek. It took Connie several heartbeats to realize it had to be a mountain lion. Then the scream was repeated.

"Wow," he said again, a lot louder. "That's close."

He hurried into the bunkhouse, threw another chunk of pine into the stove and pulled the covers up to his chin. *Welcome to Montana.*

Chapter 14, Trouble

Being Sunday, breakfast would be at seven thirty, an hour later than usual. At seven, Connie was showering in the cramped confines of the tiny bathroom of his trailer. He was thinking there would have to be a better way. For occasional use, the trailer was great, but already the prospect of using this bathroom exclusively for the next eight months was bothering him. He was used to leisurely hot showers with room to move around. Banging his elbows and shoulders every time he turned was going to get old in eight days, let alone eight months.

He wondered if there was any way he could put a shower stall in the bunkhouse. There was a sink in the kitchen area so there must be some kind of drainage system. Maybe he could tap into that. He then reasoned he could buy a small gas fired water heater and put a propane tank outside next to the building. And why stop there? He could buy a composting toilet and he'd have all the comforts of home. He could take out the beds at the back of the bunkhouse and build a wall, put in a door and he'd have a master bedroom suite. He'd talk to Pete about remodeling right away to be sure there were no objections. He didn't want to be presumptuous.

He dropped the soap and the only way he could pick it up was to do a deep knee bend and then grab it. "That's what I'll do," he told himself. He couldn't imagine Pete not allowing him to make the improvements. As he toweled off, he was thinking about everything he'd need.

Connie knocked at precisely seven-thirty. Lindsey opened the door for him. "You don't have to knock every time," she told him.

"Thank you, Lindsey. You are Lindsey, right?"

"Yep, the one and only."

"Okay, so which times do I have to knock?"

She looked him with a frustrated stare. "What are you talking about?"

"Well, you said I didn't have to knock every time, but that implies I have to knock sometimes. I just want to know when to knock." He thought he had her.

She stared a bit longer. "If it's meal time you don't have to knock, but if it's after bedtime, then you do." She grabbed his hand and pulled him across the porch and into the kitchen.

Woody sat at the table with his hands wrapped around a coffee mug. Cally had her back to him. She was paying attention to the kitchen stove. Pete and Danni were nowhere to be seen.

"Have a chair, Connie." Woody told him. "You need coffee?"

Cally turned and smiled, "Good morning."

Connie returned the greeting and asked if there was anything he could do.

"No, just sit," she said and before she turned back to the stove, she poured him coffee.

"Did you hear that scream last night?" Connie asked Woody.

"I did," Lindsey said. "That's Simba, she's got cubs."

"I heard her before, but not last night," Woody said. "Pete and the girls seen her 'bout a week ago with two little cubs. Obviously, she's still hangin' around."

"I've heard her four times," Lindsey informed them. "I named her Simba. Simba means lion in African."

"It means lion in Swahili. There are a lot of African languages," Connie informed her.

"How do you know that? You been there?"

"As a matter of fact, I have been there. Swahili is spoken all over East Africa."

"Is that where you were, East Africa?"

"Yup, Kenya and Tanganyika. We even climbed Mount Kilima N'jaro."

"Who is we?"

"My wife and I."

"I didn't know you were married. Where is she? Why didn't you bring her along?"

"She died two years ago."

Lindsey paused, but only for a moment. "What did she die from?"

"Cancer."

"One of the kids in my class died from cancer last year. We were all sad, but our teacher told us we're all going to die, we just don't know when."

"Your teacher was right."

"Were you sad when your wife died?"

"Yes, I was, very sad."

"Lindsey," Cally interrupted, "That's enough now. Go find your grandpa and Danni and tell them it's time for breakfast.

"Sorry," Lindsey told Connie and dashed off on her mission.

"Sorry," Cally told Connie.

"It's okay. Like her teacher said, 'We're all going to die sometime.'"

Pete and Danni arrived shortly and breakfast commenced. It was a hearty affair with eggs, bacon, potatoes, cold and hot cereal, sourdough pancakes, toast, juice, coffee and milk. "Eat up, Connie," admonished Pete. "Bein' Sunday we only have two meals. The next one won't be until five."

Sufficiently warned, Connie packed away an amount he believed would hold him until at least five. He couldn't help it, he was ravenous. Must be the mountain air, he thought, because I sure haven't done any work.

After breakfast Pete took him down to the horse barn. "They stay outside except during the winter when I bring them in at night. They're still getting hay every day because the pasture isn't all that good yet and I give them a few oats every morning and evening so I can look them over. It also makes them easier to catch when I want to ride. They don't always come when I call."

The barn was clean, dry and well lighted. Connie counted twenty stalls, ten box stalls and ten tie stalls. There was also a small open area with a sand floor that he assumed could be used for training. The tack room was lined with saddles, bridles, bits, reins and halters. There appeared to be at least two-dozen saddles. Several of them were trophy saddles, stuffed back in the corner, draped with dusty plastic and it appeared as if they'd never held a butt.

In one corner of the barn was a large wooden box-like structure. It stood off the floor about three feet on sturdy steel legs. The bottom was sloped on all sides towards the front and there was a long handle off to one side. It looked like some kind of a prehistoric one-armed bandit.

Pete put a six-gallon bucket under the front and pulled on the handle. A slot opened at the bottom, and a golden jackpot of oats flowed into the bucket.

"That's slick," Connie told him.

"Yeah, I built it forty years ago. I was already tired of lugging oat sacks back then." He gestured towards the barn ceiling. "There's a hole in the roof and every summer when I combine the oats, I drive over and auger them in. Never have to touch them."

"How much oats do you grow?"

"Twenty acres worth. This hopper will hold a thousand bushels, but I never seem to get that much. Thought I'd come close one year, but three days before it was ready to cut, we got a hellacious hail storm that combined more than half of it right there in the field. Had to buy some that year. Usually though, I end up feeding a bunch to the cows just to get rid of it before I can cut the next year's crop."

Pete filled the bucket about two thirds full and handed it to Connie. He then proceeded to fill a second to the same level. He led the way out a side door into the adjoining pasture. The horses, including Jolena, were lined up, already waiting around four feeders.

Pete pointed to the two feeders on the left. "Take those two and put half into each one. Pay attention to your feet. Don't want to get 'em stepped on."

After the oats, Pete showed Connie how much hay to feed them. The whole operation took about half an hour. "This afternoon you and I will go for a little ride. Got to go to church this morning. You're welcome to join us, if you've got a mind."

Connie had not expected an invitation to church. He and Sarah used to attend church occasionally, but he did not consider himself deeply religious, although he knew he was a believer. "Ah, if it's okay, maybe next time." He was still mad at God for taking Sarah away.

"Whenever you'd like. I'm sure you didn't come out here to be a Lutheran."

Connie smiled, "You're right about that, but I do have a question."

"What's on your mind?"

"Where does the water from the bunkhouse sink go?"

Pete looked puzzled. "Down the drain."

"Yeah, I figured that much, but what happens to it, ultimately?"

"Oh, it's 'gray' water and it goes into a sump and when the sump is full, it's pumped onto the grass behind the bunkhouse. I just replaced the pump before you got here. Why do you ask?" Pete was

suddenly wondering if he had partnered up with an extreme
environmentalist.

"Well, while I was banging off the walls in my shower this
morning, I was wondering if I could put a shower stall in the bunkhouse.
Actually, a whole bathroom. I'd take out the four back beds, build a
wall and install everything. I'll pay for all of it."

"What would you do for a commode?"

"I'd get one of those composting toilets. I've used them when I
was fishing up in Canada. They really work well."

Pete thought for a moment. "You'd have to get another
propane tank if you want hot water. We don't want to dig a trench for a
gas line all the way from the house."

"Yeah, I thought it could go right off the back corner."

"Sounds fine with me. I'll mention to Cally what you're
doing."

"She won't object, will she? I don't want to make any trouble."

"No, she'll be fine with it. But she's got half ownership in the
ranch and it's only right she knows what's going on."

"Great, is there a home improvement store in Kalispell?"

There were two major home improvement stores in Kalispell
and while Pete, Woody, Cally and the twins, sang praises to God,
Connie roamed the aisles of first Home Depot and then Lowe's,
contemplating tankless water heaters and waterless toilets. He didn't
buy anything, but by noon, he knew what he needed.

The day had started out sunny and clear. At noon, the sky was
hazed over by high cirrus clouds. By one o-clock, while Connie lay on
his back under the bunkhouse, planning the pipe run from his new
bathroom to the drain line in the kitchen, the clouds had thickened
considerably and the humidity was building. Crawling out from under
the floor, he was greeted by two pair of feet. Looking up, he saw the
feet were connected to Lindsey and Danni.

"Mom said you were gonna build a bathroom. What are you
doing under the bunkhouse?"

"Maybe I'm going to build a basement bathroom."

"No way," said Danni, "That would be foolish. Then you'd
have to build stairs and go up and down to use the bathroom."

"Yeah," Lindsey agreed. "Might as well use the outhouse."

"Okay, if you two are so smart, why do you think I was under
the bunkhouse? I'll give you a hint. It's got something to do with
plumbing."

"We know a guy at church. His name is Ven. He's a plumber."

"What's his name?"

Danni's face flushed. "His name is Ven."

"His name is Sven," Lindsey said. "She can't say Sven so she calls him Ven."

Connie turned to Danni. "I can teach you to say Sven."

"Okay."

"Good. Say es."

"Es."

"Say it again, a few times."

"Es, es, es, es, es, es. Is that enough?

"Okay, now say ven."

"Ven, ven, ven, ven."

"Okay, that's enough. Now say es and then right away say ven."

"Es ven, es ven, es ven."

"Faster."

"Esven, esven, sven, sven, sven." She stopped and smiled. "Hey, I did it. I said Sven."

"Of course you did. No problem."

"You know any other words like Sven?"

"Well there's not too many. Try svelte."

"Svelte, svelte, svelte. What's it mean?"

"Oh, I guess slim and graceful, having a nice figure. Your mother is svelte."

"Cool. You know any more es vee words?"

"There might be more, but I can't think of any right now."

"You still haven't told us why you were under the bunkhouse. I give up on your hint anyway," Lindsey said.

"I wanted to see how much pipe I needed to get from the new shower to the drain for the kitchen sink."

"Boring," said Danni. "I bet Lindsey you were looking for rats."

"Sorry. How much did you bet?"

"Dishes, but it doesn't matter. She was wrong too."

Connie looked over at Lindsey. "What did you think I was doing?"

"I thought you were looking for money."

"Why would I be looking under the bunkhouse for money?"

"One time Woody crawled under the bunkhouse looking for money. We saw him under there and when we asked him what he was doing, he said he dropped a hundred dollar bill and the wind blew it under the bunkhouse. That's what I thought happened to you. Some of your money blew under the bunkhouse."

"I'm real sorry to disappoint you girls, but I wasn't looking for rats or money. I was just seeing where the pipe would go."

Lindsey decided to change the subject. "Grandpa said you and him were gonna go for a ride."

"That's what he told me this morning."

"You better hurry up because it's gonna rain like a cow pissin' on a flat rock," Danni nonchalantly told him.

Connie had not heard that colorful expression for a rainstorm since he'd left the army. One of the platoon sergeants from his command used it frequently. Coming from a tough old soldier was one thing; coming from a nine year old girl was something else. He almost burst out laughing, but instead gave her a stern look. "Is that any way for a young lady to talk?" he asked.

Danni looked away. "Woody says it all the time," she said defensively.

"That's no excuse. Young ladies shouldn't use that kind of language."

Danni was crushed. She turned and ran away, up to the house. Connie watched her. "Gee," he said to Lindsey, "I didn't expect that."

"She's the sensitive one. She's always crying about something."

"I had no idea. I'm sorry I said anything."

Lindsey shrugged her shoulders. "She'll get over it. I'll go talk to her."

A half hour later, while Connie was sitting at the bunkhouse table making his building material list, Pete came in. "Still remember how to saddle a horse?"

"Yeah, I think so."

"Good. Let's you and me go for a ride. Show me what you can do."

Pete told Connie to watch him and then do what he did. When he finished, it was Connie's turn. Using a hoof pick, Connie cleaned and inspected all four hooves of his mount and brushed the horse's back before throwing on a blanket and the saddle. He pulled the cinch strap tight, but left a bit of slack in the girth strap. He had a little trouble with the bit and bridle, but got it eventually. He was surprised he remembered everything.

Pete checked out the tension on the cinch. "Good job. Now, if you remember how to ride, you'll be cuttin' cattle in no time."

As the afternoon clouds grew darker, they rode out across the little bridge spanning Rogers Creek, through the hay meadow, and up the ranch road into the hills. The steady swinging motion of the horse dredged up old memories of his summers on the dude ranch. The feel of his butt in the saddle was as if he had last ridden the day before. The smell of the horse, the pines and the saddle leather was like familiar cologne. The apprehensions he had harbored about being able to ride were evaporating faster than spilled whiskey on a concrete sidewalk at high noon on a hot summer day. He patted his steed on the neck and grinned.

Pete was watching. "Feels good, don't it?"

"Yeah. I'd forgotten."

"There's an old Mongolian saying, 'It's the breath of heaven that blows upon you from between the ears of a horse.' Or something like that."

"Mongolian?"

"Persian, Mongolian—it's not important, but I understand the gist of it."

"Yeah, I guess I do too."

"Just up ahead, this trail straightens out for about two hundred yards. That horse you're riding ain't the greatest cutter, he's a bit too tall, but he can run a twenty-eight second quarter. You can air him out a little if you think you can handle it."

"Will I be able to stop him once he gets going?"

"Certainly. He's fast, but he's also lazy."

As soon as they reached the spot, Pete shouted to Connie, "Race ya!" and was off like a shot.

Connie gave his horse some leg pressure and the acceleration almost rolled him backwards out of the saddle. He leaned ahead, found the horse's center of gravity and they flew. The scenery blew past and in seconds, they caught and passed Pete. They reached the end of the straight stretch of trail and Connie, having no desire to push his luck, eased back on the reins. The horse quickly slowed to a walk and dutifully stopped.

Pete was grinning when he pulled up and stopped. "You win."

"What's the prize?"

"You get to ride some more."

By the time, they got back to the barn and turned out their mounts, it was almost five. "Time for supper," Pete said. "You ready to eat?"

"I am. I don't know why. I haven't done anything all day."

"It's just bein' out. Fresh air is good for you. I don't understand how anybody can work indoors all the time. That would've killed me forty years ago."

"I did it for twenty years."

"Yeah and I'll bet you don't want to do it again."

Connie thought a minute, "Probably not."

The girls, all three of them, were fairly subdued during dinner or so it seemed to Connie. He, Pete, and Woody did most of the talking, although Lindsey wanted to know if they had seen Simba during their ride in the woods. She was disappointed that they hadn't.

"I hope nothing has happened to her."

"What's gonna happen to a mountain lion?" Woody asked. "It ain't huntin' season and nothin's gonna attack her."

"I suppose," Lindsey acquiesced.

Connie was tired and excused himself from the table as soon as they were finished eating. "See you at six-thirty," Pete said as he left the house. Cally followed him out.

Away from the house, she called to him, "Mister Bradley, a word please."

Connie stopped and turned. He hadn't realized she was behind him. "Yes, ma'am." He didn't have time to consider what she might want.

"In the future, please do not feel the need to discipline my daughters. I can manage that on my own. Thank you." The three-sentence speech was terse and tense. She turned and walked away, disappearing as fast as she had appeared.

Connie stood staring, until he heard the porch door close. "Wow," he whispered. "I didn't even get a chance to explain." He realized this was about chiding Danni for her graphic weather forecast.

He walked slowly down to the bunkhouse. His emotions were churning. *Who the hell does she think she is? Fool woman didn't even let me explain. Maybe somebody's trying to tell me something. Maybe I should pack up and get out of here.* Then he wondered where he would go. *Can't go home, my house is gone. Texas. Weatherford, Texas. That's where Pete said most all the cutting horse trainers were. I'll load up my horse and go down there and find one that can teach me how to ride.* The prospect lacked any real appeal.

"Damn," he almost shouted, "and I was getting to like it here—a lot." He went out to his truck to find his cell phone. He called his sister, but got no answer. He threw the phone on the seat next to him. He decided to go for a ride.

Two hours later he was back. He'd found a bar and had a drink before he discovered there'd be no answer at the bottom of a whisky glass. Cally had hurt his feelings. She had unjustly accused him and then ran away. Connie was fair-minded and Cally had violated the rules. He had no desire to get even, but he also didn't want to be forced to deal with a person whom, as far as he knew, might be unstable. He hated to disappoint Pete, but there was no way he'd put up with nonsense from a temperamental woman for eight months, no matter how good looking she was and how well she could cook.

Not knowing what else to do, he went to bed. Surprisingly, he fell asleep almost immediately. However, he woke up at four in the morning and flipped around like a fish out of water until he finally got up at six. He'd made up his mind.

Chapter 15, Lessons

Cally consulted the kitchen clock. It was six thirty-five. "Lindsey, run down to the bunkhouse and tell Mister Bradley, breakfast is ready."

"I can go," Danni volunteered.

"You stay put, I told Lindsey to go."

Lindsey was already on her way. She liked Connie. Other than Mister Jaxon, her third grade teacher, on whom she'd had a giant crush, Connie was the coolest guy she'd ever met. She knocked on the door and entered before he could get to it. She was horrified to see him packing his bags.

"Where are you going?" And without waiting for an answer, she told him, "You can't leave. You just got here." She was immediately in a panic.

"Good morning, to you too, Lindsey." He smiled at her.

"Why are you packing up all your stuff? It's time for breakfast." She walked over and sat down on the edge of the bed.

"Well, Sweetie, I might have made a mistake coming here."

She didn't let him finish. "But where will you go?" Tears had started to well up in her big brown eyes. "You're wife is dead and everything."

Good Lord, now I've made another one of them cry. "Come on, Lindsey, don't cry."

"I'll stop crying if you stop packing. Please don't go. I thought you could be my friend. I don't have all that many friends, you know."

He imagined she didn't have a lot of friends other than at school. The nearest neighbors were more than a mile away. Not many kids to play with during the summer. "Oh, come on now. I'll bet you have a lot of friends at school."

"What do you have to leave for?" She ignored his attempt to change the subject. Then she stopped crying and looked him in the eyes. "Did Mom have a talk with you?"

"Ah, not really. It wasn't much of a conversation. At least I don't remember getting a chance to talk back."

"That's how Mom is when she's giving you a talk. You don't get to talk back."

Connie smiled, "You're right about that. Does she have many talks with you?"

"No, not too many. Only when I do something she doesn't like."

"Is that often?"

"No. I'll bet she talked to you about Danni. Didn't she?"

"Well, yeah, but its no big deal."

"Well then, how come you have to leave? Danni's just a drama queen. She'll get over it. She really likes you, too."

Connie had to laugh. "A drama queen, huh? I'm too old to have to worry about pleasing a nine-year old drama queen."

"Come on, you can't go. Don't be a girly girl."

"A girly girl? What's that?"

"That's what Woody calls me when I'm feeling sorry for myself."

What's wrong with me? Here I am, a decorated former soldier, a competent, battle tempered, leader of men and a nine-year-old child is calling me a girly girl. Could I possibly be feeling sorry for myself?
"What does he call you when you aren't feeling sorry for yourself?"

"He just calls me Lindsey. Please stay."

"Okay. I'll come to breakfast, but you have to dry your eyes or your mother will have another talk with me."

"Yippee." She jumped up, wiped her eyes on the back of her sleeve and grabbed him by the hand. "Where were you going to go anyway?"

"Texas."

"Texas? What's there?"

"Probably nothing."

She pulled him into the kitchen and announced, "Connie was going to Texas, but I talked him out of it."

Connie grinned rather sheepishly, "Sorry I'm late for breakfast."

After breakfast, the school bus swallowed up the twins and Pete and Connie fed the horses. Woody and Cally took care of the breakfast mess.

"You hear it rain last night?" Pete asked Connie as they saddled horses for the morning's riding lesson.

"Nope, didn't hear a thing. Why?"

"Oh, it was something. Rained like a cow pissin' on a flat rock."

Connie looked over at Pete, but Pete was looking at the bottom of a horse's hoof. "That must have been some rain. Strange I didn't hear it."

"Yeah, I reckon. Must not have had anything on your mind to sleep so sound."

"I guess. I was thinking about what I had to get to build the bathroom, but it didn't keep me awake."

"You should think about doing that project real soon. We can ride in the mornings and you can build in the afternoon, but in a couple weeks we're gonna get real busy makin' hay. Cally's a slave driver when it comes to the hay, but I can't argue. It's what pays the bills. She might have another fault or two if you know what I mean."

"I noticed, but then again, don't we all have a fault or two?"

"I'm sure. I know I might have one or possibly even two. Some people hide their faults real good though. You don't discover them until you've known them for a long time. Then you find out and it's a mighty powerful surprise. Other people carry them right out in the open and you see them right away. It doesn't mean they have any more faults than any one else, you just get to see them sooner."

Connie didn't need a PhD from MIT to know what this was about. "So, you're telling me your daughter, the lovely Cally, is in the latter group, those who demonstrate their faults immediately?"

Pete grinned. "You never had any kids and I assume you never lived with a woman who had kids."

"Yeah, that's right. So?"

"So a woman with kids is different than a woman without kids. They usually have more maternal instinct and are very protective of their children. Of course that's not true of all women, but I'm confident in saying most women would defend their babies to the death. Just like that mama lion we got hanging around. You see her in the woods and she'll run off. Woe unto you, however, if you go after her babies. Even if she only thinks you're threatening her kittens, she'll shred you like taco meat and not wait a second for you to explain."

"Very interesting, Pete. Why are you telling me all this?"

Pete draped an arm over the back of his horse and looked Connie in the eyes. "I'm old enough to be your father. Course I ain't your father, but I knew him and I don't think he'd mind if I gave you a little fatherly advice. You got a job to do. You made a commitment; said you'd try and I'm holding you to it. Don't let my daughter run you off over her little misunderstanding. I believe she likes you and if she doesn't now, she will. She's just distrustful of strangers and very protective of her children. You were lucky. The last guy we had around here she ran off the property with my thirty-thirty Winchester."

"Comforting. I'm glad I'm one of her favorites."

Pete swung into the saddle. "Let's go find some cows."

Like the day before, they crossed the creek and traversed the hay meadow, but when they reached the trees Pete turned to the left and they followed a more obscure trail up the hill. Pete had four thousand acres in these hills, all leased from the US Forest Service. It was originally a ninety-nine year lease and he'd held it for fifty years. If the United States kept to their end of the bargain, Cally would have it long after Pete was gone. It was a good arrangement. The grazing cattle kept the grass and brush down which greatly reduced the chances for fire, and the rancher got cattle feed for a low lease fee. There were some people not happy with this arrangement, but most of those people lived back east in tall buildings.

"So, where are we going?" Connie asked

"Just up the hill a ways. I'm sure there's some cows back in here and I want you to follow them.

"Follow them?"

"Yup, just follow them, slow and steady, whichever way they go. You'll be doin' two things at the same time, watching and riding. Be surprised how hard that can be sometimes. The first rule of cutting is, 'Always watch the cow.'"

"What's the second rule?"

"Never take your eyes off the cow."

"How many rules are there?"

"Just three."

"Okay, I'll bite. What's the third rule?" He was expecting something more about watching the cow.

"Well ordinarily the third rule would be to always pay strict attention to the cow, but in your case, the third rule will be, 'Don't try to outsmart your horse.'"

"Why are the rules different for me?"

"Because you'll be riding Jolena and she'll be a better judge of any cow than you, or I will ever be. You, my boy, are merely going to be a passenger."

"Sounds a little boring."

Pete laughed. "Just you wait."

Then they found some grazing cattle and for the next hour Connie and Pete trailed cows through the trees. For something that sounded so easy, Connie was surprised by how much attention it took.

On the way back to the barn, Pete told Connie they'd be doing this for the rest of the week and next week he would get face to face with a cow in the arena. Connie wanted to know when he could ride Jolena.

"You can take her for a short ride any time, but I don't want you cutting cows off her before you know what you're doing. I don't want either one of you getting hurt."

That afternoon, Connie and Woody went to town. Connie bought everything he thought he'd need to build the bunkhouse bathroom. He spent three thousand dollars and Woody was impressed, not by the money, but by Connie's attention to detail. It appeared to Woody as if he'd thought of everything, but when they returned home and began unloading the truck, Connie discovered he forgot to buy the shower stall. He had picked one out, but after buying everything else, he'd forgotten the most important item.

"Nuts. Now I have to make another trip to town."

"Just as well. In case you didn't notice, what with all them two by fours and pipe and floor tile and a sink and commode and a water heater and everything else, there wasn't no more room for a shower stall."

"You're right. What time is supper?"

"Tonight is a week night. Supper will be at six o-clock sharp."

"How does she do it?"

"What? You mean how does Cally have meals ready at the same time every day?"

"Yeah. My wife and I always ate supper together, but sometimes it was at five-thirty, sometimes it was at seven. Cally's got breakfast at six-thirty, lunch at twelve and supper at six each and every day, except Sunday."

"Wait 'til we start hayin'. You'll get breakfast at six-thirty, a morning snack at nine-thirty, lunch at twelve, an afternoon snack at three and supper at six."

"How do you eat it all?"

"Wait 'til we start hayin.'"

"Okay. It's three now. I'm going to run back to town and get the shower. You want to come along?"

"Yeah, I do, but I'm gonna stay and help Cally get supper goin'. Plus the twins will be home and I like to help 'em with their homework, if they need help. I got a PhD you know."

Connie assumed Woody was putting him on so he played along. "Sure. If they need help with their physics, you're just the man to bail them out. See you at supper."

Woody didn't know how Connie knew he had a PhD in physics; he assumed Pete must have told him. "Deal." Handing Connie a twenty-dollar bill, he said, "Get us some beer if you got time."

Connie was back well before six with a fiberglass shower enclosure, a leather recliner, matching couch, two floor lamps, beer, and a bottle of highland single malt whisky. What good was having a little money if you couldn't spend it?

The rest of the week blitzed by. The days were used up riding in the morning and working on the bunkhouse in the afternoon. By Saturday night he could trail a cow through the trees without spooking it, and then take a hot shower in the bunkhouse. Life was good. He and Cally were polite, but cool to one another. Connie didn't spend any more time in the big house than it took him to eat. The girls were friendly, especially Lindsey. Danni was more aloof, but Connie thought it was because she was perhaps a little embarrassed by the situation. Lindsey had told her Connie almost went to Texas because of the way she had reacted to being chided.

"You didn't have to tell Mom," Lindsey chastised.

"Yeah, I know. I was silly. I'm sorry."

"What'd you tell Mom, anyway?"

"I said Connie scolded me."

Lindsey rolled her eyes. "You are such a girly girl. He was just teasing."

"What'd Mom say to him?"

"I don't know, she wouldn't tell me."

"Why don't you ask him what she said?"

"You ask him, I don't want to remind him about it. He's real happy right now and I like him."

"Well, I like him too, that's why I felt so bad. You sure he was only teasing?"

"Positive and if you feel so bad and like him, you should tell him you're sorry."

"Maybe I will," Danni said.

Sunday came and went. Pete didn't invite him to go to church and Connie didn't volunteer. Woody came down to the bunkhouse after supper and the two of them swapped lies for an hour. Connie was in bed by nine o'clock. Wow, what a party animal I am, he thought as he turned out the light.

At breakfast, the first thing Pete said to Connie after, "Good morning," was, "We're gonna ride out and bring a few cows down to the pasture. Maybe that bunch we were pushing around on Friday."

Between forkfuls of steak, sourdough flapjacks, and eggs, Connie managed a reply. "Good, that'll be fun."

Pete grinned. "No, that'll be work, the fun won't start 'til you get on Fritz and face off with a cow."

"Which one is Fritz?"

"Fritz is the black gelding with the long tail. He's comin' twenty, but he'll surprise you. He can still move like a cat, just not for long."

Connie took a long pull on his orange juice. "I'm ready."

It was almost noon when Pete and Connie finished pulling the saddles off their mounts. They had brought about forty head of cattle, cow calf pairs, down from the hills. "Let's eat lunch before we do anything else," suggested Pete.

"Good idea, I'm actually kind of hungry."

At lunch, Cally asked, "Is there anything anyone needs, I'm going downtown later?"

"Just some apples," Woody said. "I promised Connie apple pie when he showed up and I ain't made good on my word yet."

"Okay. Dad? Mister Bradley?"

Pete waved his hand and shook his head. He had a mouthful of food. Connie replied, "Nothing for me, ma'am." It was a bit awkward calling her ma'am, but he couldn't very well call her Cally if she insisted on calling him Mister Bradley.

"Well if you think of anything before I go, come tell me."

At two o-clock, Connie was sitting on Fritz and Fritz was standing quietly at the back of the riding arena located just across the driveway from the barn. Connie had ridden Fritz around the arena for almost twenty minutes to loosen him up. Pete had been watching and although he wasn't overly impressed with Connie's skill, he was satisfied for now. He'll improve fast, once we start workin' cows, Pete speculated to himself. He's doin' okay for having been out of the saddle for almost thirty years.

"Wait there," Pete told him, "I'll get some cattle in here."

The cattle, about a dozen head, were just outside the arena in a pen. Pete rode over to the gate connecting the pen to the arena and swung it open. Woody hollered and slapped the boards at the back of the pen. The cows moved into the arena. Pete closed the gate and then slowly rode around and through the cows to settle them down. After a few minutes he rode back over to Connie, leaving the cows huddled at the back of the arena.

"First of all, this arena is a replicate of the arena in the Will Rogers Auditorium where the Futurity is held. At least dimension and shape wise it is, obviously it's not covered and doesn't have bleachers. But all the important features are the same."

Connie regarded the arena without comment.

"Okay, you and I are going to slowly ride over to the cows and then I want you to try to push one of them out of the herd. It doesn't matter which one, just pick one and let Fritz walk right up to it. He knows what to do. If you can separate one, push it down to about the middle of the arena here and stop. I'll be in front of it and turn it back to face you. You with me so far?"

"Yup."

"Good. Now, when the cow faces you, lower the reins down on Fritz's neck like I showed you and hang on tight to the horn.

Connie nodded. He was nervous.

"Remember now. Pull on the horn when Fritz starts to move forward and push on it when he's stopping. Don't be afraid of breaking it off. It's not going anywhere." Then Pete waved a finger at him. "Go ahead."

Connie cued Fritz to walk and guided him towards the cows. They bunched tighter as the horse and rider approached. Pete had told him to imagine the herd as a flexible bubble and push in slow but deliberate. Just before reaching them, the cattle started to slide off to the left. Before Connie could react, Fritz calmly turned to intercept them. The cattle stopped and when they did, Fritz moved into them and turned one away from the rest. Connie finally exhaled. That was easy, he thought. Cautiously, he trailed the cow into the center of the arena, towards Pete.

The cow, being pushed forward, was quickly presented with a dilemma. Behind her was a horse and now in front of her was another horse. The cow stopped and slowly turned. Behind the horse that pushed her out, was the herd. There was safety in the herd. There was no safety out here between the two horses.

"Get ready," Pete told Connie. Connie got ready. When he urged Fritz towards the cow, she made her decision to break for the herd. Connie dropped his left hand to Fritz's neck.

The sudden acceleration was astounding. He found his right hand slipping from the saddle horn. He dug his fingers in and hung on. Her advance to the herd cut off, the cow stopped and Fritz slammed on the brakes. Connie was now being thrown forward, immediately in danger of being catapulted right over Fritz's head. Pete's words came back to him, "Push on the horn when the horse stops." Connie pushed for all he was worth.

No problem, his launch was aborted, but then the cow cut to the right and Fritz was off again. Time to pull, Connie thought and although he looked as sloppy as a hog in a wallow, he stayed in the saddle. Twenty seconds and four turns later, the cow made a long horizontal run to the fence, turned back and blew past Pete. He stopped at the far end of the arena, sulking. Connie's was breathing hard and sweating.

Pete rode over. "What do you think?"

"That was amazing! Can I do another one?"

"Absolutely," Pete was smiling. "That's why you came here." He looked at Connie's rigid posture. "Loosen up. Open your index finger off the horn."

"That'll relax me?"

Pete nodded. "Just do it."

Chapter 16, Truce

Cally decided to walk down to the cutting arena before she went to town. She thought she would check one more time with the men to see if they had remembered there was anything they needed. Besides, she thought she'd show Connie what she looked like in something besides blue jeans and an apron. It was a warm afternoon. She was wearing a short, casual skirt that displayed plenty of smooth, shapely leg and a short-sleeved shirt that ended just at her waist where the skirt started. Her shoes were open toed with fat, wedged soles that made her taller. She wasn't really certain why she wanted to impress Connie. He was, as near as she figured, at least thirteen years older. She considered that to be a bit much for her, although he was handsome. A final check in the mirror and she was on her way.

As she approached the arena, Connie and Fritz had just extracted another cow from the herd and were trailing it to the center of the arena. Connie was watching the steer with all his might. He reasoned correctly, by watching the cow, he would know when to push on the horn and when to pull. When the cow stopped to turn, Fritz would have to stop and Connie would push. When the cow started moving forward, Fritz would lunge forward and Connie would have to pull on the horn to stay in the saddle. Really, it was all very simple and after the first cow, Connie was feeling rather smug.

He dropped the reins on Fritz's neck and pulled hard as Fritz exploded after the cow. But then a flash of white and leg caught his eye. He looked up to see Cally put her foot up on the bottom fence rail. He forgot about the cow and stared. At that instant the cow and Fritz stopped and Connie, still pulling when he should be pushing, departed the saddle. He flew off Fritz's back. Then he was falling. Time slowed, as it always does in moments of great intensity, and Connie saw the ground coming up. He reached his left hand out to break his fall and reasoned he should tuck his head in and roll over to his shoulders and onto his back, if he could.

It was a good plan, but the arena floor was six inches of sand and his open hand buried itself. Even though Connie tucked his head, his shallow trajectory prevented him from rolling to his shoulders. He landed hard on his pelvis and slid forward on his forehead in the soft sand.

His first concern was embarrassment, but after lifting his head, he found it impossible to stand and his left wrist was in great pain. He decided to stay where he was for a minute and collect his thoughts.

Woody piped up from the back of the arena, "You doin' a gravity check?"

Connie winced and thought nasty thoughts about Woody.

"What's the first rule of cutting?" Pete asked.

Connie mumbled into the sand, "Watch the stupid cow." Although he was the one laying in the dirt and the stupid cow was watching him.

Pete grinned, "Well, you certainly loosened up. You gonna get up, or do you need a hand?"

Groaning, Connie rolled onto his back, "I'll get up, just give me a minute."

He breathed deeply. Nothing felt or looked broken. He slowly got to his feet. He looked at Pete, then over to Woody and last, at Cally. No one was laughing, but they were all smiling. "Ta da!" he announced and bowed to his audience. "For my next trick I'll actually get back on my horse."

Fritz had stopped and was standing about where Connie had left him. He limped over and remounted. Pete rode over to him. "Let me see your arm."

Connie held up his right arm.

"Your other arm."

He held up his left arm, the one that hurt. He was wearing a tee shirt. "Your wrist is already starting to swell. Can you move your fingers?"

Connie wiggled his fingers. Pete called over to Woody. "Woody, will you get some ice and a towel?"

"I'll get it, Dad," said Cally. Connie watched her as she walked away. The sight was almost worth it.

"You were doing real good 'til you got distracted," Pete told him.

"Tell me about it."

Pete was watching Connie's wrist grow. "It's swelling fast, you might have broke it."

"I doubt it. Bent it maybe, but it's not all that easy to break titanium rods."

Pete looked at him. "You get banged on the head too?"

Connie laughed even though it hurt. "No, this arm is full of exotic metals. One of the doctors that fixed it told me I'd have to try real hard to break it once it healed."

"What'd you do to it?"

"Took a couple bullets through it about twenty years ago."

"Well if it ain't broke, it is most certainly sprained. I think you should go see the doctor."

Connie regarded his damaged arm. "Yeah, I suppose."

"You get down off Fritz and let Cally put ice on it. I'll put these horses away and we'll decide what to do."

Connie complied and ducked out of the arena through the fence. Woody chased the cows from the arena to the pen and then pushed them down a fenced aisle back into a small pasture. When Pete returned, Cally was holding an icepack against Connie's forearm. In spite of his situation, Connie thought she smelled wonderful.

"Did you give it a good look?" Pete asked Cally.

"Yeah, I don't like it."

"What do you think, Connie?"

"I don't know. I hate to be a bother."

"It's not a bother," Cally told him. "I was going to town regardless. I can drop you at the clinic and by the time I'm done shopping, you should be ready to come home."

Pete looked at Connie, "Well?"

"All right. Sorry."

Cally took his right hand and put it on the icepack. "Hold it in place. I'll get my car."

"How about we take my truck?" Connie suggested. "I'm not sure I can fold my legs into your car right now."

"Sure, I love driving big pickups."

For the first few miles they were both silent, neither of them certain of how to start. Finally Cally broke the ice. "Does it hurt much?"

"Only when I'm conscious," Connie said with a grin.

She smiled back. "You think it's broken?"

"I doubt it. I can wiggle my fingers."

"That just means your fingers aren't broken."

"Yeah, you're right, but it's already starting to feel better."

"That's the ice."

"Yeah, you're probably right about that, too."

She was quiet for a while. "I'm sorry for what I said to you the other day."

On the inside, Connie smiled. "That's okay. I understand. You're dad told me about the last hired man you had."

"Well, yeah, but he was a special case. You're nothing like that."

"Good to know."

"Anyway, I apologize. Danni can be a real drama queen sometimes. I should have gotten your side of the story."

"Lindsey called her that, too. She also said she's the sensitive one."

"Lindsey's right, although I don't want you to tell her I told you that. They're both great kids, just total opposites."

They talked about the twins until they reached the urgent care center. Cally parked at the front door and got out. She opened Connie's door and attempted to help him out. His left hip had stiffened up considerably.

"You want me to get a wheel chair?"

"Oh, please no. Falling off a horse was bad enough. A wheel chair might just put me away." He limped into the facility and up to the reception counter. His ice pack left a trail of drips across the floor.

A man in a white lab coat, Connie assumed he was a doctor, immediately came over. "Hello, Cally. What a pleasant surprise." He was smiling for all he was worth.

"Hi, Jim, how are you?"

"I'm good," and turning to Connie, "What did you bring me?"

If Cally hadn't been there, he probably would have slapped the guy. He wasn't used to being referred to as an inanimate object. Furthermore, they obviously knew each other and Connie was somewhat jealous.

"This is Conrad Bradley. He's a friend of my dad's and he hurt his wrist."

"Well, Mister Bradley," Jim said, "let's take a little peek at that wrist."

Connie pulled the icepack away. He was certain he'd have to slap him.

"Yes, you did injure that wrist," Doctor Jim confirmed. We're going to x-ray that right away."

Cally patted Connie on the shoulder. "I'll be back for you in an hour or so." She turned to Jim. "Take good care of him. I'll see you later."

"Of course, Cally, we take good care of all our patients." He watched her walk away while Connie seethed.

"Mister Bradley, if you'll step over here and talk to Melissa for a minute, she has some forms for you to fill out."

Twenty minutes after talking to Melissa, he went in to radiology where his wrist, arm, pelvis, and hip were all x-rayed. Thirty minutes after that, Doctor Jim came into the room with a sheaf of x-rays in his hand.

"What on earth did you do to your arm?" He slid the pictures of Connie's arm up under the clips on the light box. "I've never seen anything like it."

Connie grinned wickedly at Doctor Jim, "You're just young, Doc."

Doctor Jim blushed slightly. "Seriously, Mister Bradley, what happened to your arm?"

"I was shot some years ago. It took several surgeons a great deal of effort to put me back together."

"God, I'll say. There's more metal in there than what's in my golf bag. Was it an accident?"

"Of course, I didn't intend to fall off the horse."

"No, I mean getting shot."

"Sorry Doc, you don't have a need to know." Connie didn't want to talk about the incident. "So, what's the verdict? Is it broken?"

If Doctor Jim was rebuffed he didn't let it show. "No, not at all. All the muscles and tendons in your lower arm and wrist are surely strained as evidenced by the swelling, however three of us looked at it and we couldn't find any evidence of a fracture anywhere. I'm going to wrap it and give you a sling. I suggest you refrain from using it for at least a week"

"How about my hip?"

"Your hip and pelvis are fine. Bruised, but not broken. I'm also going to give you some pain medication. You're going to be sore for a while."

"Don't bother, I'm allergic to most pain pills. I'll get by on ibuprofen."

After a nurse wrapped his arm, he limped back to Melissa's desk to settle his bill. Cally had already returned and, lo and behold, Doctor Jim was at her side, either trying to make, or actually making time. Connie couldn't believe he was jealous. He paid cash to hurry the process, and he requested all the x-rays and his newly created medical record. He considered his arm to be a private matter and didn't want Doctor Jim playing show and tell.

"The doctor said he'd never seen anything like the repair that was done on your arm," said Cally after they were back in the truck on the way home.

"Yeah, well, he's just young." *So much for doctor patient privilege*

"What happened?"

"He didn't tell you that, too?"

She didn't catch the sarcasm. "No, he just said your arm had more metal in it than he thought was possible."

"I was shot."

"I'm sorry. How did that happen?"

"It's nothing I really want to talk about. There was a fire fight. I was shot. The bones in my lower arm were shattered and some army surgeons did everything they could to save it.

"They did a good job?" Now Cally was curious.

"Yeah, I've been happy with the results. Is Jim your doctor?"

"Oh, no. My doctor is a sixty-year old woman. She's in an office downtown. She delivered the twins, and I take them to her, too."

Connie didn't like where this headed. "So, Jim, Doctor Jim, is a friend?"

"I guess. I've dated him a couple of times."

"Oh."

Cally wondered why Connie was interested. "He's okay, although, like you said, 'he's young.' What did you think of him?"

"He's okay. Are there a lot of doctors in town?" He didn't mention he'd wanted to slap her doctor friend on general principles.

"You'd be surprised. Most of them live around Whitefish. They come for the skiing and if real estate in that area keeps going up the way it's been, doctors and movie stars are going to be the only ones who can afford to live there."

"Interesting. I was told there are PhDs in Bozeman flipping burgers."

"Yeah, that's true, but not a big deal. We have our own resident PhD."

"Who, your dad? I thought he was a DVM."

"He is. I'm talking about Woody. He's got a PhD in physics from MIT."

"You're joking?"

"Nope, it's true. Helped design the Verrazano Narrows Bridge in New York."

"How did he ever end up out here?"

"It's a sad story, but you'll never hear it from him unless you're around when he gets drunk. His family was from Grosse Pointe, Michigan and after he graduated, he went home and married his childhood sweetheart. He had a job with the firm that was selected to build the Verrazano Bridge so they moved to New York. They lived in the city and loved it. Then, about a year after they were married, his wife was shot and killed during a jewelry store robbery. She just happened to be in the wrong place at a bad time."

"He mentioned his wife had been shot, but I had no idea of the whole story."

"He was devastated. He stayed in New York long enough to see his wife's killer stand trial and then he left town. He's never been east of the Mississippi since. Although he said he promised the judge at the trial he'd come back to kill the murderer when he got out of jail."

"He ever try to make good on that promise?"

"No, he didn't have to. The guy was killed in a riot at Attica Prison."

"Sometimes things have a way of working out. How did he meet your dad?"

"Woody wanted to get as far away from civilization as possible. From New York, he eventually drifted into Wyoming and got a summer job herding sheep. He went out as an apprentice for two seasons before he got his own flock. During the winters he would bum around to various places in Montana, Wyoming, Idaho, and Colorado. He wandered onto this ranch about forty years ago and he and Dad became fast friends. He came back every winter and when he quit herding sheep, Dad invited him to stay for as long as he wanted."

"Wow, and I thought I had done some living. I figured he was kidding me when he said he had a PhD."

"He told you that?"

"Yeah, last week. We had gone to town to get the stuff for the bathroom I put in the bunkhouse, but I forgot a few things, like the shower stall. When I asked him if he wanted to go back to town with me, he said he wanted to be around when the girls got home from school in case they needed help with their homework. He said he was qualified because he had a PhD. I thought he was joking and told him if the girls needed help with their physics, he was the man."

She laughed. "I'll bet that made him wonder. He really does help the girls with their homework. I hope he stays healthy so he can help them all the way through college."

As their conversation continued, Connie forgot about Doctor Jim. When they pulled into the driveway, Connie asked Cally, "Do me one favor?"

"Sure, I guess I owe you at least one for snapping at you last week. What?"

"Please don't call me Mister Bradley."

"It's a deal, if you stop calling me ma'am. You can't imagine how old that makes me feel."

"Probably about as old as I am."

"You don't seem that old to me."

"Well you can't be riding Fritz for the rest of the week, but I think you and Jolena could probably do some simple things." The family was seated around the kitchen table.

"That would be good," Connie told Pete. "Now that I've started, I don't want to stop and wait."

"I'm not talking about you doin' any cutting, but we can at least get you and your horse used to each other."

"Why can't I cut with Jolena? You said you don't train her real hard yet."

"I don't ride her for very long just yet, but when she's cuttin' a cow, she's not coasting. If you think Fritz is quick, wait 'til you and Jo cut a cow."

"So what can we do?"

"Just ride. Nothing fancy. Walk her up the hill into the trees. Talk to her, brush her; keep each other company, that's all. Get to know each other."

Danni piped up, "Sounds like a date."

"What would you know about dating?" her mother asked. "And where did you learn it?"

"Woody told me."

Cally looked at Woody. "Woodruff MacPherson, is that true? Are you giving my girls dating instructions?"

"Guilty as charged, Miss Cally. She asked me what a date was. First I told her it was a little fruit that grew on a date palm tree, but she told me that didn't make no sense."

"Yeah, how can you date somebody with a fruit?" Danni added.

"So I merely told her a date was somethin' where a man and a woman spent time together for the purpose of gettin' to know each other."

"To see if they like each other, too," said Lindsey.

"Well," said Connie, "I guess Jolena and I will start dating." He pushed his chair back. "If you'll excuse me, I'll be on my way to the bunkhouse. Thanks for the wonderful dinner, Cally." His arm was throbbing and what he needed to do was take four ibuprofen and wash them down with at least two beers.

He was no sooner resting comfortably in his new recliner with a beer in his hand, when there was a rap at the door. "Come in." It was Woody. Connie motioned towards the refrigerator with the hand holding the bottle. "Grab one. Half of them are yours."

"Thank you. Don't mind if I do. I just came down to congratulate you on resolvin' your differences with the women of the house."

"Women? I didn't think the twins were upset with me too."

"You're right, only one of the twins was upset with you. Danni's the soft one. Gotta be careful what you say to her."

"Woody, if one more person tells me how sensitive Danni is, I'll scream."

"Fine." Woody grinned. "Just don't scream at her or she'll be upset all over again."

"I'll remember that."

Woody looked around the bunkhouse. "Looks real nice in here, now. I think after you move on, I'll take it over."

"Might be a little chilly in the winter, especially in the bathroom."

"Shouldn't be a problem now you got the propane tank. I'll get me a couple gas space heaters and it'll be snug as sleepin' with a pretty woman in a single bed under a down comforter."

"Hey, good idea. I mean the space heater thing. I think I'll do you a favor and get one for the bathroom. Using the toilet at night is still pretty chilly."

Woody agreed. "Nights up here never do get real warm. But then again, winters ain't all that cold here either."

"Cally told me you've been here every winter for forty years."

"More like thirty-six, but, I was here the winter she was born. That'll be thirty-three years this December. She was born on the twenty-fourth, right up there in the house. A real Christmas present she was. Pete and Renee didn't think they could have no kids and then one day Renee ain't feelin' so hot and she's been puttin' on a few pounds. Pete joked about it, said she should go see the Doc, she's probably just pregnant. They told me the news when I got here in October, not that I couldn't notice. They were happy as they could be. I was somewhat sad. I liked the both of 'em, but figured I'd have to find another spot to winter over. I didn't think they'd be wantin' me around when they had a kid and all. Things turned out just the opposite. They needed me more then ever and the little kid seemed to like me and I been here ever since. Good friends ain't easy to find."

Not much more was said until Woody finished his beer. "Thanks, Connie. Gotta go."

"Already?" Connie was enjoying the company.

"I gotta help the twins with their physics." He winked at Connie, threw the empty in the trash and made his way out.

Connie got another beer for himself and leaned deeply back into the recliner. "You're so right, Doctor Woodruff MacPherson, good friends are hard to find."

The next thing he knew, it was almost midnight. He got up, washed down four more ibuprofen with warm beer and went off to bed. "Nothing' like a little nap before bedtime," he told himself.

Chapter 17, Dating Game

The next morning, after chores, Pete saddled Jolena and while Connie watched from the sidelines, Pete and Jo cut some cows. After each cow, Pete critiqued his performance for Connie. He pointed out subtleties that Connie had never seen and frankly, could not have imagined.

"There'll be five judges looking at your performance. Every move you make, once the clock starts, will be scrutinized. You have to be careful with all your movements. The judges don't want to see any heavy cueing with your hands or legs. Remember this is a contest for the horses, more than the riders. The best horses aren't going to need a lot of direction and the best riders aren't going to be jerkin' their horses around. Once you cut a cow out of the herd and start working it, you don't want to rein the horse at all, period. You'll be riding in what's called the Open class. That means just what it says. It's open to anyone and everyone. You'll be competing against the best riders in the country, maybe even some that aren't from this country."

At this point, Connie was much more confused than he was intimidated. His friend, John, had explained the scoring system to him on their way home from the auction where he'd bought Jolena. It seemed to Connie to be highly subjective, but at the time he had no clear comprehension of the mechanics involved. Now that he had some indication of the cutting process, albeit fleeting, he had a much better understanding of how it could be scored. An untimely dismount, like the one he suffered yesterday, ended your chances immediately.

"You start with eighty points from each of five judges. Then, as you ride, they subtract points for any mistake or omission of a requirement. You can also get credit for certain things like 'eye appeal'. When you're done, each judge calculates his score. The high and the low get thrown out, and the three middle scores are added together for your final score. To see if he understood, Pete asked him, "So what's the highest score you could possibly get?"

Connie had been paying close attention. "Two hundred and forty."

"Correct. Two forty is a perfect score and to my knowledge, the highest score anyone has ever received in a sanctioned event, was two thirty-three."

"What about style? Let's say there are two riders. They both cut three cows, neither makes any mistakes and both horses do everything they're supposed to, but one rider is smoother. Who gets the higher score?"

"What do you think?"

"I think the better rider wins."

"I think you're right, the better rider would probably get a higher 'run content' score based on eye appeal, but at this point, I wouldn't be worried about that. Unless you're noticeably sloppy, it's not going to be a big issue. From what I've seen so far, you weren't born in the saddle, but we should be able to get you to a point where you'll be able to fool most of the spectators and maybe even two of the judges."

"That's a comfort."

Pete laughed. "Pay attention. I'm going to cut one more cow out of this herd and then you can have Jolena. I'm gonna push all the way back into the herd and pull out that little calf with the big white mark around his left eye. See him? He's tucked tight against his mama." Pete pushed his hat back and scratched his forehead. "What I'm going to do is referred to as a deep cut and it's a requirement. It shows the judges how well your horse is focused."

Connie dutifully scanned the herd bunched at the fence until he thought he saw the cow Pete had referred to. "Yeah," he pointed. "Right there."

"Yup, that's him. Now watch carefully. I want you to see if you can tell when I cue Jolena. Watch my left hand. Now, all I'm gonna do is cut that calf away from his mama and push him out of the herd. Once we clear the herd, he'll probably try to cut back immediately.

Jolena's going to want to work him, but I'm not going to allow it. Watch what I do and there will be a quiz."

Pete's heels gave Jo the slightest nudge and she started forward, towards the herd. As she came closer, the cows began slipping off to both sides of her advance. Pete's hand barely moved as he brought the reins against Jo's neck, first right, then left, directing her towards the cow he had selected. Jo was alert, intensely focused; attempting to discover which cow Pete was leading her to. They were a team. Even Connie could see it and he was actually jealous. As horse and rider pushed deeper into the cattle, Jolena focused ahead, ignoring the cows they passed until only two remained. Pete tipped his hand slightly to the left, bringing the right rein against Jo's neck. She turned her head to the left and stared at the calf with the white around its left eye.

Eye to eye contact between different species of animals causes varying degrees of nervousness in the subordinate species. Horses generally dominate cattle and the little calf immediately was intimidated. His mother was also, and started to move away. Jolena eased between the cow calf pair and pushed slowly to her left. The calf was suddenly on his own. Jolena moved steadily and confidently, pushing the calf farther away. In just a few seconds, she had it separated from its mother. Pete cued her again to the left and Jo began moving the calf straight towards Connie, sitting on the fence at the middle of the arena.

Pete knew he was pushing his luck and suddenly the calf bolted for home. Pete whispered whoa to Jolena, who even though she was dying to cut off the calf's escape route, stopped and stood like a statue. Pete grinned.

Connie was impressed. He had seen at least two of the subtle commands to Jolena that caused her to change direction, but he hadn't seen Pete pull back on the reins to stop her.

"What do you think?"

"I saw you rein her a couple of times, although it seemed like once you had the cow moving you didn't do anything. I have no idea how you stopped her."

"Yeah, you're correct. I nudged her to start moving. I steered her to the cow I wanted and then I pretty much let her take over. She knew what I wanted her to do and I only cued her once more to start the calf back towards you. I didn't want her to chase the calf. She stopped because I didn't drop the reins down on her neck and I whispered whoa."

"Very impressive."

"It was and in a couple months you'll be doin' the same. If you can stay in the saddle when she's turnin' and let her do the thinking, there's no reason you can't bring it all home."

Connie sincerely wished he hadn't taken a dive off Fritz's back and sprained his wrist. As bizarre as it seemed, a month ago he would have considered cutting cattle to be an obscure sport, had he even considered it. Today, counting horse, truck and trailer, and bunkhouse modifications he had close to two hundred thousand dollars invested in the obscure sport, and mastering the fine points had become his sole mission. He was not a compulsive person, and it was difficult for him to understand how this transformation had occurred. It had all started when he first laid eyes on Jolena. Now he was finally going to ride her. "Sounds like a plan," he told Pete and he believed it.

Pete dismounted and handed the reins to Connie. "Take her in the barn. Pull off this saddle and put on the one you were using last week. I'm going to turn these cows back into the pasture and run up to the house. I'll meet you back in the barn in a few minutes."

After Connie had switched saddles, Pete had him mount up and ride Jolena around in the small arena in the barn. He showed him how little rein was necessary. "Don't go jerkin' her face around. Pretend the reins are spider webs and any heavy pressure will snap them. Talk to her. Whisper 'left' when you rein her left and 'right' when you rein her right. Whispering will remind you to go easy on the rein."

After a few turns, when Pete was satisfied Connie understood what he meant, he stopped them. "Okay, take her for a walk. You can trot her and lope her, but don't lope her for more than twenty minutes and don't gallop. I don't want you to work her too hard on rough ground."

"Where should I go?"

"Take her up the hill where we've been goin'." He looked at his watch. "You've got about two hours. Don't be late for lunch."

Jolena clip-clopped across the wooden bridge spanning the creek still fat with runoff from snowmelt. She sashayed through the grass in the meadow that was growing almost fast enough to watch. When she hit the trail into the hills, the smell of pine was thick enough to slice and pass around. The sky above was electric blue and the sunshine was warm, not hot. It was springtime in the Rockies, and Connie could not imagine a more perfect day. As he and Jolena ambled through the trees, the only thing wrong was that Sarah wasn't here, riding beside him. She would have loved this. Jolena nickered and Connie reached forward to pat her neck.

"You're a good girl, Jo. Sarah would have loved you too."

At the fork in the trail leading to Rogers Lake, Connie consulted his watch. It was almost eleven. Pete said the lake was two miles out. Not enough time. Connie turned Jo around and they started back. "Another day Jo," he told the horse. "We'll get an early start. Maybe we can even go for a swim."

Pete was hanging around the barn when they got there. "How did she go?" Pete asked him when he dismounted. Connie felt as if Pete's concern was not unlike that of the father whose daughter he was bringing home from a date.

"Just fine. We just walked and talked." Jolena nudged Pete's hand. She was looking for oats.

"Good, good, no need to take things too fast. You two have a lot of work to do together in the next seven and a half months. We don't want anyone getting hurt," and he added, "more than you already have."

Connie's damaged wrist had stopped its throbbing and had entered the dull ache phase. "I'll be good to go by next week, maybe sooner." He flipped the left stirrup over the saddle horn and began loosening the cinch strap. "What are we doin' this afternoon?"

"I thought about knocking down some hay, but I think I'll give it 'til Monday. Another four, five days of this weather, it should be about prime. But, we've got plenty of odd jobs to keep us busy."

And so odd jobs it was. Even with his bad wrist he was able to do a fair amount. He cleaned the cow barn with a five-foot bucket mounted on a small tractor. He helped Woody mend some fence. He helped Pete service three tractors, a hay baler, and a mower conditioner, a piece of equipment that cut hay and crushed the stalks so it dried faster. He ate breakfast at six thirty, lunch at twelve, and supper at six. Every morning he took Jolena for a ride and groomed her afterward. With every brush stroke, he appreciated her more.

Connie had never owned any kind of animal until after he was married and Sarah adopted a stray cat. He liked animals, especially dogs, but always found it more convenient not to own one, which made buying a horse all the more out of character. He was glad he bought her, but pondered his present situation of horse owner long and hard that first week he started riding Jolena. He even wondered if there were some sort of special providence involved. Was somebody up there looking out for him? Was Jolena an answer to somebody's prayer for him? Whose? Who knew him well enough to ask the Almighty for mercy on his soul? Who cared about him enough to want to see him delivered from the path to self-destruction he had been following? Both his parents were dead. Sarah was dead.

His sister and his good friend John had been concerned, but neither had lectured him about his drinking, although John had convinced him to go to the horse auction over his protests. He'd decided to go to the sale and on a whim, bought a horse. That horse happened to come with a trainer who talked him into entering a contest. Pure circumstance and nothing more, forget the fact Jolena caught his eye because her birthday happened to be the same day Sarah had died. Ignore the fact Jo could be one of the best cutting horses in the country and came with one of the best trainers in the business. Don't consider the fact Pete had known his father and used that old relationship to persuade him to take Jolena to the premier cutting horse event in the world. Really, stranger things had happened. His present situation was only the culmination of a number of happenstances and could have gone in any one of a number of ways.

"Yeah right," he told himself as he inspected the frogs of Jolena's hoofs prior to saddling her. "As silly as it sounds, Jo, somebody is looking out for me." The horse bent her head down to nuzzle the back of his neck.

"What do you think?" He placed her foot back on the ground. "Did I pick you out or did you pick me out?"

Jo nickered softly.

"What kind of answer is that? Yes, no, maybe? Could you be a little more specific? He brushed her back in preparation for the saddle blanket.

The horse stood quietly.

"Come on, Jo, give me something to work with here. I'd like to know if I have any free will in this deal, or am I just being led down the garden path. Who's running this show?"

He lifted the saddle onto her back. "I think you know what's going on, but you're not talking." He shifted the saddle around until he got it settled in just right. "You know, if we're gonna be real partners, you can't have any secrets." He started the cinch strap through the ring. "If I knew, I'd tell you." He pulled the strap through once and fed it back through the ring. "Maybe you don't know either, but if you find out, promise you'll tell me." He worked the strap tight.

Jolena turned her head and nickered. Connie looked up and saw Cally leaning against the wall about ten feet away. He wondered how long she had been there. His face flushed red. "Hello, Cally."

"Hi Connie." She pushed away from the wall and walked over to him. She petted Jolena's nose. "I need to run into town quick for a few things and wondered if there was anything I could get for you."

He gave her a silly grin. "Ah, no. I can't think of anything. How long have you been standing there?"

She had heard most of his one sided conversation with the horse, but she didn't think it was odd in the least. Actually, she was thinking he looked somewhat desirable. She gave him back a silly grin. "Don't worry, I won't tell anybody you talk to your horse." She turned to leave, "Don't be late for lunch."

He watched her walk away and thought once again how good looking she was. "I don't know if she even likes me a little. What do you think, Jo?"

Jo pawed her right front on the barn floor. She wanted to go. Connie grabbed the saddle horn and swung into the saddle. *Ambiguous answer.* He rode out of the barn.

It was Saturday and another sweet, early summer day. He and Pete had hooked up the mower conditioner to one of the tractors earlier in the morning and made it ready. Pete intended to start cutting hay as soon as the dew was off the grass come Monday morning. It hadn't taken very long and Connie had at least two hours before lunch would be served. His wrist was still tender, but he didn't need the compression bandage any longer and he'd told Pete he'd be ready to start lessons again on Monday afternoon. He didn't know if he'd get a chance to ride Jolena tomorrow or not. The twins had made him promise to go to church with them and after church there was supposed to be a barbecue somewhere. He didn't know when they would get back.

"Better make the most of this ride, Jo. It seems we could be gettin' busy for a while." He loped her through the meadow to the bridge across the creek and up the trail into the hills. At the cut off to Rogers Lake, they turned towards the lake and Connie slowed Jolena to a walk. He wondered how far she could comfortably travel at a lope. Even though she had a smooth ride, Connie suspected she was capable of traveling more distance than he wanted. He thought he'd read somewhere that a horse in good condition could do fifty miles in a day, but he didn't remember if that was carrying a rider. Although, even if the horse could do half that with a rider, it was still impressive.

"Remind me to ask Pete about that," he told Jolena. "Not that we're going to be doing any endurance races. I'd still like to know."

"Another thing that would be nice to know is how long Cally was standing behind us listening to me talking to you. You should let me know when there's somebody else around. I'm sure she's got enough doubts about me without her thinking I talk to you all the time."

Connie was silent for a few minutes pondering one of life's big questions for a man, that being, whether he could live without a woman's charms. Of course he could live, but could he be happy? He'd been happily married. Not once had he regretted his life with Sarah. He couldn't imagine finding another woman to compare to her, however that didn't stop him from wondering about Cally. She was definitely good looking and she certainly seemed capable, probably she was intelligent too. Connie knew she loved her daughters, and Pete and Woody, and it appeared she was kind and generous. He wondered how classy she might be. Discovering that could take some time.

"Jo, you been hangin' around Cally for three years, you should know what she's like. Is she a class act or does she have a bunch of issues? I sure don't need a woman with issues. I don't have any. At least as far as I know I don't."

Jolena nickered and Connie stretched forward to pat her neck. "That's just what I thought, another maybe answer."

A half hour later, they walked up to the edge of a sand beach on Rogers Lake. Connie dismounted and led Jolena to the water. The water was clear as gin and he could see the sandy bottom gradually sloping away for fifty feet. He dropped the reins and knelt down. The shallow water was warm, but he guessed it would be cold if he waded out a ways. Then on a whim he decided to test his theory. He pulled off his boots and socks and unbuckled his belt. He stepped out of his jeans and gingerly waded in. Jolena followed without being asked.

He went in to mid-thigh and stopped, deciding he'd been right. Any deeper and things would really get uncomfortable. He had no desire to take the big plunge. But in a week or two, when the temperature had come up another ten degrees, he'd be back. As he and Jo waded out, he realized how ridiculous he must look in his underwear leading a horse. "Oh well," he told Jo, "it's only me and you and I know you're not going to tell."

Finding a rock to sit on while the sun dried him off, he allowed Jolena to graze unattended. He was certain she wouldn't run off and she didn't disappoint him. He wondered what Pete would think if he knew he didn't have Jolena under tight control. But then again, Jolena was his horse, not Pete's. As he watched her delicately work her lips around what must be the choicest morsels of vegetation and then precisely nip them off with her front teeth, he came to a momentous thought. He loved Jolena.

The Greeks had four words for love, the English language only one, but Connie knew exactly what he meant when he thought it. Jolena was dear to him in a way that was unique. She was big and powerful, and Connie was impressed with her strength. She was smart and Connie knew it. And she also possessed a definite spirit that Connie could recognize. She was friendly, kind, and thoughtful. She didn't just react, she responded and provided tangible feedback. She knew, she was aware, and she could communicate. Whether or not anyone else recognized her attributes was immaterial. Connie could sense her soul and it pleased him greatly.

The sun was warm and Connie's eyes grew heavy. Fortunately, the rock upon which he perched was becoming hard in direct proportion to the weight of his eyelids. After ten minutes he shook his head. "Hey, Jo, we gotta go. Can't be late for lunch."

He pulled on his pants, socks and boots. They wandered back to the ranch where they were met by the twins who demanded a full report of where they had gone and what all they had done.

"We went swimming in Rogers Lake."

"Did not," Danni accused. "The water's still too cold."

"Maybe I'm part Eskimo and I like cold water."

"You're not any part Eskimo," Lindsey chimed in. "You're from Indiana. Mom said."

"Okay, so I'm not an Eskimo, but I did go in the lake."

"Not all the way, I'll bet," Lindsey defied.

Connie laughed. "Yeah, you're right, not all the way."

"Did Jo go in too?" Lindsey wanted to know. "Neither one of you looks very wet."

Connie pulled the saddle off Jolena. "Have either one of you been swimming in Rogers Lake."

"Oh yeah," Lindsey told him. "When the water warms up, we go up there all the time. Mom goes with us and sometimes Grandpa and Woody too."

"Yeah," Danni agreed. "Sometimes we take lunch along and have a picnic"

"Sounds idyllic. The next time you go up there for a picnic, invite me, okay?"

"Sure," Danni said. "What's idyllic?"

"Idyllic is what it would be if you and me and your mom went to Rogers lake for a picnic." He regretted it as soon as he had said it.

Those two would have it back to Cally before lunch. "Ah, idyllic means okay." He made an attempt at damage control.

Lindsey looked at him like she knew what he was thinking. "Just okay?"

"Well maybe a little better than okay."

"How much better?"

"Oh, I don't know, maybe nice. Yeah nice would explain it." He was being outsmarted by two nine-year olds. He was embarrassed.

Danni turned and dashed off. "Where's she going?" Connie asked Lindsey although he was certain he already knew.

Lindsey shrugged. "Who knows about that girl? Probably to ask mom if we can go have a picnic at Rogers Lake."

Connie wanted to groan, but decided against it. Maybe if he downplayed the issue at least Lindsey would forget it. "So where are your grandpa and Woody hiding?"

"They're not hiding, they're up at the house."

Connie checked his watch. It was ten minutes before noon. "I'm not late for lunch am I?"

"No we got a few minutes yet"

Connie was about to ask Lindsey if she ever got tired of always eating every meal at the same time every day. Fortunately he thought better of it. "Do I have enough time to brush Jo off quick?"

"Oh sure, that'll only take a minute."

Five minutes later, Connie had Jo unsaddled, turned out to pasture and Lindsey had him by the hand leading him to the house for lunch. His anticipation and apprehension over what Danni would say about a picnic had him worried. "Come on, Connie, you're walking too slow. Aren't you hungry?" Lindsey cajoled.

Other than what seemed to be a more generous smile than usual from Cally, lunch passed without incident. Pete wanted to know how Jolena rode, Woody made his usual wry comments about everything and anything, and the twins monopolized all discussion in between. The topic of picnics at Rogers Lake failed to materialize, much to Connie's relief. And then lunch was over and for Connie the weekend had officially begun.

Chapter 18, Options

Connie really did have some errands in town, but they were things he couldn't have had Cally do for him. Most importantly, he needed clean clothes. Nothing had ever been said about laundry privileges and he was too inhibited to ask Cally to use her washer and drier. That left him two choices, buy all new clothes or go to town and find a Laundromat. After careful consideration, he decided to do both. He stuffed three weeks of dirty laundry into a couple of heavy plastic trash bags and headed for downtown Kalispell. It would be an adventure.

He made his first stop at an upscale strip mall on the northwest edge of town. "The Tack Room" advertised 'Tack and Western Wear'. The parking lot was full of shiny SUVs. On entering, he was run into by an attractive woman. She was talking over her shoulder to a younger woman, perhaps her daughter, behind her rather then watching where she was going. Connie started to step to his right, but the woman caught him in her peripheral vision just as he did and stepped to her left. He put his hands up and caught her at the hips as she collided with him. He gently pushed her back a half step and released her.

"Excuse me," he told her.

She smiled and then laughed. "No, excuse me." She pulled down her sunglasses, looked at him over the rims and added, "Cowboy." Pushing her glasses back up, she and the younger woman continued out the door.

Connie watched them go. She looked familiar. He had seen her someplace before, it could have even been in the movies, but he couldn't recall when or where. The two women folded themselves into a black, Cadillac Escalade and were gone. Connie shook his head.

Forty minutes later he left the store with five pairs of Cinch blue jeans, three, bold colored Roper shirts, and a pair of Tony Lama boots, using up the best part of a five hundred dollar bill. He had briefly flirted with a Resistol hat, but decided he needed a second opinion from Pete on what kind to get.

His next stop was another, larger mall that had a Penny's department store where he stocked up on socks, underwear and five more pairs of classic western wear jeans. They fit well, a little different than the others and were ten dollars cheaper. He also bought some shorts, tennis shoes and a bathing suit. This time the tab was over three hundred. He calculated if he continued at his present rate, by the time the stores closed, he'd spend well over five thousand. *Time to find the Laundromat.*

It took twenty minutes of driving before he found one on the south end of town, in a small, run down strip mall. It was dark, dingy, and the scent of laundry detergent mingled with mildew, but it had one redeeming feature. Directly across the street was a decent looking restaurant and saloon called "Boot Hill" and as soon as Connie had filled six washers with dirty clothes, he made his way across the street.

Replicas of long-barreled, Colt forty-four, six shooters were attached to the doors to serve as handles. A complicated neon sign that showed two cowboys standing and drawing down on each other that would be impressive at night was not so much in the afternoon sun. The doors looked heavy, but when Connie tugged on the faux pistol, the door practically blew open. The same woman he'd bumped into at The Tack Room came flying out. Just as Connie pulled on the door from the outside she pushed from the inside. He caught her again.

"Ah, Miss, we really have to stop meeting like this. One of us is going to get hurt."

She blushed and smiled. "Are you following me, Cowboy?" She didn't make an immediate effort to back away from him.

Cowboy. He smiled back. "Now if I were following you, wouldn't I be behind you?"

She wasn't wearing her sunglasses and when she laughed, her eyes sparkled like clear blue sapphires. "Good point." She stuck out her hand. "Myra Foxx."

He took her hand firmly. "Connie Bradley, pleased to meet you Myra Foxx. Will I be running into you again?" He wanted to ask her if she was in movies, but decided if she were, he'd feel stupid for asking. He didn't recognize her name.

She peered at him with interest, as if she were assessing his looks. "Maybe, if you want to. I'll be at Rustlers later." She released her grip on his hand. "Nice meeting you, Connie."

"Likewise, Miss Foxx." He didn't ask where or what Rustlers was. He assumed it was a restaurant and if he were interested he'd be able to find it. The woman still looked familiar, a little older than he had initially thought, but he was certain he had seen her somewhere.

For three o-clock in the afternoon on a beautiful day, the Boot Hill was reasonably well populated. Connie had been hoping for a quiet, cool oasis with a long bar of some old dark wood and a big mirror behind it so he could watch what was going on without turning around. Instead, he walked into a well-lit sports bar with a phony Wild West theme. There was a large U-shaped bar more or less in the center of the room, flanked by tables, that were in turn, surrounded by booths at the perimeter. The walls were covered with used barn siding and festooned with replicas of old rifles, pistols and new copies of old photographs of famous sheriffs, cowboys, and dead outlaws. Connie guessed all the hardware was plastic, but he didn't bother to check.

TVs hung from the ceiling at strategic locations and he felt out of place wearing blue jeans, boots, and a long-sleeved, western cut shirt. Most everyone else was in shorts and tee shirts. No wonder the mystery woman kept referring to him as 'Cowboy'.

Glancing at a TV, Connie deduced the reason for the large number of patrons was a post-season basketball game. He didn't follow pro sports and he had never watched much television so it was difficult for him to understand how the combination could lure so many people into spending a perfectly good afternoon in a crowded bar. He suspected the real draw was the alcohol and the sporting event was the excuse.

He took a seat at the bar right behind a set of tap handles. There were the usual domestics and several imports including Guinness and Bass Ale. The bartender was a middle-aged man sporting a ponytail and a handle bar moustache.

"Howdy, Cowboy. What'll it be?"

Connie pointed to the beer taps. "You've got Guinness and Bass Ale. How about you pour me a black and tan?"

"Absolutely, and if I might add, an excellent choice. I get real tired of pouring lite beer and stuffing lemon wedges into Corona bottles."

Connie smiled. "I never could tell the difference between Corona and any lite beer."

"Well, the Mexicans brew some great beers, but in my humble opinion, Corona ain't one of them."

While he carefully layered the two beers into a tall glass, Connie asked, "Did you see the two women that just left?"

"Like about a minute ago?"

"Yeah, just as I walked in, they were leaving. Do you happen to know who they were?"

"Sure, that was our resident movie star, Brianna Lane, and her daughter." He leaned a little closer to Connie. "She owns this place and Rustlers and a couple of western stores. Oh yeah, and the strip mall across the street. She'll be tearing that down soon though. Gonna put in some higher class stuff."

Connie was confused. He recognized the name. She'd been in several movies about ten or fifteen years ago, and then dropped out of sight. "She told me her name was Myra Foxx."

"She was born in Whitefish as Myra Foxx, but, we all refer to her by her stage name. Helps with the mystique." The bartender leaned another bit closer. "Not bad for forty-five wouldn't you say?"

The bartender was now close enough to be in Connie's space and it made him uncomfortable. He hoped the bartender was still referring to Myra, not himself.

"Ah, yeah, not bad at all." He leaned back on his stool just a bit. "What's Rustlers?"

The bartender straightened up. "Another joint, in Whitefish, a lot like this one only bigger, but no TVs and they've got live music after nine." He laughed. "Actually it's not at all like this place."

Connie suddenly wondered if Cally ever went there, maybe with her doctor friend. "Really, what kind of music?"

The bartender noticed he was being summoned by a waitress. "Friday night is rock, Saturday is country western," he answered as he left Connie.

Connie drank his beer, watched people watching television and wondered if he should put in an appearance at the Rustlers. He could dance, but not country western style. Those dances looked like they had a million steps and he seriously doubted real cowboys ever danced like that. Then, on further contemplation, he doubted if there were many real cowboys left on the planet. Maybe in Argentina or Australia, but he wondered how many remained in the Western United States. If this bar in the middle of the American "Wild West" was any indication, Pete Browning was probably one of the last surviving cowboys in the state of Montana.

The beer went down smoothly and Connie contemplated another, but decided his laundry had precedence. He left the bartender a dollar tip and made his way out of the Boot Hill back across the street to the dingy Laundromat. All six washers were spooling down when he arrived so he repacked his clothes into three driers and sat down to wait.

It was a depressing place and he was glad its days were numbered. The plastic chair in which he was sitting was cracked and soiled, the plaster board on the walls and ceiling was stained and yellowed from cigarette smoke and the linoleum on the floor was bubbled in some spots and worn through in others. He was surprised the machines all worked. No one else came in to use the facility while he was there and as soon as his clothes were dry and folded, he quickly departed.

It was too nice a day to go back and sit in the bunkhouse so he decided to drive to Whitefish to see if he could find Rustlers. He didn't intend to go in, just find it. Whitefish being a small town with a big ski resort about ten miles north of Kalispell he assumed it would be a quick leisurely drive.

Back in the seventies when he spent his summers on the dude ranch just west of Livingston, Montana hadn't yet been discovered by disillusioned Californians. His brown haired girlfriend was a skier and she told him all about Big Mountain, the ski resort at Whitefish. She had said things like "fabulous powder, no lift lines, cheap lift tickets, sunny weather, and friendly people". And at that time, almost thirty years ago, it was true except the weather wasn't always sunny. Today, things were quite different all across western Montana. The small towns were no longer so small. In fact, in some of them like Whitefish, many of the longtime residents had been either forced to sell out or were struggling mightily to pay property taxes driven into the ozone by the prices displaced Californians were willing to pay for even the poorest pieces of real estate. They had become victims of prosperity. Towns like Kalispell had tripled in size, sprawling in wild abandon. Traffic had become nightmarish and people were no longer as friendly as they once were. The powder was still fabulous, but lift tickets were no longer cheap and the lines were long at Big Mountain.

By the time Connie arrived in Whitefish, he was wondering if he hadn't made a detour to Orange County, California. He wasn't certain where Kalispell ended and Whitefish started. The ten miles between them were being overgrown with all manners of suburban sprawl. On the plus side, he easily found Rustlers. It was just across the street from the turn off to Big Mountain ski resort. It was a low rambling building with a high false front built to resemble a whole street of old western town. There was a bank, a general store, a hotel and a saloon. The saloon section was the biggest and framed the main entrance. Seeing what Myra Foxx had built, Connie wondered what the future held for the little strip mall where he'd washed his clothes.

He would have liked to do a little more exploring, but Cally was expecting him for dinner and he'd left his cell phone back in the bunkhouse. He had less than an hour to get back to the ranch. Fortunately, he found a less traveled road that connected with US 2 on the west side of Kalispell, and arrived home with five minutes to spare. He was glad he got back in time because Cally had baked three of the free range chickens he'd brought when he first arrived. His initial reaction when he sat down to dinner and saw the big platter piled high, was to wonder who else was invited. But when the meal was over, he knew why Cally had fixed three. The twins finished off almost a whole chicken by themselves and no one else including Connie, held back.

"Cally," he said when the platter was mostly empty, "I believe that was the best chicken dinner I have ever eaten. Thank you."

He was rewarded by a smile and a promise. "Thank you, Connie. You furnished the chicken and since I know you like it, we'll have it again some time."

"How about tomorrow?" Danni asked.

"We're goin' to the barbecue tomorrow," Lindsey reminded her.

"Oh yeah, that's right. I forgot."

"How could you forget that? We won't have to do dishes afterwards."

Danni smiled, "Yippee!" Then immediately lost the smile. "But we have to do them now."

It was Connie's turn to smile. "Dinner was so good, how about I help you two with the dishes. I can wash and you both can dry."

Woody chimed in. "Here's another deal. If you girls want to go play, I'll dry and you're off the hook altogether."

"Wow," Danni exclaimed and then looked to Cally. "Can we, Mom?"

"Don't ask me. If Connie and Woody are volunteering to do your chores, I'm not going to interfere. They're big boys."

Both girls jumped up from the table and hugged Woody and then Connie. Connie was slightly embarrassed and didn't really hug back. He smiled though and caught Cally watching him watch the girls run out the back door. "Almost makes me wish I'd had some kids," he said quietly.

Cally smiled. "Yeah, well, I wouldn't sell them to you for a billion dollars and I wouldn't give you a dime for another one." She turned to Woody. "Knowing that my kitchen is in capable hands, I believe I'll excuse myself."

Pete got up and poured himself another cup of coffee. "I believe I'll just sit here and watch these two big boys work."

An hour later, the dishes were done, the kitchen was close to spotless and Woody and Connie were sitting on the back steps of the bunkhouse smoking Casa Blanca cigars, while watching the girls splash around in the creek. There was still an hour of daylight.

Woody leaned back and blew a fat smoke ring. "Nice and mild. Where'd you come by these?" He waved the cigar at Connie.

"Mail order from a place in Meban, North Carolina."

"Good, nice and mild." He waved the cigar towards the south. "Neighbor, just down the road that way got himself a mail order bride about fifty years ago. Still has her too."

"Oh yeah. I didn't think that still happened only fifty years ago."

"Well it didn't, at least to him anyway. The way he tells the story is he ordered some stuff from Sears and when he went in to pick it up, there was this pretty little thing behind the counter. He started talkin' to her and she'd just moved out to Kalispell from Williston, North Dakota to escape some guy she couldn't stand. Got hired by the Sears store, was her first day at work. Well, they started datin' and in six months they were married. Still calls her his mail order bride."

"I don't get it."

Woody looked at him rather critically. "How old are you, boy?"

"Forty-six."

"Well, at least in this part of the country, Sears, at that time, was only a mail order store. They didn't have no inventory, only a catalog. You found what you wanted outta the catalog. You ordered it, then when it arrived, you went down to the local store and fetched it."

"Why didn't they just send it to your house?"

"Well, I don't know. You messed up the story by not bein' old enough.'

"If I get us a beer, will you forgive me?"

"Yeah, I guess, but it might take more than one."

Connie fetched a couple bottles and sat down on the step again. Handing one to Woody, he asked, "Ever hear of a woman by the name of Brianna Lane?"

Woody's eyes sparkled. "Oh yeah, fine lookin' woman. Was a movie star about ten, fifteen years back. Lives in Whitefish with her daughter."

"Any husband?"

"No, apparently the guy was just a sperm donor who gave her the daughter. She's never said who he was. She owns a couple of restaurants, one downtown and one in Whitefish. I been in both of 'em."

"You've been to Rustlers in Whitefish?"

"Yeah, lots of times. It's kind of a classy dump."

"Classy dump? Isn't that a contradiction in terms?"

"You mean an oxymoron? I don't think so. Long time ago I decided all saloons are dumps. They charge an exorbitant price for a bottle of beer, drunks go there, and at quittin' time, most everybody looks bad. Course that don't mean I don't patronize 'em. I just don't have any illusions about where I am and what I'm doin' there."

"Interesting. But isn't Rustlers a cut above the ordinary dump?"

"Oh, at least two, three cuts above. It's real clean, you don't see no cowboys with horseshit on their boots. They get decent music too and the thing I like the best, is it ain't overpowering loud. Course they still dance them silly line dances, but you can actually make conversation when the band is playin'." Woody took a long pull off his beer bottle. "That's real important because I am a serious conversationalist, especially when I'm talkin' to ladies in a saloon. Where'd you hear about Brianna Lane?"

"I met her this afternoon. Twice, actually."

"You don't say. How did that happen?"

"I literally ran into her, twice, and the second time, we introduced ourselves. When I asked her if I was going to bump into her again, she told me she'd be at the Rustlers later in the evening."

"Now, boy, that's impressive." Woody meant it too. "She's my consummate woman, least one of 'em. She's smart, good lookin', lots of money, might be a little tall for me, but I think I could work that out, and you met her. What you gonna do about her invitation?"

"I'm not sure. I'm not even sure it was an invitation." Connie explained in detail how he'd met her and what she'd said.

Woody finished his beer. "That was an invitation as overt as I ever heard. Why don't you and me take a spin over to Whitefish and stop in Rustlers to see what we can see? You can look for the lovely Myra Foxx and I'll provide backup."

"You sure?"

"Course I'm sure. Neither one of us needs permission and life is short. I know for a fact mine is gettin' shorter as we speak." He handed Connie his empty and stood. "I'll put on a clean pair of blue jeans and I'll be ready." He called out to the twins, "Girls, you get out of the crick now and come up to the house."

He walked off and the twins followed behind him about a minute later, wrapped in towels and shivering, their lips blue from splashing in the cold water.

Connie took a quick shower, pulled on a new pair of Cinch jeans, a red, white, and blue Roper shirt, and his new Tony Lama boots. Woody was waiting by the back door. "My my, Connie, you are one fine lookin' scissorbill."

"Jeez, Woody why didn't you come in, sit down? You didn't have to wait outside. What's a scissorbill?"

Woody held up a bottle. "I came in and got a beer, but I came back out to watch the sunset. Didn't know how long you were gonna take." He set the empty gently on the step. "A scissorbill is a drugstore cowboy. You know what that is?"

"A cowboy hooked on oxycodone?"

Woody slowly shook his head. "I'll tell you what. When we get to Rustlers, most of the guys doin' the dancin' will be drugstore cowboys. A scissorbill is a pretend cowboy, you know, some guy who just bought the outfit and doesn't know which end of a steer the steak comes from."

"And I look like one of those guys? Maybe I should change clothes. I don't want to look like no stinking scissorbill."

"I regret calling you that. You don't really look like a scissorbill and besides the women all seem to like pretend cowboys. Some women even like real ones and the smartest women can tell the difference."

Connie laughed, slapped Woody gently on the back and the two cowboys rode off in Connie's trusty steed—his one-ton, dually pickup. From the kitchen window, Cally watched them go.

"Hey, Dad, do you know where Woody and Connie are going?"

Pete called back from the living room; "Woody said they were going to Rustlers for a beer. Asked me if I wanted to go along, but I figured you needed me to baby sit." He waited a bit for her reply, but when it didn't come, he added, "I thought you were going out with your doctor friend tonight."

She was still staring out the window at nothing in particular. She would have liked to gone with Woody and Connie. "Sorry, Dad, I forgot to tell you, I canceled out."

"Oh yeah, something the matter with the Doc?"

"Not really, he's just awfully young is all."

"Isn't he about your age?"

"Yeah, but sometimes he acts terribly immature." She left her post at the window when the taillights of Connie's truck disappeared from view. "I don't think we have a lot in common," she said as she dropped onto the couch across from the chair where Pete was sitting.

Pete lowered the book he was reading. "No, I don't imagine you do, although he seems nice enough."

"Yeah, he's nice enough, but he wants to get serious and that scares me. I can't explain it, but sometimes he acts like he's socially retarded or something. He can be so awfully juvenile."

Pete smiled. "Well, Honey, I've heard medical school can do that do you. Takes about fifteen years after internship to catch up."

She stretched out on the couch. "That'll be ten more years. No way I'm holding my breath for him."

Chapter 19, More Options

The Rustlers' parking lot was already nearly full when Connie and Woody arrived. "Must be a good crowd for dinner," Woody offered. "There's no music for another half-hour."

"You ever eat here?"

"Yeah, couple a times. I took Cally here for her birthday last year. Food is good but it ain't cheap."

"Cally's birthday is the day before Christmas, right?"

"Yup. Gotta do something. She takes awfully good care of me, but I don't know what I'll do for her this year."

"Well, I can imagine she likes going out for a good meal she doesn't have to cook."

"I guess, although she has said many times she loves to cook."

Connie had a flashback. "My wife was a fabulous cook and she loved doing it, but she also enjoyed going out to a restaurant that served good food. Didn't have to be a fancy place, but the food had to be good. Don't let Cally fool you, she appreciates going out for dinner once in a while."

Connie stepped in front of Woody and pulled the door open for him. "I reckon that's correct, maybe we'll just come back here," and he walked in, Connie close on his heels.

A large sign hanging from the ceiling of the vestibule announced in flowery script, 'Saloon' and 'Dining Hall'. Graphic hands wearing white gloves and the pointer finger extended, pointed left and right respectively. Woody turned left and Connie followed him into a large room decorated to resemble an 1890s or at least Hollywood's interpretation of an 1890s saloon and dance hall. The dark mahogany bar stretched the entire length of one wall and was backed by a series of elaborately framed mirrors. Booze bottles of every imaginable variety stood on the counter in front of the mirrors. Opposite the bar was a small elevated stage with a dance floor in front and close to a hundred tables for four. There was a piano player beating out a rag on a honky-tonk piano in front of the stage, but it was immediately apparent the piano was electronically amplified to fill the big room.

More than half the tables were filled, but the bar was wide open. Connie followed Woody to two seats part way down its length. They sat and a familiar looking bartender stepped over.

"Hello gents. What'll it be?" And then she looked a little closer. "Hello, Cowboy, we meet again."

"Hello, Myra. When you said you'd be at Rustlers, I didn't know you owned the place."

"Yeah, and when I said I'd be here, I didn't expect I'd be working, but I had a bartender call up about six o'clock to inform me she was quitting and wouldn't be in tonight."

"Don't you just love it when they give you adequate notice?"

Myra smiled. "Just as well. Saves me the trouble of firing her. She was not a model employee and I don't mind working." She looked to Woody, "Who's your friend, Connie?"

Connie turned on his stool towards Woody. "Doctor Woodruff MacPherson, meet Myra Foxx. Myra this is Woody."

She extended her hand across the bar and Woody took it in both of his. "Miss Foxx, it is to my eternal delight to make your acquaintance. I was a fan of your escapades on the silver screen and greatly disappointed when you took your leave of Hollywood. And you may call me Woody."

"Oh my, aren't you just the sweetest thing. If the people I had to work with had been half as magnanimous as you, I'd still be there. Let me buy you two gentlemen a drink. What'll it be?"

"I had a black and tan at the Boot Hill this afternoon," Connie told her, "Can you pour that here too?"

"I can. How about you, Woody?"

"I believe I'll have that also, Miss Foxx."

She left them then to get the beers. "Woody, I had no idea you were such a silver tongued fox. Did you really see her movies?"

"Well, of course I did. You think I could lie to a beautiful woman like that?"

"Jeez, I don't know. Can you lie to an ugly old man like me?"

Woody inspected him. "You ain't that old, but even if you were, I wouldn't lie to you. I might embellish the truth a tad, but I'd never lie. For instance, when I tell Pete and Cally I met Brianna Lane, I may add a few details in which I explain how taken she was with me. Now, Pete and Cally have some experience with my tendency to, to, ah shall we say, overstate the truth, so they'll believe me when I tell 'em I met Miss Lane, or Foxx as the case may be, but they'll blow off the part about her bein' enamored with me. However," and he winked at Connie, "if I tell 'em she's enamored with you, they might believe that."

"Why would you tell them that? I just met her this afternoon and I'm sure she has a veritable army of admirers with whom to be enamored. All of them certainly a lot more desirable than me."

"Never, ever, sell yourself short when it comes to pursuing a woman. There is no way to figure what attracts them. I have seen some of the best looking women with the ugliest men imaginable, although those guys might've been nine feet tall when there were sittin' down on their wallets. And you ain't ugly and don't appear to be a pauper."

"So you're saying I could have half a chance if I were to pursue our bartender?"

"Abso-lutely. Shoot, Boy! You're grade A, prime for a lot of women, anywhere from the age of thirty to as old as you're heart desires. You got most all your hair and teeth and your face in between is okay. You stand nice and straight and don't clean up too bad and ain't got no spare tire hangin' 'round your middle."

"How about Cally? You think I'd have a chance with her?" The question slipped out unintended. He was embarrassed he'd said it.

Woody looked at him rather critically. "You might. That somethin' you plan to try?"

"No. Of course not. I'm not planning to pursue any woman right now. I was just testing you're theory about being desirable to a woman fifteen years my junior."

"You weren't listenin' real close. I didn't say 'every' woman between thirty and ninety, I said 'a lot of' women."

"I know what you said, I'm just wondering which category Cally was in, the category that would find me desirable or the category that would find me disgusting for looking. Forget it. If I keep talking you'll think I have designs on her."

It was at this time Myra came back with their beers. She served them up and said, "Here you are, gentlemen. Enjoy them in good health."

Connie and Woody lifted their glasses and thanked her. "I wish you could join us on this side of the bar," Connie said.

She gave him that blue eyed, sparkly smile he had seen earlier in the day. "I'd like that too. Do I get a rain check?"

Connie might have blushed just a little, but came back strong. "Abso-lutely. We'll have to exchange schedules."

That comment led to Myra's roundabout question. "So, Connie, you look like a cowboy, you're wearing a western shirt, and boots, and jeans like a cowboy, but where's your hat? All real cowboys wear hats." She waved her hand out towards the tables. "Look at all those cowboys out there. They're all wearing hats."

Connie looked behind him. There were a number of men sitting at tables duded up like cowboys, complete with Stetsons. There was even one guy who looked like he could have had his hat on backwards, but being a novice cowboy himself, Connie couldn't be sure.

He turned back to the lovely Myra. "Guess I'm not really much of cowboy."

Woody spoke up. "You are so. You're more of a cowboy than all them scissorbills out there. At least you capture the essence of a cowboy. Boy, you even got a horse that's smarter than you. If that don't make you a bona fide cowboy, nothin' does."

Connie said, "You'll have to excuse Woody, he's an old sheepherder with a PhD and somewhat jealous of us cowboys."

Myra laughed. "Don't you two go anywhere. I'll be right back as soon as I pour some drinks. I have to hear all about this."

And so, in between pouring drinks for customers, Myra heard most of Connie's life story and at least half of Woody's. Connie switched to ginger ale after two beers, but Woody had a few more. When they left at eleven he was speaking perfect English.

"That was fun, Connie, we'll have to do it again sometime. I think Myra or Brianna or whatever her name is, likes you. Even when she was talking to me, she was looking at you. You should seriously consider a relationship with her."

Connie laughed. "Is that right, Doctor MacPherson? Are you some sort of relationship expert?"

"I'm no expert at anything, but you'd have to be blind not to have seen the lady's interest. It was patently obvious the woman was eager to become at least a little more intimate with you."

Connie believed Woody was correct, but he wasn't going to admit it. "You saw all that? I think you had too many black and tans. How many did you have anyway?"

"Oh I don't know, five, six, you ought to know. You picked up the tab. How much was it?"

"Hard to tell how many you had. We ordered those appetizers and I'm not sure if Myra charged us for all the drinks. Regardless, you must have had enough to mildly influence your powers of perception."

Woody was silent for a bit. There was only the sound of the truck going down the highway. Connie looked over to see if he had fallen asleep. Woody was staring straight ahead. Finally he spoke. "You know why I'm living with Pete and Cally?"

"Because you get along, and you're friends, and they want you to be there?"

"That's all correct, but do you know the basis of our friendship?"

"Well, you've known Pete for years and you respect each other and ..."

Woody cut him off. "I'm talking about the basic reason that underlies all the other stuff."

"Ah, no, I guess I'm not sure what you mean."

"We can communicate, on every level. Think back on your relationship with your wife. From all I've heard you say, you two had a wonderful relationship. Why? I'll bet it was because you could communicate with each other. I'm not talking about agreeing on which movie to see or what kind of car to buy, I'm referring to being able to share your thoughts, ideas, hopes, prayers, and plans with no threat of misunderstanding. You didn't always have to agree, but even when you didn't there was no confusion or bruising of egos. I am of the opinion that effective communication between individuals is the single most important factor in any relationship."

Connie was tired. He'd been up since five-thirty and he'd become accustomed to going to bed early. He suspected Woody was correct, but there was no way he could effectively comprehend Woody's premise let alone debate it. "Woody, you're a good man and probably right, but what you just said is going to require serious thought on my part. Right now, I'm at a disadvantage because you've had at least twenty more years than I have to think this through. Do me a favor and remind me tomorrow of what you just said."

Connie was concentrating on the road and couldn't see Woody smile. "That bunkhouse mattress is looking good right now, isn't it?"

"Real good. I've only had two beers, but I feel as if I haven't slept for a week."

"That's just the rarefied mountain air. You'll get used to it."

"If that's what's doing it, I don't want to get used to it. I haven't slept as well in years."

"It gets better the higher up you go. When I was tending sheep in the high mountain pastures, the dogs would have to lick my face to wake me in the morning. I'd have preferred a woman's touch, but they were scarce where I was." He chuckled. "Although, one summer I talked this young lady into coming along with me. She stayed for three weeks. Used up all her vacation and sick time from her job and then went back to Cheyenne. I thought she'd had a good time, but when I returned to see her in the fall, she had a new beau. Alas, it was fun while it lasted."

"Fun while it lasted. That's a good thing to be able to say about an experience no matter how long or short."

Woody turned to Connie, "You know, boy, I believe you and I will be able to communicate."

The next morning at seven twenty-five, as Connie hoofed up to the big house for breakfast, he wondered how Woody was doing. They had gotten back before eleven-thirty so he should have been able to get almost eight hours of sleep. He hoped Woody wasn't late for breakfast. Connie didn't want to be accused of abetting delinquency in an old man. He need not have been concerned. When he entered the kitchen, everyone, but him was already seated at the table. He checked his watch and then the clock on the wall.

"I'm sorry. Am I late?"

Pete and Woody were chewing and didn't answer. The girls just giggled, but Cally got up and retrieved the coffee pot for him. "No, we just got started a little early is all. Woody was entertaining us with your exploits last night and I started cooking while I was listening. Please sit down. How many eggs would you like?"

"I'm having two," Lindsey announced. "Danni's only having one."

"Yeah, but I've got more pancakes than you, bacon too."

"Girls, girls, girls, give it a rest. It's Sunday you know. You're supposed to rest on Sunday and that goes for your mouths as well." Pete had finished chewing. "Let Connie talk to your mother."

"Thanks, Cally, but no eggs for me this morning. I think I'll just have cakes and bacon."

"What's the matter, Connie," asked Woody, "them two beers you had last night put you off your feed? I had three eggs."

"Were you in a contest with the girls?" Pete asked.

Connie laughed. Woody didn't. Cally changed the subject. "Woody tells us you met our resident retired movie star."

Cally was smiling when she said it, but Connie thought he detected just a subtle edge to her voice. He also wondered if he'd heard her stress the word "retired" as in old.

"Well, yeah, I guess we did. Seems nice enough for a Hollywood type." He wanted to minimize the conversation on this particular topic. He wondered how much Woody had already said.

"We know her daughter," Danni said.

"Yeah, she's gonna teach us how to ski this winter," offered Lindsey.

"Her name is Cyan," Danni again.

"Cyan is a color, not a name for a girl, especially a young woman," Connie told them.

"Well, that's her name. I think it's cool," responded Danni.

"She's a really good skier, Olympic quality," said Lindsey.

Connie smiled. "Oh yeah, that good?" It was much better to be talking about the movie star's daughter than the movie star. "And how is it she's going to teach you two how to ski?"

"She gives lessons at the ski school at Big Mountain. She teaches intermediates and since we already know how to ski, were not beginners anymore."

"Now girls," interrupted Cally, "it's not certain you'll be in her class. You have to pass the test first."

As if she refused to think about it, Lindsey changed the subject. "Will you come skiing with us Connie? If you don't know how, we can teach you."

"That's very kind of you, but I have no idea where I'll be this winter, after the futurity I mean." It suddenly dawned on him, he had no plans for the rest of his life after the futurity was over. That would be sometime shortly before Christmas. He could always haul Jolena back to Indianapolis, buy a hobby farm and ride with John and his wife.

Danni looked at him. "We don't want you to go."

"Well, Sweetie, that's very nice of you to say, but when the big contest is over, I'll have to be getting home." He had only been here just over two weeks and already the thought of leaving saddened him.

No one said anything for a while. The only sounds were forks clicking against plates. At least they were off the topic of Myra Foxx. Feeling responsible for killing the conversation, Connie tried to start it back up. "So where is this barbecue after church?"

"Billy Boissvert's ranch," Pete said. "He's had it every year since he's been a member of the church and that's been thirty years now. Puts on quite a spread; beef, chicken, pork, and all the trimmings. He and his wife take care of everything."

"Very impressive, not to mention generous."

"Yeah," said Woody, "He told me he had a debt he could never repay. Don't know what he did that was so bad, but when I'm eatin' his beef and chicken, I'm kinda glad he did it."

"Oh, Woody," Cally said, "That's no way to talk. He's just grateful to the church and demonstrating his hospitality."

"I'll agree, he is certainly demonstrating his hospitality."

Connie said. "I can't wait to meet him." He glanced at the clock. "What time do we leave for church?"

"Service starts at ten thirty. We should leave here by ten," Pete said. "The barbecue starts as soon as you get there after church."

"So do you dress for church or the picnic?"

"Most everyone dresses for church and then changes at the church. In our case, we stop back here because Boissvert's place is just up the road about five miles."

Okay, Connie thought, that made things easy. He drained his coffee cup, pushed back his chair and excused himself. He had things to do. "I'll see to the horses," he told Pete.

Lindsey jumped up. "I want to help. Can I?"

"Sit back down, young lady, and finish your breakfast. As I recall you were just bragging about how many eggs you were having."

"She just wants to get out of dishes," Danni said.

Connie heard a brief flurry of words exchanged between the girls as he went out the door. He smiled. "Firecrackers, I believe that's how Woody referred to them," he said out loud.

Later, after he had tended to Jolena and the rest of the horses, he inventoried the clothing he'd brought with him. He finally settled on dark blue, lightweight wool slacks and a silk cotton blend, khaki colored, sport coat over an all cotton, white shirt with a multicolored silk tie that defied description. He was the picture of casual elegance. He wondered if Myra would still think he looked like a cowboy. A knock on his door ended the thought.

It was Danni. "Wow," she told him, "you look really nice."

"Well, thank you, Danni. You look really nice yourself." She was wearing a dress.

She blushed and informed him they were ready to leave. "Can I ride with you? Mom says we'll have to take two cars."

"Sure you can ride with me if you don't mind riding in a truck."

" Yippee, your truck is way cool. Can I sit in the front seat?"

"Sure, I can turn off the airbag, but you have to wear your seatbelt."

"Oh wow, let's go."

When Lindsey saw Danni in the front seat, she wanted to ride with Connie too, but Cally told her to stay put and if it was okay with Connie, she could ride back with him. So Connie and Danni in Connie's truck followed the rest of the family in Cally's sedan.

"So are you gonna go on a date with Brianna? Woody says she likes you."

"Woody said that?"

"Yeah, he told us that at breakfast. He said it was real obvious she was 'enamored' with you? What 's enamored mean?"

"It means fascinated. Do you believe everything Woody tells you?"

"No, he's a big fibber. One time he told us there were fish in the creek that were bigger than we were. "

"Well, this might be a time when Woody is telling you a big fish story."

"You mean she's not fascinated with you?"

"I don't think she is."

"Do you think she likes you?"

"I don't know."

"Do you like her?"

Connie was beginning to wonder if Danni wasn't sent along for the sole purpose of extracting information from him. "She seems very nice and I generally like most people who are nice to me."

"Mom is nice to you. Do you like her too?"

"Yes, I do. I think your mother is a wonderful person."

Danni was quiet for a moment, contemplating her next question. "So are you going to take her on a date?"

"Who are we talking about, Brianna or your mom?"

"Either one."

"Well, Miss Nosey, I don't think it would be appropriate for me to ask your mother for a date and as far as the movie star is concerned, I don't think I know her well enough to ask her for a date either."

"If you did take her out, where would you go?"

Connie laughed. "Why are you so interested in me and Brianna anyway?"

"Just curious. I mean she's a big star. Where could you take her around here? Mom says she owns the best place for a hundred miles."

So, thought Connie, some of this is coming from Cally. He wondered why. "Okay, Danni, here's the deal. If two people like each other it doesn't matter where they go as long as they're with each other. Or, maybe I'll just take her to the airport and we'll fly to New York City and we'll go to the fanciest restaurant in town."

"That would cost a lot."

"Didn't Woody tell you? I've got tons of money." He was relieved when they finally arrived at the church.

Chapter 20, Too Many Options

The church building surprised Connie. He had pictured a classic white chapel somewhere in or near downtown Kalispell. This facility was a sprawling affair of brick and stone, located on the southwest edge of town and recognizable as a church only by the cross and bell tower.

"How many people go to your church?" he asked Danni as they walked from the truck to where the rest of the family had parked.

"I don't know, lots I guess. Grandpa says only half of them ever show up. Did you go to church where you used to live?"

"Sometimes."

"Didn't you like to go all the time?"

How could Connie explain to a nine year old his concept of organized religion when he wasn't certain of it himself? For years he'd harbored a nagging suspicion that highly organized religion was more often than not, the enemy of God. He was dead certain it was highly political, and beyond that he suspected it was seriously compromised by ego, greed, and the desire for domination. It wasn't just Christianity that suffered these hypocritical abuses, but all religions conceived and practiced by man.

"No, not all the time."

"Me either, Lindsey always likes to go, but sometimes I'd rather stay home and go for a walk by myself." She took Connie's hand. "You ever feel like that?"

Connie was amazed. He was certain he didn't have thoughts like this when he was only nine. If he did, he definitely couldn't remember talking about them. "Well, yes, I guess I have."

Lindsey came running up, latched on to his other hand and the two of them swept him into the church. Connie was thoroughly noticed and scrutinized as he was led down an aisle by the twins as they followed close behind Cally, Pete, and Woody. There was a fair amount of speculation on whom Connie might be. A visiting relative maybe, or some out of town friend of the family perhaps, or could it be Cally had found a man after all these years? It was apparent the twins were fond of him whoever he was.

The guessing continued until shortly before the sermon when the minister asked if there were any visitors in the congregation. Connie would have blown off the invitation to stand and be recognized, but the twins wouldn't allow it. He stood, gave his name, and said he was a guest of Pete Browning. Fortunately there were several other visitors in the crowd and he was welcomed, but not asked for more details. Some of the more inquisitive members of the congregation weren't satisfied by Connie's response and continued to speculate on his true nature. Several female members, in particular, hoped he would also be tagging along with the Browning family to the barbecue because they definitely wanted to meet him.

The minister spoke about new beginnings and second chances and how with God there can always be another chance to get yourself right. Connie found himself thinking about all the things that had changed for him since Sarah had gotten sick and died. He remembered how she'd suffered and how he'd agonized while she did, and then mourned her passing. He considered his near disastrous bout with alcoholism and self-pity and how a little paint horse had lifted him up and brought him here. Coincidence or divine design, he didn't know and didn't care; he was pleased with the new beginning that had found him. Just before the minister said the final "Amen", he wondered where it would lead.

After the service, Lindsey and Danni led him out the same way they led him in. It was as if they were showing him off, which even if they didn't realize it, was exactly what they were doing. They paraded him through the reception line where he shook hands with the preacher, a man about at least ten years younger than Connie with the build of a professional bull rider, short, stocky, and muscular. Up close, several scars on the preacher's face were prominent. Connie made a mental note to find out more about him.

Woody was right behind Connie in the line and when he cleared the preacher, he said to Connie, "Let's vamoose. I told Pete and Cally I was ridin' with you and the young ladies."

"Young ladies? You know some nice young ladies? All I see around here are these two wood ticks hangin' on me."

Lindsey slapped him with her free hand and Danni laughed. "That's me, a giant wood tick and I'm never gonna let you go."

"You'll have to go back to school in the fall."

"I'll take you with me."

"Will your teacher be cute?"

Lindsey made a face. "No way, it's gonna be crabby Missus Getzke. She's mean."

"Well then, you are definitely going back to school in the fall without me. Besides I have to ride Jolena."

"Well, Miss Tick," said Woody, "you're gonna have to let him go right now cuz he's gotta drive us home so we can change clothes for the barbecue."

The twins reluctantly released Connie and hopped into the back seat of the truck. "Buckle up, young ladies or ticks, whichever the case may be," Connie commanded and they were off. Connie's departure without Cally was noted by at least two interested parties.

It was warm, but not hot, so Connie exchanged his church clothes for blue jeans and a polo shirt. He thought it would be a good time to break in one of his new pairs of Cinch jeans. He hoped they wouldn't shrink much when he washed them because they already fit him snug enough. Woody and Pete were attired likewise and all the girls wore shorts, but they all had the legs for them. It was decided that taking two vehicles to go only a few miles would be silly, so everyone piled into Connie's pickup. Cally, Woody and the twins rode in the back, Danni sharing Cally's seatbelt and Pete rode shotgun.

Boissvert already had half a crowd when they got there, and the twins vaporized into the swirling mist of kids. Cally went off to see if she could help Missus Boissvert. Pete, Woody, and Connie drifted over to where a group of about forty men were standing around the barbecue pit watching the meat cook. The beef and pork had been slow-cooking since sunrise. The chickens had gone on about eight. Connie was impressed. He'd heard the term "open pit barbecue', but this was the genuine article, a hole in the ground three feet wide and eight feet long, full of glowing hardwood coals. Suspended over the top of the pit were sturdy, stainless steel rods laden with beef roasts, quartered pigs, and whole chickens. Connie was reminded of a poster he had once seen for a medieval renaissance fair. "Authentic Middle Ages Food" the poster had proclaimed and except for the clothing worn by the people standing and watching, the two scenes were almost identical. *Must be something innately interesting about watching meat roast,* Connie mused.

Pete and Woody knew everybody and took turns introducing Connie. Pete referred to him as the son of a respected friend whom he was coaching to ride in the cutting horse futurity. Connie was surprised by how many people knew nothing about cutting horses or the futurity. Here he was in the middle of the Old West, prime horse country, and at least a third of the men he met had never been on a horse. Connie even met a guy who owned a plastic pipe and fitting business. He wanted to talk shop and, no surprise, Connie found the topic incredibly boring. Maybe Woody had been correct when he told Myra Foxx that Connie was a real cowboy.

As more people arrived, the number of women whose services were not needed by Missus Boissvert increased dramatically and the group of men quickly became populated with wives, sweethearts, and unattached females. It was by this latter category of women that Connie suddenly found himself to be an item. First there was, a nice looking lady Connie guessed to be in her late forties who knew Woody and asked him to introduce Connie. Then Pete introduced him to another who looked to be younger and just as attractive as the first woman. Pete explained she was the daughter of an old friend, long since gone. She was almost as tall as Connie. And then there was a third woman who walked up and introduced herself. She was a short, good looking, blonde with a great physique, and couldn't have been a day over thirty-two. The other two women seemed to resent the intrusion, but no one made a move to leave.

They wanted to know all about Connie, where he was from, what he did, why he was here, and how long was he planning to stay. None of them were captivated by his story of buying Jolena and entering the futurity, but they were all encouraged by the fact he would be around until at least the middle of December. They thought that would be plenty of time to get something going, and all three were doing mental gymnastics over how to proceed. These women, who had sought Connie out, were not desperate but they were lonely. They all had a desire to be loved.

It didn't take Connie long to become uncomfortable with the attention. Even though they seemed nice enough, he suddenly wanted to extricate himself from their conversational clutches. He now had some indication of how Sarah felt at his sister's party the night he met her. He wanted to be rescued.

Fortunately, Cally had been relieved of her duties in the kitchen and had observed the development of Connie's dilemma. Initially she found it humorous, but when the blonde with the knockout body stepped in, she actually became jealous and then wondered why. Finally, she saw Connie's posture stiffen and took it as a sign he was uncomfortable. She scanned the roving cyclone of kids for her daughters.

Spotting them, she was able to motion them over. "Hey girls, are you having fun?"

"We were," Lindsey told her. "What do you want?"

She nodded in Connie's direction. "You see Connie over there?"

"Yeah, with all the ladies," said Danni.

"You two go and get him for me, will you please?" Without a word and no hesitation, they blasted off on their mission. Cally smiled. What were kids for if you couldn't get them to do a little dirty work for you once in a while?

Suddenly, much to Connie's relief, not one, but two damsels burst upon the scene to rescue him from the dragons. "Mom says she wants you," Lindsey told him and she and Danni each grabbed a hand and pulled him out of the fire. Connie had another fleeting thought, this time about Cally wanting him, but quickly decided he couldn't be too literal with anything a nine-year old would say. He was, however grateful for the interruption. The three ladies weren't happy with Lindsey's choice of words, but still remained optimistic.

When he was delivered to Cally, he said, "Thank you and how can I possibly make your day any better?'

Cally laughed. "I just need to get your keys so I can get my purse. I left it in your truck."

"I'll go retrieve it for you and save you the trip."

"Why don't we go together? I could use the exercise. I've been grazing on all the food in the kitchen."

To an observer knowing nothing of Connie and Cally's relationship, it could have appeared as if a wife just sent her children to retrieve her husband. The wife seemed amused, the husband seemed appreciative, and then they walked off together. The three women who had corralled Connie didn't see it quite that way because they had additional information, but the nature of Connie and Cally's involvement was puzzling. Two of the women decided they needed to do more covert research before they made any overt moves. The third was wondering if Connie and Cally had a relationship; could she separate Connie from Cally? While seduction was not her primary specialty, she had the tools and she knew how to use them.

"Certainly is a friendly group of people," Connie said as he and Cally walked to the field where all the vehicles were parked.

"For the most part. You're also new. Everyone wants to know how you're connected."

"Is there a pecking order?"

"That might be a little harsh, but there is an order of sorts."

"Where do you fit in?"

She smiled. "Oh, way up at the top. I was born into it. Dad and Mom were charter members. They helped build the first church over fifty years ago."

"Was it a little white chapel in town?"

"Yeah, you've seen it?"

"No, but that's how I pictured it."

"You got it right. It's still there, but we outgrew it about twenty years ago."

"That's when you built the new one?"

"No, that's only eight years old. We rented a building on the east side of town for twelve years. It wasn't supposed to be that long, but the congregation seemed to stagnate and we weren't growing."

"You get a new preacher after you moved out of the little white chapel?"

"Yeah, the old one got sick and died and we were sent one right out of divinity school. I don't know if he was tired, lazy or incompetent. He certainly wasn't inspirational. We finally booted him out after six years. That was messy, but then we got lucky with Sean, the preacher we have now. He was a rodeo cowboy until the day he was thrown from a bull, stomped on, and tossed around enough to where he saw the light. Went back to school to become a minister. You'll have to ask him to tell you the story."

"I thought he looked a bit indelicate to be your ordinary Doctor of Divinity."

"He claims he learned more in the hospital and physical therapy about the true nature of God than he did in four years of seminary."

Connie laughed. He'd never thought of that, but he knew what the preacher meant. "Yeah, I'll bet he's right." He dug in his pocket for the key to his pickup. He punched the button. "Pain has a way of cutting through the mundane."

Cally opened the back door and looked for her purse. "Not there. I must have carried it up to the house."

"Sure you brought it?"

"You ever forget your wallet?"

"Rarely, if ever," and then he realized the implication of the question. "Sorry, dumb question."

She closed the door. Patting him gently on the shoulder she said. "That's okay, you can't help it, you're a man." She knew exactly where her purse was. She'd needed a reason to have the twins summon him and retrieving her purse from his truck was the best thing she could think of. Her purse was in Missus Boissvert's bedroom along with those of a dozen other women. "Let's go back to the house. I must have set it down somewhere in there."

"You suppose you could introduce me to Sean sometime?"

"I'll introduce you now if you want. I saw his little boy just a few minutes ago, so I'm sure he and his wife are here." She was tempted to add she'd much prefer Connie talking to the preacher than that little blonde bimbo and for the life of her she couldn't understand why she was being jealous. She thought about her recent comment about Connie being a man and therefore asking dumb questions. Maybe it was woman's nature to be jealous of other women or at least jealous of good-looking women with great bodies.

As they walked back to the house, Cally scanned the crowd for the preacher. When she spotted him she steered Connie that way and they spent the next twenty minutes talking to Sean and his wife. Connie immediately liked them. They knew all about cutting horses and both of them had even ridden a few. Connie's newly acquainted lady friends took this long conversation with the preacher as a bad sign. For all they could guess, Connie and Cally could be asking Sean to marry them. One of the three decided she needed to act fast. She'd have to make some type of move today. The dinner bell started ringing. She'd have to wait at least a little while.

Billy Boissvert announced dinner over a loudspeaker. After explaining how the food was laid out on four separate tables, all identical, he called on Sean for grace. After the brief prayer, Billy took the microphone back and welcomed the congregation to dig in. Pete, Cally, and Connie sat at a table with the preacher and his wife. Preacher Sean wanted to hear all about Jolena. Connie couldn't tell him much but Pete could, and Connie heard a few things about her he didn't know.

"I was real surprised by her color," Pete said. "I'm still not sure where the grulla came from."

"Well, grulla is black modified by the dun factor," said the preacher's wife who had knowledge of equine color genetics, "So she has to have at least one gene for black and there must be a dun or buckskin in there somewhere."

Pete considered this for a moment. "Okay, so where did the white come from?"

"You said Doc Olena was her grandsire. He produced a fair number of paint crop outs. No one is sure why that happens, but it has been happening for a long time. There are pictures of paint horses on the walls of the tombs of the ancient Egyptian pharaohs."

"I know Doc Olena made some paint babies, but I don't think he ever produced one as flashy as Jolena."

"Some people think parti-colored horses aren't as tough as solids," offered Sean.

"Yeah, I've heard that said. I've also never seen any evidence to prove them right. Not even anecdotal," countered Pete.

"Define tough," said Connie.

"I don't buy it either," said Sean, 'but the belief is that fair skinned horses are generally less durable in all ways."

"They must have some durability if they've been around since the pharaohs. Jolena was foaled the same day my wife died. That's what drew my attention to her at the auction. Now that I've been associated with her for several weeks, I believe she'll be as durable as she needs to be."

"What time of day did your wife die?" Pete asked.

"Late evening, I'm not sure exactly. Why?"

"Jolena was born shortly before ten at night."

Connie smiled just to reassure everyone he was okay talking about his wife's death. "Well, taking the time zones into consideration, Jolena could be a reincarnation of my wife. In that case, I'm glad I ended up with her."

Sean laughed. "I doubt your horse is anyone's reincarnation, but I know for a fact there's a Charbray bull by the name of Bodacious that is a close relative of Satan himself."

"I've heard of him. No one's ever successfully ridden him, right?"

"Six cowboys out of a hundred and thirty-five and I'm told I was one who didn't, although my memory of the actual ride is a bit unclear. I recall sitting on him in the chute. He was calm and I was thinking I'd drawn a winner. I was only the second rider to get on his back, at least officially. I don't know what happened to the first,

Bodacious didn't have a reputation yet. In fact his name at the time was 'J thirty-one' and he was an eighteen hundred pound Charlais cow and Brahma bull cross. I helped establish his reputation. When the gate opened he took two steps and started jumping. I banged my face against his head almost immediately and things got hazy."

His wife, Ellie, laughed. "Not for me they didn't. We were recently engaged, and when he went flying I can remember thinking I must be crazy to take up with a bull rider. I was horrified when he hit the ground and the bull went after him. I can still see it as if it just happened. He was groggy and couldn't get out of the way fast enough.

First he was kicked by the bull's back legs. Then Bodacious stomped him, rolled him a few times, stomped him some more, and then flipped him over the fence, right out of the arena He looked like a rag doll flying, which he was with all his broken bones.

Connie was amazed. "Jesus, oops sorry. I mean, golly, what did he do to you?"

Sean laughed. "If I'd been conscious, I'd have been calling for Jesus too, but I didn't wake up for a week and when I did I wanted to be back in a coma. He broke my arms, one leg, half-a-dozen ribs, and cracked my pelvis and sternum. I had over a hundred stitches in my head and face, and another two hundred in the rest of me. I had a fractured skull and a subdural hematoma. That was the most dangerous. Everything else just hurt."

"It's amazing you're not in a wheelchair."

"Spent some time in one. You know, for about a month after I regained consciousness I thought I was going to ride again."

"What changed your mind?"

"I believe life altering experiences have two distinct parts. First there is the action, which in my case was getting beat up by a nasty bovine. The second part of the experience is the reaction. Now that a bull has kicked my butt and I'm half dead, what do I do about it? The reaction can be a planned or unplanned response, spontaneous or well thought out. Initially, my thought was to get back on, not necessarily that bull, but a different, kinder, more gentle bull. Then I began to wonder if there was any future in what I was doing. I was good, but so what, I was almost killed. Who really wants to be good at almost getting killed? Well, after about a month of lying in bed encased in plaster, I began to get scared and anxious. The days weren't so bad, but the nights were horrible. Sometimes I'd wake up all disoriented and confused. I'd start screaming. Eventually a nurse would show up and talk me down. I became claustrophobic and probably neurotic, and I believe I came close to a complete breakdown. That's when I finally prayed for help. That same night I woke up in a panic and was about to start screaming when I noticed someone sitting at the end of my bed. I couldn't tell if it was a man or a woman, the person had his back towards me. I said something about I was glad he was here. That's when the person turned and I beheld the calmest face I'd ever seen, but I still couldn't tell if the person was male or female. No words were spoken, I just received the thought, 'Follow me,' and wondered what it meant.

"I can tell you it used to be the motto of the US Army Infantry School at Fort Benning, Georgia," said Connie.

"It's also what Jesus said when choosing some of his disciples. In any case, I didn't have a clue, but when I thought about asking my visitor for clarification, he or she was gone. It took me another week to decide I'd had a vision and that I was supposed to become a preacher. I had been called, so to speak."

"And so here you are."

'Yup, and how about you? Your wife died, and on what would appear to be a whim, you bought a cutting horse and here you are. Sounds to me as if you've had a life altering experience, also."

Connie thought briefly. "I suspect you're right. Not the first. The most profound so far, but not the first and there may even be more to come. I do like your theory though, about them having two parts."

"Yeah, I think you always get a choice."

And the choices for the rest of the afternoon were plentiful. There were games and races for the kids, horseshoe pitching and softball for the adults, and plenty of socializing. It was a good, old-fashioned picnic with terrific food. Over five hundred souls attended the affair. Connie played second base in the softball game for a while, long enough for his blonde admirer to get on base. Cally was playing center field and saw the woman put her hand on Connie's shoulder and hand him a slip of paper. She correctly assumed it was a phone number, but she didn't see Connie throw it away after the game.

Chapter 21, The Grind

They left Boissvert's at six in the afternoon as the barbecue was wearing down. Most everyone had eaten seconds and thirds and others quit counting. Connie was in this latter group. It was, food wise, the best outdoor meal of any kind he'd ever attended. He'd amazed himself with his intake. At eight thirty, after seeing to Jolena and the other horses, he dropped on his bed in the bunkhouse and was asleep as his head made contact with the pillow.

Cally woke at two in the morning and, rolling over in bed, looked out her window and saw the light on in the bunk house. It had been on when she'd gone to bed at ten and it was still on. She wondered if she should pull on a robe and investigate. She could knock quietly on the back door. Maybe peek in to see how he was doing if he didn't answer. *No, I can't do that.* She rolled over, turning her back on her window and the bunk house light. She had all kinds of confusing thoughts as she tried to get back to sleep. Foremost among them was wondering if Connie would take the blonde from the picnic up on surely what must have been her offer of something.

Cally hadn't shared her bed with a man for almost eight years. She suddenly felt as if she had missed a lot. If she'd known Connie better, a lot better, she might have gone down to say goodnight. But she didn't know him nearly well enough for that. Sleep eluded her for the rest of the night. She was too concerned about what she imagined had transpired on second base between Connie and the blonde. *Second base is within scoring distance.*

After breakfast and morning chores, Connie and Pete saddled two horses and rode out to one of the back pastures where Pete was grazing about fifty head of cattle. They split the little herd in half and pushed two dozen cows back to the arena.

Connie started his training with a couple of succinct words of advice from Pete. "What's the first rule?"

"Watch the cow."

"Correct. If you're working a cow, I don't care if Cally walks up to the fence stark naked, don't take your eyes off the cow. You were lucky last time. We can't afford any more down time."

Connie smiled. "Yes, sir!" although he knew if Cally showed up naked, he'd have to peek, at least once.

After each cow, Pete critiqued him. Mostly it was so obvious that even Connie knew what he'd done wrong. Cows blew past him and his mount as if they weren't there. Pete was patient and thorough, but after two hours and three horses, he called a halt.

"We'll let it rest until tomorrow. Any more and you'll be going backwards."

Slouching in the saddle, Connie allowed his disappointment to show.

"Connie, I've been doin' this for seventy years. The reason I'm still doin' it is because I haven't mastered it yet. You weren't good, but you will get better. You didn't fall, and that's a major improvement over last time. How long did it take you before you could coax anything resembling music out of that fiddle you got in the bunkhouse?"

"I don't know, three or four weeks maybe."

"Well, I guarantee you that in three or four weeks you'll be playin' sweet music with those cows. In fact, in five weeks you'll be riding in a competition in Polson.

"Serious?"

"Yup. It'll be your first competition. Now, I don't expect you to win it, but I'll be surprised if you don't do well—maybe even finish in the money."

"Does that mean I really didn't do all that bad this morning?"

"Oh no, you were terrible, but you have good balance and in a month, you'll know enough to be able to follow Billy's lead."

"Billy's lead?"

"Yeah, you'll be ridin' Billy?"

"Billy? What about Jolena? I'm confused. Who's Billy?"

Pete chuckled. "I guess I didn't explain the rules real well. You can't ride Jolena in any kind of contest before the Futurity itself."

"She doesn't get to practice?"

"She gets to practice plenty, just not in organized contests. The Futurity is her big debut."

"Wow. So this Billy, he's good, too?"

"Good enough to win the Polson contest and then some."

Pete motioned to the cows bunched up at the back of the arena. "You want to ride Jo, do it quick. I'll chase these cows back into the pasture. Be back by noon. We've got to start makin' hay after lunch."

Connie rode Jo out across the creek and started up the trail into the hills where he had ridden all last week. Then on a whim he turned off the trail and into the timber. Dodging trees might be a little like cutting cows he thought. After less than two minutes he decided it wasn't at all like cutting cows. He decided to get back to the trail before he got lost with all the twisting and turning he was doing. Then he recognized a path of some sort just ahead. Taking careful note of where the trail was, he pushed ahead another fifty yards and found himself on another old trail of sorts. It ran at an oblique angle to the trail he was familiar with and if he followed it to the left, he correctly surmised, it would eventually take him back to the ranch southeast of where he had entered the woods.

After several minutes of following the track, he decided it must be an old overgrown logging road, only a narrow track of which had been kept open by deer and elk. As he and Jo meandered quietly along, aspen leaves and pine needles brushed and tugged at them, but no big trees blocked the path. It was as if they were riding down a long green tunnel. Just as they were approaching the end of the trees, Jolena stopped and snorted. Her head was up, her eyes wide and her ears pinned back. Connie felt the hair on the back of his neck rise. Then there was a flash of yellow and then another and another. If he'd have blinked, he'd have missed it. A lion and her two cubs had dashed across the path in front of him and were gone in two heartbeats, one of his and one of Jo's.

"Wow, Jo! Did you see that?" Obviously she had, she'd warned him. "I've never seen a mountain lion before." Neither had Jo, but instinctive, tribal memory recognized her mortal enemy.

Connie had been told lions kill by jumping on the horse's back and biting through the neck to the spine, avoiding the animal's powerful kicking hooves. He suddenly realized they must be the primary reason horses have to be trained to allow a rider on their back. "Wait 'til I tell the girls I saw Simba."

Thinking of the twins reminded him of the time. Checking his watch, he was running late. When he and Jolena made their exit from the trees onto the ranch road along the big hay meadow, Connie turned Jo towards the house and asked her for some speed. Anticipating the acceleration, he leaned forward, but still felt Jo's powerful take off trying to roll him backwards. In about ten strides she was up to full speed and the first quarter mile flicked past in less than thirty seconds. Then Connie remembered what Pete had said about not galloping her and gently reined her back down to a smooth lope. She got him back to the barn in plenty of time to make lunch.

"Hey, Lindsey," he said when there was a lull in the conversation. "Guess what I saw this morning."

"I don't know, give me a hint."

"No hints, not yet. Danni, you want to guess?"

Tilting her head to one side, she made an elaborate gesture of great thought. "The tooth fairy?" and she giggled.

"No, not the tooth fairy, but something real and almost as hard to see."

Now she was interested. What could be real and as hard to see as the tooth fairy? "I don't know. I need a hint."

"You were talking about it just a few days ago."

"Um, a picnic at Rogers Lake."

Lindsey rolled her eyes. "Sure Danni, picnics are real hard to see. We just saw one yesterday."

"Well I don't know. I can't remember what we were talking about a few days ago."

"I'll bet I know," said Woody.

"How would you know? I was talking about it."

"Well, you mighta been talkin' about it, but I was listenin' and unlike you, I can remember somethin' for more than two minutes."

"Okay, smarty, what was it?"

"Sure you want me to say? You all done guessin'?"

Danni thought a minute. "Yeah, you can guess. I'll bet you're not right anyway."

"Connie saw a mountain lion."

Both girls looked at Connie. "Is Woody right? Did you see Simba?"

"Well I didn't inquire as to what her name was, but I did see a lion and she had two kittens."

"It must be Simba," insisted Lindsey.

"Mom, can we go look for her after lunch?" Danni asked.

Cally smiled when she answered, "Yes, but you have to stay in the yard. You can sit on the porch and look for her with the binoculars."

"Aw Mom, we want to ride out to where Connie saw her and look for her."

"Don't be silly. I'm not going to let two little girls ride out into the woods to look for lions and furthermore if I hear any more about it, you won't even get to look for her from the porch."

The ultimatum had been delivered and they knew further discussion would be pointless and could even get them in trouble."

"I get to use the binoculars first," said Danni.

Lindsey shrugged, "There's two pair and besides it'll be boring to just sit on the porch and watch for her."

"You don't have to watch, I can do it all by myself."

"Girls, girls, girls, school hasn't been out one whole day and I'm already waiting for it to start." Cally slowly shook her head.

"I could use help in the arena," Pete said. "How about tomorrow you two ladies ride turn back for Connie?"

They quickly agreed that would be far superior to anything else they could be doing including sitting on the porch staring at the tree line through binoculars. And they didn't even complain about doing the dishes.

By two o-clock, after an intensive lesson in cutting hay, Connie was blissfully knocking down grass with the mower conditioner at the rate of about four acres per hour all by himself. He did the math and decided he'd either have to cut faster or start earlier in the day if Pete intended to get his entire five hundred acres of hay cut and baled in two weeks. He made a note to talk to Pete. At three o-clock, Cally brought him some lemonade and cookies, and at six after cutting about twenty acres, he rolled his rig back up to the barn. For sitting all afternoon, he was surprisingly tired.

At dinner he asked Pete how he planned to get all the meadow cut in just two weeks and Pete explained the process. Hopefully while you're cutting tomorrow, I can bale up what you cut today. I've got another mower and Woody will start cutting tomorrow too. It's not as big as the one you're using, but with both of you cutting and me baling, we'll get it all done in two weeks or less. I called the hay broker this afternoon and they'll be here on Wednesday to start picking up what we get baled."

"You sell it all to a broker?"

"Almost all of it. They charge fifteen percent, but they pick it up and I don't have to store it or deliver it. It's well worth it."

"Yeah, we don't have to deal with the customer neither," added Woody. People are absolutely goofy about hay, specially horse people. Some of 'em want all grass, some want half grass and half alfalfa, and some want all alfalfa. The best hay is whatever each one of 'em thinks is the best."

"So what is the best?" asked Connie.

"As long as it's clean and fresh, it really doesn't matter," Pete said. "It doesn't take as much alfalfa as grass, but you usually don't have to worry about them overeating with grass hay."

"So what am I cutting? All grass?"

"Yeah, it's a mixture of five different grasses. We can sell it all because not many people specialize in grass hay. Most everybody favors alfalfa and clean grass hay is not always easy to find."

"Yeah," Woody chimed in, "We're what you call a niche farm."

Back in the bunkhouse, after supper, Connie was tired, but restless. He wanted to do something, but didn't know what. He sat in his new chair and looked around him. There were no books, no TV, no computer and he suddenly felt lonely, detached from his former life, the pleasant life he had lived with Sarah back east in the city. Here he was, sitting in a rustic bunkhouse, by himself, fifteen miles from town and Sarah was gone. He thought about jumping in the truck and driving to Whitefish. Maybe Myra would be at the Rustlers and they could talk. Consulting his watch, he realized it was too late. He needed a shower, the round trip to Whitefish would take an hour and he had to get up at five in the morning. He laughed. "Not even eight and it's too late. Wow, am I a player or what?"

He looked around the room again. He saw his fiddle sitting on the shelf where he had placed it when he'd first arrived. He pulled himself out of his chair to retrieve it. For a while he just held it, examining and inspecting it almost as looking for a flaw or some reason not to attempt to play it. Finding only meticulous craftsmanship and the beauty of highly figured wood, he slowly became interested. He plucked the strings one at a time. The instrument was horribly out of tune. He went to find the case. In there was an electronic tuner, rosin, and his old music books.

An hour later, he placed the violin and bow back on the shelf. He was pleased, no longer itching with restlessness. He'd been as bad with the fiddle as he'd been at cutting cows in the morning. *Why is it nothing good comes easy*? He didn't know the answer, but decided he was ultimately going to find one.

The next morning, he, Pete and the twins started in the arena at eight. Woody volunteered to do dishes so the girls could ride. They and Pete would ride turn back to prevent the cow Connie was cutting from running away to the opposite end of the arena. They would keep the cow turned back in front of Connie.

"Remember," cautioned Pete, "you're on a different horse. Billy is a stick of dynamite compared to Fritz. But, he's no smarter, just a lot quicker. Try to anticipate."

Connie was initially nervous, but quickly discovered he wasn't any worse riding Billy. He also discovered Lindsey and Danni were better riders than he was. In the process of turning the cows back to him, he saw them both make more than one maneuver he'd be proud to have accomplished. Danni and her mount, in particular, made a long sliding stop up against the fence and rolled back immediately in front of the cow, sending it back to Connie who cleverly let it blow right past.

Later, when he and Pete were alone, Connie asked, "Why don't you have one of those girls ride Jolena? They're both better than I'll ever be." Connie was only half joking.

"You feeling sorry for yourself?"

It wasn't the response Connie was expecting. "Huh? No. Why?"

"Connie, those two little girls can ride, but they're little girls. They have fun, but it's fun because they're out with you and me. They aren't motivated by any contest or show of skill. They're helping us. They're interested because we are, not because they have a goal to be the best."

Connie wondered what his motivation was. "I'm not feeling sorry for myself." It was the only thing he could think of saying.

"Good, because you have no reason to. I'd like you to take this serious, but I don't want it to be a chore. If it is, you might as well hang up your saddle now, because if you're not having fun, you're not ever going to get better. Relax, sit easy in the saddle. If you blow a cow, there's another, and another after that, and when your horse gets tired, there's more of them, too. But if you get tired of it you're done."

"When you're training a horse, you always want to stop for the day on a positive note. It doesn't have to be much, maybe just one step in the right direction or a good stop when you say whoa. Just that simple bit of correct behavior means a lot to a horse. They have terrific memories and tomorrow, they'll be a little better." He looked at Connie eye to eye. "Am I making any sense?"

"Yeah, I guess. Maybe I was feeling somewhat sorry for myself."

"Well you don't want to or need to. That last cow you worked quit. He didn't get past you; he quit in front of you. That was good. You're also not a bad rider. Your timing could use improvement, but that will happen without you trying."

"Thanks, Pete, I'll remember that for tomorrow."

Pete laughed. "I hope your memory is as good as a horse's."

It was eleven by the time Connie started cutting hay and after lunch he was back at it, joined by Woody pulling another mower and Pete with the baler. Pete soon had everything Connie had cut the day before baled up and was long gone when he and Woody quit for the day.

That evening after supper he had a beer with Woody and later when Woody went back up to the big house, he practiced playing his fiddle until the tips of the fingers on his left hand were sore. At nine-thirty, just before he fell asleep, he thought maybe he'd go to the Rustlers on Saturday.

The following day was a repeat of the previous, except just about the time Connie figured the lesson was due to end, Pete told him, "I've got to run up to the house. Why don't you saddle up Jolena and you can try her on a cow or two."

Connie had her tacked up and was warming her up in the arena before Pete returned. When he finished, Jo stood calmly, but sitting on her back Connie felt as if he was wound like a tightly coiled spring.

"Go in the herd and bring out a cow," said Pete. "If it runs off, let it go and go back in and get another."

They had been working this little herd for two hours and the cows were starting to sour. As he steered Jolena into the herd, Connie searched for one he hadn't worked yet. He settled on a medium sized bull calf with no outstanding markings that he thought he hadn't chased before. Moving the reins left and right he gently walked Jo towards it. Suddenly there was a defining moment when Jo recognized the cow he had chosen and he in turn recognized Jo's awareness. It was then, he knew that she knew and the realization that they were a team hit home. He wasn't going to work this cow on his own, he had help. He hadn't felt this with either Fritz or Billy. A smile slowly eased across his face. "Okay, Jo," he whispered, "let's see what we can do."

The two of them cleanly separated the calf from the herd and turned it easily towards Pete and the girls. As Connie moved the cow in their direction, they began slowly riding towards Connie and Jo. Faced with the two mounted riders, the cow turned back towards Connie and stopped. Connie and Jo stopped. There was a brief standoff until Connie dropped the reins firmly on Jo's neck and tightened his grip on the saddle horn. Good thing too, because when Jo felt his hand come down she lunged towards the calf. The calf squirted off to its left, but Jo was there, in its face. He lunged right and then left and then right again, but each time Jo was in front of him. Finally he made a long dash towards the fence and when he realized he was not going to get past Jolena, he spun around and blew through the turn back riders all the way to the far end of the arena.

"Sorry, Connie," Lindsey called out. "I couldn't stop him."

Pete was laughing. "Nothing to be sorry for, Lindsey. Connie just had the best ride of his life." He rode over to Connie and extended his hand. "You do three in a row like that in two and a half minutes and you'll win every time."

Connie was breathing hard. Jolena wasn't. He took Pete's hand and shook it. "Yeah, it felt good," was all he could say.

"Let's end on that note. You and me and the girls can walk these cows back to the pasture and we'll call it a morning."

Connie put that ride on an endless loop and played it over and over as he cut hay. He was distracted by lunch and afterward was glad to be back in the tractor where he could again replay the thirty-second tape that had suddenly given him understanding. He now knew why Pete was still riding and why his friend John drove all the way to the auction in Oklahoma to find the best cutting horses he could afford. It had been an amazing, exhilarating, adrenaline-pumping rush. Hooves were pounding, sand was flying, his heart was in his throat, and he'd been carried about as if he were less then a leaf in a tornado. And the absolute best part was he'd managed to stay on Jo's back. He had new affection and admiration for her. "Good thing I went to that auction," he said. He fell asleep that night still reliving the ride.

The rest of the week was a blur, taken up by cutting hay, cutting cows, eating, playing the fiddle, having a beer with Woody, and sleeping. Every day Pete had him finish off the day's training session by riding Jolena. "All the other horses you ride will require some input. They'll help you understand the cows and the mechanics of the game. Jolena will give you confidence."

They should have stopped work by noon Saturday, but they had about fifty tons of hay bales lying in the field and the broker couldn't get a trailer out to pick them up until Monday. Rain was forecast for Saturday night so Connie, Pete and Woody worked until two to get everything into the barn. It was only a hundred bales, but they could only move twenty at a time on the old hay trailer so it took a while.

Cally stalled off lunch until they were finished and by the time Connie ate lunch and cleaned up, it was well into mid-afternoon.

Contemplating the pile of dirty blue jeans, tee shirts and underwear he'd amassed during the week, he decided to seek out another Laundromat, not the same one he'd used last time, perhaps one in Whitefish. Then he could go to the Rustlers and hopefully, find Myra. If he couldn't buy her dinner tonight, he could try to arrange something for next week. He'd better tell Cally not to set a place for him at dinner. Better yet, he'd remember his phone and call her a little later.

When Cally watched him drive away, she assumed he was headed for a rendezvous with the blond he'd met at the picnic. *My fault.* She watched the truck disappear out the driveway. *I invited him to the picnic. He'll probably call in a while to say he won't be around for dinner.*

He found a Laundromat in Whitefish right away and since he didn't want to interrupt his visit with Myra, he stayed close by while his clothes washed and dried. It was five when he got to the Rustlers. Some early diners were just starting to arrive. He went in and ordered a beer. Myra was not behind the bar. He asked the bartender Myra was around.

"Who?"

"Myra, the owner." Then he remembered her stage name. "Brianna."

"Oh, Miss Lane. No, I think somebody said she went out of town for a few days. I'm not really sure though. I'm kinda new. Just started Tuesday."

Connie nodded. "Thanks." Well so much for a big Saturday night he thought. He finished his beer quickly and headed his pickup back to the ranch.

Cally was surprised when she saw him drive back into the driveway. When Connie pulled up to the bunkhouse, Woody was sitting on the bunkhouse back step watching the twins splash in the creek. Connie pulled a couple of brews out of his fridge and joined him. They made meaningless banter for a while and then Connie decided to join the girls. He put on his new swimming trunks and waded in. The water was colder than he thought it would be, but after the girls splashed him wet it wasn't too bad. He slid forward on his chest into the deeper water and let the current take him. It slowly pulled him along the beach and around the first turn. Before standing and wading back to where the girls were, he made a note to get some inner tubes. They could float this thing for the entire length of the ranch and Cally could pick them up in his truck, or maybe Cally would like to join them and Pete could pick them up.

After a later than usual supper, Connie sprawled in his recliner, reading one of a dozen books he'd bought at a bookstore in Whitefish, across the street from the Laundromat. He nodded off a couple of times before he decided to go to bed. "What a life," he mumbled just before he fell asleep.

From the big house, Cally looked down at the bunkhouse on her way to bed. The lights were off, and Connie's truck was next to the building. She was secretly pleased.

Chapter 22, First Blood

For the next two weeks, Connie's routine remained fixed, making hay and riding horses. Towards the end of June, he was beginning to look as if he knew what he was doing. He did okay on Billy and better on Jo. Only a few cows ever beat her, and the ones that did never beat her a second time. She was smart and athletic; good attributes for any game. Billy was quick and agile, but nowhere near as smooth as Jo. She amazed Connie on a daily basis with her abilities. Pete had been correct when he said she would give him confidence.

At the beginning of the last week in June, Pete reminded Connie about the cutting contest in Polson. "It's not a major event so don't get all nervous on me. Just do what you've been doing and we'll see what happens."

Easy for him to say, but Connie started to get nervous as soon as the words were out of Pete's mouth. "Ah, how many riders will there be?"

"Depends on how many show up, twenty, maybe twenty-five at the most. It's not a major event by any means. I didn't go last year, but the year before, I think there were eighteen or nineteen riders in the open class."

"They have classes? I thought that was only for big events."

"No, usually any competition with prize money has at least two classes."

"Where's the prize money coming from?"

"Well now, that's where you and your wallet come in. There's a hundred dollar entry fee."

"A hundred dollar entry fee for a minor event? Seems a bit steep."

Pete laughed, "I know you don't need to borrow a C note."

"No, I'm merely trying to determine how minor an event this is."

"You have to start sometime and believe me, a hundred is nothing. I've been to unsanctioned events at private ranches where you had to throw in a thousand. Course you got a pretty nice steak dinner out of it. You'll have to buy your own hotdogs at this one."

Connie knew he'd have to start competing in public sooner or later. He'd have preferred later, but he realized sooner would be better. He sighed, but smiled when he did. "Who do I pay and when?"

"That's the spirit. You can register when we get there. We'll have to be at the Polson Fairgrounds, Saturday by ten. The game starts at eleven. Also, your association with me makes you a professional. You'll be in the open class."

"How can that be? It was less than six weeks ago I fell off my horse."

"I didn't say you were a good professional, but according to the rules, if you stay with me and get any kind of remuneration, because I'm a pro, so are you."

"What remuneration?"

"All of Cally's home cooked meals and the magnificent accommodations of the bunkhouse are the remuneration. We could probably argue the point, but there's no reason. You're going to the futurity to ride in the open class, might as well get used to it now."

"Great, two months ago I was a rank amateur, today I'm a pro. I can't wait for Saturday."

"It won't be any different than what you've been doin' right here. There'll just be some people standing around watching and telling each other lies about why they're not riding, and an announcer, and some judges. We'll take both Jolena and Billy. You'll be able to exercise Jolena in the arena which will help her get used to a crowd. After that, you'll warm up Billy for the event. When they call your name, you ride out and start cutting."

"Who determines the riding order?"

"I'm not sure. It'll either be the order you registered in or they'll throw all the names in somebody's hat and draw them back out. Hey, speaking of hats, you got one?"

"No, not yet. I was going to buy one, but I wasn't sure what kind to get."

"You're going to need one. You'll have to wear boots, blue jeans, a long sleeve western shirt and a hat. Remind me to get you a current rule book."

"I'll go get a hat after supper tonight. What kind is best?"

"I like Stetsons and Resistols, but there's others. Find a style you like and get a size that fits well, nice and snug without giving you a headache."

Connie already knew the one he wanted. He had seen it at the tack store where he first collided with Myra Foxx, aka Brianna Lane. He hoped some non-pro, pseudo-cowboy hadn't bought it yet.

Anticipating Saturday, the rest of Connie's day dragged along until it was time for supper. He showered and put on clean clothes so he could run to the tack store as soon as he finished eating.

The girls were quick to notice. "Whatcha all dressed up for, Connie?" Lindsey asked.

The question caused Danni to re-examine Connie's attire. "Yeah, Connie, you got a date?"

He rolled his eyes in mock frustration. "What do know about dates?"

"You told me once, you could take out Brianna and fly to New York for dinner."

My God, he thought, you can't say anything to these kids. "I'm going to buy a hat," he said. "You wouldn't want me to go to the store all dirty and smelly would you?"

"Dirty would be okay, but not smelly," Lindsey said.

"Well, if I'm not going to stink, I might as well wear clean clothes too."

"What store you goin' to?" Danni wanted to know.

Cally interrupted the interrogation. "Are you writing a book? Stop being so nosey. Connie can go to any store he wants. He doesn't have to report to you two."

"We were just making conversation," Lindsey protested.

"Yeah, Mom, we like talking to Connie about stuff," Danni agreed.

"Yes, and I'm reasonably sure Connie likes talking to both of you too, but you can make conversation without being nosey."

Connie laughed. "Well ladies, if I knew where I was going to find the hat I want, I would certainly share that information with you, however I'm not sure. How about tomorrow, I tell you where I bought it?"

"Okay, but you have to show us the hat you got."

"Yeah, you have to model it for us."

"I'll do that, but now I need to be excused so I can go to town." He pushed back from the table. "Thanks, Cally, everything was delicious, as usual."

She acknowledged the compliment and he was out the door. "He's kind of in a hurry," Lindsey said.

"It's after seven, stores will be closing soon," Pete told her.

"Why doesn't he get a hat on Saturday? He'd have more time to shop?"

"He has to have the hat on his head Saturday morning when he rides. Besides that, not everybody needs a lot of time to shop."

"I do," Danni said.

"You need a lot of time to do most anything," Woody suggested.

"I do dishes fast," she protested.

"Yes, you do. I apologize, you're quick with a dish cloth."

"Can we go to Polson to watch Connie ride, Grandpa?" Lindsey asked Pete.

"No, but you can go to the rodeo in Kalispell next weekend and watch him ride."

"Why can't we go to Polson?"

"I think your mother has other plans for you."

Lindsey looked to Cally. "What are we doing?"

"You're going to town with me to get groceries and then we're going to buy you some summer clothes and shoes. Nothing fits from last summer. You two grow like weeds. And when we get home, you're going to help me make a nice picnic lunch. We're going to ride up to Rogers Lake on Sunday."

"Yippee. Can we swim?"

"Yes, but we have to get you both new swim suits."

"Can Connie come along? He told us a picnic with you at Rogers Lake would be idyllic," volunteered Danni.

"He did, did he?"

"Yeah, but he never really explained what idyllic meant."

Cally smiled, almost wistfully it seemed to Pete, as he was paying close attention to the conversation.

"Well, he is certainly invited."

This information pleased the twins and they decided they could wait until the rodeo in Kalispell to watch Connie ride. Connie would have probably preferred to go shopping with the girls than ride in the competition in Polson, but he'd signed up for this tour of duty and he couldn't back out now. Rolling into the parking lot of Brianna's tack store, he was already contemplating the possibilities of his performance.

Entering the store, with one purpose in mind, he went straight to the area where a myriad of hats hung on display. He grabbed the one he'd liked last week and dropped it on his head. "What?" he muttered when it settled down on his ears. Someone must have bought the one he tried before because that one had fit him.

"Hey, cowboy, can I help you?" asked a friendly, familiar voice.

He turned to regard Myra looking quite fetching in a short, skimpy tee shirt and tight blue jeans. "Hello," and he almost forgot about everything that had just previously occupied his mind. "Ah, I have to get a hat and you had one last week like this that fit me," he waved the too big hat at her, "but this one is way too big."

Smiling, she took the hat from him and looked inside at the model number. "You decided you needed a hat to be a real cowboy?"

"No, ah well, actually yes," and he told her the reason he needed a hat.

"Wow," she said, "You really are a cowboy, or at least you will be as of Saturday."

"Yeah," and then he admitted. "I'm kind of nervous."

She put her hand on his shoulder. "You'll do just fine. Let me run in back, I'm sure we have more of these."

He looked at the rest of the hats while she was gone, but none of them grabbed him like the one he first picked. Then he wondered if he should try to get a date with her. Where would he take her? He didn't really want to buy her dinner at her own restaurant. Maybe there was a good Italian restaurant around somewhere. He'd never met a woman who didn't like Italian food. Just as she returned with three boxes, he decided to go for it.

"Okay, Connie, I have a six and seven eighths, a seven, and a seven and a quarter, all in the style you like. One of them has to fit."

The size seven was the winner, just snug enough to stay on and not tight enough to hurt. "This is the first hat I've worn since I got out of the army," he told her.

"Well, I think you look nice. You'll have to wear it often, not just when you're riding."

"Any chance I can take you to dinner Saturday night? I should be back in town by six. I could pick you up by seven."

She smiled. "Connie, I'd love to go to dinner with you, but I'm flying out to San Diego Saturday afternoon." She lowered her voice. "My daughter decided she wanted to attempt to establish a relationship with her father and has been staying with some friends of mine in La Jolla since last week. I'm meeting her down there Saturday night." The disappointment on his face was readable. She put her hand on his shoulder again, "But I definitely want a rain check, I'll be back in a few days."

He liked her touch, it was assuring, but not overpowering. Brightening, he said, "Okay, I'll try again."

On the way home, he had something to contemplate besides the cutting contest on Saturday. This time he'd even remembered to get Myra's phone number. He wasn't certain why he was attracted to her. She was pretty, not as pretty as his wife had been, but she had other, similar qualities. She seemed intelligent, calm, and was a good listener, things he admired in anyone, but found lacking in so many. Actually, besides his wife, Myra reminded him of Cally. Both women expressed confidence and competence without arrogance. And after his initial misunderstanding with Cally, he was quite enamored with her. Too bad she wasn't ten years older or better yet, he was ten years younger. And why was he having these thoughts anyway? His hormones had stopped raging some years ago. Stopped raging maybe, but apparently not completely turned off because he found both women highly desirable. *Forget it. I don't need to be thinking about women right now. I need to focus on riding.*

The next four days went by in a blur. In his cutting arena, Pete simulated the conditions Connie would operate under at the contest. He had him warm up Billy at the back of the arena and then wait for Woody to officially announce him. Lindsey, Danni, and Pete were the herd handlers and turn back riders and there was even a big cardboard box where the judges stand would be. The girls loved the game. They were having more fun this summer than they'd imagined. Never having known a father, they had secretly adopted Connie. He might be a little old, but he didn't look it or act it and he was the nicest man, other than Pete or Woody, they had ever known. They both decided he was better even than Mister Jaxon, the hottie grade school teacher all the little girls liked. The twins could tell most all the girl teachers liked him too.

Friday night after supper, Pete came down to the bunkhouse. "Show me the clothes you're going to wear tomorrow."

Connie felt like a little kid, but dutifully pulled out the Cinch blue jeans and the shirt he had selected. "Meet your approval?"

Taking the pants and shirt, Pete said, "Almost," and started out the door with them.

"Hey, where're you going?"

"I'm going to get them ironed."

"You going to do it?"

"No, Cally is."

"Oh no," Connie said taking back his clothes. "I don't want her to have to iron my clothes."

Pete gently pulled them back, "Relax. She volunteered."

Connie loosened his grip. "She did?"

"Yes she did. She must like you. Now give 'em up. I'll bring 'em back in a few minutes. We want you to look like a pro rider, not some dusty old cowboy that just rode in off the range. You'll have to give Billy and Jolena a bath in the morning too, so don't be sleeping in." Pete took Connie's clothes and left.

Connie tried playing his fiddle a bit, but he couldn't concentrate, kept making simple mistakes. He put the fiddle back on the shelf and got a beer. Two minutes after he'd dropped into his recliner, Pete was back. He handed Connie his clothes on a hanger and a piece of paper.

"What's this?"

"You've never seen a hanger before?"

"I mean this," and he waved the slip of paper at Pete.

"I don't know. Cally gave it to me, said it was for you. Looks like a note to me. Got any more of those?" He pointed at the beer bottle.

"Yeah, sorry. They're in the reefer. Help yourself." He unfolded the paper.

"Phone call for you," it said. "She said to call her back." There was a vaguely familiar phone number.

Recognizing the phone number of the blonde from Boissvert's barbecue, he crumpled the paper and pitched it at the trashcan. It hit the rim and toppled in.

Pete had been watching. Connie looked up and saw him. "I wonder how many times I'll have to throw her phone number away."

"Anybody I know?"

"You might, I met her at Boissvert's barbecue."

"Oh yeah, which one?"

Connie laughed. "The good looking blonde with the dynamite body, the personality of a pecan tree and the subtlety of a sledge hammer."

"Rather forward and kind of nutty, yeah, that's Colleen. I'm not certain she attends church for its spiritual aspect. You didn't like her?"

"Not enough to find out any more about her than I learned in the first fifteen minutes of talking with her, or rather listening to her."

"As far as havin' issues, she's probably the least dangerous of the three you met."

"You don't say?"

Yeah, the first one is still struggling with the demise of her husband as the result of an armed conflict. Not while serving in the military, but rather in a shoot out with the Missoula Police Department."

"Was he a criminal?"

"Not until then, but he'd always been volatile and so the story goes, one day he heard a voice in his head telling him to 'Kill a cop.' Deciding to listen, he started blasting away at the Missoula County Courthouse with his .300 Winchester magnum, elk hunting rifle. He only had one box of ammo, twenty rounds, and when he finished firing, he stood up, and was dropped by a SWAT sniper. Must have thought a truce had been declared. His widow, the woman you met, moved to Kalispell and has been trying to forget the past. After ten years I figure she thinks she's forgotten, and is ready to trust another man. I doubt it. She keeps talkin' about the incident like it happened last week, how betrayed she feels."

"The guy didn't betray her, he was schizophrenic."

"Perhaps, but she has issues now."

"How about the other woman, the tall lawyer?"

"I knew her father well. She's never married; prefers long-term affairs. I don't know the cause of her insecurity, but I believe she's scared to death of commitment. Unless you're lookin' for an affair, I'd avoid her, too."

"Colleen on the other hand, least I believe, is hunting for a husband. She's already had two and listenin' to her, she was blameless for the failures. She might still be somewhat immature. Fine lookin' though."

"Her desire to find another husband isn't unusual. Might be foolish though. You're old enough. You obviously know there are worse things than being alone."

"You could still date her. Who said you had to marry her?"

"She'd be demanding it after a month."

Woody knocked and entered before Connie could tell him to come in. He pointed at the bottles that Pete and Connie held. "Any more of those?"

Connie pointed at the refrigerator. "Bring three."

Woody passed out fresh ones to Connie and Pete. "You two havin' an intellectual debate or can anyone join in?"

"Connie was just telling me about his not so secret admirer."

"That'd be Colleen, I'd guess."

"How do you know that?"

"I was listenin' when Cally took the call. I heard her say Colleen's name. Fine lookin' woman."

"Yeah, and she's lookin' real hard for a husband. Pete says she's already had two and I don't want to be any part of her third."

"Probably a wise choice. She's one a them women who for all their life have been told how beautiful they are, and now she expects preferential treatment from everybody 'cause of the way she looks."

"Not my problem, Woody. I have enough trouble without starting a relationship with a woman who has issues."

"Yeah, what trouble you havin'? Seems to me you got it made."

"I'd agree except for a certain cutting contest tomorrow morning."

"Why is that a problem?" Pete wanted to know.

"Because I'm nervous, that's why. I don't want to blow it."

"You told me you were in combat. Were you nervous then?"

"Not once the shooting started."

"Well, this'll be the same deal. Once you cross the time line, you'll be just fine. Actually, you'll be better than fine because no one will be shooting at you."

Woody spoke up. "If it'll help, I could maybe bring my rifle, fire a couple of rounds over your head just to settle you."

"You two are so comforting. I've never done anything like this. Cut me a little slack, okay?"

"Well if it makes you feel any better, the last time I rode in competition, I was a little nervous myself."

"When was that?"

"Summer before last, when I won the cutting you're gonna be in ridin' Billy."

Connie was puzzled. "If you were competing then, why aren't you riding Jolena and getting ready for the futurity? Why'd you sell her to me?"

First Pete looked at the floor, then he looked at Woody who was looking at the floor and finally, he looked at Connie. "I ain't all that healthy."

Connie started to make the comment that he was no spring chicken himself and had his share of aches and pains, but realized there must be a lot more to Pete's condition than a little arthritis. "Anything you care to tell me?"

"How about if I tell you, you swear not to tell Cally? I'll tell her myself when the time is right."

"Of course I won't tell Cally. Pete, you don't even have to tell me if you're uncomfortable with it."

"I was going to tell you soon anyway. Figured I owed you some kind of explanation. I apparently have an advanced case of prostate cancer."

"Advanced, as in inoperable? Are they certain?"

"No, they can operate, but the outcome is doubtful. I told them they could take anything they could find down there, and they said they just might have to do that."

"When is this supposed to happen?"

"The doctor in Kalispell wanted to get right on it, but since the only real symptom I have is reduced bladder capacity, I decided to get a second opinion. I'm going to the Mayo Clinic in Minnesota in three weeks. I figure if those doctors agree with the doctors in Kalispell, I'll have done whatever they want to do right then and there."

"Jeez, Pete, is there anything I can do to help? I could go with you. If you need any money, anything, let me help."

"Well first off, you can start by stop bein' up tight about tomorrow. Now if that's not completely possible, I can understand, so just doing your best will be helpful. I'm sure Cally's going to want to go with me and won't take no for an answer, so you and Woody will have to stay and take care of the girls and everything else while we're gone. But, there'll be plenty of time to get those details sorted out."

"When are you going to tell her?"

"Right after you win the cutting on the Fourth of July in Kalispell."

"Terrific. No pressure there."

Pete laughed. "How about another beer? If I'm gonna feel like I have to go, there might as well be a reason."

They partied until nine-thirty and were all in bed by ten. Connie flipped around for a while thinking about Pete and Cally and the contest and even Myra Foxx before finally falling into an uninterrupted sleep. By eight the next morning all three men were loaded in Connie's pickup headed down the road towards Polson. Billy and Jolena, freshly bathed, rode behind in Connie's fancy trailer, and if the truth were known, were far more relaxed than Connie.

The portion of the parking lot at the rodeo grounds in Polson reserved for trucks with trailers was already almost full. As Connie cruised through the rows of rigs, some of them sporting dents and leaking rust, Woody commented, "Too bad the judges don't take your truck and trailer into consideration, you'd win hands down."

"Yeah, Pete, what's with all the trailers? You said there'd be twenty-five riders max."

"Well, there's other events. It's a rodeo too. There'll be ropin' and reinin' and even barrel racin'. It is a two-day deal. Gotta fill it up with something."

Connie wheeled into one of the last available parking slots. "Where do the poor cowboys who come late get to park?"

"There's another forty acres on the other side of the street."

"Well, let's hope that doesn't fill up too."

When he registered, he found out there were already forty-six riders in the open class. Names had been drawn at nine for everyone who had registered by then and anyone signing up after that would ride after the others in the order in which they registered. Unless someone else showed up, Connie would be riding last. The guy that took his money also told him they'd be starting some time around eleven and would go through about twelve riders per hour. That would put him up at about three PM, almost four hours to kill.

Pete laughed when Connie told him how far off his estimate had been. "That's good. More riders, more rides for you to analyze. See where they made their mistakes so you don't have to make the same ones. Usually best to ride towards the end. Did you get an entrants list?"

Connie handed him all the papers he'd received when he'd checked in. Pete quickly scanned the list of riders. Connie's name and two others were penciled in at the bottom. Pete's finger stabbed at the name two above Connie's, 'Gilly Bedfort'. "Here's the guy you'll have to beat, Gilliam Bedfort, Junior. His old man, Gilliam Senior, has got lots of money, but Junior is all hat and no cows. However, he can ride, and thanks to Daddy, he always has a decent horse."

"Well, Pete, the way I see it, I've got at least forty-five riders to beat. I don't think I'll worry about Gilly more than any of the rest of them."

"That's the spirit. Let's hang out in your trailer 'til noon."

The back end of Connie's trailer had accommodations for three horses, but Connie had rearranged the dividers so Jolena and Billy each had an eight by four foot stall and were more comfortable there than in the temporary stalls that were set up behind the arena. Connie fidgeted while Pete talked strategy and Woody inspected his eyelids for holes. At noon, Pete woke Woody from his nap and the three of them went into the stands to watch the action.

There were a few good rides, but a lot of the cows insisted on running from one side of the arena to the other, proving disastrous for some of the riders and boring for the spectators. When rider number thirty started his run, Pete suggested they get ready.

"You change into your ridin' duds and I'll saddle Jolena. While you're riding her around in the back of the arena, I'll saddle Billy. Next time you can saddle your own horses, but you're so blasted nervous right now I don't want you makin' a mistake."

Woody asked, "Think you can dress yourself? I don't want to make it a habit, but I'll help you this one time if you don't think you can."

Connie gave him a dirty look. "Be nice to me, old man, or you won't get any more of my beer, let alone single malt."

Ten minutes later, Jolena was tacked up and Connie was sporting his new duds. Both the blue jeans and the shirt had creases in them capable of slicing cold butter.

Checking his watch, Pete instructed, "Walk her over to the back end of the arena and loosen her up. Lope some circles, do a few sliding stops, some roll backs, lead changes, and then walk her back here in twenty minutes."

Connie obeyed and twenty minutes later brought Jo back to the trailer and swapped her out for Billy. He didn't know about Jo, but he was a little less tense. He hoped this would get easier the more he did it. If it didn't, he'd be a white haired old man by the time he went to the futurity. He checked the cinch strap and climbed on Billy, not aware his warm up ride on Jolena had been thoroughly scrutinized.

"Okay, while you were gone. I checked the arena office. You're still last and they're doing a cow change at number forty so you shouldn't get any sour old alligators. And the highest score so far is two sixteen."

"What's the good news?"

"You're girl friend is here," said Woody.

"Oh no, not Colleen what's her name. How did she know about this?"

"I don't know about Colleen, I'm talking about the movie star."

"Myra? That's almost as bad. What if I blow it big time?"

"She'll still love ya."

"Yeah," agreed Pete, "Think of her as good luck. Let's go, Cowboy, show time." He winked at Woody.

When he entered the back of the arena, there were five riders there. He wondered which was Gilly. Rather than watch the action, he claimed a small space in a back corner and worked Billy. He tried to ignore the sporadic crowd noise and twenty minutes later it was his turn. The gate opened for him and, doing his best to concentrate on his mission, he slowly approached the time line, hanging onto the words Pete had left with him. "Don't try to do it on your own."

When he crossed the line, the crowd went away. He aimed Billy at the pack of cows and decided to go for his deep cut first. It went just like he had practiced it. Once Billy understood which cow he had selected, he pushed it out in front of the judges without a hitch. The cow turned and made an immediate lunge to the right to get back to the herd. Billy jumped in front of it to turn it to the left and then pounced in front of it again. This brought a few whistles and cheers from the bleachers, but the cow did a one eighty, blasted between the turn back riders and skidded to a stop up against the back fence. Connie lifted the reins from Jo's neck and went back to the herd.

The next cow must have practiced for an Olympic running event. It ran from fence to fence four times, failing to get past Billy before it quit. Connie suspected he still had plenty of time and turned back into the herd. He didn't get a chance to pick out a cow before the herd started to spill off to his left. He aimed Billy towards the back and they were able to pick one off the trailing end of the herd without incident. When he got the little heifer out in front of the judges, she froze. Not knowing exactly what to do, he dropped the reins.

Billy crouched down it front of the cow and stared like a cat eyeing a mouse. The audience came alive and after a long moment, the cow bolted. Connie figured it was going to get past Billy, but hung on when he erupted and turned the heifer with inches to spare. Blasting back in the opposite direction, the cow aimed for the fence. When she decided to cut her run to the fence short, Billy dropped his butt, locked his back legs and slid about fifteen feet. Connie's butt lifted out of the saddle and he dug his right hand into the saddle horn so hard, he later inspected his fingers for damage. He was almost catapulted from

Billy's back and there was a collective gasp from the stands. Sloppy, but he had no time to consider it because Billy had changed direction and was back after the cow in two heartbeats. Connie was beginning to sweat. Half the audience was on their feet.

Five more times Billy cut off the little heifer's escape attempts, and finally the cow stopped and walked slowly towards the turn back riders. Connie lifted the reins as the buzzer sounded. He walked out to a nice round of applause.

He'd cut three cows and satisfied the deep cut requirement and could recall making no major mistakes. Almost getting pitched out of the saddle onto his head shouldn't be counted as a serious mistake, but he knew he'd lose eye appeal points for it. His intention was to walk Billy back to the trailer to unsaddle him when he heard his name called over the PA system. "Would the last rider, Conrad Bradley, please not leave the arena, also the rider just prior to that, Gilly Bedfort? Would you two hang around for a minute while I do some calculating?"

Connie glanced over at Gilly who had parked his mount in the back where he could watch Connie. He raised his right forefinger to the brim of his Stetson to acknowledge Connie. Connie nodded in return.

The loudspeaker crackled again. "Is Miss Livinwell in the audience by any chance? Miss Corinne Livinwell you are the number three finisher. Conrad Bradley you are runner up and Gilly Bedfort is our winner. Conrad and Gilly why don't you ride out here in front of the announcer's stand and Corinne, if you're around, you come down here too."

By the time Gilly rode, Corinne knew she had at least third place in the bag. The high point leader with only two riders left, she was relatively certain she'd take second because she knew Gilly was tough. She'd never heard of Conrad Bradley. Nice looking horse though, that was certain. At fifty-three, she'd been riding cutting horses since she was seven. An excellent rider, she'd never had a great horse. She'd had a few good ones, but never a great one. After Connie's ride, she recognized Billy's ability, but to her experienced eye, the horse's rider looked to be a work in progress even though he managed to finish ahead of her.

Corinne had ridden an hour earlier and her mount was back in the trailer, but anticipating the outcome, she'd situated herself as close to the announcer's booth as possible. When he called, she was ready. She was in front of the judges' stand before Connie and Gilly.

Somewhat entranced, Connie followed Gilly back into the arena to where Corinne was standing and they parked their mounts on either side of her. Connie finally dared to look up into the bleachers. He spotted Myra immediately. She was sitting between Pete and Woody and as soon as she realized Connie had seen her, she started waving. Connie smiled and waved. About thirty people in his line of sight waved back. He smiled. He never imagined being in the winner's circle.

For his efforts, he received an envelope and the biggest belt buckle he'd ever seen. It was the only thing he'd ever won. The envelope contained fifteen, one hundred dollar bills, less than one percent of what he'd invested in the sport so far. But he was happy as he rode out of the arena. He felt he really was a cowboy and a pro rider.

Chapter 23, Life is Idyllic

He had Billy in the trailer with his tack off by the time his fan club arrived. Pete and Woody shook his hand. Myra hugged him and kissed his cheek. "You were wonderful," she said.

"So does this mean you'll have dinner with me tonight after all?"

"I wish I could, but I have to leave ten minutes ago. My flight takes off from Kalispell in less than two hours. I wanted to see you ride and now I have to run."

"Where'd you park? I can at least walk you to your car."

She pointed to her Escalade in the row immediately behind Connie's trailer. "Sorry, a guy was leaving just as I drove up." She was thinking it would have been nice to be alone with him for at least a minute.

She shook hands with Pete and told him it was nice meeting him. He told her the pleasure was all his. She gave Woody a quick hug and Connie a longer one. "I really have to go, guys. See you later, Connie."

She was no sooner off when a man, maybe fifteen years Connie's senior, walked up. "Howdy, Pete."

"Howdy, Gilliam. It's been a while. What can I do for you?"

"Well, for starters, you can introduce me to your friend with the good looking paint horse. I was watching them in the back of the arena."

Pete did that, referring to Connie as his protégé. For some reason Connie felt like counting his fingers after shaking hands with Gilly senior.

"Your protégé, eh? I thought you'd already packed it in, Pete?"

"Almost Gilly, almost. Right after Connie and Jolena win the futurity, I'll officially retire."

Gilliam laughed. "I hope you have lots of time to practice between now and then, Connie."

Connie ignored the cheap shot to his less than professional, near-departure from Billy's back while chasing the last cow. "Seems to me your son only beat me by a point. What is it you want Mister Bedfort?" He'd ignore one insult, but really didn't want to endure a conversation of any length with this bore.

"Very direct, I appreciate that in a man, Conrad. I'm rather direct myself also."

Not to mention pompous and obnoxious. "I'm listening, Mister Bedfort."

"I'd like to buy the horse you were riding today, the paint horse that is. I'll pay more than a fair price."

"She's not for sale, Mister Bedfort, not at any price. Now if you'll excuse me, I'll be taking my horse home." He turned towards his pickup.

"Now wait, son. Don't be too hasty. Hear me out."

Connie stopped and turned back towards Bedfort. "Is Gilly junior riding in Kalispell on the Fourth?"

"Certainly, why?"

"How much money do you have in your wallet right now?"

"Not enough to buy your horse, that's for sure."

"I already told you, that horse isn't for sale. I just want to know if you'd like to make a wager on the outcome of the Kalispell Days cutting contest. I'll match whatever you have in your wallet right now; I finish with more points than Junior."

Bedfort reached for his wallet. "By God, you're on." He fished out six, one hundred dollar bills. "Is that too much?"

"No, not at all, if that's all you can afford, it's fine. Connie took six, C-notes out of his wallet. "Pete can hold the money, if that's all right with you."

Bedfort was embarrassed. His bluff was rarely called. "Sure, I trust Pete." He handed his cash to Pete.

"Well then, Mister Bedfort, I'll see you in Kalispell on the Fourth, but now I'm going home—to practice."

Connie had a Cheshire cat grin on his face as he, Pete, and Woody pulled out of the parking lot. "That might have been rash," Pete commented. "I liked it a lot, but it still may have been rash."

"Probably," Connie admitted, "but in spite of the fact I almost got launched, I can beat Gilly next time around."

"You should have beaten him this time, although your misstep cost you at least three points."

"You said to always watch the cow. I was watching this one and I figured it was going all the way to the fence. I was as surprised as anyone when it decided to cut back. And if that wasn't enough, I was really surprised when Billy hit the brakes and turned."

"Something else to think about and be prepared for next time. Did you have fun?"

"Yeah, I think so. It's kind of blurry already."

"Well, you'll get to see it again, I videotaped it and your girl friend had a fancy digital camera with a long lens."

"She's not my girlfriend."

"She can be mine, if'n you don't want her," Woody said from the back seat.

"You still awake?" Connie asked. "We've been on the road for almost a minute and a half, I'm surprised you're not comatose by now."

"Well, I woulda been nappin' if you and Pete weren't makin' so much noise up there. And you can direct Brianna my way if you ain't interested yourself."

"It's not that I'm not interested, I'm not sure what I'll do if she is. I don't need a romantic interlude right now."

"Maybe you ought to tell her that," Pete suggested, "because she's powerful sure interested in you."

"Yeah," said Woody, "and I been tryin' to figure out why that is. She's probably got more money than you do and I know for a fact there's better lookin' men hangin' 'round her. Rumor has it, even Gilly Junior has been pursuin' her some and while I never much cared for either him or his old man, I do believe when it comes to looks, he got a slight edge over you. Course he's kinda short."

"Are the Bedforts some sort of celebrities around here? "

"Actually, notorious would be a better way of describin' 'em. At least the old man. Senior's been involved in more than one questionable deal and Junior was the classic ne'er do well 'til Senior bought him a horse and he started cuttin' cows. He's become rather good wouldn't you say, Pete?"

"He's not bad, although I don't like his style. Too aggressive. Uses his hands more than his head."

"I suspect he's got LMS. He's only five foot five."

"Come on, Woody," said Connie. "You're only an inch taller than him."

"Yeah, but I ain't a little guy with something to prove. Not all us short guys have little man's syndrome."

"His old man isn't so short. Obnoxious, but not short. He's also a good judge of horse flesh."

"Senior's father, Gerhardt, was short. He and Gilly senior came up here from Texas about fifty years ago. Just the two of them, and they brought lots of money along. Senior was about nineteen at the time and the first thing he did was to get one of Kalispell's finest young ladies pregnant. Her folks sent her away and when she came back, four years later, she had a degree from some old school back east and no child. By then, Senior had a wife and two kids, but she left him two years later and took the kids. Took a bunch of his money with her, too."

"Good for her." Connie said. "Where did all this money come from?"

"According to Gerhardt, he made it big in Texas oil."

"If he was big in Texas oil, why'd he leave Texas?"

"Excellent question. I have several friends down that way, cutting horse people, who are actually still in the oil business. About forty years ago, I did a little checking on Gerhardt. There was a Bedfort Oil Company in Houston, but it was owned by a different family. The only thing my friends could discover was that Gerhardt had been married to an heiress and when she died, he pulled up stakes and came to Montana."

"Be interesting to know the whole story."

"Yeah," agreed Woody. "It would probably be all about some silly, rich woman fallin' for the wrong guy."

"So, what happened when Junior made a play for Myra?"

"About two years ago, Myra helped organize a rodeo in Whitefish for some charity or other. She got a bunch of Hollywood celebrities to show up. The thing was a huge success, at least in terms of increasing newspaper sales and traffic jams downtown. Anyway, Myra and Gilly were photographed arm in arm at one of the events and the rumor was they were dating."

"How old is he?"

"He's about five years older than Cally. He tried to date her a year ago."

Woody chimed in, "Both Cally and Myra are too smart to take up with the likes of him."

"I imagine both of them have had their fair share of practice in avoiding unwanted attention."

"Well, you be careful," said Pete. "In Myra's case the converse is also probably true."

"What would that be? That she's had a fair share of practice in encouraging wanted attention."

"Something like that."

"I'll be watching the cow."

The twins were thrilled when the boys returned home and told them the news. Lindsey had an inexpensive digital camera Pete had given her because he could never get it to work, although Lindsey had no trouble with it. Connie had to pose for what seemed to be an entire memory card full of pictures. Lindsey's favorite, the one she enlarged and had framed to set on the dresser in her bedroom was one of Cally and Connie. Danni posed them together with Connie holding his belt buckle and wearing his hat. On an impulse, Connie put his arm around Cally's shoulders and she slipped her arm around his waist. They were both a bit surprised and looked at each other and smiled.

Pete watched the videotape several times and made notes. Only three minutes long, it showed Connie and Billy from the time they entered the business end of the arena until the buzzer rang and they walked out. Pete actually was impressed. Except for the one time when he almost left the saddle, Connie's riding was acceptable considering the short time he'd been riding. His timing still needed improvement, but that couldn't be taught. It would take practice and Pete intended for Connie to practice like it was tantamount to his very survival. He had a couple of reining horses and decided he would get Connie on them doing spins and sliding stops. That should help. The other thing the tape showed was Connie should have had a higher score.

He wished he'd thought to tape Gilly's ride. He probably could have filed a protest. He knew at least two of the judges were well known to Gilly Senior. He'd have to find out who was judging next week's contest in Kalispell. If Connie could ride this well then, he didn't want Gilly stealing another one. He smiled when he thought about the way Connie had handled old man Bedfort.

"He did well, Dad. You should be proud." Standing behind him, Cally had quietly watched the last replay.

"Cally. I didn't know you were there. Yes, he did and yes I am. I was also proud of the way he handled Gilliam Senior when he came up afterwards and tried to buy Jolena."

"Seriously? Senior asked to buy Jo? What did Connie say?"

Pete related the incident to Cally, omitting any reference to Myra Foxx. Pete knew his daughter well enough to see that she had some affection for Connie, how much he wasn't certain. She didn't wear her heart on her sleeve, but Connie had been around for almost two months and in that time, Pete had caught his daughter looking somewhat wistfully at Connie more than once. She probably didn't even realize she was doing it, but Pete could tell she was interested, a lot more interested in Connie than she'd been in the doctor from Kalispell. But if Cally were interested, Pete wouldn't interfere. He'd attempted to give advice on Cally's romantic adventure with the girls' father and that got him nowhere, although it produced two wonderful grandchildren. He smiled.

"What's funny?" Cally asked.

"Oh, nothing, just remembering the look on Bedfort's face when Connie told him six hundred dollars was fine, if that was all he could afford."

"You think Connie always carries that much cash around?"

"No, I believe the money he won for finishing second was paid in cash and Connie is a quick thinker."

"You think he has a chance of winning the bet?"

"Junior is a good rider, but I'm certain Connie will have to beat better riders than him next week. And you know what else? I believe he can do it. I might have gotten lucky twice, once with Jo and again with Connie. Those two have already developed a bond."

"I know, I've overheard him talking to her."

"Well, I hope he keeps it up. He's becoming a decent rider, but I've noticed he always rides better on her than any of the other horses and Jolena doesn't pull any punches with him either. Yeah, he can beat Gilly. All he has to do is stay on and work with Billy. Too bad he can't ride Jolena."

Connie wanted to celebrate his victory, but wasn't sure how. Taking Myra out to dinner would have worked just fine, but by now she was well on her way to La Jolla. Saturday afternoon was his customary laundry day, yet he didn't think sitting in the Laundromat constituted much of a celebration. What if he took everybody out to dinner? On his way up to the big house to offer his invitation, he met the girls coming down. They were wearing their new swimsuits.

"Connie, can you watch us swim?" asked Lindsey. "We can't go in without adult supervision."

"Yeah, please Connie. Grandpa and Woody are napping and Mom's really busy making the picnic for tomorrow."

"What picnic for tomorrow, Danni?"

"We're all gonna ride up to Rogers Lake for a picnic. Did you forget?"

"I don't think so. You sure I'm invited?"

"Of course, silly," chided Lindsey, "Mom wants you to come with."

"You two wait for me at the creek. Don't go in until I get back."

Cally was in the kitchen. It seemed as if she was always in the kitchen. *She works too hard.*

She looked up when Connie rapped on the screen door. "Come on in, Connie. I think Pete's upstairs napping."

"Ah, actually, I wanted to talk to you."

"Sure, what's up?"

"Well I'd like to take you and the girls and Pete and Woody out to dinner tonight if that's okay, kind of a little celebration. We could go to the Rustlers. Woody said you liked the place."

Cally smiled at him. "That's a wonderful offer, Connie, but by the time I get finished with the picnic food for tomorrow, I think it'll be a little late."

Connie wondered why it was so difficult to get anyone to go out to dinner with him. "There's a picnic tomorrow?"

"Did you forget?" and then she thought. "I'm sorry. I'll bet we discussed it right after you left the table the other night. I think it might have been when you went into town to get your hat. Anyway, I thought we'd all ride up to Rogers Lake for a picnic tomorrow afternoon. We usually do it two or three times a summer. It's idyllic"

"Wouldn't miss it for the world." The reference to the comment he'd once made to Lindsey regarding picnicking with her mother went right past him. "Well, with all this cooking for the picnic you sure don't want to have to make dinner tonight."

She'd thought about having Pete throw some steaks and potatoes on the grill for supper so she wouldn't have to cook anything, but if Connie were volunteering, she had another idea. "How's this? While I'd really like to go to the Rustlers, the saloon just down the road

in Kila makes fantastic pizza. We all love it. If you want to treat us, we
haven't had pizza for a long time."

"Okay, it's settled. How about when the girls are done
swimming, we'll go to Kila and get pizza?"

"That would be nice, thanks." She watched him as he went out.
She considered telling him she'd like a rain check on the invitation to
dinner, but held back.

When Woody woke up from his nap and wandered down to
Connie's back step, he found him watching the girls, his hands clamped
around a pair of binoculars. "Your eyes that bad?"

"Huh, what do you mean?"

"The girls are only twenty feet away."

"I'm watching the tree line for Simba."

"What are you going to do if you see her?"

"Tell the girls and let them look."

Woody yawned and stood. "You ain't gonna see her. Got any
beer?"

"Yeah, I know. Help yourself."

"Want one?"

"No, I'm going to wait until pizza time."

Woody returned and settled down on the step below Connie.
"Cally makin' pizza for supper? That don't happen very often."

"No, I'm going down to the Kila saloon to pick some up. I
offered to take everybody out to the Rustlers, but Cally said she was too
busy."

"S'matter, Boy, you can't get anybody to go to dinner with you
can you?"

"I bet I could get Colleen Husbandhunter to go with me."

"Yeah, and then some. When you goin' to Kila?"

"I don't know. Whenever the girls are done splashing around."

"Can I ride along? There's a woman who works in there on
occasion who likes me a little bit."

"How much is a little bit?"

"We went out a couple of times. She drove, I paid."

"Interesting, I'd like to meet her."

Connie didn't spot the mountain lion and Woody's friend
wasn't working. The pizza however, was excellent and all in all, Connie
was satisfied with his scaled down celebration. He went to bed tired,
happy and comfortably full, a combination hard to beat.

Sometime in the early morning hours he thought he heard the mountain lion screaming. He got up, grabbed his rifle and went out. He didn't want to shoot anything, but he also didn't want any lion jumping on Jolena's back. Looking up, he saw so many stars it made him dizzy. When he walked behind the barn to the horse pasture, there was no indication the horses had heard a lion. The young ones were lying down, the older ones were asleep on their feet. While he stood there listening to them breathe, Jolena woke up. She smelled him and came to investigate.

"Hey, Jo, how ya doin'? Any lions hangin' around out here tonight?" She nickered softly and nuzzled her nose against his outstretched hand. "Some guy tried to buy you today. Pete said he was a good judge of horse flesh. I didn't like him, but he obviously can see a good horse when he's looking at it." With the tips of his fingers, he massaged her forehead. "Don't worry, Jo, Now that I've got you, you'll never be for sale again."

He stayed for a time, just stroking her face while his mind wandered and wondered. It wandered to thoughts of Sarah and wondered why she had to die when she did. "Doesn't seem right Jo, just when you think everything is going along just swell, bang, you get cut off at the knees. Now I find out Pete is sick too. Damn cancer. I'd like to say that life isn't fair, but I don't have a clue if it's fair, foul or indifferent. Better I don't know. All I can promise is I'll do my best to take care of you." She nickered again as if she was in complete understanding. Connie laughed softly. "You don't have a clue either, do you girl."

He patted her on the neck. "Go to sleep," he told her and went back to his bed in the bunkhouse.

No one had invited him to church since the barbecue. They all figured if he wanted to go again, he'd say something. That was fine with him. He'd probably go again, but he didn't know when. When he felt like it, he supposed. Mostly what he did when everyone else was gone was to just sit on his back step, or on the corral fence, with a cup of coffee and listen to the murmur of the breeze in the pines, smell the scented air, feel the thick sunshine on his bare arms, and watch the creek burbling past on it's way to the ocean. If it was raining, he lounged in the barn on a hay bale with a cup of coffee, played with the cats, and talked to the horses. Some times he took his fiddle outside and returned nature's serenade. Generally he contemplated life, especially the life he was living and enjoyed God's creation.

This Sunday was no different, although he did have more to contemplate. It seemed as if the troops had no sooner left for church, than they were returning. He was leaning against the bunkhouse back door, legs sprawled half way down the steps when Pete's vehicle rolled into the driveway. Connie checked his watch in disbelief. "Where does the time go?" he asked. Groaning as he stood, he vowed that after Kalispell Days, he would build a proper deck to replace these uncomfortable steps.

The girls saw him and started his way when Cally reined them in. "Danni and Lindsey, you change clothes before you do anything. I want those new dresses to last for more than one day." The girls settled for waving at Connie and went to the house to change.

Pete however, walked down to the bunkhouse. "Colleen asked about you. Wanted to know if you were still around or if you went back east."

"What did you tell her?"

"Well, I was at church. I couldn't lie. Told her you were still around, but I was keepin' you so busy, Sunday morning was the only free time you had."

"She buy that?"

"I'm not sure. After the service, she gave me this." Pete handed Connie a folded piece of paper.

Connie took and unfolded it. He read it aloud. "'Dear Conrad, I'd really like to see you again. If you're not seeing anyone, please give me a call. I think we could have some fun together. Colleen.' Well, that's about as direct as any invitation I've ever gotten." He crumpled the note. "If you see her again and she asks, tell her I'm seeing someone."

"Yeah, and who might that be?"

"Well, for starters, I'm going on a picnic with Cally this afternoon and maybe next week sometime I'll be taking Myra to dinner. Pete, I have to say, I'm a dating maniac."

"Yeah, and I'm the next president. Why don't you just tell her you're not interested? I'm sure her phone number is on that note."

Connie smoothed out the paper. "Yeah, it is. I'll call her. I don't know why she's after me anyway. The way she looks, she shouldn't be lonely."

"Well, according to Cally, there's a lot of guys out there, but there's not a lot of classy guys. She was sort of seeing a doctor, but she dumped him because he was too immature."

Connie had wondered what happened to Doctor Jim. "Hey, you don't suppose Cally could arrange for the doctor to meet Colleen do you? That would be a match made in heaven or maybe somewhere else, but it would get me off the hook."

Just then, the twins came roaring up. "Come on, Grandpa, we've got to saddle horses," Lindsey said.

Danni chimed in, "Yeah, Mom's already packing up the food. She needs the panniers."

"The panniers are on the porch," Pete told her. "I cleaned them and brought them up last night."

"Where on the porch?"

"Never mind. I'll get them to her. I have to go up to change clothes. You two go help Connie with the horses. Saddle up Bojo, Reba, Dunner, Socks, and Hope, and we'll put the packs on Katy and Tess. I imagine you'll be ridin' Jolena," he said to Connie.

Connie nodded. "Come on, you two, let's get movin'. I'm as ready for a swim in the lake as you are."

As Connie and the girls moved off to the barn Pete watched them go. He was thinking how much he loved the girls and that Connie was probably one of the classier guys out there. He sure hoped he had enough time left to see how this all played out.

Chapter 24, The Flirtation

Connie could have sworn the horses knew something big was up as soon as he and the twins walked into the pasture. Half of them ran up to meet them; the other half ran away. It took almost forty-five minutes to catch and saddle all the riding horses. It took Pete's help to catch Katy and Tess and cinch on the pack frames. When all was finally ready, the parade started with the girls racing each other across the creek for the lead. They were followed at a more sedate pace by Woody, Cally, and Pete leading the pack horses while Connie and Jolena brought up the rear.

Lindsey and Danni were already standing in ankle deep water, their swimsuits on, waiting for adult supervision, when Woody, Cally, and Pete arrived. Just before they reached the lake, Connie had turned off the trail, pulled off all Jo's tack and changed into his swim trunks. As the rest of the group dismounted, he rode up, passed them and splashed into the lake. When the water hit Jo's belly, he stopped her, stood up on her butt and dove in. Surfacing, he called Jo out to him and the two of them swam a lazy circle in front of their audience.

"Well, I'll be go to hell," said Woody. "That boy'll be takin' over from you as head horse trainer any day now, Pete."

"It's the horse, Woody. I believe even you could train Jolena." He wouldn't admit it, but he was impressed.

Connie returned to the cheers of the twins and Cally who whistled and clapped. He bowed and gestured to Jo who whinnied and walked off to graze. Connie made no move to restrain her. He'd been coming up here whenever he had the chance for the past month to swim with Jo. They both had the routine down pat.

Pete somewhat nervously watched Jolena walk over to where the rest of the horses were picketed. "That's a cutting horse you got there, son, not a circus horse."

"I believe that horse can do anything and in fact, just as soon as the futurity is over, Jolena and I are joining the circus."

"Can I go with you?" asked Danni.

"Yeah, me too," said Lindsey.

Cally laughed. "Neither one of you is joining the circus and I seriously doubt that Connie is either. We came up here to swim." She pulled off her tee shirt and stepped out of her jeans, revealing a very fit physique in a skimpy one-piece bathing suit. It was the sexiest thing Connie had seen in more than three years and Cally could tell the maneuver had the intended effect. "I'll race all of you to the bar."

Connie didn't know where or what the bar was, but if Cally was going there, so was he. He ran in after the girls. After two minutes, he wondered if he was the only one getting tired and just where was this bar? Then he felt the bottom come up quickly and suddenly they were all standing on a sandbar in ankle deep water. The girls ran along following the bar as it arced back in towards shore somewhere down the line. He and Cally were left alone.

"I think I won," she said.

"I'm sure you did. Why is this sandbar here?"

She pointed in the direction the girls were going. "I don't know. It comes from that little point over there. It's always been here. Dad says there must be springs in the lake that create enough of a current to form it and keep it here, although over the years it seems to wander around some."

Connie's eyes were doing some serious wandering of their own and he found it difficult not to stare at her. If only he were ten years younger. "Did Pete bring you up here to swim when you were a little girl?"

"All the time. It was my most favorite thing to do in the summer. My mother used to tell me I was going to grow webs between my toes. When I got older, I'd bring girlfriends up here. We had a rule though, no boys. It was for girls only. In fact, you're the only man I've ever been out here with, except Dad and Woody of course."

"I'm flattered and I'll never show it to anyone except Jolena."

"Horses are always accepted."

"So how wide is this thing?"

She pointed out across the lake. "Try walking that way."

He took three steps and was up to his waist. "I suppose it's all down hill from here?"

"Yeah, about ten feet in front of you it's ten feet deep. We used to see who could swim the farthest out and still touch bottom."

"I'm sure you always won."

"No, I had this friend, Leslie, I'm positive she was part turtle. She could bring up a hand full of sand from thirty feet. None of the rest of us could ever come close."

By this time the girls had followed the bar to the point and were splashing their way along the beach back to where Pete and Woody were unpacking the picnic. Cally watched the girls until she was sure Pete knew where they were and then moved over to where Connie was standing and sat down in the shallow water behind him.

"So Conrad Bradley, you've been out here almost two months, what do you think of the wild west?"

Taking a step backwards, Connie sat next to her. "Well, I don't think it's all that wild. It's different than back east, most everyone seems to be friendlier and probably more relaxed. I don't feel like there's as much competition for everything out here as there is where I lived. I doubt if I'll ever live back there when this is over."

"So what do you think you'll do after the futurity. And by the way, the girls already expect you to have Christmas with us."

"Christmas? It's not even the first of July. How did that come up?"

"In case you don't know it by now, Danni is very sensitive." Cally smiled, referring to the incident that almost chased him off the ranch.

"Yeah, I picked right up on that. I also discovered her mother is very sensitive about her kids."

"Come on, Connie, you've forgiven me for that little misunderstanding by now, haven't you?"

"Yeah, as soon as I heard the story about you chasing off the previous hired hand at gunpoint."

"You're hardly a hired hand and the one you're referring to, was a pervert. If he would have touched those girls, I'd have shot him dead."

"Yeah, and if I'd been around when you did, I would have helped you hide the body. I love those two kids."

"Well, they're smitten with you, too. So much so they're worried about you not having a home to go to for Christmas. Danni

wanted to know when the futurity was over and I told her it was just
before Christmas. Then she wanted to know what you would do and
where you would go when it was over. I truthfully told her I didn't
know. She insisted I invite you to stay, at least through Christmas. So,
consider yourself invited. They're already contemplating what they can
give you. Lindsey says you're a man that has everything."

"I'm touched," and he really was. "Well, it's Christmas with
you and the girls then."

"I'll tell them." She'd been looking out at the lake while she
talked, but now she turned to look Connie in the eyes. "What will you
do when this is over?" She gave him her best smile. "And don't tell me
you're running off to join the circus or I'll have to smack you."

He smiled back. "I don't know yet. I've thought about it.
When I'm on the tractor cutting hay, there's plenty of time to think.
Woody told me about an area in Idaho that sounds pretty nice. Maybe
I'll spend the winter in Texas and wander up to Idaho in the spring. If I
like it, I'll look for a little ranch to buy. I think I'd have a tough time
going back to the big city. If my memory serves me, one of my
classmates and best buddies from West Point was from somewhere
around Grangeville, Idaho. I might go look him up."

"You could always spend the winter here. You'll be here for
Christmas anyway and it's a lot closer to Idaho from here than it is from
Texas."

"That's a fantastic offer. I'll have to consider it, but by the time
Christmas is over, you'll all probably be tired of having me around."

"I doubt that very much," and then deciding she'd probably said
enough, she stood and took Connie by the hand. She pulled hard.
"Come on, I'll give you another chance. Race you back to the beach."

Connie let her stay in front so he could keep his eyes on her.
He lost again

While Connie played with the twins in the warm shallows,
Cally assembled lunch on the log table Pete had built thirty years ago. It
was over twelve feet long, weighed about six hundred pounds and was
in need of some maintenance. Woody and Pete reclined on aluminum
chaise lounge chairs from a stash Pete kept hidden in the woods and
watched Connie launch the girls over his shoulder into deeper water.
Pete and Woody sipped from large plastic tumblers containing heavily
iced gin and tonics.

About two o-clock, Cally poured herself a large gin and tonic
and announced that lunch was ready. Connie was relieved. The twins
thought the launch game was the coolest thing they'd ever done.

Connie's arms and shoulders disagreed. He threw a beach towel across
his back and took a seat in front of an empty plate
        Cally looked at him. "Here's how this works. All the food is at
this end, bring your plate over here, fill it up, go back, and sit down.
That way no one has to pass anything and you can come back for more
when you're ready."
        "I can do that," he said and before the picnic was officially over,
he made four trips to the food end of the table. There was a raw
vegetable plate, a fresh fruit plate, a cold shrimp plate, three different
cold salads, two kinds of beans, a huge plate of fried chicken, still warm,
and a desert plate. Connie could understand why they had taken two
packhorses.
        After eating, Pete and Woody zoned out in their lounge chairs
while Connie and Cally sat at the table talking and watching the girls
play in the shallow water.
        "When I was a kid," Connie told her, "most of my swimming
was in pools at officers' clubs on army bases. I didn't swim in a lake
until I was fourteen."
        "You poor deprived child. Where was the lake?"
        "Montana, down around Livingston."
        "You're kidding. What were you doing down there?"
        "Working."
        "Working, at fourteen? Doing what?"
        "Same thing I'm doing here, ranch work. Only it was a dude
ranch and I didn't drive tractor and bale hay, but I did saddle horses and
ride with the dudes. Not my first year though. I seem to remember
cleaning lots of stables and grooming horses that first summer."
        "I had no idea you were already a cowboy when you came out
here. Was there a lake like this one back in the hills where you went
swimming?"
        "Well, not as nice as this one. The bottom was rocky. You had
to wear tennis shoes when you went in and I don't think it was as clear
as this one, but we had fun."
        "How did you ever come to Montana to work on a dude
ranch?"
        "One of my dad's best army friends was from Montana and
when he retired, he went back, bought an old run down cattle ranch,
refurbished it and opened a dude ranch. Two years later, my dad retired
and we went out for a visit. I was twelve and his friend told my dad that
in a couple years, I could come out for the summer and he'd put me to
work. I wanted to stay then, except everybody but me realized I was a

little too young. I whined so much about it for the next two years that
when I turned fourteen, we drove out again and my parents left me there.
I was still a bit young, but after two weeks, I could have stayed forever.
In fact, my last summer there, after I graduated from high school, I was
planning on staying. I wanted to be a rodeo cowboy and then buy a
ranch of my own."

"That certainly explains a lot. When you showed up, I thought
you were just another city boy with a fat wallet. I didn't think you'd last
a week."

"I almost didn't. If Lindsey hadn't given me a pep talk, I would
have been on my way to Texas."

Cally laughed. "You mean she actually did change your mind?
What did she say?"

"She asked me if you had a 'talk' with me. I told her it was a
one sided conversation and she told me that's how it was when you gave
a talk. She said you were basically harmless and I shouldn't be a girly
girl. She also told me there was nothing in Texas, so I might as well
stay right here."

"She was right about everything except me being harmless. I'm
ferocious if I need to be."

"I'm sure you are. Anybody who can't be tough when they
need to be isn't worth much in a pinch. Anyway, after Lindsey and I
talked, I decided to stay. I really like the place."

"I'm glad you did. All of us are glad you're here. Dad just said
again yesterday he thinks he got lucky twice, once with Jolena and again
with you."

Connie suddenly felt guilty. Pete had definitely been lucky
with Jo and maybe even with him, but he wasn't so lucky with his health.
Connie wanted to say something to Cally, however he'd promised Pete
not to and really, it was up to Pete, not him. "I'm flattered," he told her.
"I'm the lucky one."

Danni came running up, rubbing her eyes, "Lindsey threw sand
at me."

Cally looked over to Lindsey. "What's going on?"

From the water, Lindsey shouted back, "It was an accident,
honest."

Danni's condition didn't look too serious. Connie scooped her
up in his arms and carried her into the lake. "We'll just have to wash
your eyes out." He held her out by the ankles and dunked her head in
the water several times. She squealed with delight. Then Lindsey
jumped on his back and for two minutes there was a massive water fight

with no clear winner until Cally joined in on the girls' side and soon
Connie had to cry for mercy. Pete, wakened by the commotion, thought
Cally looked happier than he could remember.

After Connie's surrender, Pete called over to her "Cally, you
think it's time we head back?"

Her watch told her it was after four. "Yeah, I'll start clearing
up."

From the water, Connie watched Cally start packing things and
told the girls he had to go help. They protested and he told them,
"We've had a great time and we can do it again soon, but now it's time
to go. You can't always do what you want, when you want."

"Yeah, we know," Lindsey said.

"It's the same thing Mom tells us except she never tells us
why," added Danni.

Connie slipped one arm around each girl's waist, lifted them
easily and started back to shore. They hugged his neck tightly. "I'm not
sure why either, but come on. Let's go help."

It took a half hour to pack up and saddle the horses, and by five
thirty they were back at the house. After seeing to the horses, Connie
opened a beer and dropped into his chair. He attempted to contemplate
the afternoon's event, from the way Cally looked to what she said, but
fell asleep. It wasn't until Woody knocked on his door an hour and a
half later that he woke.

"Takin' a little nap before you go to bed?" Woody asked.

"I didn't intend to, but I guess I was." He felt his beer bottle.
Warm. "You know what I'd really like?"

"A cold beer?"

"Yeah, that and fresh, hot popcorn."

"How can you be hungry? I saw you eat at the picnic. You
keep doin' that, you're gonna end up lookin' like you swallowed a
Shetland pony."

"I doubt it. You know I've lost seven pounds since I came
here."

"If that's true, you gotta have a more inefficient digestive
system than a horse."

"I think I'm just working too hard."

"The only one of us around here who works too hard is Cally,
but that would explain why she is in such fine physical form."

Connie shook his head. "She looks as good in a swimsuit as any
woman I've ever seen."

"Yeah, I never saw her in that suit before. She usually doesn't wear 'em quite so skimpy."

"You complaining?"

"Of course not, but a man in my condition shouldn't be exposed to so much pulchritude. Not good for the heart. I'm thinkin' she must have worn that suit specifically to catch your attention." He pronounced specifically with a long e.

"It certainly worked. I can't think of anything that's maintained my attention in the last two years like she did this afternoon. You really think she wore it for me?"

Woody got up, went to Connie's refrigerator and extracted two beers. He handed one to Connie, "There's so much you don't know 'bout women, I hardly know where to start."

Two hours later, Woody had gone back to the big house and Connie was lying in bed. He was still having trouble believing Cally was interested in him. Woody's theories on the feminine mind were fascinating, but they were just that—theories. Connie had truly known only one woman and most of what Woody thought about what motivated women didn't apply to her. If Cally were trying to get his attention, what should he do about it? If she were merely being nice, he didn't want to make a fool of himself. There's no bigger fool than an old fool especially if he's being a fool over a woman. *Better wait and see what happens. Play it cool, Connie, play it cool.* With that thought, he fell asleep.

Chapter 25, The Streak

The competition in Kalispell was on the Fourth of July, a Thursday. To prepare for it, Pete had Connie riding his two reining horses until Connie had mastered the sliding stop and was no longer dizzy from spinning. That was in addition to cutting practice on both Billy and Jolena. Connie rode four hours every day. Then he cut and baled hay from right after lunch until almost sunset. It was a tough three days. Cally could have showed up at the bunkhouse any time after supper wearing only a smile and Connie would have slept through it.

Thursday dawned bright and clear. Cally had told everyone to sleep in. She wouldn't make breakfast until eight, but Connie woke at his normal time. He got up, made coffee, and went outside to watch the morning begin. Cally was awake too, and saw him park a folding chair by the creek. She debated going down to sit with him and finally decided against it. Then she attempted to analyze her attraction to him and finally decided she didn't know exactly what it was. There were the obvious reasons of course; he was handsome, his body was in better condition than that of most men her age, he apparently had money, class, and taste. He liked kids, at least hers anyway, and he was certainly intelligent. Then there were a few not so obvious things. He seemed to be thoughtful, patient, and kind and if the way he first looked at her in her new bathing suit last Sunday was any indication, she suspected he could be passionate, too. All these things were important, but there was more and she couldn't put her finger on what exactly it was.

She watched him for a while, looking down from her bedroom window across the yard to the creek. As she watched, the thought she was being what Lindsey called a girly-girl came to her. She'd given Connie enough hints. If he couldn't figure it out from here, he might not be as smart as she thought. She left the window and went back to bed, but she didn't sleep.

Down by the creek, Connie's head was as full of thoughts as Cally's. He hadn't come out here to find romance; a replacement for his wife wasn't an issue. Meeting Cally was not fate, it was merely chance; nothing more. He could choose to act on it or ignore it, the choice was his. He didn't owe anybody anything, except he'd promised Pete he'd try to take Jolena to the futurity. That was a deal and now it was something he wanted as much or more than Pete. And there was Pete's cancer. *How would that play out? It always killed. But when? You never beat it, you merely postponed it.* To Connie, cancer was the ultimate physical sickness.

The morning sun washed the little valley with an ocean of light. The creek rippled and popped, the pines stood in jagged, green symmetry against the impossibly blue sky, and Connie found it difficult to be anything but content. Draining his cup, he pushed back in his chair and decided to take it slow. He'd do everything he could to be helpful, but now was not the time to get all gushy over Cally or any other woman. He'd do what he came to do, take Jolena to the futurity.

On the Fourth in Kalispell, the first go-round in the open class was scheduled to start at one in the afternoon. There were over a hundred entrants and the top twenty would ride again at seven that night to decide the winner. Connie made a couple of stupid mistakes in the first round and barely qualified. Pete didn't say anything. He knew Connie realized what he'd done wrong and knew he wouldn't make those mistakes again. Gilly Bedfort finished fifth in the first round, eight points ahead of Connie. The points didn't matter because in the final round the first score was thrown out and everyone started equal, except you rode in the same order in which you finished. Connie had finished last in the first round, which meant he rode last in the final round. This was a definite disadvantage as the cows weren't as fresh and it was difficult to find those that hadn't been worked.

It didn't matter. When Connie rode last, the score to beat was Gilly's two twenty-three. He blew the saddles off the competition and finished to a standing ovation with a two twenty-seven, beating Gilly by four points. Pete was as proud as he'd ever been, including the day he won the futurity forty-five years earlier. First prize was five grand and a fancy saddle, but the sweetest part was taking Gilly Senior's six hundred dollars.

Gilliam Bedfort Senior met him, Pete, and Woody outside the arena office after the award ceremony. "Well, you did it, Conrad. You must have practiced night and day," said Senior. Junior was nowhere to be seen.

Pete handed Connie the envelope he'd been holding since Saturday. Connie took it. "You can call me Connie, Mister Bedfort. All my friends do and I want to thank you, too. Not so much for the money, but for the motivation."

Bedfort laughed. "Connie, if I'd have known I was helpin' you, I'd never have bet you a nickel. I'd still like to buy that paint horse though. How about a hundred thousand? And you can call me Gilly."

It was Connie's turn to laugh. He threw his arm across Bedfort's shoulder. "Gilly, I've probably got as much or maybe even more money than you do so you can stop offering to buy my horse and I can stop refusing you. We're likely to be much better friends that way."

Bedfort would rather have Connie's horse than Connie's friendship, but it appeared as if he wasn't going to get her. It also appeared if he expected his son to have a serious shot at winning the futurity, he'd have to find a better three-year old than Jolena. That was probably impossible at this stage of the game. All he could hope for was that either Connie or Jolena would break a leg.

"Well, Connie, I'd rather have you as a friend than an enemy."

"Good, that's settled then." He still didn't trust Gilly farther than he could throw him, although under the right circumstances and he were mad enough, that distance would not be inconsequential.

Gilly was about to propose he buy them all a drink when the twins came rushing up. They jumped into Connie's arms and he caught them both. Gilly tipped his Stetson, "Ladies and gentlemen, another time."

Finished with hugs, Connie set Lindsey and Danni down just as Cally walked up. "Congratulations, Cowboy," she said and held out her hand.

She was smiling and she looked magnificent. He might have been semi-giddy or maybe just full of the moment, but he decided she wasn't going to get away with a mere handshake. He took her hand and pulled. The intensity of their embrace surprised both of them. Embarrassed, they quickly backed apart. Connie immediately felt as if he shouldn't have done it, but Cally was still smiling. So was the rest of his fan club, but he wasn't sure at what.

"So," he asked, "When do the fireworks start?"

"Should be real soon," Woody said and he paused a long time before he added, "It's almost nine thirty."

It was well after mid-night when Connie finally dropped into bed. He'd spent almost an hour grooming and talking to Jolena. He told her how he felt about Cally and that he wasn't sure he wanted to get involved, at least now. In short, he bared his soul—to a horse.

"Good grief," he said once he was in bed. "I must be crazy," but he didn't elaborate because he fell asleep.

The next day was tough. Cally had announced right after the fireworks that due to the extraordinary events of the evening, breakfast would again be at eight. Pete had told Connie earlier, he'd be talking to Cally about his medical condition in the morning. Connie was apprehensive at breakfast, but it was immediately apparent Pete hadn't said anything yet. He ate quickly and excused himself. Cally wondered why he left abruptly and wondered even more when Woody got out fast, too.

"Dad, what's going on?"

"Why, what's going on?"

"No, that's my line. Connie rarely rushes through breakfast and Woody never does. What's up?"

The twins were all ears. Pete looked at them. As far as he was concerned, they might as well know now. They would find out shortly anyway. They were his family.

"I have a little problem and it involves my health."

It was something she hoped she'd never hear, but something she'd always known she might. When Pete got to the details, she sent the girls to go find Connie and Woody and stay with them until she and Pete were through.

"Grandpa is sick," Lindsey told Connie.

Danni was sobbing, "I'll bet he's going to die. How can you be so sick and look so healthy at the same time?"

"Have you ever heard the word insidious?" Connie asked the girls.

They both shook their heads. "Well insidious means that something is sneaky and dangerous at the same time. Your grandfather has cancer and a lot of times cancer sneaks up on you. You feel fine, maybe for a long time, but then, very quickly, you get real sick. You grandpa is in that time where he still feels good, but when the cancer gets stronger, he'll start to get sicker."

"Can't the doctors stop it?" Danni asked, fat tears trailing down her cheeks.

"Sometimes, and they can usually slow it down. Your grandpa is going to go see some of the best doctors there are. Hopefully, they can help."

"Yeah, he's going to some clinic back east and we can't go along. Mom says we'd be in the way." Lindsey sounded resentful.

"I don't believe for a minute your mom is serious about you being in the way, but your grandpa is going to be very busy while he's there. You know, sometimes you have to travel light. You two will be better off staying here with me and Woody."

"Can we go swimming in the lake?"

"Sure. I can't make a picnic like your mom, but I can get us pizza from Kila and we can take that up to Rogers Lake."

"Yeah," agreed Woody, "We can roast hotdogs too. We'll be okay 'til your mom and grandpa get back."

Lindsey was comforted, but Danni wasn't. "Is he going to die?"

Woody put his arm around her. "Sweetie, you know what a journey is, right?"

"Sure, it's a big trip."

"Exactly. Each and every one of us is on a journey. The journey is called life. At the end of our big trip we die, each and every one of us. We all die."

"I know all that. I don't want Grandpa to die now."

"Well, that's what I'm talking about. None of us knows exactly where our journey will take us or when it will end. Your grandpa has been on a long journey. When he was little like you, he rode horses and lived on a ranch, just like you do. Then when he was a young man, he was a soldier and fought in Korea. Then he married your grandma, Renee. She was about the prettiest woman I ever saw and her and your grandpa were both horse doctors. They bought this ranch, built the house you live in and raised your mom from a baby, just like your mom is raising you. Grandpa Pete has ridden hundreds of horses and won all kinds of contests just like he showed Connie how to win. He's been to a lot of places and done a lot of things. He's had a long journey and now it could be coming to an end and there might not be a thing we can do about it except love him while he's still here and say goodbye when he leaves." He gave her a hug. "That's just the way it is."

"It sucks."

"Young ladies shouldn't talk like that, but you're right. Sometimes it does suck. But then other times it's wonderful. You had a blast up at the lake the other day, didn't you, and you have fun ridin' turn back for Connie when he's practicing, don't you?"

"Yeah, but that's different."

"Well, of course it's different. Life is always changing and it ain't always fun, that's why it's a journey. It keeps moving. But you don't have to always like everything about it either, I guess."

About then, Pete and Cally showed up, Cally to collect the girls and Pete to organize his hay making crew. Lindsey and Danni hugged Pete half to death before Cally could get them back to the house. They had to do dishes and Cally had to get organized. She was initially upset with her father for waiting so long to tell her, but he was right when he explained she would just have had longer to worry. They'd be leaving in two weeks; she'd be too busy to do much worrying.

"Let's just bale up what we've got cut and get everything into the barn. We can start haying again on Monday. Connie, there's another contest in Whitefish on Saturday you should be in, and a big one in Missoula a week after that. Then there's the one at the fair in Helena, a week later. Then I leave for the clinic, but that weekend there's a major event in Billings. I'm certain I won't be back by then, but if you and Woody could pack up the kids and take your time that would be one to make. It's three days and it'll be good practice for the futurity."

"You should take a break once in a while when you're talkin'," Woody told him. "Gives more import to what you're sayin'."

Connie couldn't help it. He burst out laughing. Both Pete and Woody regarded him somewhat critically. "Sorry, I can't help it. We just had a therapy session for two little girls, then you show up, Pete, and start talking a mile a minute with plans for the next two weeks and Woody gives advice as if he were the debating coach. What time is it? I could use a beer and maybe a cigar too."

Pete looked at his watch. It's not quite ten."

"Too early. How'd it go with Cally?"

"She was plenty upset, initially, but the girls were there so she had to restrain herself. Then she settled down and listened. She insists on going with me, just like I predicted and I agreed. We also agreed you two could take care of the girls and the ranch, if that's okay."

"Course it is, Pete," Woody said, "you been lookin' after me for at least thirty years, it's time I paid you back a little."

Connie nodded. "I'm in, Buddy, for whatever you need."

"Thank you, both. This could be a hell of a ride before it's over."

When they had the downed hay baled and stored in the barn, they packed it in. Connie saddled Jolena and went for a ride. Pete took a nap and Woody took one of the tractors down to the Kila saloon. He'd never gotten a drivers license, but he didn't need it to drive farm machinery. He parked behind the building and spent a couple of hours at the bar talking to his lady friend while she poured drinks.

The next day, Connie and Billy drove alone to Whitefish, but by the time the contest started, his fan club was in the stands. He treated them to a winning performance and then to dinner at Rustlers. In spite of the concern over Pete's health, they all managed to have a good time. The girls especially, since they didn't have to do dishes afterwards. Connie asked around about Myra, but apparently she was still out of town. Too bad, he thought, Cally and the girls might have liked to meet her.

A week later, Pete and Connie made the two-hour drive to Missoula and Connie won all the marbles again, his third win in a row. If he could keep this up, he might eventually get back his investment.

The next weekend was the contest in Helena and the following Monday morning, Pete and Cally had a flight to Minneapolis. All the arrangements had been made, the only uncertainty was Pete's condition. The way Pete saw it, he'd either be back home in a week on his feet or he'd be home in a box. He didn't share his opinion, but he did tell Cally to remember that anything was possible.

Connie suggested that they all go to Helena as sort of a mini vacation and going away party. It was quickly agreed to by everyone except Woody who had a date for Saturday night with the woman who worked at the Kila saloon. The girls were wild with anticipation because they would get to stay in Connie's trailer. Cally was glad to have a diversion and Pete would be going regardless. They left at noon on Friday and by five that afternoon they were parked with about two hundred other trailers in the parking lot next to the fairgrounds.

Pete was tired so Cally and Connie took the girls and did the fair, or at least the rides and the food. Cally made an exception to the fast food rule and they all over indulged on everything from fried cheese curds to pork chops on a stick. The next morning Connie regretted some of his culinary choices, but by the time he had to ride, his stomach was back where it belonged. He finished first in the first round and won the final round by three points. Billy was impressive and Connie was good enough. He now had four first place finishes in a row.

They left for home early Sunday morning. Pete spent considerable time talking about the time he'd won the futurity, forty-five years ago.

"I could do no wrong," he said. "Everything went my way, every time. I had a good horse, Czar, he wasn't a great horse like Jolena, but he was good. I'd trained Czar myself and was real proud of him. I was certain if we could pick out some decent cows, we had a good shot at the title. When I got there, I watched each cowboy, hoping to spot anything I could use. I memorized the cows that had been cut once so I'd find fresh ones. And I tried to analyze every ride to see what I'd have done different. Funny thing was, when I crossed the time line, I forgot everything I was trying so hard to remember and put it on automatic pilot. I did what came natural and Czar and I got lucky.

"Don't think for a minute luck doesn't play a part in this game because it does. Personally, I'd rather be good than lucky, but I know a few cowboys who are more lucky than good and they do okay." It was his last chance to talk to Connie before he departed on another segment of his long journey. He wanted very much for Connie to remember what he said.

Connie smiled. "So you're saying that I'll need to be lucky to win?"

"Your luck is Jolena. I've been watching the horses you've been riding against these last couple weeks. I've only seen one that even begins to come up to Jo's level and since she's been ridden in competition, she won't be at Fort Worth."

"Well, not to worry then," said Connie. Although he was worried and would continue to be.

Chapter 26, Take a Break

Woody and the girls said their goodbyes to Pete and Cally at home, before Connie drove them to the airport. They had a direct flight to Minneapolis and from there, a limo ride to the Mayo Clinic in Rochester, courtesy of Connie. Once at the clinic, Cally could walk to everything she'd need. The town catered to visitors from all over the world and it was possible to get most anything in the way of food, clothing, and medical supplies within a half mile radius of the clinic.

Before Cally and Pete got on the plane Connie handed Pete a bag.

"What's this?"

"Something to keep you from getting bored out of your skull, hopefully."

Pete hefted the bag. "It's kind of heavy." He peeked inside. It was a portable DVD player and some DVDs including *Band of Brothers*, *Saving Private Ryan* and a documentary on the Korean War. "Wow! Hey Cally, Connie got me my own private theater. Thanks, Connie."

"You're welcome and don't you two worry about anything back here. Just get done what needs to be done and come home as soon as you can. We'll be waiting. Call often."

Blinking back tears, Cally told herself not to make a scene. She hugged Connie, "You're a good friend. Take care of my girls and Woody and yourself too." Then she hugged him again and held on.

Pete shook his hand. "What's the first rule?"

"Watch the cow."

"What's the third rule?"

"Jolena knows best."

"You're good to go. I'll see you in a week or two."

Clearing security, Pete and Cally turned and waved from the other side. And then they were gone.

The drive back to the ranch was depressing. Connie prayed to heaven he'd see Pete alive again. He wasn't sure he could do this on his own. The girls and Woody were mopey when he got back, but he promised them dinner at the Rustlers if they'd cheer up and it worked.

Then he made a deal with Woody. "I'll cut and bale if you'll watch the girls and make breakfast and lunch. We'll go out for dinners, my treat. What good is all this prize money I've been winning if I don't spend it?"

"That sounds good to me. Are we still fixin' to leave for Billings early Thursday morning?"

"Thursday is pushin' it. I'm thinking we should leave Wednesday early afternoon. That'll put us in there before sunset. We can sleep in and take it easy Thursday. The first round starts at nine Friday morning."

"Okay, you're the boss. I'll get a hold of Boissvert to have him look in on the place twice a day."

"Deal," said Connie, and he went out to start knocking down hay.

Myra was the hostess at Rustlers when they got there. "Cowboy," she greeted Connie with a big hug. Then she saw Woody and the girls. "And look, you have a family since I last saw you."

Connie introduced the girls and explained about Pete's medical problem. He also explained he'd been rather busy of late.

"You cowboys are all alike. It's just like the song says, 'You love that damned old rodeo more than you love me.' " She showed them to a table and had the waitress deliver black and tans to Woody and Connie and Shirley Temples to Danni and Lindsey.

"She sure is nice," said Lindsey

"Yeah, pretty too. Do you love her?" Danni asked.

Connie almost spit beer across the room. "What? Where did you get that idea from?"

"Well, she said something about how you loved the rodeo more than her."

"Yeah," Woody put in, "Maybe you'd care to explain that to all of us."

"There's nothing to explain. She was joking because about three weeks ago, I told her I'd call her, but first she was out of town for a week and then I was busy for two weeks. I never called her. That's all there is to it."

"Since you guys are in love," said Lindsey. "Do you think you could ask her if her daughter will give us ski lessons for free?"

"Lindsey, we are not in love. We've never even been on a date. I'll pay for your ski lessons. Don't worry about it."

Woody was grinning at him from across the table. "Nice job with the explanation. If I ask you to get me dinner every week 'cause you and Myra are in love will you buy it for me too?"

Connie rolled his eyes. "Just keep it up and instead of taking you three out for dinner, I'll make hotdogs or something equally as tasty every night."

The girls giggled and Woody drained half his glass. "Order big tonight, ladies, we might be goin' hungry for a few days."

They continued to pick on him until the food arrived and all foolishness ceased. For skinny, nine-year-old girls they had powerful appetites. They ate like sixteen-year-old boys, just a little slower.

When the waitress brought the check and it showed, 'No charge', Connie excused himself and went looking for Myra. He went to the lobby where he found a hostess who was not Myra.

"Miss, I need to talk to Miss Foxx."

She looked at him rather critically. "I'm sorry, sir, who are you looking for?"

He sighed. It was really a problem to have two names. "Miss Lane."

"Yes, sir, and can I tell her your name?"

"Connie."

"I'm sorry sir, did you say, Connie?"

"Yeah, Connie. Conrad Bradley."

She punched a button on her phone. "Miss Lane, Conrad Bradley would like to talk to you." There was a brief pause. "Thank you."

The woman hung up the phone and smiled sweetly at Connie, "Miss Lane is in her office and you can talk to her there."

"That's cool. Where might I find her office?"

"Oh, sorry." She pointed to the right. "Go into the other room, behind the bar, there's a sign on the door that says office."

"How convenient. What do I tell the bartender?"

"Just tell him you have an appointment with Miss Lane."

"I can't let you pick up this tab," Connie told Myra when he got into her office.

"Of course you can. I own the joint." She came out from behind her desk. "You can buy next time. Maybe we'll even get to eat together." Her smile was near intoxicating to Connie.

He knew arguing would be futile. "Okay, but I'll be in Billings this weekend."

"You'll be coming back, right?"

"Well yes, but…"

She took two steps forward and kissed him. He kissed back. "Call me when you do."

"Okay, boys and girls, let's head back to the ranch," he said when he returned to the table. He left the waitress a twenty dollar tip.

He had a lot to tell Jolena that night before he went to bed. He told her about Pete and Cally going away and how he hoped Pete would be okay, at least for a while. He told her what an evil thing cancer was and how much he despised it. He told her all about Myra Foxx and that he thought he'd better be very careful. "I don't need any more complications right now." Jo nickered, but whether it was in agreement or merely because she liked the sound of his voice was impossible to say.

The last thing he talked about was the trip to Billings and how he thought they could win again and how great it would be to be able to tell Pete they pulled off another one.

He didn't sleep well that night, tossing, turning and dreaming bizarre dreams. At breakfast, Woody reminded him there were trucks coming for all the hay they had in the barn and since they were leaving Wednesday, at noon, better not cut anymore, just bale up what they had on the ground. "Besides, we got everything cut once, it won't hurt to wait a few days before we start over."

Connie pushed his sourdough flapjacks around his plate and nodded in agreement. Woody watched him with some concern. "You're off your feed this morning. What's the matter?"

Connie yawned. "I couldn't sleep last night. I'm just a little tired."

"Have anything to do with a foxy lady."

Connie looked at Danni and Lindsey. They were feigning indifference as well as they could, but it was obvious they were on full alert. Connie laughed and then lied. "Not a thing. I think it was something I ate."

Woody winked at him. "Yeah, I had a little trouble sleepin' too, but in my case it was everything I ate. How about you ladies, you have any trouble sleepin' last night?"

Before either girl could comment, the phone rang. Woody answered. It was Cally. She'd called yesterday after her and Pete were settled in the hotel and now she was calling to report that Pete had started his tests. It would be late in the afternoon or more likely tomorrow before they had any results. She talked to each girl for ten minutes and in the meantime, a semi pulled into the driveway. By the time she asked to talk to Connie, he was out loading hay.

Before the first truck was loaded, the second pulled in and Connie was loading hay until almost nine. Woody and the girls had cleaned the kitchen and fed the horses before he was through. The day was becoming warm with a breeze out of the southeast.

"I'm thinkin'," Woody, told Connie, "if we turn over the hay you cut yesterday right now, we can start balin' it by four. I'll be real surprised if it don't rain tomorrow."

They hooked up the rakes and well before noon had turned the hay. The day continued to heat up and was becoming what Woody called a "real scorcher". But the humidity was staying down and they could practically hear the hay crackle as it dried in the steady breeze. Connie started baling at four and just before sunset, he finished. Now he was really tired, but if the trucks showed up in the morning, they'd have everything cleaned up and moved out before they left. He took Woody and the kids to the Kila saloon for pizza and later, as soon as his head hit the pillow, had no problem sleeping the night through.

In the morning everything went as planned. They pulled away from the ranch about ten minutes after noon, Billy and Jolena in the trailer. They stopped at the Boot Hill on the south end of Kalispell for lunch. Connie spotted a black Escalade in the parking lot, but it must have belonged to a customer because Myra was nowhere in sight. With full bellies, they headed down the road to Polson and then I-90. Missoula came next, then Butte, then Bozeman and finally Billings. The girls looked like a lazy set of bookends, tilted towards each other, sound asleep in the back seat when Connie parked the rig at the Cottonwoods RV Park and Mare Motel. It was a good thing they left when they did, the place was already well over half full.

It was seven-thirty, sinfully late, before Connie finally rolled out of bed in the morning. He put on coffee, used the bathroom and took the horses for a stretch. When he came back, Woody and the girls were at the table eating fresh blueberries swimming in heavy cream while waiting for the fried egg sandwiches with bacon that Woody was making. They goofed around at the breakfast table until almost nine.

The beauty of this particular park was that it was within easy walking distance of the arena and fair grounds. At ten, Connie hoofed over to pay his two hundred and fifty dollar entry fee. Over three hundred cowgirls and cowboys were already registered in the open class. The top sixty would qualify for the second go-round and the twenty with the highest scores would ride in the final on Saturday night. Connie found a few names he recognized from Kalispell, but Gilly Bedfort wasn't one of them. There were cows available to rent for practice and a number of riders were out working their horses.

Top prize in the open division was twenty grand and Chevrolet was throwing in a new pickup. Connie debated buying some practice time, but the more he debated, the less appealing it was. It wasn't that he was so good he didn't need practice, he was merely spoiled by having his own private trainer and arena. He watched for a while before he returned to the trailer.

There were new neighbors on both sides of them when Connie returned. Woody and the twins were sitting under the awning drinking lemonade with a young couple who had just moved in next door. The woman was short, pretty, and plump. Sitting next to her on one side was a cute, pudgy, two-year old with dark hair and on the other side, a cowboy who looked to be in his late twenties, short and built like a bull rider. After introductions, Connie learned the cowboy, Cody, was thirty-two, a professional cutting horse trainer and in this particular show, was riding three horses for three separate clients. His goal was to some day find that one great horse and take it to the top, the futurity in Fort Worth.

Connie was suddenly disheartened. *What am I doing here? This kid probably has thirty thousand hours in the saddle, cut fifty thousand head of cattle, and trained two hundred cutting horses. And I think I can win against the likes of him?* What Connie said was, "So are you taking a horse to Fort Worth?"

"Yes sir," Cody replied, "Two of 'em. How about you?"

"Yes, I am. Me and Jolena."

"Jolena?" Cody asked. "She one of 'em your trailer?"

"Yup, want a look at her?"

"Absolutely. Always nice to get a preview of the competition."

Cody followed Connie into the trailer through the side door. "Nice," Cody said, "Air conditioning."

Connie smiled. "Yeah, the front's air conditioned and for only a little more, I had the back done, too. So far it's been a good investment." He slipped a halter on Jolena and led her out.

Cody walked all around her, taking note of every detail. "Well, she looks like a cutter. Where did you get her?"

"Bought her at an auction from Pete Browning. Maybe you've heard of him?"

"Heard of him? I've studied his methods. He's one of the best in the country. He still working horses?"

"Yeah, but I believe this will be his last big project," and Connie proceeded to tell him about his involvement with Pete.

"Nuts," said Cody when Connie was through, "I won't stand a chance against you two."

"Oh, I don't think I'd throw in the towel just yet. I'm not much of a rider and you're a real pro."

"Doesn't mean a lot any more. Non-pros have won twice in the last five years. It's ninety percent horse and ten percent rider."

"Yeah, I don't know a lot, but I know you need a good horse."

"This game is all about the horse. That's why it's so much fun. You've got to find one that's smart, quick, strong, and athletic. Then, if that's not enough, she has to have the soul to want to win and the heart to pull it off. Horses like that are scarce. All horses are strong and most are quick. A few of those are athletic enough and some less are smart enough. But when it comes to the heart and soul part," Cody shook his head slowly, "those horses are few and far between."

Just before he rode in the first go around the next morning, Cody's words came back to Connie. He patted Billy gently on the neck as they walked into the arena. Crossing the time line, he felt a chill run up his spine. He grinned and then he and Billy gave a performance that easily qualified them for the semi-finals. Cody, in between rides, watched from the bleachers. It was immediately obvious to him Connie was only an adequate rider, but riding a powerfully good horse. *And the horse back in his trailer is supposed to be a lot better.* Cody leaned over to his wife, "If he can keep his seat, he's got a chance."

The semi-final in the open class started the next afternoon at one. Connie rode fourth and turned in a score that earned him part of a three-way tie for first place in the final. When the scores for the first go around and the semi-final were added together, Connie was high point man. He'd be riding first in the final. Even though the cows were the freshest, he didn't consider riding first to be an advantage; too much tension. He'd almost rather ride last.

Woody grilled steaks and fried potatoes at five, but Connie was too nervous to eat much. "Butterflies? " Woody asked.

"Yeah, big time."

Connie picked up a spoon and held it at the very end between his thumb and forefinger. The bowl end of it hopped around like the ball in a roulette wheel.

"You're just doing that," Lindsey told him.

"You're right, but I don't want to."

Danni was sitting next to him. She stood up and put her arms around him and hugged. "Don't be nervous. It's only a game."

Connie laughed. "Thanks, Danni. You're right, it is only a game."

After a brief opening ceremony, the announcer introduced them, "Our first horse tonight is Billy ridden by Connie Bradley out of Kalispell. Good luck to both of you."

He crossed the timeline and the butterflies were gone. He pushed into the herd for a deep cut and all went well, the cow giving a brief, but spirited attempt to rejoin the herd. The next cow performed a number of serious maneuvers, but Billy handled her with ease and they received some nice applause. Connie was thinking it wasn't all that bad to ride first as they went back to the herd. He steered Billy towards a smaller cow with an alert, almost desperate look in her eye as she peeked out from under the belly of a bigger herd mate. Connie and Billy brought her out in front of the judges. As soon as Connie dropped the reins, the cow took off like a shot. Billy dug in for all he was worth and got in front of it. The cow turned faster than Connie had ever seen a cow turn and high tailed it for the fence. Billy was barely able to beat it, but in his haste he misjudged the distance to the fence and slid into it. He didn't bump it that hard and Connie stayed on, but he lost his rhythm. Then three things happened almost simultaneously. The crowd gasped collectively, the cow spun and blasted past Billy, and the horn signaled the end of the run.

The judges may have had some doubts as to whether the cow got past them before the horn sounded, but Connie knew instantly they'd been beaten. Billy knew it too and as they walked out to a polite round of applause, he hung his head. They had gone from top contender to big loser in the blink of an eye.

From the stands, Cody, who hadn't made the final round with either of his horses, watched with a critical eye.

Chapter 27, The Gelding

"Did ya think you couldn't lose?" Woody asked Connie when they got back to the trailer. "Billy's a good horse, not perfect. Nothin' in this world is since Adam sinned."

"I know that. It's only that I'm used to making the mistakes, I wonder how Jolena would have done against that cow."

"Well, I got it all on video. We'll see what Pete says. Maybe nobody made a mistake. Maybe that little heifer just beat you."

"Yeah maybe, and I don't even care that we didn't win. Like Danni said, 'it's just a game.' But the thing that really bothers me is how fast it ended for us. One instant we were in the lead, favorites to finish first, or at least finish in the money. The very next instant we're history, low score, no standing, no money, no nothin'. We might as well have stayed home. What if we do this at the futurity?"

"You're bein' kind of a girly man about this. You pays your money and you takes your chances. Life is hardly ever fair, in fact sometimes, it's exceeding dangerous."

Connie was upset. "Don't tell me about dangerous. I've been there and done that and I'm not whining like a girly man. I'm making a statement of fact, maybe it's philosophical fact, but it's still true. Things happen fast. Fortune changes quickly and most times it's a shock. That's all. I was up for three weeks and now I'm down and it happened in a heartbeat."

"You're correct in sayin' things happen fast, however if you'd stayed home you'd missed all the experience you got. You beat almost three hundred riders to get to the finals. Our neighbor, Cody over there, he's a pro, he's ridin' two supposed hotshot horses and you beat him. How about that?"

Connie sighed. "How about a beer? I think I want a cigar too. Let's go out and watch the moon rise." He called up to the girls who were in the queen bed at the front of the trailer. "You ladies need anything? Pete and I are going outside to smoke a cigar."

They both said no thank you and he and Pete went out.

"You talk to Cally today?" Connie fired up his cigar and passed the lighter to Woody.

Woody reached for the lighter as he spit out the end of his cigar. Distaining civilized tools designed to neatly nip off the tip of the cigar, he preferred to bite his off with his front teeth. "Yup," he said when his mouth was empty. Once he had the heater lit, he continued, "Pete's finally done with all his tests as of noon today."

"I'll remind you that he was supposed to be done on Wednesday, then Thursday, then Friday,"

"I know, I know. Apparently, the place is as big a bureaucracy as the federal government. All the decisions are made by committee and they won't say nothin' 'til they're ready."

"It's been five days."

"Same thing I told Cally. She said the doctors told her he had prostrate cancer for certain and they were runnin' all these other tests to determine the extent of it."

"We knew all that when he left here. I don't like it. It sounds ominous."

"Well, apparently Cally doesn't like it either. She said she gave them an ultimatum. Monday mornin' she wants a diagnosis and a course of treatment or they're packing it out."

"Sounds fair. More than fair really. Connie blew a ring of blue smoke. "These are supposed to be the best doctors in the world.""

"Yeah, actually Cally said she liked the place and everybody seemed competent, but she's frustrated with all the waitin'."

"How about Pete? He's got to be going crazy."

"Apparently other than all the pokin' and proddin', he's doin' fine. Watches that thing you gave him all the time. Cally's gone out several times to get him more movies."

"So what's she doing for excitement?"

"A little shoppin' I guess. She mentioned there were fancy clothing stores everywhere."

Connie hoped she'd buy some and was trying to imagine her in a fancy party dress. Just then Cody and his wife came home. Connie offered them a beer. Cody's wife declined, but told Cody to go ahead. He handed off the two year old and sat down. Woody got up to get the beer.

"Like a cigar with that beer?" Connie asked.

"Thanks, but I can't. They make me dizzy."

"Yeah, they used to do that to me, but now I'm too old to tell the difference."

"You didn't look too old out in the arena tonight."

"Thanks, but I'd feel a lot different about it if I'd finished in the money."

"You just had a bit of bad luck is all. You beat me and three hundred other guys."

"Same thing I told his sorry ass," Woody commented as he passed out beers. "He's been whinin' for an hour about how just one little thing like a cow getting past you is the end of the world."

Cody smiled, "Maybe not the world, but your chance for finishing in the money for sure. I wouldn't feel too bad about it. That little heifer had you beat one way or the other."

"What do you mean? There was nothing Billy could do to stop her?"

"From where I was sittin', you two were behind as soon as you dropped the reins. I was amazed your horse turned her the first time. I never figured she'd get to the fence first either. That was about the quickest cow I've ever seen."

"So you think it was a fluke?"

"Pretty much. Horses have the fastest reflexes of any domesticated animal, but that doesn't mean they'll never get beat. Your horse was merely outmaneuvered by an extremely fast and agile cow. It may never happen again, at least in that particular fashion."

"Any advice on what to do if I run into another lighting quick one?"

"Never pick a cow with wild eyes or shit on its tail."

"I don't get it."

"Cows that have been soiling themselves are nervous, always moving, skittish. Cows with wild eyes are the same, only more so."

"Wild eyes? I don't know if I'd recognize wild eyes on a cow if I saw them."

"It looked to me like it was eyeballin' you from under the belly of another cow. You definitely want to avoid a cow doin' that."

Connie considered buying the cow to bring it home and use it to practice. He decided he'd check the pens in the morning. If he could find it, he'd buy it.

Cody hung around for two beers and by the time he left, Connie was feeling much better about getting beat and his long-term chances for success. "Don't pick out the smallest cows either," was Cody's final advice.

He had a long talk with Jolena after Woody had gone to bed, explaining to her how he and Billy had lost. "Well at least I got some practice and you got some exposure at the back of the stadium. Sure wish the rules would let me ride you in competition." Her calm eyes said she agreed with him and so he went to bed.

They rose early the next morning and, after checking around for the cow that beat him, Connie pointed the rig west towards home. He thought he'd never forget what that cow looked like, but after a few minutes of inspecting the stock pens, he gave it up. *I made a bad pick, the cow beat us, I lost, get over it. Like both Cody and Woody said, I beat more than three hundred other contestants.* They stopped once in Bozeman for a leisurely breakfast and were home by mid-afternoon.

Woody and the kids were at the house and Connie had just turned Jo and Billy out to pasture when his phone rang. It was Cally. "Hi, Cally. How you two holding up?"

"We're okay, but I'll sure be glad when we can get out of here. I miss you all."

"Well, I miss you and Pete too, especially today. I lost yesterday and I could use a couple of friendly shoulders to cry on."

"What happened? When I talked to Woody yesterday afternoon, it sounded like you were leading going into the final."

"We were," and Connie related the whole sad story, although he no longer was sad about it. "But, enough of that. What's going on there? Are you getting a diagnosis tomorrow? Woody said you had laid down the law."

"Yeah, well I thought I had, but this place not only marches to its own drummer, it has its own orchestra and chorus, and they don't play requests. I was informed this morning that, 'While every attempt will be made to have all test findings analyzed and a diagnosis prepared, we can't guarantee we can meet your request to have everything finalized for Monday morning.' "

"I guess they told you. You going to call their bluff?"

"They have until noon. If we don't have either a diagnosis or a good reason why not, we're leaving."

"How does Pete feel about that?"

"It's basically his idea. He said the doctors in Kalispell told him more in four hours than these people have in a week."

"Yeah, but is there more to the story?"

"If there is, hopefully we'll know by tomorrow noon."

"I hope so too. What are you doing for excitement?"

"I've read three books. Taken some walks. Gone shopping a few times."

"Buy anything?"

"I bought some stuff for the girls and a couple of things for me. Lot's of clothing stores around here and I think I've been in all of them. I hope I don't have to visit them again."

When Connie started talking to Cally, he'd started walking up to the house. He was now there. "Cally, I'm at the house. Who do you want to talk to first?"

"How about Woody, if he's there?"

"Comin' right up, bye Cally."

"Bye, Connie, see you soon."

He gave the phone to Woody and went back down to the bunkhouse. He had a few things to do before they went out to dinner. Other than breakfast this morning, they had eaten all their meals since Thursday in the trailer. He wanted to clean up the trailer while he was thinking about it. He'd have to start cutting hay again tomorrow and he didn't want to deal with the mess later. Actually Woody had taken good care of the living quarters so it wasn't much of a problem. The two horses had made a much bigger mess in the back end of the trailer and it took Connie an hour before he was satisfied with both he front and the back.

Connie decided to stay away from the Rustlers. He now had an approach avoidance thing about Myra. Part of him was thinking he wanted a relationship with her while the other part wanted to steer clear. What he'd seen of her so far, he liked, but he realized he was too busy to carry on a romance. And then there was Cally. His thoughts about her weren't exactly platonic. *One or the other, or neither? Neither is the safest bet for right now.*

They went to a barbecue place downtown and ate ribs. The girls liked the arrangement of eating out. "I miss Mom and Grandpa a lot," said Lindsey, "but going out is so great. No dishes."

Danni took a break from eating for a moment to agree, "Yeah, this is like heaven. Could we keep doing it when they come back?"

"I doubt it," said Woody. "Your mother has specific ideas about what and where we eat. Besides, it's expensive to go out all the time."

Lindsey turned to Connie with a questioning look and barbecue sauce on her face. "Is it lots of money?"

Connie wiped her chin with his napkin. "Well, it does cost money, but it depends on your definition of 'lots'." And to avoid further discussion of money he asked, "Why don't you have a dishwasher?"

"Mom says there's no place to put one," Lindsey said. "She's saving her money to remodel the kitchen. Then she'll get one."

"Oh yeah? Interesting. When does she plan on remodeling the kitchen?"

Lindsey shrugged. "I don't know. A few years I guess."

"Probably when we're old ladies," Danni said.

Connie laughed. "I doubt she'll wait that long. She'll be an old lady before you two will."

"Did you have to do dishes when you were a kid?"

"Yes, I did. My sister and I washed dishes almost every night."

"How old were you when you didn't have to do them anymore?"

"I was seventeen, and I left home."

"You left home when you were seventeen? Where'd you go?"

"First, I went to Livingston, Montana for three months to work on a ranch and then I went to college in West Point, New York."

"What kind of college did you go to?"

"It was a military college."

"Did you have to do dishes there?"

"Nope, not even once. You two certainly have a thing about doing dishes."

"We hate it," they chimed in unison.

Later that night, when Connie couldn't sleep, he went to the barn to talk to Jolena. He called softly and she walked up as if she'd been waiting. He scratched her face gently with his fingertips while he told her his thoughts. He was worried about Pete and what might happen if he couldn't keep instructing him. "We'd still have to try to keep going without him, but it wouldn't be easy. See, just like yesterday I got beat, Pete would be able to tell me what happened and how I could fix it. Without him it's a mystery.

"Another thing, what are we going to do when this is over? I don't want to move back east. Neither one of us would be happy there. There's no mountains where I lived. I'd miss the mountains now. It's hotter there, humid too. You wouldn't like it. Maybe we can find us a neat little ranch in Idaho. What do you think about that, Buddy?"

He babbled on for another fifteen minutes sharing his hopes and fears, Jolena standing quietly, eyes closed, breathing deep and slow. She might have been asleep. When he finally felt drowsy, he went back to the bunkhouse to bed.

The next day, at lunch, Woody had news. "Cally called. They'll be operatin' on Pete tomorrow."

"What's the diagnosis?"

"Prostrate and testicular cancer, but his lymph glands and every thing else looks clean, although they said they would be taking the lymph nodes in the immediate vicinity as insurance. He said they also told him a lot of old men die with prostrate cancer, but not from it. His apparently is quite advanced."

"So they'll be removing both his prostate and testes?"

"Yup, he'll be comin' home a gelding."

"When's he supposed to be back?"

"If everything goes as scheduled and there ain't complications, they can check out some time late Friday afternoon. Cally figured they'd leave Rochester early Saturday morning. There's a flight out of Minneapolis at ten in the morning. Should put them in here by one in the afternoon. She's checkin' the availability now and is gonna call back as soon as she's confirmed.

Cally had not called back by the time lunch was over and Connie went back to work mowing. Rain was possible later in the week, and he wanted to get as much cut and baled as he could before Friday. They had commitments for at least eighty tons for the week. He was concerned about Cally getting out on Saturday. Air traffic into Kalispell on the weekends was high during the summer with all the tourists visiting Glacier Park. She might have to fly into Missoula.

Woody and the girls brought him lemonade and cookies in the middle of the afternoon. "Cally wants you to call her," Woody said. "She's havin' trouble gettin' a flight back."

Connie drained half a glass of lemonade and called Cally's cell phone. She answered on the first ring. "You weren't waiting by the phone, where you?"

"Hi, Connie. I'm so frustrated I could spit. Everybody and his brother want to go to Montana on Saturday and Sunday."

"How close can you get?"

"We might be able to get to Great Falls on Sunday afternoon."

"That's bogus. What about Spokane? That's only three or four hours from here."

"I never thought about Spokane. I'll call right now."

"Give me the number and I'll call."

She gave it to him and he used his finger to write it in the dust on a tractor fender. "Call you back in a few minutes," he said.

He called and had no problem getting two first class seats out of Minneapolis to Spokane on an eleven AM flight. He booked the seats and called Cally back. "Hey, Cally, you get to come home after all." He gave her all the information.

"I'll pay you for the tickets when we get home."

"Get home first and then we'll discuss it. I also called that limo service for your ride back to the airport. They'll pick you from your hotel at seven AM."

"Thanks, Connie. I really appreciate this."

"My pleasure. I'll see you in Spokane shortly after noon Saturday."

He ended the call and regarded his audience. "Nothin' to it. I'll have them back at the ranch by three o'clock Saturday afternoon."

Woody addressed the twins. "See, ladies, I told you Connie would think of something."

The twins ran to Connie and hugged him. "I love you, Connie," Danni said.

"Me too," Lindsey agreed.

"Well, thank you girls. No one has said that to me for almost three years. I love you both, too." It was nice to be appreciated.

Chapter 28, Pete's Return

According to the physicians in attendance, Pete's surgery went well. "Routine," they said, "No surprises," and they had him up moving around Wednesday morning. But he was sore and had absolutely no control over his bladder, so it wasn't routine as far as he was concerned. They told him he should regain control of his bladder in about six months, but that wasn't a certainty; it could be three months, a year, or it could be never. The thought of wearing a diaper for the rest of his life was not at all appealing, although the rest of his life might not be all that long. He had yet to find the inherent dignity in growing old. He suspected there was none. *Golden years, my ass*, he thought when he had to change his diaper by himself the first time. Still, he was alive and hopefully he'd be able to continue to coach Connie and see his last good horse perform in the Will Rogers Cow Palace. That would be worth a few diaper changes.

The rest of the week went fast for Connie as he scrambled to meet the delivery schedule. He lost a day on Friday because of rain, but Woody said he could load the truck on Saturday while Connie went to Spokane to fetch Pete and Cally. Even without Pete helping, they figured they'd have the second cutting finished by the end of the second week of August and that would fulfill their contract. If they made a limited third cutting, the broker said he would be glad to take it, but it wasn't anything they had to do.

After Friday's on again, off again, all day rain, Saturday dawned crisp and clear. As Connie hoofed it up to the big house, his

breath fogged in front of him. The scent of wet aspen leaves gave the
air a hint of the coming fall. It was the first of August. Snow would be
falling in the upper elevations in a month. He'd never been a fan of
winter, but he suspected winter out here was a lot different than winter
in the big city back east. *I might even enjoy it.*

The girls wanted to ride with him, but he turned them down.
"Your grandpa might not be feeling too good and want to stretch out in
the back seat. Besides, it's almost four hours each way and we're not
doing any sightseeing. If your grandpa is up to it, we'll go out for
dinner. How's that?"

They decided Connie's offer was a reasonable alternative.
"Where will we go?" Danni asked.

"I don't know. Why don't you two find a new place? I like
Chinese and Italian food. Any of those restaurants around?"

"Grandpa hates Chinese food," Lindsey said.

Connie looked at Woody and Woody nodded. "Says it all
tastes the same—bad."

"He's obviously never had good Chinese food. Oh well, pick
something he'll like. I'm going to feed Jo and the other horses, clean up,
and get on the road no later than eight." He looked at his watch, "And
since I'm already running late, I won't stop up here before I leave. You
girls be good."

They hugged him and told him to drive carefully. "Call us
when you start back," Woody said. "If Pete don't want to go out, I can
start fixin' an early supper."

Before I-94 and I-90 existed, US 2 was a major east west route,
running between the eastern border of Maine all the way west to Seattle.
It was the northern equivalent of Route 66 and had been heavily traveled.
Since the interstates had been developed, most of the old US highways
were either integrated into the interstates or had become second-rate
roads, used mostly by locals or the occasional sentimental sojourner
looking for the real America. As Connie traveled this former main
artery, he once again pondered his new life. He'd been living with
Pete's family only ten weeks and already felt like a member. He just
wasn't certain which member. Was he a father figure for the girls or
something less, like an uncle? He didn't think he was a surrogate son
for Pete, although at times he found himself responding to Pete the same
way he had to his father in his latter years. He tried to think of Cally as
a younger sister, but he had a sister and what he felt for Cally was no
way near the same. He thought she might have similar feelings for him,
but was almost afraid to find out. About the only relationship he was

sure of was the one he had with Woody. The difference in their ages
was immaterial. As Woody had said, they could communicate and that
made them friends.

He was still pondering his place as he idled through Libby, over
an hour later. He stopped at a coffee shop for a cup to go, nursing it
well into Idaho, the big diesel engine pulling him well past eighty
whenever possible. When he wheeled into the short-term parking lot of
Spokane International, it was noon sharp. He found Pete and Cally in
baggage claim waiting for their luggage. Cally looked tired and Pete
looked old, but they brightened when they saw him and Pete's grip was
still firm when he shook Connie's hand.

"It's good to be home," Pete said. "Almost home anyway. At
least we're back on the right side of the Rockies."

Cally thanked him for the ride in First Class. "I couldn't have
taken another day there. I was getting claustrophobic. The weather was
horrible, hot, and humid. I didn't want to be outside, but I was going
crazy sitting in the hotel room. I hope we don't have to go back there
again."

"We don't," Pete told her. "It either worked or it didn't, but
I'm not goin' back."

Connie got them and their luggage into the truck and they
hadn't cleared Coeur d'Alene before they were both asleep. Cally curled
up on the back seat and Pete reclined as far back as he could in the front
passenger seat. Connie smiled, "Welcome home," he said softly to them.

Just after passing through Libby, some three hours later, Cally
woke and started talking. "I'm sorry, Connie. I was so tired. I think I
was awake most of last night and I didn't sleep on the plane. That was
about the longest two weeks of my life."

"Yeah, I know what you mean. When my wife was sick and we
were going from clinic to clinic, I was a wreck. I think she held up
better than I did."

Cally asked him what type of cancer she had and he talked
about her at length. He surprised himself. The memories were still
painful, but it was almost a relief to discuss it. He'd never told anybody
the whole story of Sarah's ordeal. Cally listened sympathetically,
realizing some day, she could be telling someone about how her father
was claimed by cancer. When he finished, she put her hand on his
shoulder and told him she was sorry.

"It's funny," he said. "I thought I might never get over it, but
now," he shrugged, "I think I'm all right again. I'll never forget her and

I'll always love her memory, but I'm okay with it." He looked up into the rear view mirror and caught Cally's eye. "You know what I mean?"

She patted his shoulder and nodded. There was silence for a while before she asked how everybody fared in her and Pete's absence. "The girls miss you, big time, although, they won't be real excited about eating suppers at home again." He explained how they went out every night and how the girls loved not having to do dishes.

Cally laughed. "I really should get the kitchen redone and put in a dishwasher. I'm probably the only person in North America without one."

"I'd be glad to help you with that if you'd let me. I figure I owe you. You have no idea what fate Pete and Jolena saved me from."

"Really, what fate was that?"

"Suicide, probably. I was pretty well convinced I was going to kill myself, I just wasn't certain how quickly to do it."

"You can't be serious. You seem far too strong for that."

Connie shrugged. "Once you allow depression to get a hold of you, all bets are off." He told her a condensed version of his life after Sarah died up to the time he'd arrived on their doorstep.

"Wow, that's amazing; all of it, especially finding Jolena and buying her. I had no idea."

"Yeah, it is amazing. I think about it all the time, so much coincidence." He didn't tell her how much she resembled the first love of his life, the curly haired brunette from the dude ranch. "I'd really like to know if there's a grand plan for all of us."

"I don't know. Sometimes I think so. Other times, I think God doesn't even know my name."

"How about right now?"

"Right now, as in this instant?"

"Yeah," he consulted his watch, "Today at three, twelve PM."

She put her head back and ran the fingers of both hands through her hair and shook her head quickly from side to side. "I don't know, Connie. I'm grateful you showed up on our doorstep. You've been a huge help. I guess we could have gotten through the last two weeks without you, but it would have been a lot more difficult. After hearing your story, the fact you're here just when we needed you, gives the grand plan theory some credibility. I used to believe everything happened for a purpose, but so much happens, it's impossible to see it all, and sometimes, even any of the connections. Really, right now, this very instant, I think it's better not to know."

"Yeah, you're right. Even though I always think about it, not knowing is better. I can't believe I'd be any happier or better off if I'd known the future."

Pete had been awake for the last few minutes and decided to join the conversation. "You two can stay in the dark, but I'd like a little reassurance that everything is going according to plan. I'd hate to think I invested all that time showing Connie how to cut cattle for nothing."

"Good morning," Connie told him, "We were thinking we'd have to carry you in and put you to bed."

"I heard every word you two said. Been awake for hours."

"Really?" Cally asked, "Because I just woke up and started talking about twenty minutes ago."

"Well maybe I did doze off for a minute or two. Where we at?" He pushed the button that brought his seat up. After looking out the window for a few seconds, he commented. "Well, we're almost there. We're not far from Boissvert's place."

"Yeah, you're right. We should be home in about ten minutes," Connie said.

Cally smiled at his comment about being home, but wouldn't tell him why when he asked what was so funny.

Pete didn't catch it either. "Must be a real private joke," he said.

Ten minutes later, Pete and Cally were being mugged by the girls. "Oh. Mom," I missed you so much," Danni said, tears in her eyes.

"Yeah," Lindsey agreed. "You guys were gone so long."

While Pete and Cally, flanked by Danni and Lindsey led the way to the house, Connie and Woody followed with all the baggage. Connie chuckled.

"What's funny?" Woody wanted to know.

"I've been trying to figure out my place in this family for the past couple of days and I finally got it. I'm the butler."

"That ain't so blasted funny. Means I could be the downstairs maid."

When Connie met Cally and Pete in Spokane, he'd asked if they were up for going out to dinner. They quickly decided they weren't, so Connie had called Woody and told him to start cooking. When they walked in the house, the rich smells of roasting beef, apple pie, and fresh coffee hit them like a tsunami, overwhelming their senses with a flood of hominess.

Inhaling deeply, Pete sat at the table. "Wow! Is there any way I can have coffee and pie before dinner?"

"Sure," Woody told him. "You just have to promise you'll eat all your dinner."

Pete held up his hand. "I promise."

Cally grabbed the chair next to Pete. "I promise too."

"How about you, Connie? You promise too?

"Sure," he said and went through the kitchen with a double handful of luggage, ultimately dropping it all at the top of the stairs. When he came back into the kitchen and sat down, he asked Woody, "What did I just sign up for?"

"We're havin' dessert before dinner. You just promised you wouldn't spoil your appetite."

"If Cally and Pete can do it, so can I. They had lunch on the plane. I had a cup of coffee about ten."

They all ate a slice of apple pie and when they were finished, Woody told them to go get ready for dinner. "You got about thirty minutes, so do what you have to do and be back here at five sharp with your appetites like you all promised."

Pete was clearly exhausted, and Cally shooed him off to bed shortly after supper. Connie and Woody did the dishes so Cally could spend some time with the girls. By eight o'clock Woody and Connie were sitting on the back step of the bunkhouse smoking cigars and sipping single malt whisky in the retreating sunlight. They had quietly discussed Pete's appearance at length, finally deciding, all things considered, he looked pretty good. They could only hope he would heal and the cancer hadn't spread and wouldn't be back.

After a long pensive silence, Woody changed the subject. "You ain't been out to see your girlfriend lately. You givin' her the heave ho already?"

Connie leaned back against the bunkhouse door. "You think Pete would mind if I built a nice big deck so we could sit out here and sip scotch like civilized men in deck chairs instead of crouching on this miserable step?"

"I reckon, but what about the movie star? I'll bet her house has a deck the size of New Jersey. Probably backs right up on Whitefish Lake, too."

"Probably."

Woody waited. "That's it? 'Probably'? I'm talkin' about a perfectly good woman here and you sound about as interested as if I had brought up the subject of zucchini squash. Actually she's a lot better than perfectly good, she's outstandin'."

"Oh, she's a lot more interesting than any kind of squash, I just don't know what to do about her. If I start an affair and it gets complicated, then what?"

"Then enjoy it. That's what."

Connie waved away the cloud of cigar smoke he'd just exhaled. "I don't see it being all that simple. I believe it was you who once told me, women always want something. I'm not sure I want to find out what Miss Foxx wants from me. Paying a lot of attention to a charming woman could be a detriment to my education. You have any idea how much money I've got invested in going to the futurity? And that reminds me, I have to send in the rest of my entry fee."

Woody reflected on that for a bit. "Well, okay, but in less than five months you're gonna know if you invested your money wisely or squandered it. What's your plan for life after the futurity? That woman could keep you mighty cozy through the winter."

Connie considered the prospect of cuddling with Myra through the winter. Tempting, but he couldn't take Cally's offer to stay here and be with Myra at the same time.

"I'm sure she could. I'm not sure what I'll do after Christmas. I might go some place warm for the winter or Cally said I could stay here. I'm thinking of looking for a little ranch in Idaho or along the Clark Fork River in the spring. I don't want to go back east again. Too crowded."

"Yeah, that's different country. I ain't been east of the Mississippi for over forty years. Don't see no reason ever to cross it again neither. Stayin' here through the winter would be good. I have to admit, I'll miss you when you leave. You got real good taste in whisky, cigars, and women."

"Well, what else is there, except horses? And I've got the best horse on the planet."

"She must be, both you and Pete say so."

Connie swirled the scotch around in his glass before he downed it. "Yup, and I also say we should taste a little more of this."

Woody tossed down what was left in his glass. "Suits me."

As Connie stood, he heard the back door of the big house slam shut and looked up to see the twins headed his way. He postponed his trip to the bunkhouse kitchen.

"Well, well," Woody greeted the girls. "What brings you two lovely young ladies down here to see us two old men?"

The twins were wearing flannel pajamas and bedroom slippers. "Oh, Woody, you're not old," Lindsey told him.

"No, and Connie's not old either. He's hot," Danni said.

Connie laughed. "I knew I loved you two. Now I know why."

Danni hugged him. "We have to go to bed. We came down to say goodnight."

"Kinda early," Woody said.

"It's nine-thirty and there's church tomorrow," Lindsey informed him. "Are you going?"

"I'll let you know in the morning." He hugged Lindsey. "Goodnight Sweetie."

After their hugs, the girls hung around long enough so Cally had to call for them, and then they were gone.

"Be tough to say good bye to those two," Connie told Woody as he headed in to fetch the single malt. He visited the bathroom while he was at it and when he returned to the back steps, Cally was sitting in his place.

"What a pleasant surprise," he told her and holding the bottle so she could see it, he asked, "Can I get you a glass?"

"Yeah," she said. "I could use a taste."

"Good. Why don't we move inside? I don't think I can sit on the steps much longer."

"Great idea," Woody agreed, and the three of them went into the bunkhouse where they sat around the kitchen table, sipped single malt and talked, mostly about Pete, until ten-thirty.

When Cally left, she hugged Connie and kissed him. "Thanks again, Connie. I appreciate everything you've done for us."

He held on to her for a bit wondering whether he should kiss her back. "Anything I can do, Cally, anything at all. Let me know." He relaxed his embrace.

Woody left behind her. "See you in the morning," and he winked.

Connie went out to the paddock behind the barn to talk to Jolena. He had a lot to say and he didn't come in to bed until after midnight.

Chapter 29, The Assignment

After watching the tape Woody had made of Connie and Billy getting beat by the little heifer in the finals at Billings, Pete chuckled. It was Sunday afternoon just before supper.

"What's funny?" demanded Connie.

Pete backed up the tape to the beginning and stopped it. "That wasn't Supercow, she just outsmarted you. Watch close." He started the tape again. Connie watched as he and Billy brought the cow out in front of the judges. There was the briefest of pauses, Connie dropped reins and in three moves they were beat. "Did you see it?"

Connie shook his head. "No."

"Watch again. Watch the cow's head."

He did. "Play it again." He watched it again. When filming, Woody had zoomed in on them and had a good image of the cow from head on. "Once more."

Pete played it again and when it was over he smiled. "You see it, don't you?"

"I think so. She makes a little move with her head before she takes off. I missed that and I dropped the reins a split second too late. That put Billy behind, trying to play catch up and the cow beats us. And then each judge whacks us five points and we lose."

"Yup. It's hard to say if Billy saw it or not, because regardless, he waited for you and that made you both late. Although, I'll have to say that's about the fastest little heifer I ever saw. Be nice to own one like that."

"I tried to find her the next day and buy her, but they all looked alike. I felt silly after a while and gave up."

"No matter. You learned a valuable lesson. You just picked an extremely bad time to learn it. Probably cost you some serious money."

"It cost you a new pickup. I just wanted the belt buckle."

"Well, next time the grand prize is a pickup, watch the cow."

"I was watching the cow."

"Yeah, but you were watching her feet. Watch her eyes."

"So now I'm supposed to able to figure out what they're going to do by staring into their eyes?"

"No, but if you're watching her eyes, you'll be lookin' at her head. She'll go the way her head is pointing. You ever play football?"

"Yeah, in high school. I wasn't all that good."

"Did you play any defense?"

"I was an offensive end with bad hands, so I played more defense than a normal offensive end would play."

"Ever make any tackles?"

"Lots of them."

"Did you ever hear your coach tell you or any other defensive players to watch the runner's head to know which way he's going?"

"Yeah, I guess. You telling me it works for animals too?"

"It especially works for animals because they're not trying to trick you out of your jock strap by giving you conflicting signals. A good running back will turn his head one way and try to go the other way. A cow isn't trying to score a touchdown, it's just trying to get back to the herd. It always goes the way its head is turned."

"Is that what Jolena does? Watch the cow's head?"

"Tomorrow morning, when we start workin' cows again, once you drop the reins and this is for one time only, don't look at the cow, watch Jo's head. She and every other good cow horse will lock onto the cow's head the way you'd hang onto the winning lottery ticket. I'll video tape her head from the front while you're riding and you can see how focused she is."

"Poor Billy, I know he felt bad when that cow beat us. Seemed like he actually hung his head when we walked out of the arena."

"I could have taken Billy to the futurity three years ago. He was good enough, but he lacked maturity. He'd be great one day, impossible the next. He was just too young. However he's matured in the past two years and now he almost always gets it right. He's not as smooth or smart as Jolena, but I expect he probably thought he should have been able to correct for your mistake and was surprised when he couldn't. Not that he reasoned in those terms of course, but I do believe horses can reason, especially smart ones."

"I let him down."

"Get over it, he has."

"Yeah, I guess I have too. Would have been a nice one to win though."

"Every one you win is nice. We'll start practicing again tomorrow morning."

"You feel okay for that?"

"I feel pretty good. I'm still sore where they cut me so I won't be riding, but the girls are good enough to ride turn back without me. We'll manage."

The next morning they all started back on the old routine, except breakfast was at seven to give Pete a little more rest. Connie was used to getting up at five-thirty so he took care of the horses before breakfast instead of after. Then after breakfast, he rounded up some cattle and spent the next couple hours practicing. The girls rode turn back, he worked the cows and Pete critiqued. They knocked off about eleven. Connie and the twins put the cows back out to pasture and groomed the horses they had ridden. By then it was time for lunch. After lunch, Woody and Connie made hay while Pete took it easy. Lindsey and Danni helped Cally and then it was time for supper.

By the middle of August, they'd made two cuttings of hay, Pete had seemingly improved and most of the cows had become too tame for cutting practice. They were no longer intimidated by the horses and mostly refused any attempt at being worked.

The third Sunday in August, they rode up to Rogers Lake for swimming and a picnic. In a couple more weeks the water would be cooling off and the girls would be back in school. Picnic season would be over. But this day was sunny and warm. Connie bought ten pounds of fresh jumbo shrimp, sweet corn, potato salad, watermelon, strawberries and short cake. After splashing around in the tepid shallows of the lake, they grilled the shrimp and sweet corn and ate until they all needed naps. After they wandered back home about five, there was no mention of, nor need for supper.

Later that evening, Pete came down to the bunkhouse with a proposal for Connie. "You know, Connie, I think it's time you and Billy took your show on the road. I made up a little schedule for the next four weeks, and you could make five NCHA shows. It'll be some serious driving followed by some long periods of boredom, but you'll get competition experience and that's what you're lacking. I'd like to go with you, but I don't quite feel up to it. Woody might enjoy it if you can stand each other's company."

Connie wasn't totally unprepared for this news. He knew he'd have to find fresh cows, and this was the best way to do it short of buying a new herd. There was also the experience of the competition itself, something Pete could not provide. What he wasn't looking forward to was the grind of traveling from one contest to the next for weeks on end. He would miss the ranch and its people.

"Where do I start?"

"There's a big show at Fort Klamath, Oregon in about a week. It lasts about ten days but you can probably get in at least two contests and still get over to Henry's Lake in Idaho by the thirty-first. Then on the fifth of September there's the Colorado State Fair in Pueblo. Four days later there's a big contest in Nampa, Idaho and when that one is over there's another good one in Casper, Wyoming. Now when you get in with all those other cowboys, you're gonna hear about other shows along the way. Some of them might be worth your while. You get to Colorado, there's contests all over the place, especially up around Gunnison. Some of those might be worth your while too. You'll have to take it as it comes, but don't go crazy. You have to pace yourself and don't rush. You want experience not an injury. And one other thing." There was a pause as if what Pete had to say next was of great import.

"Yeah, what might this other thing be?"

"Well, I never had a son, but I can think of all kinds of things I would have told him if I did. I also know you're a little old for me to be giving you any fatherly advice, but I have to caution you anyway."

"Come on, Dad, give it up. I'm not too old to listen to good advice." Connie was smiling.

"Well, some of these other cowboys you'll meet might not be quite as scrupulous as they should be. If someone tries to get you into a 'private' contest with only a few competitors, a high entry fee and the winner takes all, be careful.

"Are you saying if it sounds too good to be true, it probably is?"

"Precisely what I'm saying."

"I appreciate the reminder and I'll stick to public contests. I'll also have to get out my road atlas and start planning."

"I got everything you'll need up at the house. I didn't bring it with me because I wasn't certain you'd be agreeable."

"I can hardly quit now, can I? The way I see it, I'm past the point of no return. I have to keep going and if you figure this is what I should do, I'm ready to try."

"Glad to hear you say that, Connie. By the time you get back, our cows will be ready for you and Jolena to workin' 'em again. I'll give you all the stuff I have tomorrow morning after breakfast."

There was a knock on the bunkhouse door. Lindsey and Danni made an entrance. They were wearing new dresses.

"I didn't know there was a party up at the house," Pete said.

Connie whistled. "Look at you two. You look mighty fetching."

"What's fetching?" Danni asked.

"It's a good thing," Lindsey told her. "Mom got us these new dresses when she was gone with Grandpa and we wanted to show them to you."

"Well, I'm glad you did. You're both very stunning."

"Mom got a new dress too, but she's not coming down to show you," Danni confided.

"Pity," said Connie. "I'll bet she looks stunning too."

"Oh, she looks way better than that. She's beautiful in it."

"I'll bet she is. I can't wait to see her wear it."

"It's pretty fancy. She said she wasn't sure if she'd ever get to wear it."

"Well, I've got a fancy suit. Maybe we'll all have to get dressed up and go out some time soon."

"Really," Danni asked. "Me and Lindsey too?"

"Especially you and Lindsey. You're grandpa and Woody too if they want to come."

"When will we go? I can't wait?"

"How about as soon as I get back from the assignment your grandpa has given me?"

Lindsey looked at Pete. "What does he have to do, Grandpa?"

"Billy and him and maybe Woody too, are going on a little road trip."

"Can we come along?" Danni asked.

"We went to Missoula and we were good. We won't be any trouble," Lindsey reasoned.

"Connie's going to be gone a few weeks and school starts soon. I'm afraid it won't work out for you girls to go along."

"When are you leaving?" asked Lindsey

"In about a week?"

"When are you coming back home?" asked Danni.

"Towards the end of September."

"That's almost five weeks," said Lindsey.

"Five weeks," Danni almost wailed. "You can't go away for five weeks. We'll miss you too much." She threw her arms around Connie. "You can't go."

There was another knock on the door and Cally and Woody came in. Danni released Connie and ran to Cally. "Mom, Connie's going away." She had tears in her eyes.

"It's okay, honey, he's just going for a little while and he's coming right back."

"Five weeks! He's gonna be gone five weeks."

"I don't like it either, Danni," Lindsey said. "But I'm not cryin' about it."

"You two go up to the house and get ready for bed. We'll talk about this later. And hang up those dresses where I told you," she called out as they headed out the back door.

"Sorry about that, Connie," she said when the girls had gone.

"I'm not," he told her, "I haven't had a woman cry for me because I was leaving for over twenty years. The last one that did was married to someone else when I came back."

"You were probably lucky. If she'd been waiting, you would have never met your wife."

"Good point. I hope Danni and Lindsey won't forget who I am in a month."

"Not likely. They were thrilled when I told them you'd be here for Christmas. I don't think they'll forget you in a month, but can't you work it so you'll be able to stop in once in a while?"

Pete answered for him. "Of course he can. He'll be going right past at least twice."

Connie looked at Woody. "There you have it, Buddy. Care to join me?"

"Love to. It's been a while since I did any serious bummin' around. You goin' anywhere near south central Colorado? There's a deputy sheriff down that way I'd like to visit with one more time before one of us tips over for good."

"Pete mentioned Pueblo. Is that near where you want to be?"

"It'll be a detour, but probably not more than a hundred and fifty miles."

"Shouldn't be a problem. I wouldn't mind stopping off in Longmount if we get up that way." Cally was listening and he didn't want to mention the reason would be a woman. "I know some people around there."

"When we leavin'. It'll be fun."

Pete was suddenly jealous. He wished he hadn't gotten sick. Oh well, it probably wouldn't be the last thing his condition prevented him from doing. Still, he thought, I'd rather be going to Fort Worth in December than driving around for a month now. And if the truth were known, even Cally felt some jealousy as Connie and Woody discussed their plans. *When Connie goes to Fort Worth, I'm certainly going along on that trip.*

"Okay, boys," she said, "I'm going to leave you to your fun. Dad, don't stay up too late."

"Good night, Cally," Connie said. "I'll send him along in a bit."

Pete and Woody left about an hour later, and Connie went out into the horse pasture to find Jolena. He told her all about the plans he made. How there'd be a lot of traveling and probably a lot of standing around and waiting too, but there would also be fresh cows to chase and crowds to cheer them. He told her she wouldn't be going, but when he came back, he'd be riding her full time. No more Billy.

When he ran out of things to say, he just stroked her head and neck. Not all horses like to be petted, but Jolena would stand as long as Connie would continue. She liked it as much as he did and he thoroughly enjoyed having an intelligent, eleven hundred pound animal for a partner and friend. They were a team.

"Well, Jo," he finally told her when it was dark and all the lights in the big house were off, "I better get to bed. I'll see you in the morning."

She nickered softly as he walked away. She had bonded strongly to Connie. What she felt for him was great trust. She would use her heart and soul to attempt whatever he asked. And her heart was the powerful heart of a beast and her soul was tender, yet tenacious, like the soul of a competent woman.

Chapter 30, Confusion

After the contest in Kalispell on the fourth of July, Connie and Pete had made a quick trip to Coeur d'Alene to see an old friend of Pete's who made custom saddles. Pete explained he'd first met Mac in Weatherford, Texas about fifty years earlier when they were both young men. Mac had since retired and moved to Idaho to be close to his daughter and her family. However, he quickly became bored so he set up shop on a limited basis. He made about ten saddles a year and had a waiting list as long as his arm. Over the years, Mac had built at least a half-dozen saddles for Pete and when Pete wanted a saddle, his name always went to the top of the list.

Mac spent close to a half hour sketching and measuring Jolena. He spent about thirty seconds with Connie. "How much you weigh, son?"

"Two hundred even."

"You about six feet tall."

"Yes sir. Six feet even."

Mac pulled out an old tape measure, its numbers barely legible and slipped it around Connie's waist. "Hmmm," he muttered. Dropping the tape lower, he measured Connie's girth around the hips. He muttered some more. "How old are you, son." He made a notation on the paper with all the measurements he made of Jolena.

"Forty-six."

"Well, you're in fine shape. Whatever you're doin', keep doin' it." He turned his attention back to Jolena.

"That all you need from me?" Connie asked.

"Yup. You're not the important one, she is. This little mare has to carry your two hundred pounds and I want to make sure the saddle I build for her does exactly that. All I needed from you is how big your butt is and how much you weigh."

On the way home, Connie told Pete. "He didn't even ask me what color I wanted it to be."

"You know what the saddle you been using looks like, don't you?"

"Yeah, of course."

"Well, Mac made that one about twenty years ago and yours is going to look just like it except it'll fit Jo perfectly."

Now, five weeks later, the saddle was finished. "Okay," Pete told Connie, "first stop is at Mac's place to pick up your new saddle. I know it was made for Jolena, but I want you to break it in on Billy. Put it on him when you're warming up and then put his regular saddle on him when you're ridin' for real.

"After leavin' Coeur d'Alene you'll want to head over to Fort Klamath. Stay on I-Ninety through Spokane and down to Ritzville." He stabbed at a spot on the map with his finger. "Then you have to take US Three-Ninety-Five south to I Eighty-Four and go west to here," and he traced the spider web network of highways that plied western Oregon until his finger came to rest on the tiny town of Fort Klamath. "Now that show is a big futurity that you won't be able to get into, but they'll also have a derby you can enter. As soon as it's over, you'll need to make tracks for Henry's Lake back in Idaho and you'll probably have only two or three days to get there, so you can't waste any time."

For the next hour Pete and Connie poured over the maps and Connie's itinerary. "I wish you could join us," Connie told him when they finished.

"I do too, but I'm saving myself for the futurity and somebody's got to be here with Cally and the girls."

"Woody said if you wanted, he'd trade places and you could go."

"Well I appreciate that, but if the truth be known, as much as I'd like to go with you, I don't feel all that hot just yet. I'm still sore and this diaper business is a real pain you know where. Riding in your truck for hours wouldn't be real convenient for either one of us. We'd be stopping all the time."

"Yeah, I'm sure you're right. Best if you stay here for a month and heal." Connie really would have preferred Pete coming along because of his knowledge. Woody was great company, but he knew less about cutting than Connie. It was equivalent to being on the high school football team and going on a five game road trip without the coach. You were going to have fun and you'd probably learn a lot, but would you win any games? Whatever, Connie decided he'd said enough. He'd just have to do his best without Pete.

One thing he wanted to do was see if Myra was available before he left, and he needed to act fast. The cutting in Oregon started in six days and he needed three days to pick up his new saddle and get there. Monday afternoon, he dialed Myra's number and got the answering service. Rather than leave a message, he told Cally he wouldn't be up to the house for supper and then drove to Whitefish. Hopefully Myra was taking care of business at the Rustlers and they could at least talk. He almost felt guilty about not keeping in touch.

"So why isn't Connie here for supper?" Danni asked.

"Danni, I've told you three times," Cally said. "He didn't say where he was going, I didn't think it was polite to ask and I'm not a mind reader, so stop asking me."

"Did he tell you, Woody?"

"Nope, he just got cleaned up and left. He must have some business somewhere."

"Yeah," Lindsey agreed. "He probably went to the bank to get some money for the trip."

"I'll bet he went to see Brianna at the Rustlers," Danni offered.

"Maybe he did," Cally said, "but he's a big boy and that's his business."

"I don't like her," Danni said belligerently.

"Why? What's wrong with her?" Cally asked.

"I don't know. I just don't like her."

"That's silly. Would you like her if she didn't like Connie?" Danni had relayed the details of their night out at the Rustlers to Cally.

Danni stared at her plate and pushed a chunk of grade-A beef around in circles. Tears were filling her eyes. She didn't answer.

"Danni, we don't own Connie. He's here because your grandpa is teaching him how to ride Jolena. In return for that, he's helped make hay all summer, and he took good care of you two when I was gone. If anything, we owe him. And most important, he's free to go anywhere and see anyone he wants. I know you like him a lot, but he's a grown man and if he wants to see Brianna, he can."

Danni blurted out, her voice cracking, "We found him first. If you loved him, he wouldn't go see Brianna." Pushing back from the table, she ran out of the kitchen, sobbing mightily.

Blushing, Cally looked from Pete to Woody. "Good grief," she muttered and went after Danni.

Pete had a wry smile on his face and Woody was grinning.

"What's so funny?" Lindsey asked.

Woody dumped his smile. "Nothin' particular. Just seems to me your sister is overdoin' it a bit."

Lindsey's eyes were moistening up too. "Well she's right this time." And then she also, left the table crying.

Pete slowly shook his head. "I think the family has started a transition from two girls and a woman to three women."

"That little horse of yours sure has created a situation."

"It's her new owner that created the situation not Jo. And if it hadn't have been Connie, it would have been something else sooner or later. They weren't going to stay little girls forever."

"That's not exactly what I mean. What about their mother? You don't think she's interested in Connie also do ya?"

"You know something I don't?"

"No, sir. I'm just askin' your opinion."

Pete shrugged his shoulders. "Pass me that beef, will you? I know Cally likes him, but I don't know if she's romantically inclined." He pulled a piece of steak off the serving plate and regarded Woody. "What do you think?"

"You 'member that bet we made when we was drivin' down to the auction in Oklahoma? The one where I said Cally'd be gettin' married sometime soon. I wrote it all down."

"Yeah, I remember."

"Good, because I think you'll be payin' me off before long."

Pete chuckled. "Woody, he's going to see the movie star. If he gets involved with anybody, it'll be her."

"Care to double the bet?"

Shaking his head, Pete admitted, "No."

Cally returned with her daughters who sat and ate their supper without further comment on Connie's whereabouts.

Meanwhile, Connie was cooling his heels, sitting at the bar waiting while Myra made phone calls in an attempt to get someone in to take over as the hostess. She wasn't having any luck and they were short handed as it was. She couldn't spare a waitress or waiter.

Good Lord, you'd think I was old enough to know better than to jump through hoops for some cowboy, was what she was thinking, but she also believed Connie to be worth the effort so she continued. Fifteen minutes later it became apparent she was not going to be able to line up a substitute tonight or for tomorrow night either.

"I'm sorry, Connie, I just can't get anyone in to take over for me," she told him.

"It's okay. It's my fault. I can't expect you to drop everything on such short notice. How does tomorrow night look?"

She gave him a sad smile. "The best I can do is Wednesday."

"Wednesday would be good. I'd just like to see you before I hit the road for a month."

She reached across the bar to take his hand. "I'd like that too."

They made their arrangements for Wednesday and Connie left. Myra offered to buy him dinner, but he declined. Instead, he stopped at a fast food joint on the way back to the ranch and had serious indigestion all night long.

Everyone except Woody seemed somewhat subdued at breakfast. Connie wondered if perhaps he was the cause. Oh well, he wasn't about to offer an explanation. He was a big boy and free to come and go as he pleased. He ate quickly, excused himself and went to do his chores.

Danni came to see him before the school bus arrived. "Hi, Danni," Connie said when she showed up in the barn. "To what do I owe the honor of your presence this fine morning?"

"You didn't come to supper last night. I missed you."

"Well, that's very thoughtful of you, Sweetie. I missed you too."

Danni stared at the barn floor for a while, kicking bits of discarded hay. "Where did you go?"

If Connie had thought the undiplomatic question was anyone's idea other than Danni's, he would not have given a straight answer, but Danni was an original and he was certain no one had put her up to this. "I went to the Rustlers."

"Did you see Brianna?"

"Yes, I did."

"Did you have a date?"

Connie laughed. "No, I didn't have a date."

"Then why did you go?"

"To see Brianna."

"Well, if you saw her, how come you didn't have a date?"

"Because she was busy and couldn't get away."

Danni was happy to hear that, but she wasn't through. "Do you love her?"

"No, I don't love her. I just wanted to see her. Where are you going with this?"

"I got to go to school now." She gave him a hug and ran out.

Connie shook his head and went to talk to Jolena about the nature of women. An hour later, neither of them had learned anything new and since Connie was no longer making hay, he decided to go up to the house to see if he could be helpful.

He put new washers in the faucets on the sink in Cally's bathroom. The leaks had been driving her slowly out of her mind and she was grateful, but it was the extent of the minor repairs she needed. He was disappointed. He'd been working from sunup to sundown for almost three months and instead of being weary, he wanted something to do. "How about I remodel your kitchen?"

"Can you be finished in three days?" Cally asked.

"No, probably not."

"I'd love to have you remodel the kitchen, but as much as I appreciate the offer, you're leaving for a month on Thursday morning.

"Yeah, you're right. Be a little tough to work around it for that long."

"Why don't you just take it easy for a while? Go for a ride. It's still warm enough. You could go up to Rogers Lake for a swim."

"I will if you will."

She looked at the clock. "Ten thirty. I should start lunch. Then by the time I get that cleaned up, it'll be time to start supper." Actually, his invitation sounded terrific and she was thinking how she could make it work.

"Okay, here's a deal. You make lunch. I'll help you clean up quick. We ride up to the lake, go for a swim and then instead of you cooking supper, we'll all go out to a restaurant. I'm really hungry for some Italian food. There's got to be an Italian place somewhere around here."

She looked at him for a minute without speaking. She was feeling some strong emotions. "You know what? You've got a deal."

"Great. I'll get a few things ready before lunch and as soon as the dishes are done, I'll saddle the horses."

"Okay, and there are two good Italian places in town." She was smiling as she watched him walk down to the barn.

It was the last day of August and the afternoon was warm as they rode lazily up the trail to Rogers Lake. There was a different quality to the sunlight however. It was more golden, and when combined with a little extra humidity, it gave the countryside a soft, slightly out of focus appearance. The yellowing aspen leaves completed the effect. The woods looked cozy, comfortable, and friendly. Connie hoped the water was still warm enough for swimming. He wanted another good look at Cally's bathing suit.

Where the trail was wide enough, they rode side-by-side, talking and laughing. When there was a narrow spot overgrown with young pines or aspen saplings, Connie dropped back and let Cally lead. Once through the restriction, Cally stopped her horse and waited until he pulled up even before starting again. It took them a bit longer to reach the lake, but they weren't counting minutes. When they arrived, Cally gave the water a check with her toes and pronounced it fit for at least a quick dip.

Once again Connie was impressed by her physique, and once again found himself wishing mightily to be ten years younger. When they had splashed around for as long as they were comfortable, they headed for shore and the blanket Cally had thrown out on the sand. Connie had an almost overwhelming urge to help her dry off with the thick beach towels she had packed along, but somehow resisted. Wrapping the oversized towel around her, she proceeded to produce a bottle of wine, three kinds of cheese and four varieties of crackers. The wine was from a dinner she'd planned to cook for her doctor friend, but decided he wasn't worth it. Connie was.

They talked, ate cheese and crackers, and drank wine until everything was gone. Some high cirrus clouds moved in after three o'clock and lowered the temperature just enough to make them cool even though their bathing suits were dry. They decided to pack up and head for home. They weren't as talkative on the way down as they had been on the ride up. They were each thinking thoughts about the other. Connie's thoughts were centered mostly on how much he liked her and how much older he was. Cally's thoughts had nothing to do with their relative ages. She was wondering how far his relationship with Brianna Lane had progressed.

The twins were home when Connie and Cally arrived and they had a million questions for Cally, all of which she dismissed by telling them to clean up and put on different clothes because Connie was taking them all out for dinner. While Cally was in the shower, they ran down to see if they could get any information out of Connie. They were unsuccessful there also, because Connie was in the shower and didn't hear them knocking. Feeling very frustrated, they went back up to the house to wait for everyone else to get ready.

Dinner was at an Italian place that had great food, but almost no ambiance. *If you could get this food and an intimate café setting, you'd really have something.* Connie made a mental note not to bring Myra or any other date to this place.

"Was the water cold?" Lindsey asked.

"A little," Connie said, "But we didn't stay in the water all afternoon like you two do."

"Well, if you weren't swimming, what did you do?" Danni asked.

"Talked, ate cheese, and drank wine."

Danni smiled, "So, like you had a date?"

Connie refused to be intimidated by a blunt talking nine year old, "Yeah, you could call it a date if you were so inclined. What do you think Cally, was it a date?"

"Yes, I believe it was a date, and so is this except all of us are on this date."

That night when the girls had gone to bed, their lights-out conversation was centered on the fact their mother and Connie had gone on a real date. They tried to talk about it for a long time, to ponder the mystery of it, and savor the romance they imagined, but sleep won out and by ten they were in the arms of Morpheus.

Meanwhile, Connie was in the barn grooming Jolena and filling her in on all his thoughts. "I don't know what to do, Jo. I really like her, but have you ever heard the expression, 'There's no fool like an old fool,'? The last thing I want to do is make an old fool of myself by making a pass at her and have her shoot me down. I suppose I could just ask her for a real date and see what happens. I know she likes me a little bit. Too bad I asked Myra out for tomorrow, I'd really rather be with Cally." Jo gave a little nicker as if she understood, but she was perhaps only responding to the way he was gently scratching her face.

"You know, Jo, right now I miss Sarah more than I did two years ago. You would have liked her, but then again, if she'd lived, I doubt I'd have ever found you." Jo put her heavy head on his shoulder. "I'd never be doing what we're doing. I'd still be back in Indiana living in that big beautiful house we built, not in Montana in a little old bunkhouse. Not that I mind. In fact I like it here. The bunkhouse is cozy and I like Pete. Woody is a great friend and I love those two little girls. I'm not sure about their mother, I might even love her too. So I'm not complaining. It's that sometimes I miss Sarah so much it hurts."

Jo lifted her head from his shoulder and put her nose against his neck. Connie put his arm around the horse's neck and hugged. "Yes, I love you too, Jo. Whatever happens, girl, we're stayin' together. Win, lose or draw, we're goin' together." He patted her neck. "I'm going in. You go to sleep."

Cally's bedroom window was open and she heard Connie close the barn door. She got up and watched him walk from the barn to the bunkhouse. She thought about going down to talk to him, but decided against it. Instead, she stared out the window at the bunkhouse long after the lights went out.

Chapter 31, A Date With A Star

Myra Foxx, aka Brianna Lane, had been blessed not only with beauty, but also with skin, bones, and flesh that seemed to defy the normal human aging process. At forty-six with the right makeup, she could pass for twenty-six. Tall and fair-haired, a classic Nordic beauty, she bore a slight resemblance to Connie's late wife. The physical resemblance part however, was incidental in her appeal to him. After her looks had initially attracted him, it was her self-assurance that made him interested. It appeared to Connie as if she knew exactly who and what she was and while it didn't make her think she was any better than anyone else, she definitely knew what she could do. As he made the drive to Whitefish, Connie was wondering if he were out of his league. *I'm not much of a social butterfly. That's my sister's job. I've never traveled in the circles Myra has. This is probably a bad idea. What do I have to offer her that she hasn't been offered before by men a lot richer, younger, and better looking than me? I can't even take her to a great restaurant because she owns the best one within a hundred miles.* He felt a lot like he had after purchasing Jolena and agreeing with Pete to learn how to ride her. Dating a movie star, or at least a retired movie star, seemed even more intimidating then riding a high performance cutting horse. He wished he'd put off this rendezvous until he got back to town in October, but it was too late now.

Danni and Lindsey were visibly upset when they discovered Connie wouldn't be home for dinner again. They immediately assumed the worst which was Connie must be going to see Brianna. Once again, Cally reminded them Connie was an adult and quite capable of making his decisions without their input. Lindsey was mad and Danni was crushed.

"Why is he going to see her?" Lindsey demanded, "He just took us on a date last night."

"Yeah, he's cheating on us," Danni wailed.

"You two stop it right now. I doubt Connie has ever cheated, or cheated on anyone in his entire life. He doesn't owe us a thing and if he wants to see Brianna, he's free to do it. I know you like him a lot, but you have to let this go."

"Well, how do you like it?" Lindsey asked, defying the order.

"It doesn't matter what I like, it's what Connie likes. That's what I've been trying to get through your two, thick heads."

"Don't you like him too?" Danni took up the offensive.

"Of course I like him."

"How much? Do you love him?"

"I don't know, I mean, I don't know him well enough to know that." The girls were going where Cally didn't want to go. "Okay, look here. From now on, there'll be no more discussion of Connie's business or what I think about it. You two want to talk about it, keep it between yourselves. It's not going to be a topic for discussion at mealtime or any other time either." She gave them the look. "Do you understand?"

Even though they both acceded to the look, they had a feeling they'd somehow won the debate. That didn't help their depression over Connie's absence at supper or his impending departure tomorrow morning. They were sullen and gloomy through the evening meal and spoke only to each other in whispers while they did the dishes. Their displeasure over Connie's apparent lack of loyalty to them was contagious, and by eight, Cally was infected with the same symptoms as her daughters. She was angry at Connie for seeing Myra, worried the two of them would hit it off, and depressed because it was Myra and not her that Connie had chosen to be with on his last night before leaving for a month. In short, Cally was jealous.

Connie, meanwhile, was seated next to Myra in a back booth in the other Italian restaurant in town. This one had decent ambiance; the verdict on the food would take a while. Their waiter recognized Myra immediately and she and Connie were given preferential service including a complimentary bottle of the house's best wine, a pinot noir, from grapes grown in western Oregon, a strange choice for an Italian restaurant Connie thought. He also thought the waiter, a slight, handsome man is his mid-thirties, was being overly solicitous. Myra appeared to enjoy it however. Connie was somewhat surprised.

"Are you encouraging this guy?" Connie asked when the waiter left their table.

She smiled sweetly. "Actually, yes. I'm trying to determine if he's worth stealing. I'm a little short handed at the Rustlers. I could use a good waiter who could also fill in as host." She reached over and tapped his hand with her finger. "Then if a certain cowboy showed up at the last minute looking for a date I could oblige him."

"How would you feel about your waiter giving away your best wine?"

"I'm assuming he had permission to do that, because I don't allow my wait staff to give out complimentary anything."

"I could get the manager or maitre d' and thank him. We'd find out."

"Let's wait a bit and see what happens."

They sipped their wine and waited while they talked. Connie asked her about her acting career and she told him most everything, how she got started, how she initially loved it, but then after several years how it became tedious and finally, how she came to detest it and why she left. "I came to the point where I no longer knew myself. I felt like there was someone else living in my skin and I didn't like that person. I was doing what I had to do to stay connected and I decided it wasn't worth it. Fortunately I'd saved a lot of my money and even made some decent investments. I thank my father for that. He was very diligent about encouraging me to put away at least half my income. That's what I did. When I knew it was time to leave, I could."

"I'm impressed. I understand you own the strip mall across the street from the Boot Hill. What do you intend to do with that?"

"How did you know I owned that?"

"The bartender told me. About a week after I got into town I went looking for a Laundromat to wash my clothes and that's where I ended up. When I'd loaded up the washing machines, I went across the street for a beer and that's when I ran into you the second time. I asked the bartender if he knew who you were and he told me. He also told me you owned the joint and had just bought the property across the street."

"Interesting. What else did he tell you about me?"

"He told me you were forty-six and how good he thought you looked."

The part of the restaurant they were in was dimly lit, but Connie could still see her blush. "That must have been Mel. I'm glad he doesn't know anything else about me."

"He wasn't at all disrespectful, but I could tell he liked you."

"I don't know whether to be flattered or mad."

"Oh come on. You know the effect you have on the ordinary male."

"She took his hand. "So, are you an ordinary or extraordinary male?"

"I'm afraid I'm extraordinarily ordinary."

"Good," she said as their waiter arrived with their food.

The food was better than passable, and Myra wondered out loud if she should put an Italian entrée or two on the menu at her place. "What do you think, Connie, should I offer cannelloni or lasagna at Rustlers?"

"Why don't you just open another restaurant and make it Italian?"

"If you'd run it for me, I might." Then before he could answer, "No, forget that idea. We'd never see each other."

He agreed. "You're right. Years ago, I decided there were two businesses I'd never get into, diary farming or a restaurant. They're both way too much work."

"Well, I never milked cows, but I'll agree restaurants are too much work. Actually, I don't intend to stay in business that much longer. When I turn fifty, I'm selling everything and officially retiring. I want to see some of the world before it's gone."

Her comment had an immediate effect on Connie. It was what he and Sarah had intended to do just before she got sick. The sudden memory of it dumped on him like a massive avalanche of emotion and rolled him into a ball, leaving him fighting for control. He was momentarily lost in time, experiencing this conversation again, but with Sarah not Myra. Exhaling a long, slow breath as his countenance sagged, he carefully placed his fork on his plate.

"You okay, Connie?"

He nodded slowly before speaking. "Yeah, I'm fine. I just had about the most powerful deja vu sensation I've ever had," and he proceeded to tell Myra about what had happened to him and Sarah when they retired to see the world.

When he finished, Myra put her arm across his shoulders and kissed his cheek. "I'm so sorry." And she truly was and not only for him, but herself too. Just prior to Connie's story, she'd decided she was ready to take it to the next level. Actually she still was, but now she decided she should give him a little more time. She realized he wasn't ready. However, she definitely wanted a rain check when his feelings were in order, maybe in a month when he came back from riding the cutting circuit or if not then, for certain after the futurity in December. She'd decided a long time ago she'd never take advantage of a man when he was weak. It'd been done to her, more than once, but that would never happen again either. She quickly removed her arm from his shoulder and pulled back a bit.

"Thanks, it's okay. When you said you were going to retire and see the world, I got dizzy. I didn't mean to go on about my past."

"I'm glad you did. You and your wife were obviously in love. That's a good thing. I wish I could tell you I'd been in love with the father of my child, but I'm afraid I can't, not without lying."

"Speaking of your daughter," Connie decided to change the subject. "The twins, the two nine-year olds you met with me a few weeks ago, are lobbying me to convince your daughter to give them skiing lessons."

"Are they intermediates? Cyan doesn't do beginners anymore. She used to get too involved with them and if they didn't have enough interest and dropped out, she would blame herself. I finally told her to only work with kids who had some experience and knew they wanted to stay with it. She did. She's much happier teaching now."

Eventually they ordered dessert and coffee, and it was eleven before they left Kalispell for the drive back to Myra's home in Whitefish. When they arrived, Myra decided to make it short and sweet. She leaned across the center console of Connie's truck and put her arms around him. "I'd really like to take you home tonight, Cowboy, but you've got a long day ahead of you tomorrow." Connie joined her in the rather clumsy embrace the big front seat made necessary. "You be sure to come and see me when you're back in town and we'll talk some more." She kissed him and promising he would, he returned the favor.

About twenty minutes later, Cally watched the headlights from his truck spin around the house, following the driveway from the highway down to the bunkhouse. She checked her watch; just midnight. She thought that was good, probably not enough time for him to have gotten into too much trouble. She finally fell asleep after seeing him turn off the light.

Connie didn't sleep. He lay on his back thinking about the coming day and the past evening. He was both flattered and apprehensive that Myra was apparently his for the taking. He'd only had one serious relationship in his life. Well maybe there had been two if you counted the girl who promised to wait for him, but was married to someone else five months after he left. He wondered about Myra's track record. Did she love 'em and leave 'em or did she immerse herself into each and every one? He didn't want to be another notch on her belt in either case. Maybe he better extricate himself before he went any further. "No problem," he told himself just before he fell asleep, "I've got a busy two months ahead. By the time I'm done with the futurity, it'll be Christmas and I'm spending that here. No reason I have to even talk to Myra before New Years."

It was a little tough getting to breakfast on time. Fortunately, it was still at seven, not six, in deference to Pete's condition. The girls seemed to be moping, but everyone else appeared in good spirits. Woody was ready to go and Pete had some last minute advice. "Don't push too hard. Win if you can, but don't forget this is the pre-season game. You can't afford to get hurt."

The twins hung around the breakfast table until just before the school bus came. They were quiet, but when they hugged Connie goodbye, they both had tears in their eyes. Lindsey told him she loved him and Danni just clung to him.

"Hey, ladies, it's okay. I'm coming back. I'll probably be able to stop in on my way to Colorado from Idaho. Can you think of something you'd want me to bring you from Oregon or Idaho?"

"No," was all Danni could say between sobs.

"Just come back," Lindsey told him. And then they left for school.

Connie looked hopefully to Cally for an explanation.

"They love you half to death."

"I'm not sure I deserve it."

"Well, apparently they think you do. And," she added, "I happen to agree with their evaluation." Turning quickly she left the kitchen.

Connie looked to Pete and Woody who were grinning at him. He cleared his throat and pushing back his chair he said to Woody, "I'll get Billy in the trailer and be ready in about fifteen minutes." He extended his hand to Pete. "Wish me luck, Coach."

Pete shook his hand. "Remember when I told you about bein' lucky? If you're good, luck isn't all that important. Billy's pretty good and you've become a decent rider. You keep that in mind and you won't need a lot of luck."

About twenty minutes later, Woody, Connie, and Billy rolled out of the driveway as Pete and Cally waved them goodbye. "I wish you were going with them," Cally told Pete.

"Yeah, me too. If I felt a little better I would, but I don't think I could deal with the long ride. I'm saving myself for the futurity."

Cally put her arm around him. "You think he'll make it?"

"Oh he'll make it down there all right as long as he and Jo stay healthy. He's paid his money, that's all it takes to go."

"That's not what I mean. Do you think he can do anything once he gets there?"

Pete lowered his arm. Connie's truck was out of sight, climbing west up the long hill towards the Idaho border. "He seems to be a chip off the old block. His old man, Major Bradley, was a tough, capable leader. I believe Connie can do near anything he decides he wants to do. I'm more worried about him getting hurt. I almost died when he fell off Fritz that first day I had him cutting." Pete regarded his daughter. "He was looking at you when it happened, you know."

"Yeah, I thought I might have distracted him a bit."

"I think more than a bit." Pete laughed. "He likes you—a lot. You know that too?"

"I'm not so sure about that. He took out the movie star last night, not me."

"I wouldn't worry too much about that. She's got nothing on you except about fifteen years."

"That may be part of the problem."

"Are you thinking Connie believes he's too old for you?"

"Yeah, maybe. Besides, Brianna is rich and beautiful."

"Well, you're just as pretty, prettier in fact, and I doubt if Connie cares much about rich. As far as thinking he's too old for you, if your mother were around, she'd be able to tell you how to handle that little detail. Do you think he's too old for you? Seems to me, that doctor was your age, but too immature."

"No I don't think he's too old, not anymore. I did when he first got here, but that didn't last long."

"Your two girls sure are taken by him."

"They adore him. I can't imagine what will happen when he leaves after Christmas."

Pete smiled, but Cally didn't notice. She was still staring at the highway that had swallowed up Connie's truck. Pete was thinking Connie might not be going anywhere after Christmas.

Chapter 32, Start of the Circuit

The first stop for Connie and Woody was just outside the little town of Athol, Idaho, not far from Coeur d'Alene. It's where, Pete's saddle making buddy lived with his daughter and son-in-law. His workshop was in a building attached to their horse barn. Mac was in his shop sitting in a saddle reading a Louis L'Amour novel when they arrived. He appeared to be quite comfortable, as if it were normal to sit in a saddle without the horse.

"Well," he said greeting them, "You boys are right on time. I been sittin' in your saddle for about three hours now and I haven't felt any bad spots. If it fits your horse, I think it'll be good to go."

Connie explained Pete's medical condition and how their plans had changed. "Pete didn't think I should be hauling Jolena too as he couldn't come along to help."

Mac was disappointed. "Well, that's a shame, lets see how it fits the horse you brought."

Connie unloaded Billy for Mac to saddle. When he was finished, he told Connie to mount up. He pushed and tugged at the saddle for a bit. "Not perfect, but he's built a lot like the one I made it for. I believe he'll be all right with it if you want to use it on him."

Connie smiled. "That's great Mac. Pete wants me to use it when I'm warming up."

"Yeah, that'd be good."

Connie pulled out his wallet. "I believe I owe you some money."

They stayed for lunch because Mac's daughter wouldn't have it any other way. She was shaving thin slices of beef from a leftover loin roast when Connie, Mac, and Woody traipsed into the kitchen. In no time at all, they were treated to the best hot roast beef sandwich Connie had ever eaten. Smothered in thick, rich gravy, it was accompanied by mashed potatoes, green beans and a dollop of shredded fresh carrots and horseradish, mixed with some kind of mayonnaise dressing and a few raisins. It was an unusual combination and Connie normally never ate horseradish, but the stuff was so good he thought about asking for seconds. He didn't however, because desert was mentioned as in, "save room for pie," and since moving to Pete's place, he'd become something of a pie connoisseur, especially Woody's apple pies. She didn't serve apple, but pumpkin made directly from the genuine article and Connie wasn't disappointed.

He thanked her profusely for the lunch when they finally left. "My pleasure," she told him. "Thank you for keeping my dad busy making your saddle."

"Can I be real nosey?" Woody asked him when they going back down the road, "What did that saddle cost you?"

"Five large ones," Connie told him.

Woody whistled softly. "Wow, Boy, you have got expensive hobbies."

"Yeah, six months ago, I would have thought I was nuts for buying a five thousand dollar saddle, but I know better now."

"Know what better? How to squander your money?"

"It's all relative, my friend. First of all, money was made to be spent. Secondly, I consider myself extremely blessed to have enough so I don't have to worry too much about spending a disproportionate amount of it on certain non-essentials."

"Non-essential is right. It's a good thing not everybody needs a champion cuttin' horse."

Connie ignored the comment. "Thirdly, and I have this on good authority, Mac works for about half price."

Woody whistled again, louder this time. "You mean to tell me, there's fools out there who'll pay ten thousand dollars for a saddle?"

"According to Pete, yes there are and from what I understand, that's not an upper limit. It's all about fit and strength. You ever have a new pair of shoes or boots you put on and they were immediately comfortable, never hurt you're feet from day one?"

"Yeah, I've had that on several occasions. Are you suggesting this saddle ain't gonna hurt your ass from the get go?"

"My ass is relatively unimportant. I want it to be comfortable for Jolena. She's the one doing all the work. I figure she weighs about eleven hundred pounds. The saddle and I weigh about two and a quarter, which is close to one fifth of Jo's weight. Now I've humped my share of fifty-pound packs around in the heat, humidity, and mud, and the Army isn't noted for providing state of the art pack frames. If it costs me a few thousand dollars to make sure Jo is comfortable with me on her back, it was money well spent."

"When you put it like that, it does seem like a bargain." Woody was grinning.

"What? What's so blasted funny?"

"You love that horse, don't you?"

There was no hesitation. "Yes, I do. Sometimes she seems almost human, at least in regards of understanding what I'm saying. She seems to understand me almost as well as my late wife did. She doesn't mind me spending money on her either, just like my wife."

"Your wife was high maintenance?"

"Not hardly. She was at ease with whatever she had and pretty much wherever she was, but she didn't mind if I spoiled her either."

"You spoil her a lot?"

"Not nearly as much as I wished I had."

Woody frowned. "Yeah, me too. I know what you mean. I'd have done a lot more fancy livin' if I'd known mine was gonna be taken away so fast."

Connie was silent as he came down the entrance ramp onto I-90 going west to Spokane and beyond. "What happened, if you care to talk about it?"

Woody exhaled a long thin sigh. "We got married in June, right after I got my doctorate from MIT. We'd been sweethearts since the eighth grade. Twelve years we'd waited for that day, and believe me it was worth the wait. I had a job offer workin' for the engineering firm that built the Verrazano Narrows Bridge across the East River. You went to West Point, you've probably had occasion to use it a time or two."

"Yeah, I went to the 'City' more than once."

"Well, we moved to New York, found a cozy apartment and spent as much time as we could explorin' the city. It was idyllic." He looked at Connie and winked. "Like a picnic at Rogers Lake with Cally."

"Jeez, do those girls tell everyone every thing I say?"

"Pretty much."

"I was afraid of that. How did Cally react to that?"

"She just smiled. I believe that woman has plans for you."

"What kind of plans?"

"You have to ask? What are you, blind, deaf, and dumb?"

"A little hard of hearing maybe, but mostly just dumb. However you were telling me about your wife."

Woody ran his hand slowly over his face. "The wedding ring I got for her was a little big and one day she decided to get it resized." He paused. "It was a classic case of bein' in the right place at the wrong time, the wrong place at right time or the wrong place at the wrong time, I've never decided which. Regardless, when she was at the jewelers, a sub-human, son-of-Satan, decided to rob the place. When she didn't move fast enough, he shot her." Woody paused again and when he continued there were tears in his eyes and fifty-year old pain in his voice. "The godless bastard shot her in the face."

Connie waited for a while, but Woody had stopped talking. "I'm really sorry, Woody. I can't imagine how you felt." That's what he said, but he could imagine how Woody felt. More than one soldier had died in his arms, and then there was Sarah.

Swallowing hard, Woody waved a hand in the air. "I went to the trial and made certain I had a seat next to the aisle. When they led the murderin' bastard down to the front of the courtroom, I jumped up and started to pommel him. I had every intent to kill him. They pulled me away before I could, however I did manage to break his nose and jaw." Woody chuckled, "A week later when the trial started again, his lawyer referred to me as an animal. I had to sit in the back, between two bailiffs."

"Cally told me the guy died during a prison riot at Attica."

"Yeah, and I checked on that too, just to be sure. When the bastard was sentenced to life, I got up and told the court, if he were ever paroled, I'd kill him. Some of the spectators started to clap and the judge had me carried out. Can't say as I blame him."

"Is she why you left the city and came out west?"

"Yup, I didn't want nothin' more to do with civilization. If people were gonna act like animals, I might as well live in the wild. I wandered around lookin' for a remote spot and happened into a saloon in Cheyenne, Wyoming where I met a Basque sheepherder. It was early autumn and he was recently down off the mountain for the winter. All he could talk about was not bein' able to wait for spring so he could go back up. The way he described the solitude seemed perfect to me in my condition at the time. I asked him if his employer was lookin' for help and that started me off on my second career."

"That was quite a switch, from bridge designer to sheep herder."

"It's no different than what you did goin' from soldier to business owner to professional cowboy."

"Maybe, but I don't have a PhD in physics."

"You got a degree in engineering from West Point. Seems to me, by rights, you shoulda stayed in the army and been a general, not ridin' a cutting horse for fun and profit."

"Okay, I give. My history is just as checkered as yours."

Woody grinned at him. "But you're havin' fun ain't ya?"

Connie had to admit he was and the two friends went down the road swapping stories about their lives, loves, and plans. They had a reservation at a mare motel south of Pendleton, Oregon and they made it easily by six that evening. Prior to going to Oklahoma with his friend John back in April, Connie had never heard of a mare motel. Now he was actually considering the possibility of building one somewhere in central Idaho. They were great, a place where you could stay in a comfortable room or cabin and your horse or horses were stabled close by. His trailer was fine if the RV Park catered to horsemen, but that didn't always happen. At a mare motel, you knew both you and your horse would be taken care of.

After cleaning the trailer and getting Billy settled in, they found a restaurant with passable food. Woody had volunteered to cook, but they were both tired. The restaurant was quick and easy. They were back to the motel and in bed by nine. Billy's stall was six inches away on the other side of the wall. Connie slept easy.

After breakfast the next morning, they wandered the convoluted highways of central Oregon until they arrived at Fort Klamath in the middle of the afternoon. Connie found a spot for the trailer and went to the event office to enter the derby. After paying his entrance fee, on his way back to the trailer, some one called his name.

"Hey, Connie," said Gilliam Bedfort Junior, "How ya doin'?"

Connie was surprised Gilly remembered his name. "I'm doin' all right, Gilly, how about you?"

"Super," Gilly told him. "If I were any better, I'd have to be two people. I was hoping I'd run into you one of these days. I got a new horse, two actually. I'm looking for a rematch."

Glad to see a familiar face so far from home, Connie shook
Gilly's hand. "Fantastic," he told Gilly, "I'd love a rematch. Care to
make any wagers."

"You in the derby?"

"Yup. Just signed up. What about you?"

"Yeah, me too. How about a C note, high point man wins?"

"Deal," Connie said and they shook on it. Why don't you come
over to where we're parked. Woody will be grilling some steaks in
about an hour. I'll buy you a plate of beans."

Gilly laughed. "That's right magnanimous of you. I'd love to
join you and Woody."

"Come on along now. I don't want to have to draw you a
map."

Woody was just starting the coals when Connie and Gilly
walked up. "Hey, Woody, look who I found."

"Well I'll be," Woody said and shook Gilly's hand. "How you
doin' Junior? We're havin' steak and fried potatoes. Can you stay?"

"I sure can and I appreciate it. The worst part about these
contests is eating alone and driving all over creation by yourself,
although I did get lucky a few weeks ago."

"You want to define what you mean by lucky?" asked Woody.

Junior grinned. "I met a fine young lady at the rodeo in
Spokane and she took me to the best restaurant I've ever been to. Her
daddy owns the place and she has a thing about cowboys."

"So, you're sayin' the extent of your luck was getting' a good
meal with a pretty woman?"

"Well, there was more, but I'm only talking about the restaurant.
On the weekends you can't even get in without a coat and tie."

"You normally travel to the cuttin' shows with a coat and tie?"
Woody asked.

"Not hardly, but this was a Thursday night and the tie was
optional. I was probably the most casually dressed guy in the place, but
I didn't let that spoil my appetite."

"So what did you eat?" Connie asked him.

"Oh, all kinds of stuff, lobster, salmon stuffed with crab, steak
you could cut with a spoon, all types of side dishes and desserts, I had
what was called 'The Sampler'."

"A little bit of everything?"

"Actually, no. It was a lot of whatever was on the menu and
struck your fancy. You asked for what you thought sounded good and

the waiter brought out a portion. When you were done with that, you could get another and another until you called it quits."

"What's something like that cost?" Woody wanted to know.

"It wasn't cheap, but Missy, that was the woman's name, was buying and she said to get what I wanted, so that's what I had. I guess what I had was way north of a hundred dollars."

Woody whistled. "I hope you got her phone number."

"Oh yeah. I'm going back to visit just as soon as I get a break. I'm bringing a suit along next time too. On the weekends the restaurant has an orchestra. I've danced to a lot of cowboy bands, but never to a real orchestra. Hey, I might even buy her dinner this time."

Connie was listening closely, getting an idea. "What's the name of this place?"

Junior told him and he made a mental note. Woody looked at Connie as if he was reading his mind, but rather than let on, Woody asked Junior if he'd won anything. "How you doin', Junior? You finish in the money in any of the contests you been in lately?"

"Yeah, I took a second and a third in the last three weeks. I was hoping for a good ride here until I saw Connie."

"Well, don't lose heart, Connie won't stop you from having a good ride, but he just might have a better one."

"We'll find out. We've got money on it. In fact if I beat him, I can afford to take Missy out and buy the dinner this time."

"I heard that, Gilly," said Connie. "What makes you think you'll win? Your new horses that good?"

"As a matter of fact I think they might be. The one I'm saving for the futurity is a real beauty. She's the best horse I ever rode. I brought her along, but obviously I can't ride her in competition yet. The other one I'm ridin' tomorrow is at least as good as the one you rode against me in Kalispell.

"Interesting," Connie said. "Where'd you find them?"

"Your mentor, Pete, put me onto them. Gave me the name of a guy he met in Helena. Turns out this guy had three good, three-year olds and sold me the two he didn't like. He'd been plannin' on taking only one of them to Fort Worth, and decided the two I got were too independent."

"If it's the same guy he mentioned to me, Pete said he was heavy handed."

"Yeah, he said he didn't figure the guy was too bright. He also said if I expected to win I'd have to back off some on the rein."

"You been able to do that?"

Junior got a little twisted grin on his face and then laughed. "It wasn't easy, but yeah, pretty much."

"Well, that's good. Pete also said you were better than you thought you were."

"That means a lot, coming from Pete. Why isn't he with you guys?"

While the steaks grilled, Connie filled Gilly in on Pete's condition and then it was time to eat. After dinner, they swapped lies with each other and a couple of cowboys from the trailer parked next door. Junior left by nine and a half hour later, Connie and Woody packed it in.

"You know, Woody, we are a couple of real party animals." Connie was in the queen bed up front and Woody was in the queen bed that pulled out from the dinette. "Nine-thirty and we're crashed like two old men."

"We are two old men, leastwise I am. Besides that, where's the party? We're fifty miles from anywhere. The only girls around here are a few of them barrel racer types and we got here too late to snap up any of them. Shut up and go to sleep."

Connie laughed, closed his eyes and did exactly that.

Chapter 33, More of the Circuit

The next morning Connie slept as late as he could which was only six-thirty. Rather than staring at the low ceiling, he took Billy out for a walk, cleaned the mess out of the back of the trailer and when he was done, he and Woody ate a leisurely breakfast, drinking coffee until ten. The contest didn't start until one in the afternoon. At eleven, Junior came by with his new mount and Connie wondered why Pete had steered Gilly Senior onto this filly. She was well built with a big hip and short back, a lot like Jolena. She was also calm, but alert, just like Jo. Pete must have been thinking the competition between him and Gilly Junior needed to be ratcheted up a notch just for sport.

"She looks good to me, Gilly, but I'm not an expert by the stretch of anybody's imagination."

Woody piped up, "You're more than fifty miles from home, ain't ya?"

Connie looked at him critically. "Of course I'm more than fifty miles from home? What do you mean?"

If you're in the company of strangers and more than fifty miles from home, you can be any kind of an expert you want."

Shaking his head, Connie turned back to Gilly. "Like I said, I'm no expert, but she's built a lot like Jolena and I know what she can do." Actually, he was more than a little concerned about Gilly riding this horse. Pete had described the filly he'd seen as a horse that came close to Jo in ability. Now, Gilly had told him this horse was better than the one Pete had seen. Gilly had been riding a long time. If this horse were as good or even almost as good as Jo, theoretically, Gilly could beat him.

Gilly hung around for a while and talked. He seemed lonely and Connie knew if Woody hadn't decided to come along, he'd feel the same way. It wasn't until well after noon that Gilly finally left. "Gotta go, Gents, I'm riding number seventeen. See you all after the dust settles."

"I'm number eighty-four. You think you'll be riding about two?" Connie decided he wanted to watch Gilly ride.

"Yeah, but not before. I always figure twelve to fifteen riders an hour. Twelve if things don't go smooth and fifteen if they do."

"That puts me on about seven o-clock tonight."

"Yeah, about that. I heard this morning they got a bunch of late entries, so the first round will probably run into tomorrow morning."

Connie shrugged. "Oh well, we don't have anything else to do."

"Yeah, except get to the next one on time." He left them then to go warm up his horse.

"He got you a little worried?" Woody asked.

"Yeah, a little. I don't know why Pete had to find him such good horses."

"So you could discover how good yours is."

"The problem isn't the horse, Woody. I know she's good. It's me I'm worried about. Gilly on a good horse could be dangerous."

"He might beat you once, but I seriously doubt he'll do it a second time. From what I can see, you and Billy are a pretty good team. I'm bettin' Junior is still not ready to turn over control to his horse. He may think he has, but I'll bet you a C note it hasn't happened."

Sliding out of the dinette, Connie slapped Woody on the shoulder. "I hope you're right. Let's clean up so we can go watch him."

They did watch and he was impressive. He found three good cows to nail the highest score so far, bumping the previous leader down a notch. Connie was impressed, although he thought he detected Gilly still holding a tight rein. He was deep in thought as they walked back to the trailer.

Around four, he took Billy out and groomed him before he tacked him up. "Okay, it's you and me and we've got competition. I'm afraid it's all up to you, again. I'll just sit on your back and hope I can hang on." Billy merely looked at him with an inscrutable gaze.

Connie didn't pay any attention to the standings until after their ride. They had a good one, maybe as good as Junior's. He may have even beat him. He did, by only a point though, and somebody by the name of Jake Coleman was three points ahead of him. Must have had a real good ride, Connie thought.

As Connie walked Jo back to the trailer, Junior caught up to them. "Good ride, Connie, I can almost feel that hundred dollar bill tryin' to get out of my pocket."

"Yeah, well, it's only one point and who in the world is Jake Coleman? Did you see him ride?"

"He's a local cowboy from Klamath Falls and I did see him ride. I didn't think he was as good as either of us, but I figure being local, he's got the favor of at least a couple judges."

"I thought the judges were impartial."

"Mostly they are, but you know what happens when money is involved. Besides, this kid was in the local futurity and got blown out on the first round. According to what I've heard, he was supposed to do a lot better, so maybe this is a chance at redemption."

"At our expense?"

"It happens. Not often, but it happens."

"Anything we can do?"

"If it's really obvious, we can file a protest, but otherwise the decision of the judges is final. Just like it says on that form you signed when you paid your entrance fee."

"Protesting sounds time consuming. I have to be in Henry's Lake, Idaho the day after tomorrow."

"Yeah, me too. Where you going to from there?"

"Pueblo, if we can make it, and then back to Idaho unless there's anything going on in Gunnison."

"What about the one in Columbus, Montana? You thought about it?"

"Yeah, I just don't know for sure yet."

"Hey maybe after Henry's Lake, we should swing by Kalispell. I could park my rig and ride with you. Then we could take turns drivin' and share expenses."

"Sounds good to me. We've got plenty of room. Let me run it past Woody. You coming over later?"

"Thanks, but I have to scoot."

The next day, Gilly, Connie, Jake Coleman, and seventeen other cowboys rode in the final round. Jake Coleman finished first. Gilly and Connie tied for second. They both agreed they put in better rides than Jake, but they collected their prize money, loaded their trucks, and headed for the next competition. No formal protests were filed, although a case could have been made. Connie chalked it up to experience, bad judging, and politics. He wasn't in it for the money and he had places to go. He was out of there before the ink on his prize money check had dried.

"You ever been awed?" Woody asked, as they were moving across southern Oregon on the way to Henry's Lake in the northeast corner of southern Idaho. The roads in this part of the country were convoluted beyond belief and they were going to have to hustle to get there in a day and a half.

Even for Woody it was a strange question. Connie wondered where this would go. "I'm not certain what you mean."

"One summer when I was herdin' sheep, I got caught in a violent thunderstorm. When it started, I was in my wagon tryin' to stay dry. Lightnin' was walkin' all around me and when I looked out the back, all the sheep, my dogs, and my mule were laying down. Say what you will about them being stupid, they knew enough not to be the highest thing around. I wondered how smart I was by sitting in the wagon. Two quick bolts, one on each side of the wagon, got me out and I joined the flock on the ground some distance away. About twenty seconds later, a bolt struck the wagon, blew it in half and then the lightnin' intensified to the point I thought I couldn't avoid bein' blasted apart. But here's the strange thing. In spite of what was happenin', I wasn't afraid. I was, however, confounded into amazement by the sheer power and intensity of the storm. It was like bein' inside a strobe light and goin' over Niagara Falls at the same time. It was a spectacle and I was watching. Never have experienced anything like it since."

"Lose any sheep?"

"No, but the wagon was broke bad. Pete told me once that in an artillery barrage on Heartbreak Ridge when he was fightin' in Korea, he experienced the same feeling. I figured maybe you had encountered a similar situation."

Connie hesitated. "I graduated from the Point well after Vietnam ended. As a second lieutenant I was a dime a dozen, and the sad truth is, without a war, it's not easy to make rank. So I took a different approach." He paused.

"How so?" Woody asked.

"You ever heard of the 75th Ranger Regiment?"

"Can't say as I have. Should I?"

"No, of course not. Suffice to say it's where most of Delta
Force starts from. Regardless, I was in the employ of Uncle Sam in a
place where soldiers with that relationship shouldn't have been. I was
with seven other like-minded individuals and we were betrayed by one
of our 'trusted guides'. We were ambushed by about fifty members of
the opposition. We were moving as two teams, four each. My team was
in the lead. We were hit first. Two of my team were killed instantly.
The other one and I were wounded, him worse than me. I happened to
fall in a slight depression and in the ensuring two minutes, I had the hell
awed out me. Unlike you however, I was scared."

"Amazin', Boy, how is it you and me are talkin'?"

"Because the fire-team behind mine had guts, superior training,
and a belt-fed weapon. They annihilated the ambushers. I might have
helped a bit."

"So, you won."

"I suppose if you want to call it that. Big price tag. I would
have preferred never to be awed again, although after that, I saw some
action in Iraq."

Sensing an end to that conversation, Woody changed the
subject. "Do you suppose you can be awed without being in mortal
danger?"

Connie thought a bit. "Yeah, maybe so. I remember an
inexplicable detached feeling, I knew I was there, but I was also
watching myself be there. If that makes any sense.

"Perfect sense. When the lightning was cracklin' all around me,
I had the thought I was totally inconsequential and in the presence of
such fearsome power, whether I lived or died mattered not one iota."

"Interesting. I haven't thought about it for some time, although
after it happened, it was all I could think about for months. It's still
vivid. You're right about feeling inconsequential, I can remember
thinking I was very small, almost infinitely so, merely a tiny mote in a
powerful storm of red hot steel, fire, and noise."

"Well, realizin' if you lifted your head, it'd be removed had to
contribute something. I became intimate with the earth under my back.
In fact, after the lightnin' stopped, I was the last one up. The sheep
were all up grazin' before the dogs finally convinced me it was safe to
stand up straight again. Took me a while to realize I was cold, wet, and
in trouble with no wagon."

"What did you do?"

"I picked up what I could find of my supplies, made a shelter
out of what was left of the wagon and built a fire. Took me four hours

to get dried out. The next few days I got the wagon cobbled back together after a fashion. A week after the storm hit I was back in business."

"Did Pete ever say anything else about his combat experiences?"

"Very little. He's always been kind of closed mouthed about it, although he did tell me about when he got shot. He said his outfit was overrun one night and for some of them it came down to hand to hand combat. A Chicom jumped into his foxhole and when Pete pulled the trigger on his rifle, nothing happened so he smacked him with the rifle butt. The guy went down shooting at Pete and managed to hit him in the left cheek as Pete was trying to exit the foxhole. He said it hurt and made him so mad he jumped back into the hole and landed on the guy's chest. He took the rifle away and tried to shoot him with it, but it was empty too. That's when he figured he'd already killed the man by jumping on him. He said he sat there for a while before he realized he needed to find more ammo, but before he could, the attack was over. Pete said the Chinese would sometimes make what were called short attacks, usually five guys against a single position out of the line. They'd attack until they were successful or all dead and then immediately five more guys would attack. Sometimes it seemed like they wouldn't quit."

"Yeah, it was a strategy exclusive to the Chinese; the North Koreans thought they were crazy."

"As they surely were. Anyway when his own troops showed up, Pete came out the hole to greet them and promptly collapsed. He'd lost a lot of blood and didn't even know it. Said there was so much excitement he'd forgotten he was shot." Woody looked over at Conrad. "After a deal like that, how could anything ever scare you?"

Connie suddenly felt a chill. "Is Pete afraid of something?"

"Oh no, just the opposite, but I got a feelin' he knows something we don't."

"Like what? What did he say?"

"The night before we left, I asked him how he felt. He just smiled and said, 'Not great, but I can still shoot, move, and communicate.' You got an idea what he meant by that, exactly?"

"It's an infantry soldier's expression. It means exactly what it says, Pete can still function, but the not feeling great part worries me. Did he say any more?"

"Nope. That was it. I figured he was still just sore from the surgery and didn't want to complain. It's only been the last day I got to thinkin' about it again. He's not the type of person to volunteer his problems."

"Why don't you call Cally right now and ask how he's feeling, discreetly of course. After this next contest, we'll shoot up to the ranch for a quick visit like we planned, and maybe we can extract some information from him ourselves." He handed Woody the phone.

Cally answered on the second ring and she and Woody talked for the time it took Connie to drive about twenty miles. When he was done he told Connie, "She wanted to talk to you, but I wouldn't let her. Not safe while you're drivin' you know."

"Yeah, I heard that part. How's Pete?"

"She's a little concerned, too. She said she called one of doctors from the clinic that worked on him and they told her that due to Pete's age, she couldn't expect him to heal quickly. He said he might be sore for at least a month, maybe two."

"Maybe, but I think when we get back there we should convince him to go in for a check up."

Woody agreed and they were silent, each thinking private thoughts about their friend. Connie knew all too well how insidious cancer was and Woody knew Pete well enough to know they wouldn't have an easy time getting him to the doctor.

For Connie, the contest at Henry's Lake was a breeze. Everything went his way. The cattle cooperated, Billy was magnificent, and he rode like an old pro. He finished first with apologies to no one. Junior was six points behind, but finished in the money. Connie and Woody pulled away from Henry's Lake late in the afternoon and stopped for the night at a place about sixty miles east of Butte. From there they were within five hours of the ranch. If they got an early start, they could be there by noon. They'd have a day and a half respite from the road.

At six in the morning, Woody stayed in the trailer while Connie started driving. About an hour later, Woody used a two-way radio to announce breakfast was served. Connie found a place to pull over and joined Woody at the dinette in the trailer. They were already west of Butte.

"Good idea, Woody," Connie said. "This will put us home in time for lunch."

When Connie looked up from his plate, Woody was grinning at him. "What?"

"I just get a kick out of you referrin' to it as home."

"What do you think I should call it?"

"Don't get me wrong. I like you thinkin' of it that way. That means you'll think twice before leavin' when you're done playin' games."

"I'm not sure what I'll do, but it's more home now than my own house was after my wife died."

They were both quiet for a while, eating and contemplating. Woody spoke first. "What'd you think about that restaurant in Spokane that Junior told us about? You think it might be fancy enough for Cally's birthday. Be nice if she could wear that new dress she bought."

Connie had already been considering that possibility and guessed Woody suspected as much. "It's almost a four hour drive from the ranch to Spokane, Woody. I just did it a few weeks ago. That makes a long round trip for a dinner date."

Woody took a big hit off of his coffee cup and smiled innocently across the dinette table at Connie. "I remember hearin', although I'm not sure where exactly, maybe from Danni or Lindsey, something about you contemplatin' flying Brianna somewhere for a date." He put down his cup. "Any of that sound familiar or am I imaginin' things?"

Connie groaned. "I really have to be careful what I say to those two little recording machines."

"Yes, you do, but I wonder how long it would take one of those little bitty jets to get from Kalispell to Spokane. Let's see, it's probably less than a hundred and fifty air miles and they must fly at least four hundred miles per hour. So you're lookin at maybe twenty, twenty- five minutes and...."

"Yeah, yeah," Connie cut him off. "It's only probably a ten or fifteen minute limo ride to the restaurant. We could leave the ranch at five o'clock have a leisurely dinner, dance, and linger over cocktails and still be home by midnight."

Woody put down his fork and politely patted his lips with his napkin. "Why, Connie, I'm surprised, you already gave this some thought."

"No, you're not surprised, you're just nosey. What I don't understand is why you're encouraging me. I got the impression you were protective of Cally."

"I am protective of Cally if I think she's in danger, but getting remarried to the likes of you wouldn't be dangerous. And then you wouldn't have to go wanderin' off someplace else when you're done. Be great for everyone concerned if you were to hang around."

"So now you've got me married to Cally. Sounds like this would be a marriage of convenience, at least convenient for you."

"Is there something wrong with Cally? She not pretty enough for you?"

"She's gorgeous. She reminds me of the first girl I ever had a crush on. I'd sign up in a minute, but what about the fact I'm more than ten years older than she is?"

"I don't believe that's a problem for her and as far as the kids go, they're girls. You won't have to worry about playin' football with them when you're sixty."

"How do you know she's okay with the age thing? Have you talked to her?"

"Course not; you think I'd meddle in your affairs?"

"If what you're doing isn't meddling, what do you call it?"

"I call it friendly advice. Now get up there and drive. I'd like to get home."

Connie took a cup of coffee to go, told Woody he'd stop in a half hour so he could come up front, and left the trailer. Woody said he'd cleanup the breakfast dishes. In the half hour that followed, Connie made plans. Tomorrow morning he would drive to the Kalispell airport to see if there was a charter service flying bizjets.

Chapter 34, The Plan

They pulled into the driveway at eleven-thirty. Connie dropped Woody in front of the house and then drove down to the barn to turn Billy out into the pasture. After Connie pulled an armload of packages out of the truck and walked up to the house. Cally was there to open the door.

"Welcome back," she told him. She'd planned on hugging him, but his arms were full. She had to settle for patting him on the shoulder. "Congratulations. Woody said you were impressive."

He smiled back, wishing his arms were free. *I could have brought all this stuff up later.* "Thanks, Cally. I don't know if I'd call it impressive."

"A first and a second, what do you call it?"

"Ah, lucky, maybe? I have some things for you and Pete and the girls. Where can I put them?"

"That's nice. Let me help you. We'll put it all in the living room. Lunch is almost ready. How about a cup of coffee?"

"That would be great. I could use it. For some reason the last fifty miles almost put me to sleep."

She laughed. "Must have been the thought of getting back here."

"That didn't sound good did it? I've been thinking about being back here since the day we left." He followed her into the living room where they dropped all the bags and boxes.

"What is all this, Connie? It looks like Christmas?"

"Well, it's not all that much really; boots, jackets, and Tee shirts for the girls and a little something for you and Pete."

Now that his arms were free, she decided it would be an even better time to hug him. "It's very nice, Connie, thank you." He felt real good against her as he hugged back. If no one else had been around, things might have gotten interesting.

"You're welcome." He was blushing when he stepped back.

"Come on, sit down, I'll get you a cup. Dad will be down in a minute. You can tell us all about it." She poured coffee and left him and Woody at the table

Woody winked at him when he joined him. "What?"

"Welcome home."

Connie blushed some more, looked over his shoulder to make certain Cally wasn't still in the kitchen. "I can't help it if I'm lucky."

Woody agreed. "No, I don't suppose you can. Just don't screw it up."

"I don't intend to."

Then Pete was there and they all discussed recent events until Cally served lunch and they called a time out. After lunch, the discussion was resumed and continued until almost two o-clock. The consensus was, Connie and Billy had performed admirably and if Connie could continue, he had as good of a chance of winning the futurity on Jolena as anyone. Connie was especially encouraged because he believed that Pete believed it.

The question of Pete's health was not broached. Connie preferred to let Woody discuss that with Pete and he also intended to ask Cally about it in private. He thought Pete looked a bit haggard, but not much worse than when he and Woody left about nine days ago. His attitude was upbeat, same as ever, and he still had his sense of humor.

When Connie excused himself from the table, Pete asked if he was upset with him for putting Gilly onto some new horses.

"Initially, I was a little confused, but then after I left him in the dust at Henry's Lake, I forgave you."

"Then it was good training?"

Connie thought he knew what he meant. "Yeah, I believe it was." It was as Woody had suggested, attitude training designed to show Connie he could ride.

"Good, never forget it."

When Connie finally got back to the bunkhouse, he hauled out a calendar, his itinerary, the Kalispell phone book, and his cell phone. Sitting down at the bunkhouse kitchen table, he started planning.

Within the next seventeen days, he was going from the ranch to Pueblo, Colorado back to Columbus, Montana and then west to Nampa, Idaho. After that, there was a ten-day break before he had to be in Casper, Wyoming for at least four days. Then, the only things remotely close to home, were several contests in eastern Washington, spread out from the end of September into the middle of November. That would be the end of it for him until the futurity started at the end of November. If his plan was feasible, he decided to ask Cally out when he returned from Nampa. He pored over his calendar and checked off a Saturday three weeks distant. Then he looked in the Kalispell phone book for air charter services and was surprised by all the listings. He called all but those offering only sightseeing flights, and then pared his list down to two. He made back-to-back appointments to visit them the following morning. Finally, he called the restaurant in Spokane and after getting all the specifics, made a reservation. He rechecked all the details and decided he was good to go.

"Whoa," he said out loud, "I suppose I better check with Cally too." He looked at his watch. It was four. There was an impatient rap on his door and without waiting for his reply, the twins burst in.

They hugged him vigorously and repeatedly, demanding to know everything he'd done and everyplace he'd been in the last nine days. When he finished with that, they wanted to know what was in the packages he'd brought them, and when could they open them, and how long was he staying, and when would he go again, and how long would he be gone, and on and on.

"I think I'm done answering questions for now. You two go back to the house and let me get cleaned up. When I come up for supper we'll open your packages and talk some more. Deal?"

They agreed and left him. After putting away his reference material and notes, he headed for the sanctity of his shower. Later, after dinner and the girls had received their presents, Connie hung around until he caught Cally alone in the kitchen.

"I know it's a bit far out, but I'd like to take you out for dinner and dancing on the twenty-fourth. It's the only free Saturday I'll have all month."

There was absolutely no hesitation. "I'd love to. Where will we go?"

"It's a secret, but I'm certain it will be fancy enough for that new dress you bought."

She looked at him a little suspiciously. "Where in the world would that be?" She was wondering if there was a new place opening up in town.

"I can't tell you. You'll just have to trust me."

"Okay, I will, but I haven't danced in years."

"Me either, I guess we'll have to figure it out together."

"What time will we be leaving?"

The reservation was for seven-thirty. He was figuring a half hour to the airport, forty-five minutes total for the flight and another thirty minutes for the ride from the Spokane airport to the restaurant. "About five–thirty." That would leave a fifteen minute cushion.

"I'll mark it on my calendar."

"Mark what on your calendar?" asked Lindsey. "What are you guys talking about in here?"

"We were talking about what a nosey little girl you are," Cally said. "Do you have your homework done?"

"Hours ago. I'm not all that nosey, am I?"

"Who's nosey?" Danni wanted to know as she walked in on the party. "Why is everybody out here?"

"Your mother and I were trying to have a private conversation, that's all."

"Oh yeah," Lindsey said, "What about?"

Cally made a noise sounding like an unhappy bear, and Connie asked, "What part of the term 'private conversation' don't you two understand?"

Danni said, "That's easy, the private part. We're family you know. We don't have any secrets." She looked to Lindsey for backup. "Do we?"

"Nope. Well, maybe a couple like Christmas presents and stuff."

Connie decided he would win this battle of wits. "Maybe your mother and I were discussing that very thing, what I could get two little girls with big noses for Christmas."

"You were? What did you talk about?" Danni pressed.

"I said we might have been talking about that and if we were, why would I tell you? Don't you like to be surprised?"

"Sure, but …."

Connie cut her off. "No 'sure buts', you two beat it for a few minutes."

Surprisingly, they dutifully obeyed with no further protest.
They were taking no chances on compromising their chances for
Christmas presents.

"Well done, Connie. I'll have to remember how you did that."

"Sheer luck and don't forget to mark your calendar."

"No danger of that, and thanks for all the gifts. It was very nice
of you."

She was standing close to him, close enough that he could smell
a hint of perfume, and she was smiling. He didn't remember ever
smelling her perfume before. Connie suddenly felt like he had when he
first met the woman who would become his wife, a little weak in the
knees, tongue-tied and warm, very warm. He couldn't believe he was
feeling this way at his age. These were adolescent reactions. Men his
age shouldn't be affected this way. He didn't feel like this when he was
talking to Myra. If he weren't positive the twins were lurking just
around the corner, he would have embraced her. He decided to make a
hasty retreat.

"My pleasure. I'll see you at breakfast."

She told him good night, and he was on his way to the
bunkhouse. Before crashing, he went to see Jolena. She came up
immediately to greet him. He fed her half of a three-pound coffee can
of oats from his hand while he talked to her. "Well, Jo, so far I've done
good. Pete says I've improved considerably. It's the first time I've
dared to think I could have a chance. Pete also says I have to let you be
the boss. Can you do that?"

If she understood, and Connie sincerely wanted her to, she gave
no indication, only licking his open palm when the oats were gone. He
scratched her gently above her eyes. "You're a good girl. Get some
rest."

The next morning after breakfast and chores, he went to the
airport. From a kitchen window, Cally watched him drive out. "Hey,
Woody, do you know where Connie is going?"

"Maybe."

"What do you mean, maybe?"

"I mean, I may have a guess to where he's goin', but I don't
know for certain."

"Care to share your guess? You don't think he's going to see
Brianna, do you?"

"Highly unlikely," said Woody.

"So where do you think he's going?"

"I believe he may have some business in town and since my guess regardin' the nature of that business could be correct, I prefer not to share it because I don't want to compromise any secrets he may be keepin'."

Woody's cryptic answer made Cally all the more curious, but she downplayed it. "That's very noble of you." She added quietly, "Noble, but highly irritating."

After visiting the two charter services he'd called yesterday, Connie picked one and made his arrangements. This one date was going to cost him about as much as his new saddle. All things considered, he didn't think the price tag for the round trip between Kalispell and Spokane was unreasonable. When he thought about the fate his late wife had suffered, he wished they had done more extravagant things together. He had the means and he was going to use them.

He spent most of the rest of the day getting ready for the next two and a half weeks on the road. Since Gilly would be riding along, Woody decided to stay at the ranch. Even though Pete had told him he felt fine, Woody decided he'd stay just in case he wasn't. Pete didn't like his decision, but Connie did. He was glad Woody was going to be there just in case. There wasn't a lot of work to do, the cows were still on pasture for a while, and Connie had fixed all the fences that needed mending. However, things happen. Better that Woody was there to take care of them. It would give Pete more rest, if that was what he needed.

The next morning, departure day, after breakfast, the girls clung to him like wood ticks until Cally had to chase them out the door to catch the school bus. When they were gone, Connie loaded Billy and went down the road to pick up Gilly. It was almost nine when they left the Bedfort place.

Connie hoped he hadn't made a mistake by deciding to travel with Gilly. A bad traveling companion could stretch the next two and a half weeks into two and a half months. If he were half as affable as Woody, Connie would be happy. Besides, he could help with the driving. Woody couldn't do that.

By the end of their first day on the road together, Connie decided it was going to work out just fine. Gilly was polite, helpful, and entertaining; not at all arrogant and obnoxious as was his old man, Gilliam Senior. They stopped just south of Sheridan, Wyoming for the night and while Junior tended to the horses, Connie put together a late supper. They tried to stay awake and talk for a while, but by nine-thirty, they turned off the lights and called it a day.

They pulled into the State Fair Grounds at Pueblo at four the next afternoon. They took in some of the fair that evening, mostly the food, and in the morning they lounged around until they had to ride. Neither one of them finished in the money. Connie had one decent cow, but his other two picks were sour and didn't want to play. Gilly had the opposite problem. His first pick was a fast little heifer that blew past them on the third turn. He was trying too hard again.

"You have to let go of that horse, Gilly. Even I can see that," Connie told him.

"I know. I started reining her hard and I couldn't quit. The next thing I knew, I was looking at a big butt roast."

"So now what? It's not even two in the afternoon and we're both all done."

"There's a cutting in Fort Collins day after tomorrow. I saw a flyer for it on one of the bulletin boards somewhere around here."

"Where around here. This is a big place."

"It was probably in the horse barn. Let's start there."

That's where they found it, and while they were studying it Connie recalled Cindy, the woman who sold him his trailer. "Gilly, how old are you?"

"Thirty-eight. Why?"

"I've got a friend in Longmont you might like to meet. Regardless, it's on the way to Fort Collins and I'll buy dinner."

There were several of the fliers on the board. Gilly pulled one off, "Let's go."

Connie didn't remember exactly where Cindy's restaurant was so he drove to where he had picked up his trailer. "Five o'clock on a Saturday afternoon. What makes you think anybody's still here?" Gilly asked when they pulled into the lot.

"She works a lot. And if she's not, now that I'm here, I think I remember how to get to the restaurant." He turned a big circle in the lot and stopped in front of the office. A diminutive blonde in tight blue jeans came out to greet them. Gilly whistled softly.

"Howdy," she said when Connie stepped out of his truck. "What can I do for you?" Then she recognized him. "Well, if it isn't the reluctant cowboy, Conrad Bradley. How are you?"

"Hi, Cindy. I'm fine. How are you?"

"Same as always, overworked, and under appreciated."

Gilly wasted no time getting out of the truck. Connie made introductions and then suggested Cindy allow them to take her to dinner.

"That'd be great," she told them. "I sold my restaurant though. Too much work."

"All the more reason to let us take you there for dinner, you can relax while you eat."

"Good idea. I haven't been in there since I sold it. That was a month ago. It'll be interesting to see how it's doing." She nodded towards the trailer. "How's the rig working out for you?"

"Super. Want to see our trusty steeds?"

"Sure. You can walk them around the lot if they need a break. You can clean the trailer out too if you want. Throw the manure in the dumpster."

"You sure?"

"Yeah, it's organic."

So while Cindy and Gilly exercised the horses, Connie gave the back of the trailer the once over. When he was finished, they loaded the horses and followed Cindy to the restaurant that used to be hers. Most of the staff she had hired were still there so they were served extra well. The menu hadn't changed much, only a few new entrees and the steaks were still good.

"I thought the trailer building business was hectic," she said, "but this place demanded every spare minute I had and I didn't have that many." She smiled and leaned back in her chair. "It's nice to come in here and enjoy the place instead of worrying about everything."

"You ever find someone to manage the trailer business?" Connie asked.

"No, not yet. You interested?"

"No, I like retirement, but Gilly here might be in the market for a job."

"Is that right?" she asked, smiling sweetly.

"I could be, although I don't know anything about building trailers."

"You wouldn't have to actually build them. What you have to do is see that other people build them. You any good at managing people?"

"I don't know. I've never tried."

"What have you done?"

"Well, I really hate to admit this, but for the last four years, I haven't had a steady job. My father buys and sells cattle and when I'm not working for him, I'm either riding roping horses or cutting horses."

"That just great," Cindy said feigning disgust. "I meet two nice looking men and one's retired, and the other one doesn't have to work. How am I going to find help?"

"I wouldn't mind trying," Gilly told her. "Believe me, I know what a good trailer should be. Maybe I could learn to be a manager."

"When can you start?" She was serious.

"Right after the futurity."

"That's over by the middle of December, right?"

"Yes, Ma'am. I could be here right after the first of January."

They lingered over dinner until most of the patrons had left. Connie could see Gilly and Cindy were getting along famously. He suspected Gilly was probably a polar opposite of what her late husband had been, but maybe that was best. Might be just what she needed.

"Any place to go dancing around here?" Gilly asked Cindy when they finally walked out.

She told him there was and when he asked her if she'd like to go, she agreed. Connie said he was tired. "How about I take the truck and trailer back to your trailer place and you can bring Gilly back later? Two's company, three's a crowd."

The plan was quickly agreed to and Connie was sound asleep when Gilly came in about four hours later.

Chapter 35, The Long Pull

The morning after dinner and dancing with Cindy, Gilly looked remarkably fit on only five hours of sleep. "Glad we made this detour," he told Connie as they burned freeway to Fort Collins. The contest was scheduled to start at noon.

"If nothing else we had a good steak dinner. That's not always easy to find."

Gilly was grinning. "Yeah, and I met a beautiful woman and got a job offer to boot."

"You serious about the job."

Gilly lost his smile. "You have any idea what it's like being a 'Junior'?"

"Sort of. I'm a 'third', but nobody ever called me Junior."

"I don't mean the name thing. Your old man obviously let you become your own person. I've lived in my father's shadow my whole life. It hasn't been easy and it sure hasn't been fun. As a kid I got into a lot of trouble just because I wanted to do something on my own. I've thought about pulling the plug for years. I just never had the guts, until now—I think. Cindy and I did more talking than dancing last night and I believe I'm going to take her up on her offer."

"That's great, Gilly. I think it could work out for you, maybe."

Gilly turned to Connie. "What's the maybe?"

"Well, she's a strong woman and maybe she's not really looking for a manager."

"Maybe she's looking for a man?"

Connie wished he hadn't said anything. "Ah, don't take me
wrong, you probably know her better than I do by now. And whatever
you do is your business. I just think you need to be aware of all the
possibilities."

Gilly laughed. "Okay, Dad. I'll be careful."

"Hey, I'm just concerned about you. Not enough to let you
beat me in cutting, but I am concerned."

"We talked about the sexual attraction aspect."

"You did?"

"Sure and she told me even though she was attracted, she
wouldn't let that stop her from firing me if I couldn't do the job."

"You believe that?"

"Yeah, but if that happened I might just have to marry her and
make her keep me."

Connie shook his head. "Don't ever tell Senior I introduced
you to her."

The contest in Fort Collins was a local affair, held monthly, and
although there were some good cowboys and horses there, Connie and
Gilly pretty much rode rough shod over the field. There wasn't a lot of
prize money, but Connie took first and Gilly took second, leaving the
rest for the locals. By six that evening, they were west of Cheyenne,
looking for a spot to park for the night. They found a place half way to
Laramie and set up just before it got dark.

They slept in and then took their time with breakfast. They
even went on a little ride into the surrounding territory, a national forest
full of trails. They had two days to get to Columbus, Montana and it
wasn't that far away. But as soon as that one was over, they would have
to move fast to get to the next in Nampa, Idaho.

"Why can't these things be set up in a big circle with
consecutive dates? Then you could jump in, go around as far as you
wanted and get out again. You wouldn't have to drive back and forth
across the entire country."

"You actually expect me to answer that?" Connie asked Gilly.

"No, but if I do this again, I'm going to limit myself to
Washington, Oregon, California, Nevada and Utah."

"That's not exactly a local neighborhood. Besides you'll be
working, managing a horse trailer manufacturing operation."

"Yeah, I probably won't try the futurity again. This is my
fourth go at it and it's starting to wear a little thin. I've spent probably a
hundred and twenty thousand dollars so far and never even made it to

the semi finals. It doesn't favor the average cowboy. In fact, if the old man wasn't bankrollin' me, I'd never have made it to Fort Worth the first time."

"Yeah, I know exactly what you mean. One of the first things Pete told me up front was that cutting cows was a thrill, but it wasn't a cheap thrill."

"Yeah, it's like ropin'. I have a friend who was over at the place one day about five years ago and saw me rope a steer. He told his wife about it and she bought him a twenty-five dollar lariat. Well, he started throwing it at a fence post, catching it every third time, so she bought him a dummy steer head. That was great, but it wasn't long before he was looking at horses. I sold him one he could rope off, and after he roped his first steer he was hooked. Bought a fancy ropin' saddle, a truck and trailer, and started entering contests. He was doing okay except his horse was a bit slow, so he bought another one for about fifteen thousand dollars. Before he was finished, he was in debt up to his ears and his wife had left him."

"He still your friend?"

"Oh sure. He worked his way out of debt, found himself a girlfriend who runs barrels, and he still ropes steers, only now he sticks to local contests on weekends. That's what I'm going to do when this thing is over. Stick to local contests on weekends. You know cutting is a lot like golf. You can golf as long as you can swing a club and you can cut cows as long as you can stay in the saddle." Gilly looked over to Connie. "What are you going to do when it's over, go back east?"

"No, I could never go back there again. I've been thinking about buying some dirt in Idaho, maybe even put up a mare motel around Lewiston. I've got an old army buddy somewhere near Grangeville. I have to look him up after the first of the year. I promised Cally's kids I'd spend Christmas with them."

"Cally always appeared to me to be a class act."

"Did you know her husband?"

"No, I believe he was from around Billings. She didn't have him very long from what I understand. He had to have been a real dope."

"Apparently. Woody said he was a bull rider."

"That explains a lot. There are only two kinds of bull riders. Good ones and stupid ones, and the stupid ones eventually figure out they're no good and give it up."

"That's harsh. You ever try it?"

"Once, but that was enough. But speaking of Cally as we were, she got a boyfriend yet?"

"She was seeing a doctor, but I think that ended some time ago."

"Well, there you go. You couldn't do much better than her."

Connie didn't want to talk about Cally. His feelings toward her were going to stay secret for a while yet. "How about Brianna Lane? I heard you two were romantically linked at one time."

Gilly smiled. "I could only hope. Now you talk about a strong woman, she could kick Hercules' butt, metaphorically speakin' of course. You ever met her."

"Had dinner with her just a few weeks ago."

Gilly looked at him skeptically. "Serious?"

Connie told him the story.

"You going to take her out again?" Gilly wanted to know when Connie finished.

"Maybe, but it's doubtful."

"Why not? She's definitely a trophy. Not many like her around."

"Why didn't you move on her? You had a chance."

"Sort of, maybe. To be honest, I may have been intimidated."

"I know I was, but not because she's capable. I'm not much of a social animal, and I just feel her life style and mine are diametrically opposed. I don't think it would work."

"Yeah, I see your point, but it might be fun while it lasted."

Connie agreed, and they continued on down the road to the next contest. When that one was finished, they raced to the next and when that was over, they raced for home. They had gained experience, confidence, and enough prize money to pay their expenses and then some. In addition, Connie had won a new saddle and two more belt buckles. He wondered if it were possible to hammer the buckles into dinner plates. They would make for eclectic tableware and there was certainly enough metal in them. He had seven of them now. One more he'd have a place setting for eight.

Once again the twins were thrilled to have him home. Cally, Pete, and Woody were too, they just weren't quite as expressive as the girls. At the state fair in Pueblo, Connie had tried mightily to win each of the girls a huge stuffed animal, but couldn't. He even subsidized Gilly, and he couldn't do it either. After he'd given up, he found a booth where they were for sale. The two he bought cost far less than what he spent trying to win them. "There's something in the back seat of my truck for you ladies," he told them after they were done hugging him. They were gone in a flash and back almost as fast, struggling to carry teddy bears bigger than they were.

"What did ya do?" Woody asked. "Shoot a couple of yearling grizzly bear cubs and have them stuffed?

"Look, Mom," Lindsey said. "Isn't it cool?"

"Yeah, Mom," Danni said, "I'm going to name mine Sidney."

"That's a nice name, could either be a boy or a girl. How about you both take them upstairs and put them in your room."

"You shouldn't have," she said to Connie when the girls were gone. "And I mean it," but she was smiling.

"I won you a new saddle."

"If you won it, you can't give it to me."

"Sure I can. It's a fifteen inch model and there's no way my butt's going to fit."

"What else did you win?" Pete asked.

Connie told him and they discussed the four events he'd ridden in at great length.

"How did you and Junior get along?"

"Just fine, if not famously. I like the guy. He's been living in his old man's shadow, but I think that's about to change." Connie related the story of Cindy and her offer to Gilly.

"She sounds like a woman I could love," said Woody.

"You could love every woman, at least in your mind," said Cally.

Undeterred, Woody fired back, "That's what makes me so charmin' and irresistible."

"I don't suppose you could charm some apples into a pie? Connie asked him. "I've been dying for a slice of your pie since I left here two and half weeks ago."

"Way ahead of you as usual. I got two ready to bake. You'll get a piece for dessert after dinner."

Later that evening Connie was sitting at his kitchen table in the bunkhouse with his back to a crackling fire in the wood stove, sipping single malt and smoking a cigar when Woody came in. There was a cold drizzle falling and Woody shook off his oiled drovers coat before hanging it on one of the pegs by the back door.

"It's right cozy in here. What are we drinkin'?"

"I'm drinking a lowland single malt I picked up at a liquor store in Colorado."

"Never been partial to lowland Scotch."

"Me either, but this stuff is tasty. There's a bottle of Makers Mark if you'd prefer Bourbon. You know where the cigars are."

"I hear you're takin' Cally out to dinner this Saturday." Woody opted to try the lowland single malt. "Where you takin' her?"

"It's a secret."

"Can I guess?"

"If you'd like."

"You're takin' her to that place in Spokane Gilly told us about. You don't have to answer; I know I'm right. I just can't imagine how you're getting' there."

"Guess again."

"You chartered a plane I suspect. It's the only way you can get there for dinner by leavin here at five-thirty."

"I'm glad I can provide for your amusement by giving you something to ponder. Have you shared any of your speculations with Cally?"

"Of course not, but I can tell you that she's goin' crazy tryin' to figure it out."

"How close is she coming?"

"I ain't sure. She's not sayin' much about it."

"If she isn't talking about it, how do you know it's driving her crazy?"

"Because I've known her all her life." He sipped at the whisky. "Say that is good. Did you just get the one bottle?"

"Yeah, but I think I've seen at it that big place downtown. It's a popular brand; I just didn't know they made a lowland. What's Pete think about me taking his little girl out to dinner?"

"From what I can tell, he's happy with it. For some reason he likes you."

"Perfectly understandable. I'm a fine upstanding gentleman. How's he feeling? Has he said anything about that?"

"Yeah, and I got him convinced to go to the clinic. He says he aches all over like he's got the flu, and he's tired, real tired."

"That doesn't sound good. Maybe he does have the flu. How did you convince him to go see the doctor?"

"It wasn't hard and that's a concern, too. Normally, he wouldn't hear of it, but as soon as I suggested it, he agreed. I believe he's been considerin' it himself."

"What does Cally think?"

"Well, she's worried about his lack of improvement of course and happy that he's goin'. I believe she thinks he's got a problem."

"What do you think?"

Woody leaned back, exhaling a cloud of cigar smoke before answering. Then he leaned forward and looked Connie in the eyes. "I'm worried, too, Connie. I think he's not gettin' better for a reason, and I don't like the reasons that come to mind."

"You think they didn't get all the cancer?"

"Didn't get it all or he's got more that they didn't find in the first place."

"They said it hadn't spread anywhere else."

"Anywhere they looked. Did they look all over?"

"It's supposed to be one of the best clinics in the world."

"Your wife died of cancer. I assume you took her to the best places you could find. What was the outcome?"

Connie thought back. Woody was right. It took three different doctors just to diagnose that she had cancer. Admittedly, it was a rare type, but it didn't inspire a great deal of confidence in medical science. As far as treating her was concerned, nothing they tried anywhere seemed to help in the least. "You don't see any improvement in him at all?"

"He ain't lookin' bad, but he didn't look bad before the surgery either. He just seems off. He's been tireless as long as I've know him and now he seems to have lost his pep, coughin' some, too.

"Well, he is over eighty and he's had a big shock to his system. He might have picked something up at the clinic. I'm glad he's going to the doctor on Monday. Good job convincing him."

"I didn't do much. He seemed ready for it."

Then, although the subject changed and they talked about other things, Pete was still there occupying their thoughts. After Woody went up to the house, Connie walked out to the barn and talked to Jolena. She stood silently, listening, or so it appeared to Connie, while he told her about Pete and scratched her head. With the inclement weather, all the horses had opted to come into the barn. It seemed cozy to Connie to be in there with all the animals and after talking to Jolena, he lay down on the hay bales.

A crack of thunder woke him an hour later. He left the barn just before midnight and went back to the bunkhouse. The fire in the stove had all but gone out, and there was a wet chill in the air. He thought about going to town tomorrow and buying a gas stove, maybe one of those cast iron ones with a glass front and fake logs. After the trip outside for more wood, rekindling the fire, and waiting for it to come back to life, he decided for certain. He'd also visit the air charter place to reconfirm his flight.

"I'm going to town this morning," he announced at breakfast. "Anybody need anything?"

"You could pick me up a bottle of that single malt we tasted last night," Woody said.

"I need some things," Cally said, "But you can't get them for me."

"You want to ride along; I'll take you where you want to go."

She thought about it briefly. "Thanks, but I'm not sure where I have to go to find what I want."

"Sounds mysterious."

"It could be. What are you going to get?" She wasn't about to tell him she was looking for lingerie of a style she hadn't worn for years

"I want one of those little cast iron gas stoves for the bunkhouse. The kind with a fake log and glass front."

"They have some at the propane dealer. I was in there last week and they had them on display."

"That's where I'm headed then. Pete, you want anything."

"How about a bottle of water from the fountain of youth?"

"If I could find it, I'd bring the whole fountain back."

Pete was smiling. "Well, if you can't find that I'll just beg a little sip of Woody's single malt."

Connie had to settle for the green colored stove because it was the only one they had in stock. There was a blue one on display that he would have preferred, however there was a two-week delivery and they wouldn't sell him the floor model. After he had wrestled the stove and the pipe he'd need into his truck, he picked up Woody's scotch. His last stop was the airport where he was assured all was in order including the limousine services between the ranch and the Kalispell airport, and the Spokane Airport, and the restaurant. He returned to the bunk house in time to install his stove.

It was a thing of beauty. He was almost late for supper, lost in his admiration and wonder for it. It came off and on from a thermostat he'd placed on the wall opposite the stove. The stove itself was positioned in a corner near his easy chair, across the room from his couch. No big chimney was needed. A double walled pipe that went up two feet and straight through the wall, terminating outside was all that was required. The look of the fire it produced was amazingly realistic. Had there been some sort of smoke smell dispenser on the thing, it would be indistinguishable from a genuine wood fire. I've come a long way, he thought. I had a house that just sold for nine hundred thousand dollars. Now I live in a cabin smaller than my old living room and I love it. A knock at his door followed by two nine year olds calling him to supper broke the reverie.

"Connie, come on, you're going to be late for supper," Danni told him.

"Wow," said Lindsey when she saw the stove, "I want to move down here."

"Sorry, no girls allowed after bedtime."

"Our room is so cold in the winter. Maybe you can put one in for us too."

"Maybe. I'll have to check with your mother so don't try to hold me to anything. She makes the rules."

Of course as soon as they were seated at the table, they announced that Connie was getting them a stove just like his for their room. Connie could only shake his head slowly.

The rest of the week passed quickly, filled with odd jobs, riding Jolena, and small projects Pete and Woody hadn't finished. Connie was happy to help, knowing Pete and Cally wouldn't be burdened with the work. Before he knew it, Saturday afternoon was upon him.

Chapter 36, Date with Destiny

When Connie went calling for Cally he was wearing a double-breasted, medium weight wool suit. It was dark brown with pale blue pin striping. It fitted him perfectly, having been made by one of the finest custom tailors in Indiana. It was five years old and he'd only worn it twice. On both those occasions, his late wife had accompanied him. She'd picked out the material and the style. He hoped he still looked as good in it as his wife had claimed he did. He carried a small bouquet of flowers when he knocked on the door. The girls had seen him coming up the drive and were dying to go to the door, but Cally had forbidden them to interfere. She answered his knock in person.

He couldn't help staring at her. She took his breath away. "Wow," he said. "You're beautiful." Her hair was styled slightly different than normal, and she wore a hint of makeup and lipstick. She'd always looked good, and even though he knew she'd clean up nicely, he had no idea. "Wow," he said again.

"Thank you and wow, yourself," she told him. "You look terrific. You'd better come in and meet the family." She looked behind him to the driveway. "Where's the truck?"

"Truck? You can't look like that and ride in a truck." He checked his watch. "The limo should be here in five minutes."

"Wow, again." She took the flowers in one hand and his arm in the other and escorted him into the living room. "Dad, Woody, Girls, this is Conrad Bradley the Third."

The twins clapped and cheered. Connie blushed. Pete and Woody merely smiled and nodded. Cally put the flowers in water and placed them on top of a low table in front of the couch.

Lindsey had them pose together so she could take several pictures. And then, mercifully, headlights cut through the living room window announcing the limo's arrival.

"Have fun," Pete called out as they made their departure.

A cold front had followed the rains from earlier in the week. The air was brisk and Cally handed Connie a long, camel colored coat that looked new. Connie held it for her while she slipped into it. It was a soft blend of wool and cashmere. Connie thought it a shame to cover up the dress, but based on the amount of material in it, he imagined Cally would be easily chilled. They sat close together on the ride into town and Cally plied him with questions about where they were going. He wouldn't say anything until they pulled into the airport and then all he told her was they weren't going to a local restaurant.

They had no baggage and went through a security check separate from the scheduled airlines. Within a couple of minutes they were seated in the cabin of a Raytheon-Hawker 800. Seating consisted of four plush chairs and a tiny couch at the back of the cabin. They opted for the couch. The pilot gave them a briefing, opened a bottle of cold champagne, apologized for the plastic champagne flutes, and told them to have an enjoyable flight.

Connie poured them each a dollop of champagne. He lifted his glass. "Coming to Montana and finding you and your family was more than I could have ever hoped for; thank you." He tapped his plastic glass against hers. "To us."

She had a wistful look in her eyes when she agreed, "To us."

Then the plane was moving. With no traffic on the ground, the little jet rounded the corner from taxiway to runway and the pilot hammered the throttles. The plane came unstuck from earth in less than thirty seconds. Cally and Connie were comfortably nestled together in the back seat by the acceleration.

"So will you tell me now where we're going?"

"Sure, Spokane. There's a restaurant there that is allegedly renowned for its class and cuisine. We're going to find out if the rumor is true."

"You've never been there before?"

"Nope, we're in this together. I hope it's worth it."

"It's already worth it."

The pilot climbed to flight level twenty-two, leveled off and almost immediately started the descent. The entire flight took thirty-five minutes. At the Spokane airport, another limo was waiting to whisk them to the restaurant which was every bit as good as Gilly had claimed.

They dined, they danced, they sipped cocktails and liqueurs, and at eleven, they were whisked back to the airport where their plane was waiting.

On the short flight home, Cally rested her head on Connie's shoulder. She was slightly inebriated, mostly from the experience rather than any alcohol she'd consumed. "Pinch me," she whispered in his ear.

"That would be enjoyable, but how about I kiss you instead?"

"Even better. Why didn't I think of that?" Actually she had, but she wanted him to start. Much more ladylike, she reasoned.

The flight was too short and some of the spell was broken between transferring from aircraft to limousine, although not all of it and by the time they reached the ranch, they were back up to speed. The crisp night air in front of the house brought them to decision time.

"I have another bottle of champagne in the bunk house refrigerator. We could sip champagne and stare at the fire in my new gas stove."

She almost giggled. She knew what would happen if she took him up on his offer. Not that she didn't want that to happen. Her attraction for him had been building for months. She hesitated. *Is this a defining moment? If I don't make a move now, what will happen? Will the future change or is the future immutable?* In other words, should she go into the house alone or down to the bunkhouse with Connie and start something, the outcome of which was nebulous.

She put her arms around him and kissed him with passion. "This was the best date I could have possibly imagined, but I should go in."

He was disappointed, however he wasn't going to let it show. "Okay, but I'll have to stare at my fire all by myself."

It's probably for the best. It's silly for me to start something serious with Cally now. That's what he thought, but it wasn't what he wanted. He hung his suit coat in the closet. He wanted Cally. He pulled off his dress shirt, poured himself some champagne and sat down to stare at his fire.

In her bedroom, Cally was mentally kicking herself. *What is my problem?* She threw her new coat carelessly on her bed. *The best man I've ever met, I think I love him, and I just ran away.* She looked in the full length mirror next to her tall dresser. *He's the reason I bought this dress. And these shoes.* She kicked off the high heels. She slipped out of the dress and pulled off her nylons. She regarded her nearly naked reflection. *And this underwear. What am I waiting for?* As if to give her a last chance, her defining moment had returned. She watched a smile flicker across her lips. Grabbing the coat from the bed, she put it back on. She stepped into her shoes, crept out of the house and marched down to the bunk house as quietly and as daintily as she could on uneven ground in three-inch heels. No need to worry, everyone else in the house was sound asleep.

At approximately a half hour past midnight she rapped gently on his back door and without waiting for his reply she entered. The room was dark except for the glow of the little gas stove. Connie was on his feet moving towards the door when she met him. "I changed my mind," she told him and embraced him fiercely.

He was surprised, but recovered nicely. "Good." He unbuttoned her coat and got another surprise, the minimal black lingerie. "And I thought you looked good in that little black dress."

She looked up at him, her eyes half closed. He kissed her and she reached for his belt. "Let's level the playing field."

For the next couple of hours they nearly rocked the bunkhouse off its foundation. At about two-thirty she told him she had to go back up to the house.

"You didn't get to watch the fire in my new stove."

"What happened to the 'no girls after bedtime' rule?"

"Do they tell you everything?"

"They'd better."

"What I meant, was no little girls after bedtime. You're a big girl."

"Another time we'll watch the fire. In the meantime, just make sure I'm the only big girl with after bedtime privileges."

"That won't be a problem—ever."

She went back to her own bed, being very careful not to make any noise. Everyone was still asleep and shortly thereafter, so was she. Within minutes after her departure, Connie was also dead to the world. The defining moment had come and gone. Decisions had been made. Events had occurred. The future for Cally and Connie had been established.

Sunday breakfast was interesting. Cally had already talked to the girls when they woke her at seven. They sat on her bed, plying her with questions until she was forced to get up and start breakfast. Pete and Woody were duly impressed by the details of the evening, at least the details Cally was willing to share. When Connie arrived, most of the collective curiosity had been satisfied. The two lovebirds wanted to be affectionate, but neither wanted their secret out. They played it as straight as they could and fooled everyone except Woody. He'd slept through Cally's roundtrip to the bunkhouse, but he sensed a shift in their attitudes. They had a secret. Pete didn't notice, but he was hoping for the best. If it was what she wanted, then it was time for Cally to get a partner. He didn't think he'd be around much longer and Woody wasn't exactly a young man anymore. It took at least two people to work the ranch. Connie had proven capable and trustworthy. Pete liked him. If he and Cally were good together, Pete could die a happy man.

Connie volunteered to do dishes and clean up the kitchen. He thought it might get the twins out of the way so he and Cally could talk, but they stuck to him like glue. They wanted to know all about the airplane ride and the restaurant and what he thought about their mother's dress and on and on. Since she wasn't going to get the chance to be alone with Connie, Cally took the opportunity to take a little nap before they had to get ready for church. Connie declined Danni's invitation to go to church with them and after finishing in the kitchen, went down to the bunk house.

He lay down on his couch across the room from the stove, but after five minutes, he was restless. He got up and went to the barn. Grabbing a handful of oats for Jo, he called out the back door for her. She trotted up when she heard him, knowing he'd have a treat. He talked to her about the evening he had with Cally and confessed he was probably in love. Jo took the news in stride as if she not only expected it, but also approved. Connie stood petting Jo until he was tired which didn't take long. He apologized and told her he had to lie down for a minute. The hay bales were looking mighty comfortable. He was out like a light.

He awoke to the sound of his name being whispered in his ear. "Connie. Connie, move over, so I can join you," Cally told him.

He wriggled backwards. She had on jeans and a sweatshirt. "What a pleasant surprise. What are you doing home already?"

"Already? It's after one. The girls told me you were down here sleeping. I told them to get their homework done and I came down to see for myself."

"Any danger of them showing up in the immediate future?"

"No, Woody's supervising. We have at least a half hour."

He wrapped his arms around her. For the immediate future they were alone.

"When are you two going on another date?" Danni asked when they were all seated at the supper table.

"Maybe tonight, after you and your sister have gone to bed," Connie told her.

"Where will you go?" asked Lindsey.

"I'm not sure." He turned to Cally. "How would you like to go to town to see a movie?"

"That sounds wonderful. I'd like that."

Then Danni had a wonderful idea of her own. "You know, if you went right after supper, me and Lindsey could come with."

"Lindsey and I," Connie corrected, "But I don't think so. Tomorrow is a school day."

Danni turned away, obviously crushed. "However," Connie added, "Maybe if your mother is willing, I could take all you ladies to dinner and a movie as soon as I get back from my next trip."

Danni brightened at the prospect. "When will that be?"

"Let's see, I leave on Wednesday and the contest is on the weekend and I'll be back Tuesday night, so not this Friday, but the one after."

"Yippee. Can we go, Mom?'

"Well if Connie is asking me, I'm going. If he's asking you, you and Lindsey have to decide for yourselves."

"I'm going," said Lindsey.

"Me to," agreed Danni.

"Okay, that's settled then, dinner and a movie a week from this coming Friday. I'll write it down so I don't forget."

"We won't let you," Danni told him.

Connie and Cally left for town at seven and by ten, were back, snuggled on Connie's couch, the fire in the gas stove dancing for their pleasure. The door was locked and the curtains were drawn. They weren't paying any attention to the fire. At midnight Connie walked Cally up to the big house.

"We're not going to be able to keep this secret for very long."

Cally agreed. "I know. I'm sure Woody already suspects it's more than casual. What do we do? I also feel guilty"

"Okay, I know what you mean. We could announce our engagement."

Cally stopped walking and pulled him to a stop. "Are you serious?"

"Absolutely. I don't know about you, but I'm never going to find a better lover and friend. You impressed me the minute I first met you. There was one brief instant when I wasn't sure, but that didn't last long and ever since, I've been desiring you."

"If that's the case, why were you seeing Brianna?"

"I figured I was too old for you and I really only 'saw' her once."

"That was more than enough, you drove me crazy."

"Sorry. She wasn't a substitute for you."

'I hope not, I dumped a doctor for you."

"You mean the young Doctor Jim?"

"That's the one. He started getting all gushy and you were here. When I compared the two of you, he had to go."

"Interesting. So now that we've held out for each other, what do we do?"

"I thought you had just asked me to marry you?"

"The offer stands. Take your time. Just keep my advanced age in mind."

"You weren't acting that old a few minutes ago or earlier this afternoon either. I accept."

There was a timeout while they embraced. "I'm not sure we should announce it just yet. You're going to be gone for a week, let me do some preparatory work on my father."

"What about the girls."

"They've already got us married."

"Woody won't be a problem, he convinced me you weren't worried about our age difference."

"Woody had to convince you? What did you think the picnic at Rogers Lake was for? Do you have any idea what that swimsuit cost me?"

"Worth every penny and even though I thought you were trying to tell me something, I had to be positive. There's no fool like an old fool and I didn't want to be one."

"You'll never be an old fool. Old maybe, some day, but never a fool."

"You're sweet. We'll have to get you a ring."

"It can wait. But only for a little while. Let me set the stage."

"It's a deal."

Connie made a quick visit to check on Jolena and then went in to bed. A lot had happened in the past two days. He didn't regret any of it, but he'd surprised himself and he couldn't explain his actions. All he could determine was it appeared he'd been given a second chance at life and Cally was to be a big part of it, a very desirable part. He didn't know what might have happened if he'd walked away when the futurity was over and Christmas had passed. Last night he realized he couldn't walk away. His previous life was over, his future was here with Cally, the twins, Pete, and Woody.

Cally also found it hard to sleep. She was happy, happier than she'd been since the birth of her daughters. She believed she'd made the right decision. She'd had a lot of time to determine what she wanted in a man and it hadn't taken her long to recognize that Connie was the man. She smiled when she thought about her hesitation last night. She smiled more when she thought about what happened after that. She'd surprised herself with he intensity of her passion and suspected Connie had been surprised by his as well. Asking her to marry him was another surprise. Accepting his offer was the logical thing to do. She'd have been heartbroken to watch him leave in December. She was as sure of him as she could possibly be. Only the future would validate her choices.

Chapter 37 Get Ready

"I didn't realize you were a cancer specialist," Pete told Doctor Jim.

"I'm not, but Doctor Leonido asked me if I'd check you over before he sees you. I understand you had prostrate surgery a number of weeks ago and you haven't felt good since."

"Yeah, that about sums it up."

"So how do you feel?"

"I'm tired. I ache all over, especially my head and I hardly ever have headaches."

"Are you coughing much?"

"Some, not a great deal. More than normal I suppose."

"Any pain in your chest when you cough. Ever cough up anything?"

"Sometimes it hurts a little when I cough, but I don't bring up blood or anything."

Jim listened to him take several deep breaths. He looked down his throat and took his temperature. "Hmmm," he muttered. "I want to get a chest x-ray."

Pete pointed to a thick, oversized envelope he had brought with him. "There are several in that file. I had enough x-rays taken at the cancer clinic I was at I think I could light up the dark side of the moon."

"I'm sure you did, but I need a recent one, like in the next ten minutes."

"What are you thinking? The cancer spread to my lungs?"

"Nothing that serious. How's Cally doing?"

"She's fine. How are you doing?"

Jim laughed. "Okay. I'm still looking for one just like her."

Pete had a sudden inspiration or maybe it was just a whim. "You know, Doc, I might just be able to point you in the right direction. Are you a church going man at all?"

"Ah, I used to be, but I haven't gone for some time. Why do you ask?"

"Well, let's get that chest x-ray and then if you think I'm going to live long enough, I'd like you to come to church with Cally and me this Sunday. There's someone there you might like to meet."

"Really? I'm intrigued."

"You'll be more than intrigued."

Forty-five minutes later Doctor Jim was back in the exam room with the results of Pete's x-rays. "Okay, Mister Browning, here's the problem." He pointed at an area on one of the negatives he had clipped to the light box."

Pete recognized his lungs. "What is it a tumor?"

"No, nothing that dramatic, although in your situation it's probably more dangerous. You have pneumonia."

"How'd I get pneumonia?"

"You were in the hospital for how many days, five, six? Hospitals are dangerous places."

"You're telling me I have pneumonia and I caught it at the hospital when I had my surgery?"

"I'm positive you have pneumonia and you could have picked it up anywhere, but I wouldn't bet against the hospital."

"I had pneumonia once before, about sixty years ago. I remember coughing constantly. Why don't I have much of a cough?"

"That's not uncommon. The infected areas of your lungs are not near any of the major airways. If we don't stop it, your cough will get worse as the infection spreads, but we're not going to let that happen." He started scribbling on his prescription pad. When he finished, he handed the sheets to Pete. "Get these filled immediately and start them as soon as you get home. Take it easy, get plenty of rest, and if you don't start to feel better in three days, come back to see me."

There was a knock on the exam room door and one of the nurses peeked in. "Mister Browning, Doctor Leonido is tied up in surgery and I'm rescheduling all his appointments."

Jim waved her away. "Thanks, I'll handle it." She closed the door on them and he turned back to Pete. "Let's do this. I'll reschedule you with Doctor Leonido for next week and when you come in, I'll see you first. If you're improving, it'll make his job easier. In the meantime, I'll make sure he sees your records."

"Okay. I hate to come back, but if all I have is pneumonia, I'm a happy man."

"Don't underestimate the pneumonia. I'm sure it kills a lot more men your age than prostrate cancer. Now, about church on Sunday, what's the purpose?"

"The purpose is twofold," Pete said. "Number one is to save your sinful soul, and number two is to meet a fine looking lady by the name of Colleen."

Jim was grinning. "Is she as pretty as Cally?"

"Well, I might be a bit prejudiced, but I guarantee you won't be disappointed. You want to come out to the house or meet us there?"

He opted to meet them there and after giving him directions to the church, Pete got dressed and found his way back to the reception area where Cally was waiting and talking to Doctor Jim.

On the drive home, after they filled Pete's prescriptions, Cally asked him about his discussion with Jim. "I can't believe you invited him to church with us so you could introduce him to Colleen."

"Why not? I felt sorry for him."

"Great, after he meets Colleen, you can really feel sorry for him."

"Not necessarily. They could be a perfect couple. I believe each of them has exactly what the other wants. It might be a marriage made in heaven."

Cally thought about it. She doubted it, but since Pete was discussing marriage, she decided to drop a bomb of her own. "What do you think about Connie?"

"Prince of a fellow. He could be the son I never had, although his father was probably more man than I've been."

"Oh, Dad, don't be silly. There's no man better than you."

"Thank you, Cally. I knew I raised you right. What about Connie?"

"If he can't be your son, what if he were your son-in-law?"

Pete looked at her. She was smiling. *She's happy. The date on Saturday night must have been much more involved than she let on and she's not easily impressed.*

"You two have something serious in mind?"

"He asked me to marry him last night and I accepted."

"Well, I asked your mother to marry me after I had known her for only four months. It seemed right and it was, although we'd been on more than two dates." Then he had a disturbing thought, "Oh nuts!"

"Nuts? What's nuts?"

"My bet with Woody. He bet me a hundred dollars back in May you'd be married within two years. I never imagined."

"It's your fault. You brought Connie home so I was able to meet him."

"I suppose, although we could blame it all on Jolena. He fell in love with her first."

"Maybe, but you invited him to come out so you could get her to the futurity."

"Yes, I did. I'm guilty on all counts and I'm happy for you. I have good feelings about Connie. When will you tell the twins?"

"Probably when Connie takes us all out to dinner and the movies. It's like I told Connie, they've already adopted him as their father. If he'd walked away from us after the futurity was over, you'd have had three broken hearted girls to deal with."

There were two events Connie could have entered at the contest in Wyoming. He chose the one with the biggest field and decided to sit out the other. Like Pete had told him, these were preseason games, use them for practice, don't worry about winning. He took a second place on the one he entered. Gilly entered both and won the one Connie had avoided, but it came with a price. His horse was limping when he left the arena. He got off her back as soon as he felt it and immediately found the resident veterinarian.

The verdict was a strained tendon in her back left leg. It wasn't a career threatening injury, but she'd be out of any serious activity for probably a month. "Don't ride her at all for two weeks and then start in gradually. You were lucky.

Then the doctor started a general rant about the practice of working young horses too hard. "If you want my opinion," and while neither Connie nor Gilly did, he gave it anyway, "there is no reason all these performance horses couldn't start competing at four instead of three. The quality of the contest would be much better and I wouldn't be seeing so many five year old horses with chronic joint problems." He continued until he felt he had adequately made his point and then handed Gilly a bill for eighty-five dollars that included a jar of one hundred phenylbutazone tablets. The "bute" was a general pain reliever and inflammation reducer that performed much the same function as aspirin in humans.

"That last turn is when she did it," Gilly lamented as they were driving home. "I could feel just the slightest hesitation as she started to pivot. I should never have entered that second event."

Gilly had stopped his bad habit of reining his cutter as if she were a draft horse plowing the back forty. His horse had responded by giving her all for him and come up lame, at least temporarily. "I don't think it's your fault," Connie told him. She's a young horse. We're asking an awful lot of them."

"Well, I asked too much. After I get her back in shape, I'm taking it easy on her." He patted the little filly on the hip. "I'll be strictly working my futurity prospect until December."

Connie thought for a bit. "Yeah, you know what? Billy and I are done too. I'll get some fresh cows even if I have to buy them and just work with Jolena until the futurity."

Gilly was quiet for a few miles before he said anything. "I won't be going to Fort Worth with you like we talked about," he finally said.

Connie was confused. "You're kidding. You just said you were going."

"Oh, I'm going, but I'm going down with Cindy."

"Really? How'd you manage that so fast?"

"I was in Denver last weekend. I flew out there Thursday afternoon and Cindy picked me up. She showed me the trailer operation and we talked. We decided I'll drive to her place and take one of the new trailers down to Texas."

"The two of you are going to Fort Worth?"

"Yup." He grinned. "Was I stuttering?"

"No, no. I heard you. It's just so quick." *Like asking Cally to marry me wasn't quick.* "Are you going to work for her after the futurity?"

"Maybe. Well, probably. It depends on how things go between now and then. If we can't stand each other after the trip, I guess not."

"I'm surprised. I could see you two took a liking to each other, but wow, you move fast."

Gilly shrugged. "One of those things, I guess. She's a year older than me, but that's no problem. Old men are always marrying young women, what's the difference?"

Connie was smiling. "Yeah, no problem. Besides she's a little doll."

Now Gilly was smiling. "Yes she is."

"I hope everything works out for you two. You tell Senior yet?"

"Yeah, I think he's relieved. He didn't say it, but I believe he was wondering if I was going to hang around forever."

"I'm surprised again."

"Me too. I figured he'd detonate when I told him. He just said, 'Well, Son, if you go, I'll sure miss having you around, but I understand.'"

"That's it?"

"Yup. Well, that and a bunch of bad advice on how to handle a woman. Not like I haven't heard that before. I think part of his good nature is due to the fact he's got another lady hanging around. He thinks he's running the show with her, but this one is a little smarter than most. She'll have his name on a marriage license if he's not careful."

"How old is he?"

"He's only sixty?"

"How about his new lady love?"

"I'm not certain. She's no spring chicken, probably fifty plus. She owns a beauty parlor or hair styling salon I guess we call them now. Got about four stylists working for her and they're always busy. I've been getting my hair cut by one of the girls there for about five years. Twenty-five bucks, can you believe it? The middle of what was once the 'Old West' and I'm paying twenty-five dollars for a haircut."

"You could go someplace cheaper."

"Of course I could, but you're missing the point. I'm a cowboy or at least I think I am, but I'm into creature comforts and good living just as much as some stockbroker in New York City."

"I can cut your hair if you'd like. Save you some money. I won't guarantee Cindy will recognize you though."

"Shut up."

Connie laughed. "I went from living in a four bedroom, five bathroom house to a one room bunkhouse and I'm doing just fine."

"You better wise up and marry Cally, then at least you can move into the big house."

Connie almost told him that's what was about to happen. He wanted to share the news, but if he told Junior, Junior would tell Senior, Senior would tell his girl friend who owned the beauty salon and the whole town of Kalispell would know. Probably, in less than a week, Brianna would hear about it and he wanted to talk to her in person before she heard it as gossip. He didn't owe her anything, but he thought he should be the one to tell her. He kept quiet.

"Didn't you hear me? I said you ought to marry Cally."

"Yes, I heard you. I've got too much on my mind right now. I'm thinking about winning the futurity. That's probably why your horse got hurt. You were thinking about Cindy and not watching the cow."

"That's hard. There's nothing can take my mind off the cow when I'm cuttin'."

"Okay, I apologize. But not being as disciplined as you are, I have to keep my life simple. I can't be skirt chasin' like you."

"You're so full of it, I can hardly believe you're able to get on a horse let alone ride one from all the extra weight."

"Ouch. Now that's hard, although the only way you can beat me is if I don't enter."

"That's even harder. We got any bets on the futurity?"

"No, and I'm not making any either. I don't want to jinx anything. Besides you're going to need every penny you have. Cindy could be planning on starting a family. She's still young enough."

"That's cool. We could have us a Gilliam the third."

They kept up the banter all the way to the Montana border. "How do you feel about driving straight through?" Connie asked.

"Fine by me. I wouldn't mind getting back tonight."

"Good. How about driving for a while."

Gilly agreed and Connie pulled over. They were back in Kalispell by eleven. The lights were out in the big house when he drove in, but he went directly to the barn. His intention, after turning Billy out, was to go straight to bed and he did, but when he went into the bunk house, Cally was sitting in his chair, watching his fire. She was wearing only a skimpy tee shirt and a tiny pair of matching shorts, her pajamas, she said.

"I saw you drive in. I thought I'd welcome you home."

"I'm glad you're so thoughtful. Can I shower off the road dust?"

"Can I help? Maybe wash your back?"

"Of course. What about my front?"

The twins were surprised and delighted when he showed up for breakfast. The questions came fast and furious. "How come you're home already? Did you win? We missed you, did you miss us? Can we go to Texas with you?" And on and on until Cally called a halt.

"Lindsey, Danni, listen up. Stop talking and eat your breakfast or Connie might rethink his plan to take us out to dinner and a movie. He might not want to go out with girls who talk all the time."

They were only slightly intimidated, but they did slow down enough to finish their breakfast. After they left for school, Cally asked Connie, "Sure you know what you're getting into?"

Woody and Pete exchanged a knowing glance and Woody winked at Connie. Apparently Cally had broken the news.

Chapter 38, Get Set

Connie allowed the twins to pick any restaurant in Kalispell they wanted for their date. That conveniently ruled out the Rustlers and the chance of running into Brianna Lane. They picked the barbecue place that Connie had taken them and Woody to earlier in the summer when Pete and Cally were out of town. It was crowded and noisy when they arrived. After waiting a bit, they were able to get a table in the back where conversation was difficult, but possible.

"Next time, I get to choose the restaurant," Cally said.

"But, Mom, the food here is terrific," Lindsey said.

"You ordered a hamburger. How terrific can that be?"

"It's really good, Mom.

"I'm getting barbecued chicken," Danni informed her.

"I had ribs last time and they were okay. I think I might get them again," said Connie. "And what will you be having, Dear," he asked Cally.

The girls giggled. "You called her 'Dear'," Danni informed him.

"Are you two in love now? This is your third date," said Lindsey.

"As a matter of fact, we are in love," Cally told them. "And we've decided to get married."

There was a momentary silence before the twins erupted into cheering, clapping, and wild hugging of both Connie and Cally.

"Can we be in the wedding?" Lindsey asked.

"Can we call you Dad?" Danni asked.

"They seem to be taking it well," Connie told Cally.

Later, after the movie, when they were home and Cally had chased the twins off to bed, she was sitting on Connie's lap and they were actually watching the fire in his little cast iron stove. "What do you think about right after Christmas?" Cally asked.

"How about tomorrow?"

"Before Christmas?"

"Tomorrow is before Christmas."

"You're not taking this seriously."

"I'm taking it very seriously. Whenever you want as long as it's soon so we can stop sneaking around."

"We're not sneaking around. Are we?"

"What would you call it?"

"Any couple with young kids has to be discrete. We're being discrete."

"That works for me."

"We could fly to Vegas and get married tomorrow if you want."

"I want what you want," he told her.

"Okay, it's right after Christmas then, and in the meantime we'll continue to be discrete."

"How about a ring? We could get you a ring tomorrow."

"That works for me."

Both Connie and Cally had been out of the courtship loop for a long time. At this point in their lives, they didn't need or want games. They were merely being honest with themselves and were prepared to commit to each other. Time would refine and strengthen the relationship, but at this instant, they were good to go.

"Oh, one more thing," Cally said. "You have to go to church with me on Sunday. You won't have to always go if you don't want, but you have to go this Sunday for sure."

"Okay."

Cally waited for the rest of his response, but apparently that was it. "Okay? Aren't you a little curious as to why?"

"I trust you implicitly."

"That's a good answer, but I want to tell you why."

"Please tell me. I'm a good listener."

"Pete invited Doctor Jim to go to church with us."

That got his attention. "What?"

"You heard me. We're meeting Doctor Jim at church and he's going to sit with us."

"What kind of medication is your father taking?"

Cally laughed. "He has a reason. Well, plan at any rate."

"Is it like when he found a way to get Gilly a better horse so he'd be more competition for me? I hope not, Doctor Jim could be in danger. Mortal danger even."

Cally kissed him. "You're so sweet. You're jealous."

"Well, yeah." He said it like the girls did, "yea-ah".

"Relax. Dad plans to introduce Doctor Jim to Colleen. You remember her, great body, good looking, big blonde hair?"

"How could I forget Colleen Husbandhunter? Does Pete hate Doctor Jim? She'll eat him for lunch and be hungry by supper."

"Dad doesn't think so. He thinks they both have what the other wants. He thinks they might be good for each other."

"Well, if the lion is good for the lamb, then he may be right. We're sure going to get you a ring tomorrow because I want them to know we're both off limits."

Sunday was interesting. Cally had to do a fair amount of explaining about the diamond she was wearing and Connie had to be cordial to the doctor. When Colleen arrived, she noticed both Connie and Jim immediately. Then she noticed Cally's ring and realized why Connie had given her the brush off, but who was the other guy? He was handsome, well dressed and looked to be about her age. From where she was sitting, she couldn't see any ring on his finger. Very interesting she thought. Maybe this was the Sunday she had been waiting for; Lord knew she had been faithful. She might be aggressive, but she wasn't about to look for a husband in the saloon. She knew from experience that didn't work. She'd been attending Sunday services at this church for two years in hopes a desirable man would materialize. It wasn't as if she didn't get plenty of attention. Attention was no problem, but she was looking for special attention from a nice man with means. Maybe this Sunday was the day. Pondering what excuse she could contrive to meet the 'new guy' occupied her thoughts for most of the sermon and by the end of it, she had the answer. She'd noticed Cally's ring and would congratulate her. Simple.

During the coffee drinking, social period immediately following the service, Colleen stalked her prey. "Cally, what a beautiful ring. Who's the lucky guy?"

"You've met Connie, I believe."

Connie nodded, "Hi, Colleen." The twins were standing guard, one on each side of Connie, sentries, serious about their duty.

Pete stood next to Doctor Jim who was smiling. He liked what he saw. "Colleen," Pete said. "Meet my doctor. This is Jim. Jim this is Colleen."

Colleen extended her hand and Jim took it. "Pleased to meet you, Doctor," she purred.

Twenty minutes later, after Pete, Woody, Connie, Cally, the twins, and most everyone else had gone, Colleen and Jim were still talking. Colleen was pulling out all the stops and Jim appeared to like what he was hearing and seeing.

"I don't know if that was such a good idea, Dad," said Cally on the way home.

"Better him than me," Connie said.

"You're spoken for."

"All I did was introduce them," Pete replied, "I have no responsibilities as to the outcome of that simple act. Women play matchmaker all the time. Furthermore, I don't think he's a pushover. He could surprise her."

"It's all hormonal anyway," Woody chimed in. "When that dies, they'll see the truth, whatever it might be."

"When are your hormones going to die?" Pete asked.

"Knock it off, you two," Cally said. "We have impressionable minds with us."

As September ended, the presence of autumn asserted itself with crisp, frosty nights and warm sunny days. The aspens vibrated yellow against the dark green pines, and the smell of dying leaves was a bittersweet perfume. The calves born in the spring were rounded up and shipped off, never to return. The bulls had bred all the cows earlier, in the spring after they had calved, and in February there would be another crop of cow babies. The pastures had been eaten down and the breeding stock was put into a forty-acre dry pasture where they were fed hay from the ample stockpile.

Feeding took three to fours a day and the afternoons were spent on odd jobs. Pete's condition had started to improve almost immediately after starting the antibiotics. Within two weeks, he was almost back to his old self. The diaper thing irritated him greatly, but he didn't think complaining about his diaper was a manly thing to do so he kept it to himself.

Connie did all the feeding chores, refusing to allow Pete to help. Pete initially protested, but Connie found a way to control him. He merely reminded him, if he wasn't healthy when it was time to go to

Texas, he'd have to stay home. With Cally backing him up, the threat worked and Pete acquiesced. He did mutter something about not giving his blessing to their marriage if he'd known they were going to gang up on him. In spite of what he said, he was grateful to Connie for doing the heavy lifting. Woody helped when Connie had something to do that needed four hands, otherwise he helped Cally around the house.

Connie rode Jo every day. Usually they rode into the herd and cut cows, but sometimes they just rode around the ranch or up into the hills looking for strays that were incredibly happy to be found. About the middle of October, Connie and Pete took a couple of days off and hauled Billy to a contest in Eastern Washington. It was fairly well attended with some high-powered riders. Connie won by three points and Pete was impressed by the way he rode and the way he allowed Billy to do the work.

"You haven't been wasting your time," he told Connie on the way home. "You were all business and you gave your partner his head. It was fun to watch."

Coming from Pete, this was high praise. "Thanks Pete. The credit is all yours. You trained us both."

"Okay, and I'm proud of both of you. You looked like you'd been riding half your life."

"Just half?"

"That's a considerable amount. You're no kid. Remember what I told you back in May when you first showed up? I said you'd eventually be riding good enough to fool half the judges."

"I do. That was right before I almost broke my arm when I was distracted by your daughter."

Pete chuckled. "Your fault. I told you never to take your eyes off the cow. Come to think of it, falling like you did was good training. You've never taken your eyes off the cow since."

"Maybe once or twice, but I did learn from taking that dive."

"Regardless, the point is, you're at the level now that we talked about five months ago. You should be able to fool at least two of the five judges, maybe even three. Starting when you did, there's no way you could ever be the best rider, but if you and Jo can do what you and Billy did today you'll definitely finish in the money."

"Seems like a lot of how it goes depends on the cow."

"Cutting is a three species sport. There's little that can be done to make the cow perform other than attempting to pick out those cows that haven't been worked before, or avoiding those that are acting spooky. You're correct, a great deal depends on the cow. Books have been written on how to read the herd. You didn't have the time to even attempt to learn all that. You're just going to have to trust Jolena. She knows what we want and she's got the eye."

"How does she do it?"

"As far as cows are concerned, she's a member of the dominant species. In animals, theoretically speaking of course, the dominant species is supposed to be able to recognize the most easily intimidated members of the subjective species. That's as much as I can tell you. I personally believe there's more to it, but I can't explain it. I just know every great horse I ever rode had a sense of which cows to cut. Allowing them to choose was the hard part."

"I hope I can do it. There's not much time left."

"You getting nervous?"

"I suppose. Although, I wasn't very nervous on this last one."

"Nothing wrong with being a little nervous. Keeps you sharp. Have you been having fun? I don't want to think I coerced you into this."

"No one has coerced my into anything since I got out of the army, and even that wasn't coercion. A friend of mine, the guy that brought me to the auction, maybe you remember him?"

"Sure, John, the guy you were going to give Jolena to until I talked you out of it."

"Yeah, that's him. He told me cutting was the most fun he'd had since his honeymoon. I didn't believe him then, but I'd have to agree with him now. When Billy or Jo is chasing a hot cow, spinning and twisting, starting and stopping, I can't believe it's me in the saddle. I feel blessed to be associated with such a horse. Does that sound stupid?"

"I'm sure some people would think it does, but I don't. I've owned a lot of horses during my life and I've loved them all. A few of them were special, way beyond good. They had abilities that were almost unbelievable and personalities that were endearing. I know the feeling you're describing. It's not foolish or weak or trivial. I feel sorry for people who never get to experience a partnership with an animal. Ask a canine corps cop what he thinks about his dog, or somebody with a companion animal. You'll get the same answer. They feel privileged too."

"Well anyway, no matter how it goes in Fort Worth, I've had fun. It's hard to believe it's coming up in just a few more weeks."

"Yeah, and you've only been waiting since you bought Jolena. I've been waiting since she was born. I wasn't sure what God had given me that night. It was an easy birth and she was up nursing as fast as I'd ever seen a foal get its legs together. She seemed special from the get go and has been getting better ever since. You don't know how I agonized when I realized I wasn't going to be able to ride her myself. That's why I pushed you so hard."

"Yeah, you even used my old man's motivational speech on me."

"It worked on me the first time I heard it. Probably kept me alive. Even though I was cold, tired, and miserable, I knew I didn't want any heathen commie Chinese soldier killin' me. I was going to try to keep on living."

"If the truth be known, hearing it from you probably saved my life too. If you'd let me give Jolena to John and just go home, there's no telling what might have happened. I might have picked up where I left off, drowning my sorrows in vast quantities of alcohol."

"Well then, when we get home, let's hoist one to General Conrad Bradley. I'm sure he'd appreciate that comin' from two old soldiers. Or at least one old soldier and another not quite so old soldier."

When they returned home, Cally and Woody had supper on the table, fried chicken and all the trimmings. It was a preview of Thanksgiving except the birds were smaller,

Connie also got another surprise. Cally had picked up a hundred head of feeder calves so Connie and Jo would have fresh cattle to chase. She figured they had extra hay and come spring they'd at least break even on the cows

Connie and Jo spent the last weeks before the futurity training hard.

Chapter 39, Go

The National Cutting Horse Association World Championship Futurity in which Connie rode was a nineteen-day event, beginning at the end of November and continuing to the middle of December. There were several stock auctions and cutting events for all classes; amateur, non-pro and open. There was even a celebrity cutting event that drew movie stars, television and radio personalities, country western singers, doctors, business notables, professional athletes, and politicians. There was something for everybody interested in cutting. The biggest event was the open class final, held the evening of the last day, typically a Sunday.

The working orders for all the classes were established about two weeks prior to opening day and the open class, first and second rounds, occupied the entire first week. It would take that long to whittle the field of almost seven hundred entries down to a workable number for the semi-finals.

Connie didn't have to be there on opening day. He wasn't scheduled to ride until the third day. However it was an eighteen hundred mile trip, and he and Pete were planning to leave two days before the futurity started. That would give them a leisurely four-day drive. If Connie made it through the first and second rounds, he'd have to wait a full ten days for the semifinals. If they stayed to watch the finals and counting travel time, they'd be gone almost three and a half weeks. Woody, Cally and the girls with help from Boissvert would be staying home to do the chores, but if Connie got to the finals, they'd all be flying down to watch him ride.

Prior to departure, he decided to buy a couple of shirts and maybe another hat in case his fell off and a cow stepped on it. He made a trip to Brianna Lane's tack shop. He doubted she'd be there, but if she were he'd tell her about his engagement. It would no doubt be awkward. As he pulled into the parking lot, Brianna's black Escalade, driven by her daughter, was pulling out. She had a passenger, a guy who looked to be about Connie's age. There was no reason for Brianna's daughter to recognize Connie; they'd never been introduced and she drove off without acknowledging him. To his surprise Brianna was in the store, although she had her back to him while she helped a customer. He went to the men's shirts and started looking. He wanted a spectacular shirt he could wear if he got to the finals. He found three he liked and decided to get them all. Then he went over to the hats. A young woman helped him find one he thought looked okay.

After paying for everything, he looked around for Brianna. Failing to see her, he decided he could wait to talk to her, but as he went out the door, she called to him. "Connie, wait." She hurried over. "You can't get out of here without talking to me."

He didn't let on he had seen her. "I saw your truck leave when I came in. I'm surprised you're here."

"My daughter and her father dropped me off. I'm training in a new manager and I'll probably be here all day."

"How are things going? Between them, I mean."

"Unbelievably well, and since I caught you I should tell you that I've been seeing him, too."

Connie was rendered momentarily speechless. This was fabulous news, the best he could hope for. It was so good, he couldn't have imagined it.

Brianna mistook his silence for shock. "I'm so sorry, Connie. I thought there could be something between me and you, but my daughter wanted me to talk to him and when I did, well, he'd changed. He was different than when I walked away from him eighteen years ago. He's become a real gentleman, like you. For my daughter's sake I want to see where this goes."

"Just for your daughter's sake?" Connie couldn't help the grin that was starting to turn up the corners of his mouth.

"Well no, not just hers, mine too. Connie, I'm real sorry."

His grin morphed into his best smile. "It's okay. Honest. I wish you all the luck in the world. If you can reconcile things with him, it would be the best ending possible. I hope it works out for all of you."

Since he was telling her the truth, he came off sounding sincere. "I'm glad you told me."

She kissed his cheek. "Thanks, Cowboy, you're the genuine article." She was relieved, but wondered more than a little why he was taking it so well.

He decided to quit while he was ahead. He saw no purpose in telling her about him and Cally. "Thank you too, Myra. It's been my pleasure." He walked off to his pickup and she went back into her store. If only everything was so easy, Connie thought as he drove back to the ranch. He was still smiling when he got there.

Connie watched as Cally ironed the last of his new shirts. She had the ironing board temporarily set up in the kitchen. It was Sunday night. Pete and Connie would be leaving in the morning. Except for these shirts, he was all packed, ready to go. "I wish you were coming along," he told her.

"I do too, but it's probably better this way."

"Oh yeah, how so?" The girls were in bed, maybe not asleep, but in bed regardless. Pete and Woody were both in the living room and out of sight. Connie stepped up behind Cally, put his arms around her, and nibbled her ear.

"Just like this is how so." Standing the iron up, she turned around in his embrace to face him. "You might be too distracted to ride."

"Maybe, maybe not. I can be very focused when I need to be."

"I know you can, but what would you be focusing on?" She kissed him.

"Good point," he said.

"Why don't you go down to the bunkhouse and when I finish, I'll bring these shirts down?"

"Great idea. I'll make a fire."

She laughed. "You'd better get a move on then. Turning up that thermostat is a big job and I want it warm when I get there."

The next morning, Connie and Pete said their goodbyes to Lindsey and Danni after breakfast before they left for school. Connie waited outside with them until the last minute when they boarded the bus. "Take care of Grandpa and Jolena," Lindsey told him. "I love you."

"I love you too, Lindsey."

Danni clung to him. "I love you," was all she said. She was about to cry.

"I love you too, Danni. Cheer up. I'll be back. Think about the Christmas we'll have."

There were tears in her eyes when she climbed the steps into the bus. Connie waved at the bus until it disappeared around a long, sweeping corner. He never imagined there would be children in his life. He walked slowly back to the house against a blustery wind promising snotty weather. Snow had been prophesied. The air was damp, it could happen.

Woody opened the door for him. He was on his way out to feed the cattle. He extended his hand. "Have a care, friend. I expect to be comin' down to see you ride in the finals in a couple weeks."

Connie shook Woody's hand. "I hope I can do it."

"I never been to Fort Worth. I'm told Texas is full of pretty women. Be nice if I could see for myself."

"Then you'll have to do it. Take good care of my future bride and the girls for me."

"Count on it. Gotta go, Connie. Keep your eye on the cow."

Pete came out as Woody was walking away. "Give me the keys, I'll load Jo."

Connie dug in his pocket and fished out the keys. Pete jerked his thumb over his shoulder towards the kitchen. "Cally's waiting for you."

"I wish we had a little more time," she told him.

He agreed and added, "More privacy too."

A few minutes later they heard Pete drive up with the trailer in tow. "I have to go. I'll call every day."

"Better. I'll be waiting."

One more kiss, one last squeeze, and he was out the door. "Keep your eye on the cow," she called out as he got in the truck. He waved and they were on their way.

"We got everything?" Connie asked as they pulled onto the highway.

"We have your horse and your new saddle. If you didn't forget your wallet, that's all we really need."

Connie felt his left, back pocket, looked up at the TV monitor and saw Jolena standing in the trailer. She looked as if she were smiling. "We should be good. I can feel my wallet and I can see Jolena."

Grinning, Pete eased down the accelerator, "Look out, Fort Worth, here we come."

As they passed the strip mall that housed Brianna's tack shop, Connie was surprised to see the black Escalade in the parking lot. "Myra's working early," Connie commented to Pete.

Pete nodded. "Cally told me about her new beau. She was glad to hear about him."

"Me too, although I don't know if you can call the father of her nineteen year-old daughter a 'new beau'."

"I suppose not." Pete shifted in the driver's seat slightly. "None of my business, but I thought you and Myra were a little more serious than you apparently were."

"No, I never was remotely serious about her. She intimidated me."

"You're joking? I don't know her, but a woman stronger than my daughter is hard to imagine."

Connie laughed. "Yeah, but that's not why she intimidated me. How many men do you suppose a woman like that has had?"

"Hard to say. Maybe a lot less then you're imagining."

"Yeah, could be. And she's very nice, but I never really wanted a romantic relationship with her."

"She didn't want a plutonic relationship, I take it?"

"I don't think so. I'm happy she's seeing her ex, so to speak."

"She say who he is?"

"She didn't tell me. I saw him briefly as he and her daughter drove away. He didn't look familiar."

"At the time her baby was born, rumor had it the father was Henderson James, the hotshot actor with the million dollar face. Even Cally thought he was a doll, although she was only a kid when he was popular."

"Isn't he the one who was charged with rape?"

"One and the same. His defense was simple. He maintained with his looks and popularity he didn't have to rape anybody. Women simply laid down for him. I believe the judge bought it. He threw the charges out of court."

"Interesting. When his word against her word is all there is, how do you establish the truth?"

"Impossible without a witness. Maybe that's why the judge threw it out."

"I don't know if the guy I saw was James or not. I just hope Myra makes a smart choice with him."

"Not our problem," Pete said. "We got us a contest to win."

Three and a half days later, they were there. The Will Rogers
Memorial Center had two thousand stalls, enough for all the horses that
would be involved, but Connie had made reservations at a motel with
horse facilities a few miles outside of Fort Worth. They wanted to keep
Jo close at hand. After settling in, they dropped the trailer and drove
over to the coliseum to see what was happening. They ran into Cindy as
soon as they walked in the door. She had just come from wishing Gilly
good luck. Connie introduced Pete and the three of them found some
seats and waited for Gilly to ride.

The coliseum seated fifty-seven hundred, but there were
probably less than three hundred people watching. They were able to
get close to the action. The cowboy just ahead of Gilly turned in a great
performance, and what audience there was gave him a healthy round of
applause. Then Gilly turned in an even better performance and his three
person cheering section led the crowd in a round of applause just short
of a standing ovation. Connie was certain Gilly would make the second
go round.

The four of them went out to dinner that evening and Gilly and
Cindy caught Pete and Connie up on all the news. It was obvious to
both Pete and Connie that Gilly had found the woman of his dreams.
Cindy appeared to be equally as enamored.

Back at the mare motel Pete wondered out loud, "Gilly and
Cindy appear to be somewhat serious. You suppose Senior approves?"

"According to Junior he does. Regardless, I don't think he
cares. I believe we are witnessing Junior's discovery of independence."

"About time, but it would appear he's merely shifting
allegiances. He just found somebody else to take care of him."

Connie shrugged. "Maybe, but I like Cindy a lot better than
Senior. It's the same as what you said about Doctor Jim and Colleen
each having what the other wants. Is there any more than that?"

Pete thought a bit. "My wife, Renee, once told me I was
everything she ever wanted. I was flattered, of course, because I
thought she was the consummate woman and she loved me. Maybe
you're right. I had what she wanted and she had what I wanted. It's a
basic distillation of a lot more complicated thoughts and emotions, but I
suppose it's true."

Connie shrugged again. "I rest my case and not to change the
subject, what did you think of Gilly's ride."

"It was terrific. It'll get him into the second go round."

"I hope I can do as well."

"You will, probably better. There are over six hundred horses and riders down here. About a hundred of them are good. Fifty of them are excellent and ten are great. You and Jolena are in that top ten. I don't know if you'll win, but I know you have the potential. Just go out there and let Jolena play her game."

The next day, Connie did exactly that and he and Jo scored high enough to guarantee they would be in round two. Then they had to wait two full days before they rode again. Waiting was something Connie didn't do well. He was okay if he had something else to do, but just waiting was nerve wracking. Pete recognized this immediately because he was the same way. He did his best to keep Connie occupied until he rode again and wondered what he would do if they made it through round two. Two days had been hard enough; there was a ten-day wait to the semi-finals.

Connie rode early on the second day of round two. Again Jolena was brilliant and Connie helped by staying on her back while looking reasonably competent. Their score easily guaranteed them a slot in the semi-finals, ten days in the future. A number of spectators who had seen Jo work in the first round, made a point to show up to watch her again. Connie and Jo had a cheering section of more than a hundred. Seeing her work, it was hard not to root for the pretty little paint horse from Montana. The smile it put on Pete's face was as big as the sky over The Big Sky State.

Pete and Gilly shook Connie's hand and Cindy hugged him, and a number of people came over on the premise of congratulating him, but mostly they wanted a closer look at his horse. Jolena was magnanimous, standing square and straight while she was petted and praised. Connie believed she knew exactly what was happening and was enjoying it. For some reason he remembered the ten year reunion of his West Point class. Both he and his wife were thirty-one years old and made a stunning couple, she by far the more stunning. As a couple they attracted a sizeable crowd of Connie's classmates, all of them, without exception, wanting to get a closer look at Conrad's wife. She handled it well and Connie was certain she'd even enjoyed it. She treated all onlookers politely and was infinitely charming. Now his horse was acting the same way. *Was it possible the most beautiful members of every species appreciated flattery? Stupid question. What does a horse know about flattery?*

Gilly rode later in the afternoon and earned a score they all hoped would hold up for the rest of the day. "Well," he told them when he was finished, "I've never been this far before so no matter what happens, I'm still way ahead."

The four of them sat and nervously watched the last twenty riders. Cindy was a wreck and when Gilly's position in the semi-finals was finally secured, she told everyone, "I need refreshment and I'm buying."

They found the closest saloon and eatery. "Here's to the two best cowboys I've ever met," Cindy said. "Now, what do we do for the next ten days?"

"Well, for starters," Connie said, "You and Gilly could pull out of that RV park you're in and come on out to where we're staying. They've got some vacancies now, and Cindy, even though I love the trailer you built me, the accommodations are real nice. I just reserved two more rooms. Woody and Cally and the girls will be coming down on Thursday of next week."

"Oh, goodie," said Cindy, "all of us girls can go shopping. That'll take care of two days. Why can't they come down sooner?"

Connie looked at Pete. Pete shrugged. "They can come tomorrow by me. Boissvert's sons have promised to do the chores for whenever and however long we need. I don't know if Cally will want to pull the girls out of school for that long."

Connie said to Gilly, "When we get back to the motel, I'll call." He dug in his wallet for a business card. "Here's the place we're at. Call them, line up a room and come over. If nothing else, we'll just sit around and take it easy. It'll be just like when we were on the road together a couple of months ago except the girls will be prettier."

Chapter 40, Keep Going

"Their teacher won't be happy, but I'm not going to worry about it. It's only a week and they get straight As. Are you sure the Boissvert brothers are agreeable?" Cally asked.

"Your father just got off the phone with the oldest Boissvert and he said it would be no problem," Connie told her. "He's going to talk to his brother and call us right back just to make certain. They know what to do and they'll take over on Sunday morning. Your dad also talked to the old man and he volunteered to come out every day in the afternoon to check on things. Sunday morning I can get you on a plane out of Kalispell to Spokane and then to Fort Worth. You'll be here by noon. As soon as I hear from Johnny Boissvert I'll call you."

"It sounds wonderful to me. We just had six inches of snow. I wouldn't mind a little sun."

"That's all you're coming for, a little sun?"

"Well, there is this guy down there I wouldn't mind seeing. He's a hotshot cutting horse rider, apparently going to be in the finals. Maybe you know him?"

"Perhaps. Anything you want to tell him? I'll see he gets the message."

"It's quite personal. I'll have to deliver it myself."

"I'm positive he'll be eagerly anticipating your arrival."

"Make sure he is, it'll be worth his wait."

"Lucky guy."

"Lucky girl, too. Call me as soon as you know what the plan is. I'll have to get moving."

Connie promised to do that and by noon the next day, all the arrangements had been finalized. A limo would pick up Woody, Cally and the twins at eight on Sunday morning and bring them to the airport in Kalispell. From there they would take a charter flight direct to DFW. The price of four one-way tickets purchased on short notice from Kalispell to Spokane and on to Dallas was only slightly less than a charter. Connie would be waiting to collect them before noon. The Boissvert brothers would be doing the chores until the family returned.

Cindy and Gilly moved out to join Pete and Connie and for the next few days they basically goofed off. The two horses received plenty of attention. Gilly's new little mare was doing for Gilly what none of his previous horses had ever done. The fact he had gotten into the finals had affected him more than it had affected Connie. It wasn't that Connie hadn't worked hard, but he'd only worked for about six months. Ordinarily it took years to get this far and Gilly was well aware of his investment in time. He still had not allowed himself to think about winning. He'd watched almost all of the competition and from what he'd seen, Jolena was the best horse. From Gilly's analysis, the only way she could be beaten was if her rider made some major mistake. He didn't wish that on Connie, but he was going to turn in the best ride he could and whatever happened, happened. He had a good horse now, too.

After Cally, the twins and Woody arrived, instead of dragging, the next week flew by. Everybody shopped, including Pete and Woody. The Dallas, Fort Worth area was full of all types of stores, shops and restaurants. Cindy had an amazing talent for finding bargains. She, Cally, and the twins spent at least forty hours in pursuit of stuff. The twins found the perfect present for Connie, a belt buckle with a silver and black, paint cutting horse standing nose to nose with a steer. Cindy pointed it out to them. It was on sale for half off and the girls had just enough money to cover it. The problem was, it was all the money they had for all the presents they needed to buy.

"Let's keep looking," Lindsey told Danni.

"Okay," Danni reluctantly agreed.

"Hang on, ladies, let me find the manager and see if I can't do some negotiating," Cindy told them. "Stay put." She went off to find someone with authority. She knew all about retail mark-up. Five minutes later she was back. A middle-aged gentleman with whom she had already cut a deal, accompanied her.

"Danni, Lindsey, this is Mister Carson, he's the manager of the store."

Carson nodded to the girls. "Pleased to meet you. I understand you're interested in a belt buckle for a very good friend."

Lindsey volunteered, "Yeah, his name is Connie and he's going to be our dad."

Not to be upstaged Danni chimed in. "He's got a horse just like the one on the buckle and he's going to win the futurity."

"Well if that's the case," Carson said, "he needs this belt buckle. I've been trying to sell it for a long time with no luck. Maybe it's been waiting for you two. How much can you pay for it?"

Between them they had eighty dollars. They had decided to pool their funds so they could buy 'bigger' presents, but they had four presents to buy, one each for their mother, grandfather, Woody and Connie.

Danni looked to Lindsey and said, "You tell him."

"Twenty dollars," Lindsey said.

"That's it? Twenty dollars?" Carson asked.

Danni was nervous, but Lindsey didn't flinch. "Yup, that's all we can pay. Twenty dollars."

Carson made a production of considering their offer. I should have more than that, but it's been here a long time." He stroked his chin and scratched his head. "Well, okay, I shouldn't, but I will. Sold, for twenty dollars."

The girls were ecstatic. Cally was grateful and Cindy slipped Carson another thirty after the girls had gone. "Thanks," Cindy told Carson. "We all appreciate it."

"My pleasure. I used to ride cutting horses. Does their new daddy have a chance at winning the futurity?"

"It'll either be him or my boyfriend in the winner's circle Sunday night." And she laughed. "Come on out and watch Gilly Bedfort and Connie Bradley. You'll be impressed."

"I might just do that. Been a while since I've sat in the Cow Palace."

"Maybe we'll see you there. Thanks for your help." She shook his hand and went to catch up to Cally and the girls. When she did, she winked at Cally and said, "Never to early to learn how to shop."

Connie, Gilly, Pete, and Woody did an abbreviated version of the girls' shopping tour, but in total dollars spent, it was more impressive. The boys also made a trip to Weatherford to visit two old pals of Pete's he hadn't seen in years. They were younger than Pete and both still involved with horses. One had made it big, the other had been less successful, but they were both down to earth. The successful one had seen Connie and Jolena work in the second round. He'd been impressed. "I'm not much of a paint horse man and I'm not real sure why," he told Connie, "but if that little filly of yours finishes in the money, I'll pay a good price for her."

"She'll never be for sale," Connie told him politely, "at any price, but I'm flattered you asked."

Pete's buddy laughed. "I know exactly what you mean. I've had a few that were born here and died here. No way were they ever going down the road."

The time not spent shopping or visiting was occupied with sightseeing and eating. They sampled every type of cooking they could find, from Armenian to Szechwan. No cooking and no dishes for a week, Cally and the twins were in heaven. However, before they knew it, Saturday morning was upon them. It was time for Connie and Gilly to ride.

Connie rode before Gilly and almost ended his chances. His first cow was half sour and he made a rather sloppy quit, losing points. The second cow he picked, ran from fence to fence and although Jo contained it, there was no head-to-head excitement. The third cow kept him in the race. It was feisty and quick, giving Jo a chance to shine. She had the crowd on their feet cheering before she was through. All Connie had to do was worry and wait for several hours for his score to hold.

Gilly, riding towards the end of the line up, had three good cows and scored high enough to ensure his trip to the final round. He was as ecstatic as Connie was nervous. By eleven that evening, the lineup for the final round had been determined. Connie made the cut, just barely, in a tie for last place. Gilly came in fifth and while Connie was no longer nervous, Gilly was still ecstatic.

Fortunately the only thing that determined the winner would be the ride in the final, tomorrow night. Back at the motel, Pete and Connie talked until well after everyone had gone to bed. Connie wanted to know what he had done wrong or at least what he could have done better.

"It really wasn't that bad," Pete told him. "The first cow was acting sour. You should have quit her sooner and more decisively. You pulled her out of the herd just fine. You trailed her out in front of the judges just fine, but as soon as you knew she wasn't going to work for you, you should have quit. I figure you lost at least six points by trying to play her too long."

"Yeah, you're right, and I knew it at the time too. I was hoping she'd come to life even though I was fairly certain she wouldn't. Stupid mistake. I don't think I could have done much to change the second one though."

"No, you handled that one just fine. Jo made some nice sliding stops and roll backs and you stayed in the saddle so that didn't hurt. Although it wasn't terribly exciting, I couldn't see where it cost you any points. Anyway you saved the best for last. Your third cow was probably the best cut of the entire evening. I don't know if you could hear it, but by the time you finished, there were people whistling and yelling out Jolena's name. Sent chills down my spine. If you can put two runs like that together tomorrow night, you'll own the place."

"I pretty much let Jo pick that last cow. I figured we weren't going to make it anyway so I let Jo do it all. You suppose there's a lesson there?"

Pete smiled and looked up to the ceiling. He lifted his hands. "Hallelujah! Lord, your pilgrim has finally seen the light." He put down his hands and looking back to Connie, said, "Well, yea-ah. What have I been saying for the past six months?"

"I know, I know. I just have a hard time giving up all control. It seems like I should be doing something."

"You are doing something. You brought her here. I've always wondered how many first class, cutting horses and reining horses and jumping horses are out there that never get the chance to perform. They go on a trail ride once or twice a week or maybe never get ridden at all and yet they might have abilities beyond anything we have ever seen. I don't feel particularly sorry for those horses as long as they're well cared for, they don't know the difference. But I started Jolena and you finished her. Your determination and your money got her down here. Other than being her passenger, you've done about everything you can really do. There's no more time. Allow Jo to do her part and I don't know if you'll win, but I guarantee you'll be surprised." He pushed back his chair. "It's late. I'm going to bed."

When Pete was gone, Connie went out to see Jo. She was standing by the gate of the little paddock adjacent to the cabin as if waiting for him. She wasn't wearing a halter, but Connie let her out and then slipped up on her back. She stood calmly, waiting for a cue. In the past few weeks he'd ridden her this way often. The first time was a little spooky. Neither of them knew what to expect, but it didn't take either of them long to come to terms. At first Connie used leg cues to turn her. After a few rides, he realized he could turn her by telling her "left" or "right". They had never gone faster than a lope and he never intended to. Pete had seen him riding her without a saddle and bridle and even though he didn't think it was the greatest idea, he never said anything. He decided anything that fostered trust between them was okay. He remembered his first mount, Old Zipper. He rode him with nothing but a halter and baling twine reins and they'd become the best of friends.

"Walk, Jo," said Connie and Jo walked. There was a little fenced meadow at the other end of the property that "guests" were free to graze in and the gate was never locked. "Not much grass left," Connie told her as he slid off her back onto the top fence rail. "Check it out, girl. There might be a bite or two."

Jo moved around a bit, but came back and stood by the fence. She nickered.

"You want to go back and go to sleep? We don't have to get up early tomorrow." He contemplated the day. "Pete says I have to let you do it all. Can you do that?" He smiled. "Can you do it all and make sure I don't fall off besides?" He moved from the fence rail to her back. "Okay, I believe you can. Let's go back and go to bed."

The morning and afternoon went agonizingly slow. Connie didn't know what to do with himself. He walked Jo, played with the twins, talked to Cally and when they went to lunch, he picked at his food. Later, he was too nervous to eat supper and Cally was concerned.

"Are you sure you're all right? I've never seen you not eat."

"I'm fine, except for my nerves. I haven't felt this jumpy— ever."

If they'd had some privacy, Cally was reasonably certain she could relax him, but that wasn't going to happen. "You're going to do just fine. Win or lose, it doesn't matter. I'll still love you and so will Jolena."

"Me too, Connie," said Woody, "I'll still love you even though you're not really my type."

Connie laughed. "Thanks, man. That's what I really need, to be loved by a crusty, old sheepherder."

"Could be worse. At least I'm a good looking, crusty, old sheepherder."

Connie laughed some more, hugged Cally and said he wouldn't leave Cally for him. For some reason the twins found this all very amusing and started giggling. For a brief moment the tension was lifted and then Pete announced it was time to get moving.

The laughter died down, but the smiles remained. "Well, folks, the Man has spoken. We'd better get." Connie went to change into his best blue jeans, boots and fanciest shirt. He wore the belt buckle he'd won for coming in second at his first contest in Polson. A half-hour later they were out the door, heading for the Will Rogers Auditorium, The Cow Palace.

Chapter 41, Cut For the Title

The whoops, whistles, yells, and hollers for the last rider had
made a deafening din as Connie watched and waited, parked on Jolena
at the back end of the arena, well behind the judges' stand. The last
rider had found a fresh cow and his horse made an impressive cut. But
now the applause was gone, the Cow Palace was ominously quiet. He
sat in silence waiting for the announcer to tell him and everybody else it
was his turn. Jolena was perfectly calm beneath him. Connie couldn't
even feel her breathing. His own mouth was dry and he reflexively
licked his lips. He was tight as a set mousetrap. He wondered if Jo
sensed any of his tension.

*Is she as nervous as I am? No reason to think she is. She never
seems to be nervous. She doesn't realize this ride is for all the marbles.
It's just another cow for her to chase.* He smiled for himself when he
thought that. It made him relax a notch. *And she loves to chase cows!*

The announcer seemed to be taking forever. Connie wanted
this over. Win or lose he wanted to be done. He looked down at his
hands holding the reins. The long, pale scar that started on the back of
his left hand, disappeared under his shirt sleeve and ended two thirds of
the way up his forearm looked whiter than he recalled and his fingers
were going numb. He realized he was squeezing the reins. He relaxed
his grip. Gradually, the feeling came back into his fingers. He
remembered the painful therapy he'd endured trying to restore the use of
his hand after he'd been wounded. There were times he thought his
hand would be merely a club, something to use if he got into a fight.
But eventually, through hard work and constant trying, he'd regained

almost complete use of it. *It's a good thing too. I'd never be able to ride Jolena with one hand.*

Finally the announcer started, "Ladies and Gentlemen!" The loudspeaker barked. Connie flinched. "It's the moment you've been waiting for!" Connie took a deep breath. "It's all come down to this ride. This is it," the announcer droned on. "This will be the last ride." And then he added, "Unless of course, we have a tie for first place."

God forbid. I've had all the excitement I can handle for one lifetime. I don't think I can do any more rides after this one.

The announcer continued on, stroking the crowd, reminding them only one point separated the top two riders and how many points Connie would have to get to win and blah, blah, blah.

"Cut the bull," Connie mumbled. Jolena nickered softly and tossed her head in apparent agreement.

Connie was slightly startled. It was the first move Jolena had made since he reined her to a halt behind the judges' stand. He reached forward and patted her neck gently, "I hope you're readier than I am, Jo."

She nickered again. The announcer called, "Ladies and Gentlemen, here is Smokin' Jolena ridden by Conrad Bradley!"

After the echo from the PA system died and the introductory applause faded, the arena became silent in anticipation. Jolena had picked up a big following. Connie gave Jolena the smallest amount of leg pressure. He licked his lips again. "Let's go, Jo." They moved forward into the main arena.

The look of the Cow Palace arena at the instant they started toward the herd was to become indelibly etched on the retina of Connie's mind's eye. He saw the audience sitting quietly, expectantly. He saw the herd holders and turn back riders, motionless, watching him as he neared the time line. He saw the cows, frozen, huddled against the back wall watching Jolena. And in the middle of the cows was the big, red steer no one had attempted to cut. It was an alligator if ever there was one and it seemed to be glaring directly at him.

Then Connie blinked. He crossed the line. The clock started ticking. The scene changed. Jolena moved slowly towards the herd, approaching it from the right side. The cattle put their heads down to avoid eye contact with the horse, hoping to remain anonymous. The herd holders started moving up behind him, one on each side, keeping pace with Jolena. The cattle bunched tighter as the riders approached.

Connie had carefully watched the previous nine riders, hoping to remember which cows did not get worked. It was confusing, but he thought he could recognize at least three cows that hadn't been cut. One of them was the big red steer, and he really didn't want to tangle with him. There was however, a mostly all red little heifer towards the back of the herd. Connie was almost positive she hadn't been worked. He decided to push deep into the cows, and see if Jo would give her a try. It would satisfy his deep cut requirement as soon as possible. He needed to avoid any sour cows on this ride. He needed fresh meat to have a chance to make a good score. He also needed to refrain from trying to tell Jolena her job.

The herd began to part ahead of Jolena, but as she went deeper, space became limited and she was almost pushing cows with her shoulders before Connie finally confronted the timid looking little heifer. He carefully turned Jolena into her. Connie could tell Jo approved of his choice and she slowly eased the heifer out of the herd. By the time they had the cow in the center of the arena, Connie had used less than thirty seconds of his two and half minutes. He believed he would gain points for the depth of the cut and the trailing work to get her to center of the arena. As far as he could tell, he had not yet made a mistake. *God, please, give me a good ride.*

And then to Jolena he whispered, "Cut her, Partner."

He tightened his grip on the saddle horn with his right hand and dropped the reins on Jolena's neck. Jolena tossed her head. The crowd came to life and the game was on.

For a scared looking little heifer, the cow had plenty of spunk. For thirty seconds Jolena kept her in the center of the arena, making short, quick dashes back and forth before she was finally confused into submission. The crowd loved this kind of action and they made their presence known with whoops and whistles. Connie was sweating profusely when they quit and turned back into the herd for another cut. The clock had ticked away less than half their time. Connie figured he would go deep again. *It worked last time. I'll do it again.*

This time however, as they entered the herd, the cows rapidly slid away from them on both sides, flowing like a river around a boulder in midstream. This had happened to Connie before and he knew the outcome. What he didn't know was how to prevent it. The herd holders on both sides of the arena contained the cows in two bunches, one on either side of Connie and Jo. Now there were only two cows facing them. One was the big, red steer. He had a short, stubby horn sticking straight out from each side of his head and glared malevolently at them. He was the biggest, meanest looking steer Connie had ever seen in a cutting contest. Right now, the devil himself would be less intimidating.

Connie swallowed hard. He had to avoid that one at all cost. He reined Jo carefully, attempting to turn her head slightly to the right to face towards the smaller, more timid looking steer, but Jolena refused the cue. She had spotted the big red steer the first time they rode into the herd, but had deferred to Connie. Now, for whatever reason, she decided it was her turn to choose. Maybe it was the way this devilish red steer glared at them or maybe it was his size, or his posture. Maybe she just wanted a little extra challenge, a chance to show the audience how good she really was. There was no way to know what she was thinking and it didn't matter; she was going to kick this steer's big, beefy butt.

It became immediately apparent to Connie that despite his cue, Jolena was locking on the ugly red steer. *God no, Jo! Not that one!* He quickly considered turning Jo away. At this point, the judges could probably deduct for a quit, but maybe not. He didn't know how much commitment they thought he'd made. Less than twelve feet separated him and Jolena from the red steer. The rest of the herd was split off to both sides and acting nervous. As Jolena focused her attention on the devil steer, the last remaining cow bolted for the part of the herd to the left. Now there was no choice. It was either cut this steer, here and now, or quit him, go back to the herd for another, and take at least a five point deduction from each judge. That would mean if he made no other mistakes, his best possible score would be 225. He needed 226 to tie.

Connie's better judgment took over. *You fool! You didn't get here because of your abilities. You're here only because you've got the best cow horse in the country.* He allowed Jolena to approach the red steer. The steer started moving slowly away, glaring at them over his shoulder. He was not happy about being pushed. Jolena was carefully moving him to the center of the arena. Connie had suddenly become just another spectator. He watched as the steer walked grudgingly to almost dead center of the arena. When he got there, Jolena stopped. So did the steer. He had increased the ten-foot separation they had initially established to almost twenty feet. The steer turned to face them. Defy them, it seemed to Connie. The herd holders had the cows back under control and had moved them against the back fence away from Connie and Jolena. They didn't like this turn of events any more than Connie did. They felt his apprehension and he could taste it.

The center of the arena was wide open. The turn back riders were parked directly to the sides of the judges' stand. Connie, Jo, and the ugly red steer were in perfect position. "What the hell!" Connie said

out loud. *Hang on, enjoy the ride and don't do anything to screw it up.*
He dropped the reins and the action started.

  Jo charged up to the red steer. It didn't flinch. The sudden
acceleration had Connie pulling on the saddle horn for all he was worth.
To avoid a collision with the steer, Jo dropped her butt and locked her
back legs. Now Connie was pushing on the horn to prevent being
catapulted out of the saddle. The crowd cheered as the dirt furrowed out
behind Jo's back hooves, leaving an elongated "eleven" in the sand of
the arena floor. She stopped nose to nose with the steer, three feet away.
He stood fast and Jo recognized by his posture it wasn't from fear. This
cow wasn't afraid of her—not yet anyway.

  They stayed locked up, the steer standing straight, legs braced
tight, head down, glaring hard. Jolena was crouched with her butt down,
back feet well under her powerful haunches, front legs just ahead of her
shoulders. For a long two seconds Jo tolerated the standoff. The crowd
became silent, holding its collective breath.

  Connie was an emotional wreck. He tried to sit as easy as
possible, slouched back on his pockets and squarely over Jolena's center
of gravity. His right hand gripped the saddle horn tightly. His left hand
held the reins down on Jo's neck just in front of the horn. He was
sweating hard, trying to concentrate on being at ease and to not give Jo
any cues. He was acutely aware of six thousand pairs of eyes staring at
him and Jo. He wanted to be invisible.

  Then Jo made the move. To his surprise, Connie sensed it
coming and leaned back slightly to aid the horse. Jo shifted all her
weight to her haunches and slowly raised her front feet. She stood there,
her front feet completely off the ground, shifting from side to side like a
tennis player waiting for the serve. Then with her right hoof, she struck
the ground with a smack that even the sand on the arena floor couldn't
completely muffle. Spectators in the front row heard it.

  That was too much. The once defiant steer had never expected
this. When the blur of Jo's hoof hit the ground, he bolted to his right.
Connie saw the move, didn't believe it was happening, but once again
surprised himself by leaning smoothly into Jo's counter move.

  Jolena exploded to her left and cut the steer's escape before it
made four strides. The steer hit the brakes, dug in with all four and
leaped back to the right. Jo slid to a stop, spun on her back end,
reversed direction and caught it again. Connie lurched in the saddle
slightly, but held on. *Sloppy. That's not going to look good on the big
screen TV back at the ranch, but I ain't eatin' dirt.*

Four more fast cuts; the cow stopped and stared at Jo. It was a different stare this time. Last time it was a glare of defiance, now the cow was looking at Jo in exasperation. He couldn't see how to get past this horse.

In the stands, the twins had started shouting, "Go, Jo-Lena!"

Jo dropped back on her haunches and again raised her front feet off the ground. Again she swayed from side to side, toying with the steer like a cat with a mouse, defying it to move. The steer moved and so did Jolena. Back and forth they raced, the steer always cut off and forced to change direction.

A group of Jolena's fans somewhere in the arena heard the twins cheering and joined in. "Go, Jo-Lena! Go, Jo-Lena!"

The chant was picked up and, within seconds, became the mantra for the entire audience. Unified with one great voice, the crowd shouted. "Go! Jo! Lena!" reverberated through the arena.

Connie not only heard it, he could feel it. His head throbbed with the pressure of the sound. It pounded tight against his chest. There was a lump in his throat. He had goose bumps everywhere it was possible to have them. He wanted to shout with the crowd. Jolena was putting on the show of a lifetime and he had the best seat in the house. He only hoped he could keep it.

It was a perfect cut. The steer could not escape. The herd helpers had nothing to do except watch the show. The steer wanted to get past Jolena all on its own. But whatever he did, whichever way he ran, the horse was always there, in front of him, blocking his escape. He dipped and bobbed and weaved and charged, all to no avail. Jolena was eternally there, seemingly reading his mind. Connie was an extra, a non-essential, providing no input, no cues and no help. Jolena was doing it all. When it was over and he tried to recall details—he couldn't. Once he dropped the reins to turn Jo loose on that red steer, individual events merged into a twisting, turning, hooves-pounding, sand-flinging, spinning blur of movement, color and noise.

And then it stopped. After fifty seconds of constant trying, the frustrated and confused steer finally gave it up. He turned his back to Jolena and stood motionless. If Connie hadn't been breathing so hard he would have laughed out loud. It was the best quit he ever had.

He lifted the reins and began turning Jolena around, going back to the herd to find another cow to cut. He was operating automatically. The noise in the arena was deafening. He could not hear the horn that ended his ride. It was only when one of the herd holders motioned to him, pointing at the clock, did he realize his time was up. His action only made the crowd cheer louder.

He was about to explode from pride and there were tears in his eyes. He did not care he was only able to cut two cows and he no longer cared what their score would be. This was the best ride he'd ever had, maybe the best ride anyone had ever had. He slowly took Jolena behind the time line, to the back of the arena, well beyond the judges. He turned her around and dismounted. Holding the reins in his right hand, he removed his hat with his left and bowed to the audience. He held the reins high and gestured with his hat to Jolena. It seemed like the right thing for him to do. Jolena tossed her head and whinnied. The sound of it was lost to the cheering. The crowd was already on its feet. They stayed there, cheering wildly. Standing ovations were not lightly given in this game. Connie mounted up and the partners moved out of the cutting arena. On the way out, Connie looked up at the scoreboard hoping to see his score. He stopped and stared. Jolena had done it. They had won.

"You did it, Jo." Connie leaned forward in the saddle and patted her neck. "You did it all."

Dismounting in the holding area outside the cutting arena, he heard his name being shouted. "Connie! Connie!" The twins roared up, leaping into his arms. Cally was close behind.

He put the girls on Jo's back and embraced Cally. "Let's go home now. All of us. Together."

Epilogue

Connie's score of 230 beat the previous all time record by one point, giving him a decisive four point victory, and it was the first time a rider from Montana had won since Pete himself almost fifty years earlier. Gilly finished in a two-way tie for third and won forty some thousand dollars. Connie won two hundred grand, a new pickup, a saddle, a jacket and a belt buckle. He gave half his prize money to charity and traded the pickup and some additional cash for an Escalade that he gave to Cally. He kept the saddle, jacket, and the belt buckle. He also bought the big, red steer that gave him and Jo their win, saving him from the butcher. He hauled him home, and he spent the rest of his days in the pasture being lazy and looking mean.

They were all home by the twentieth of December. Cally had a wonderful birthday party and they all had a merry Christmas. It was a balmy day. After a four-inch snowfall two days before, the Chinook winds were blowing, pushing the temps into the high fifties. Just for kicks, Cally served Christmas dinner in the barn. Everyone loved it. One of the presents from Connie was a complete renovation to the old ranch house. The twins would finally have a dishwasher.

Connie and Cally were married three weeks after Christmas in a small ceremony at Cally's church, officiated by Pastor Sean, the bull rider turned preacher. Woody was Connie's best man and Cindy was the maid of honor. The wedding was followed by a huge reception at the Rustlers. Two of the more notable couples in attendance were

Doctor Jim and his fiancé, Colleen, and Brianna Lane and her new old beau, Henderson James.

Connie and Jolena retired from competition after winning the futurity, passing up the opportunity to go on to greater heights. They had signed up with Pete for the futurity only and they'd served with distinction. There was no dishonor in quitting while you were ahead.

What did Jolena think of the decision? She gave Connie no reason to suspect she missed the action. In fact, she appeared to enjoy being a normal horse for a change. She eventually produced three foals, two fillies and a colt. While none of them ever equaled Jolena in their abilities, one of the mares finished in the money at a national futurity, and the colt grew into a fine looking stallion. Some of his offspring went on to distinguish themselves in the cutting arena and elsewhere. Pete had been correct; the world would not see another horse like Smokin' Jolena for a long time.

In November of the following year, Cally gave birth to a baby boy and Connie's life changed again. For Christmas, Woody gave Connie a football. Pete didn't feel good that winter and by early spring he was diagnosed with liver cancer. He was tired and didn't like the odds he was given. He decided to forego treatment. He faded fast.

On his deathbed talking to Danni, he told her, "It's okay, Danni, I'm ready. You have to let me go. When I was a little boy, a few years younger than you, I had a horse named Zipper. Zip was old when I started riding him and he was very gentle with me. He died one day when I was riding him and I was very sad. I loved that old horse and I cried for a long time. My father told me I had to let him go. He said Old Zipper had gone to ride with the big herd in the sky. It was his destiny. My dad said I couldn't go because it wasn't my time, but now my time has come, and I so badly want to see Zipper again and ride with him in that big herd in the sky. You have to let me go." He died three days later surrounded by his family. The last thing Connie heard him say in a still, small voice as he died was, "Awesome."

A year after Pete's departure, Connie and Cally quit raising cattle. They didn't need the extra work and the money was of little consequence. Connie predicted with the advancements in genetic engineering, it wouldn't be much longer before beef roasts would be grown on bushes. Three years after that, they contracted out the hay business and basically retired. They built a small log cabin on the shores of Rogers Lake.

The girls went to college, Danni in Iowa to become a veterinarian, Lindsey in Massachusetts to become an engineer. Within two years after graduation, they were both married, living in Montana, not far from the home of their youth. The boy, Conrad Allen Bradley IV, grew up in the saddle, but for some reason developed a keen interest in the sea. He received an appointment to the US Coast Guard Academy.

Connie woke early. The sunrise was streaming in through the bedroom window. He was strangely invigorated and got up immediately. Cally stirred and mumbled something about getting up too early. He patted her hip and told her to stay put. He dressed quickly and before he went downstairs, he kissed her cheek. She smiled.

Normally he would have started coffee, but for some reason he wanted to be out as soon as possible. Pausing for a moment on the covered deck off the back of the house, he inhaled deeply. The scent of the pines mingling with that of fresh cut hay was thick and sweet. Less than an hour into the early September morning, the day was already bright, clear and warm. Somewhere, at sometime in his life, Connie had seen a movie in which an old Indian, when confronted with the news that General Custer is attacking, jumps up with a smile on his face, grabs his rifle and says, "It is a good day to die." Connie knew what happened to Custer, but couldn't remember the fate of that particular Indian. Strange that thought should come to him just now, but he knew what the old Indian had meant.

He walked briskly to the barn to see Jolena. As usual, she was there waiting for him. "How about some breakfast?" he asked her. She didn't answer, but he gave her some anyway. While she picked at the oats, Connie brushed her, and when he finished, he threw a bareback pad on her, moved her to the fence and climbed on. It was an almost everyday occurrence. They didn't go fast or far, but they usually went. On this beautiful morning they rode over the creek, across the pasture and up the trail towards Rogers Lake. Connie had no intention of going that far, he merely wanted to ride high enough up the hill to be able to look down on the ranch. Less than an hour later, they had ambled back down to the edge of the pasture where the tree line started.

Suddenly, Jo stumbled and didn't immediately recover. Connie slipped down off her back. He stood by her as she slowly settled to her knees. "What's the matter, girl?" Connie asked as she continued to lie down. She stretched out on her right side. Her breathing rapidly became labored. Her eyes were losing focus.

Connie went to his knees and caressed her head. "Jo, don't leave me now. Hang on, I'll get help." It was then he noticed the gnawing ache that was starting in his back teeth, on the left side of his jaw. The pain quickly moved down his jaw to the left side of his neck, into his left shoulder. Trying to ignore it, he sat down to cradle Jo's head in his lap. The pain in his shoulder ran all the way to his fingers and then back up his arm, finally seizing deep into the left side of his chest. His heart felt as if it were being squeezed in a vise. His last mortal thought was to call Cally and tell her goodbye. Fumbling for the phone in his vest pocket, he and Jolena died together.

Connie reached for her as they rose above the ranch and soared over the hills. He hung on tightly as they galloped wildly across a great chasm, racing together towards the light.

Cally had them both cremated and put their names next to Pete and Renee on the stone memorial by the riffle in the creek. She and Connie had been together for twenty-four years. She missed him greatly, but she had their son, plus her two daughters, their families, and Woody who was just over ninety and still hale. She also had one of Jolena's daughters and her daughter as well.

A year later, Conrad the fourth, his bride and their twin infant sons came to live with Cally. Connie's longing for the sea had been satisfied. He left the Coast Guard to raise hay and horses at the place of his youth. His father and grandfather had been cowboys and both had won the big cutting horse futurity. He decided to see if he had enough try in him to win it too.

Made in the USA
Columbia, SC
07 February 2018